Paper Cup

Also by Karen Campbell

Paper Cup

KAREN CAMPBELL

CANONGATE

First published in Great Britain, the USA and Canada in 2022
by Canongate Books Ltd, 14 High Street, Edinburgh EH1 1TE

Published in the USA by Publishers Group West and in Canada
by Publishers Group Canada

canongate.co.uk

1

British Library Cataloguing-in-Publication Data
A catalogue record for this book is available on
request from the British Library

ISBN 978 1 83885 509 3

Typeset in Sabon LT Std by
Palimpsest Book Production Ltd, Falkirk, Stirlingshire

Printed and bound in Great Britain
by Clays Ltd, Elcograf S.p.A.

I worry about the weather that's to come.

Karine Polwart, *Wind Resistance*

To Dad

Chapter 1

A flutter and a swoosh. A fairy-winged, tulle-wound woman waltzes with a chamber pot on her head. Birling in the rain. Teetering on her peerie heels, stumbling into, then onto a bench.

In memory of Jessie Keane who loved to sit here.

The bench is damp. Smells of pish. The girl shuffles into the corner. A bedraggled bride, who will wake in the morning with no memory of the grand denouement of her hen night, but with a long, moss-coloured smudge on the back of her skirt. She flexes her toes. Surveys George Square through bleary eyes. Glasgow girls don't do insouciant walking home with heels in hands after a night out. Invariably the ground is wet or covered in sick, and there will be jaggy unmentionables poised to bite your flesh.

Her shoes fall on their sides, unable to support their own height now her stockinged feet are free. It is an elongated, solid bench she sits on, built to hold many citizens. The drizzle makes a gauzy sheen of lamp posts, buses. Around her, the square is magnificent. Tinsel Town gleams, the city moist and mobile. Glasgow is a living beast of sandstone and grit, of smart-mouthed sideways humour, of traffic cones as modern art and soaring grandeur and dear, dear green places, of glittery puddles reflecting Victorian statues – men,

1

all men, and one torn-faced queen – of deer grazing by gravestones, of the Molendinar Burn and a gentle monk named Mungo, of chewing gum, pizza boxes, tumbled ginger bottles, multicoloured faces and fluttering doos. Pigeons. Hunners of them. It is a place that has welcomed her to its bosom as a dancer would drag you into a ceilidh, sweat-drenched, barely pausing for breath. Four years of study has brought her here: one MA (Hons), some decent friends, and a passable fluency in Weegie. She practised hard. Folk thought her Galloway accent was Irish at first – or worse, from Edinburgh.

The night rain, settling on her. Seeping. Home tomorrow. To her lilac and turquoise bedroom. To French toast, knitted slippers and a shelf full of Beanie Babies that her mother still dusts. The girl begins to cry. She's lost her pals and her head hurts. The veil that drapes from the potty is held by an elastic band, which cuts into her forehead. Stupid, stupid thing. It's meant to be lucky – a sign that she will soon be great with child. She cries even harder. Her ears ache – her hens have been banging the potty all night, even after they stuck it on her head. Her pockets jingle with the change they collected in the potty's plastic bowels, demanding pounds for a kiss. Selling her for kisses, to all men, any men, in the pubs they visited, even out on the streets. One old boy said he'd need to take his teeth out first. She retches, tries to remove the potty, but her hands can't make proper contact with her head. They slither and drag: there is something very wrong. Jesus, she's had a stroke. She's had a stroke and Connor is bound to call it off; who'd want a bride that canny even smile? Panicked, she tries to touch her face. Can't feel anything beyond a dull, padded sensation.

Whorls of people pass, dancing in the dark. All of them strangers. One boy showers another with the remains of his kebab; a taxi driver shouts. Contained trees drip despondently. Tonight, the City Chambers flies the rainbow flag and is lit in pink.

The smell of urine increases. She isn't that drunk, surely? A mass at the other end of the bench stirs. Lifts its head.

'Shh. Sorry, mate,' she says. 'Go back to sleep.'

The tramp adjusts his hat. In the rainburst arc of street light, his hair is glowing, and she cries all the harder.

'I'm sorry. Sorry, pal. Jus ignore me.'

The figure doesn't move. He is a statue on her bench, as stoic and weathered as the stone poets and politicians who adorn the square. The girl's voice echoes inside her body, swimming with all the cocktails and Chardonnay; it is loud and splashy, but surprisingly lucid. So. Her tongue works fine. Just her hands that are wonky.

'I'm really happy – I am, I am. I'm just a wee bit emontional. Is my hen night, see. So. I'm great. But I canny find ma pals.' She hiccups, and a taste of sick is left behind. Her feet are cold. 'Bloody went for chips 'n' cheese. The lot of them! No me. Am not blowing it now – I've lost two stone, y'know? Cause I'm getting married in the morning! Is why . . . this.' She waves dismissively at her headdress. 'Ach, it's not tomorr . . . One week tomorrow . . .' She pauses. 'Nope. Today. Wow. Canny believe it's so quick, is come round so quick, ah canny believe it. Cause you're planning and planning for ages, then whoosh! Just like that, is here it is. And there's so much to do, and this is meant to be my night out, let my hair down, y'know, and now I've got this stupid thing stuck on my head and my hands don't work and my pals have went and left me. Even my sister, and she hardly knows Glasgow at all at all.'

The tramp hasn't moved, she doesn't think he has, yet he seems more huddled, cowed in on himself. The girl's skin is clammy; freezing rods of rain run down her neck. She tries to focus on the figure, but he is blurred. A smelly blur of

3

coat and . . . cardboard? Half man, half rubbish. She giggles at her cleverness. Swallows.

'I love him. Connor. Know? I mean I really, really love him.'

Still the tramp does not move. That nasty taste, swilling in her mouth. Salt. She needs salt. She licks the back of her rained-on hand, but her tongue sticks. Her flesh feels thick and distant. Thick hands. Useless. All that rain, and the man just absorbs it. She closes one eye, to see the shape of him better. What must it feel like, to not go home tonight? To not get dry, or get a heat in you? Ach, but there will be places. Places for folk like these. There's another one over there in the doorway of the Chambers. Or maybe it's a lassie peeing? Hard to tell through the shadow and smudged, liquid light. No one has to sleep on a bench in the rain anyway, and anyway, even if they wanted to, the police would move them on. When they had the Commonwealth Games here. That had been so brilliant. You didn't see folk on benches then. The sun had blazed and the streets were shining. Blue Saltires, blue sky. Even the Clyde seemed blue. It was as if they'd lifted the giant rug that Glasgow sprawled on, and swept all the grubby bits underneath.

'My head hurts.' She cradles the pot between her muffled hands. The weight feels as if it will break her neck. 'Gonny feel like crap tomorrow. And am going back down the road. Two hours on a shoogly train. Just for the wedding, but. Not to stay. Stay in bloody Gatehouse? No way, José. Ow.'

She's forgotten not to shake her head. George Square tilts violently. Yet the people walking and smoking and waving arms for taxis, they keep going about their business fine. She grips the arm of the bench. Braces her spine against its wooden slats. The cold and miserable wet slaps in, rendering her slightly sober.

'Nobody's even heard of it; I just say Dumfries now, even

though that's nowhere near. Like when you go abroad and they say where's Scotland and you go, near— Oh!'

Through long spears of rain, she can see her tribe – ten strident woman, chucking chips, come screeching, seething towards their bartered bride.

'Where the buggery hell were you?' she yells becomingly.

'Where were you?' her tribe yell back.

The girl rises from her bench, forgets she wears no shoes. 'Shite!' Her tights, sooking puddle water. In tandem, her ballast at the other end of the bench also shifts; the tramp is throwing off his cardboard blanket, ruffling as if his rags are feathers. 'How could you all just leave me, eh? I'm supposed to be the . . . Oh! I canny even get this . . . It's stu . . .' Great juddering sobs flooding, surprising her, but it isn't the indignity of the potty stuck on her head, or that her feet are snagged and saturated – and they're Wolford tights, not cheap . . .

'I can't get . . .'

'You've still got your Marigolds on, you daft bint.'

Of course. Along with the potty and the fairy wings, they'd put her in a tutu and bagged her hands in rubber gloves.

No. It is the way the tramp is watching her, like he's hungry. God, of course he is hungry, but it is not for food, she thinks, it is for her, for this blaze of action, for being in the centre of a whole, and laughing, and going into the warm – not for jealousy, no, it is instinct, it is the instinct of the lost, and she feels she can't breathe because he has real eyes, proper ones that have a colour and everything, how they bore into her, reaching in with pale, hard determination.

The girl recoils. It is too human, this face, and she wants to get away; it's why folk fling money at them, isn't it, why you never see the white of their eyes. Money, that's it, he can have her money, all the stupid pennies that are jingling in her coat.

'Get them off me! Get these bloody . . . like slimy bloody
. . .' She flaps and flaps her hands and her sister pulls – what
has she been up to? Her lipstick's all smudged and there is
a love bite on her neck – in the queue for Pizza Crolla?
Actually in the queue for Pizza Crolla?

'Would you like a chip?' Her pal Amy is proffering a
greasy bag, and the tramp is reaching in. Such filthy fingers,
Amy is a bridesmaid, what if she catches—

'Get – them – off – me!'

A tug and a fling and a soar as hard and glittered as
diamond, because diamond is as diamond does. The gloves
come off, a splat of quiver-pink rubber strikes Amy's shoulder,
and the bride upturns her pockets so the silken lining is
hanging out, shaking dross and bits of hankie and bright
streams of golden coins around the dosser's feet. The coins
roll and bounce, some coming to rest against the discarded
rubber glove. A celestial catcher's mitt. The coins are fallen
stars.

'Here, mate. Here. Away and get . . .' She doesn't know.
'Just. Here. Please, take it.'

'Susan, don't be so stupid. There's about fifty quid . . .'
Her sister squats to retrieve the cash.

'No!' The bride-to-be is adamant. Adamant and pished.
Or else. Or else it will be bad luck. She has begun collecting
omens – black cats (different websites say they're good or
bad). Single magpies. Mirrors, ladders. You don't want to
risk fate.

'Hope you realise how lucky you are.' Sweet Amy, taking
her arm. 'She'd to kiss a hundred guys to get all that money.
C'mon, missus, and we'll get you home.'

The tramp crouches forward, a hollow, dank odour
crouching too. It smells of forgotten leaves. A skein of long
grey hair tumbles, escaping from his hat. He gathers the
coins towards him, methodically, like he is tidying a mess.

'Thank you.'

A soft voice. Such a soft voice.

'Jesusgod,' says Amy. 'That tramp's a woman!'

'Jesusgod,' say the rest, or some of them, or perhaps none. The bride feels sick. Feels really, really tired. She lets herself be absorbed into the shelter of their bodies. Her pals. Her hens. And they run for their bus, sparkling and animated in the rain.

Chapter Two

You are lying in your bed, with the covers pulled tight. Tight, because when you were wee, if everything up to your head and neck was swaddled, then the monsters wouldn't get you. Or if you had your back to the door, then the blankets had to be wound right across your back, up past your ears, and you would never turn around, even though you could feel its eyes on you in the dark, this thing, this goblin, or the shadow on the picture on the wall: the open gaping mouth, the eyes of bright black coal.

So. You are in your bed, and it is comfy. But then it is a little cold, as if the covers have slipped. You know when your shoulders are exposed, and the chill that catches you, there, migrates, like the thin metal prongs of a freezing fork on your gums can give you toothache in your head? Yes, so, the cold passes from your shoulder to your neck, and simultaneously to your stomach; it gnaws along your spine at the precise moment you realise the bed is not comfy at all, because the cold is emanating from there. You have been kidding yourself that it's soft, you have been dreaming it, but it's actually a terrible, wet, rock-hard cold that you are lying on, but it's more terrible than water, because it is solid. It is a heavy, dreadful cold that grows stronger as you screw your eyes shut. Ignoring it. Ignoring the leaping pain in your head and the dry-mouth drouth that is screaming at you. See? See what you have done, you total waste of space?

Oh, but it was lovely. Fine and lovely, the loveliest thing that has happened to you in months. First, the grip on glass. Unyielding. Yours. That first firm twist. The gorgeous click as metal cracked, green glints and the cascading spill of clear-pleated liquid, the sharp, bright glug, the glug, the luscious, gurgling glug that fills your veins and gives you what they had.

Warmth.

But you are not warm, not at all. Neither are you prone. Not even comfortably foetal. Kelly, you are propped. Discarded. Your knees are folded, hurting at your chin, which droops. Och. Your neck. Aching with weight; your swollen mega-head is too heavy to lift. And the blankets that have slipped are also heavy, but it is the heaviness of water. Damp folds chafing on your skin – but how, when it is the covers? And then you realise, they are not covers at all; they are the bulk of your clothes, layered on for warmth, and they are soaking. And that the cold moisture is coming from both outside and within. The moisture inside is your body, bleeding heat. You stink, Kelly. You must do. Great blocks of cold hammer you, thud, thud, thud. Your head. Your neck. Your knees. You need a pee. You need a drink. Imagining the heat of a cup of tea; imagine your own tea, a kettle, a heat, a hotness there, whenever you want it. Your choice.

You shift the bits of boxes you have cooried under, and the cardboard turns to pulp in your hands.

Kelly, you have woken inside a skip, although you don't yet know it. All you know is sharp edges and the light smarting above, a pale, watery square of light that is quite bright enough, thank you very much. On your breast, you cradle an empty green bottle of Gordon's gin. Beneath you, plastic crackles. It is a Tesco bag, bulging with change. You breathe the longest sigh, and pull yourself up.

'There's a queue, you know.'

The woman behind has given up sighing. Before the sighing, she had delivered two long tuts, and now she's totally had enough. Kelly stares at the postmistress. Do you still call them that when this is not really a post office? It's a wee counter at the back of Sainsbury's, with a plastic window to shield and muffle the postmistress, who is folding her arms.

'But why d'you need to know what's inside?' says Kelly.

'Because I do. It's the rules.'

'It's just one envelope. And I just need one stamp.'

She has sixty-two pee to her name.

The postmistress pokes the envelope with her pen. It lies between them, in the no-man's-land of the slotted tray through which all business is transacted.

'And that isny a proper address.'

Does the woman know how hard it was to find a decent envelope? One that was still intact, and with enough space to score out the old words and write this new, wrong address. Does she know the flap has been stuck down with liquid soap from the toilets in Buchanan Galleries, to augment any remaining tackiness? There's no way Kelly is telling her what's inside. One look at Kelly, and – fine, OK. That's all they've done since she's been queuing here. Looking at her.

It's rare she gets inside the Galleries. A long, glittering shopping palace with several entrances, it also has a crack squad of security men, who prowl and hoover up the unruly gangs of boys, the glazed-eyed and light-fingered, the strange singular man in a raincoat who watches, watches but never buys. And any threadbare soul who looks like they might need a rest, or a wee top-and-tail at the second-floor ladies' sink. Aye well. *You're no so sharp the day, boys.* Kelly knows she smells of soap, knows her hair is reasonably flat. (She's lost her bunnet somewhere in the skip.) But her greatcoat? It is a great coat; it's the snuggliest, most tough-hided, stand-up-by-itself-cause-you're-in-the-army-now piece of clothing she's ever possessed. They gave it to her one evening, the lassies who run that second-hand shop in King Street. Mr Ben's – it's been there for ever and is a glitterbox of dressing-up adventures. Vintage, beads, furs, army surplus. The two girls were pulling in the last of the clothes rails; Kelly had been there all day, sitting where the pay machine used to be in the big car park. Except the bastards went and made it one of those ones where you key in your details and do it all by card. *Spare any change?* does not work so well in a world that is cashless and slick. Maybe she was shivering, who knows, but a shadow came and stood over her, and she was gathering up her stuff, waiting for the shouting, maybe a swift kick, and this beautiful, beautiful lassie with a rolled-back fringe and gingham pinafore had gone, 'Here.' Just that. Then she laid the coat over Kelly's shoulders, pressed down with her red-polished fingernails and walked away.

'Excuse me!' The woman behind is doing her dinger. 'I've a bus to catch.'

Kelly's greatcoat has stood her in excellent stead, but it is a wee bit minging. What can you do, though, when it's your house, when you're wearing it like a turtle?

'Can you tell me what's in the envelope?'

'It's a ring,' Kelly whispers.

'A what? A ring? Like jewellery, you mean?'

'Aye.'

The postmistress snorts. What with her snorting and the woman behind snuffling, and all the folk staring, you could be in a bloody zoo.

'Well, you can't send it like that, then. No way. Not even if,' the woman clears her throat, in order to better take the pish, '"Susan who's getting married next week, Gatehouse of Fleet, Dumfries and Galloway" was an actual, legitimate address.'

The woman behind sniggers. Then remembers the time and reverts to being outraged.

'Right. That's it. This is ridiculous. Away and get me the manager.'

'I *am* the manager.'

Quietly, as they argue, Kelly places her hand over the envelope and withdraws it from the scooped tray. She'd padded the envelope with toilet paper so the ring didn't bump about. The envelope has a pleasing plumpness, sits comfortably in her hand. She was only trying to do a good thing, not sign up for a session in public humiliation. Oh, people. She feels her breath coming in short, sharp bursts. See people? No good comes from being around people.

She pushes through the shoppers, their baskets and trolleys, the shelves of quinoa (as in Winona? Who knows. Looks like maggots) and peeled satsumas rewrapped in plastic, past the aching smells of baking bread and the shrieking of all those lovely bottles, and makes it outside – where there are still people, yes, but their bulk is less compressed; you can see sky and spaces. You can feel the cold. Fuck warm. Cold keeps you moving. Keeps you sharp.

A youth bangs into her. Opens his mouth; he has an apologetic cast to his face. Then he sees who he has jostled, and flinches.

'Raa-aar!' she yells at him, like a tiger. Folk jump.

It's better when you're invisible.

Here's a joke. Why did the jakie . . . something about jackets. She tries to think of a witty double play on jakies and jackets, but her hip is smarting. It'll be purple there

12

tonight, if she looks. But she never looks at her flesh. Not at the hang of it over her bones, nor the twisty joints or unwanted greyness. Kelly is not a jakie. She is a *homeless person*. There now, doesn't that sound better? Why do homeless persons favour vast and shapeless clothing? She wonders if the people rushing past have ever wondered that. Aye, it keeps you warm. And yes, beggars cannot be choosers; that is a literal, literal truth. But your baggy gear is your armour. It hides you from yourself, and is your camouflage from the world. Her old men's breeks are nicely neutral. Be humble, meek. Do not draw attention, do not provoke debate. Eyes down. Shuffle. Whisper *thank you* when they chuck you change.

Oh, Kelly. You are such a liar. Kelly does not have sixty-two pee to her name. Under her great greatcoat, she has another forty-eight pounds fifty in change remaining, tied tight in its plastic bag. A bag she dare not open again, no, not even to buy another envelope, a bag that is the weight of a dead rodent, and which that boy just crushed against her thigh when he bumped her. It is not her money. She didn't ask for it. Cannot have it, cannot have it burning and whispering *glug glug glug*.

Further up Sauchiehall Street, away from the colossus of the Buchanan Galleries, the shops become more careworn. There is a Celtic shop and a multistorey boarded-up Dunnes, a big brash shoe store, plenty pound shops and – *hullo rerr doll* – the Suave Savvy. There used to be a nightclub in that complex, above the indoor market: a dance hall famed for its 'grab-a-granny' nights. Kelly would be a prime candidate for that now. She turns her head a little, avoiding windows, till she find the Chinese restaurant down the street. It still exists, but not the club above it. Another disco that is not there. Do folk still do that, go to discos? Or is everything online? She knows about online. Online is where everything

13

happens. Online is where if your name's not on the list, you're not getting in. But that's where they used to go. Above the Chinese restaurant. Her gang. Strutting and proud, openly mocking the denizens of the Savoy Disco as they leapt and jostled in a moving swarm of spiky black. Cool as—

'Out the road.' Another youngster, a girl with orange skin and ironed blonde hair. Her stride is hurried, heels high. 'Fucksake.'

Kelly is standing in the middle of the street. This is a problem. This part of Sauchiehall Street is pedestrianised, so there are no rules, no margins. The paved setts are a free-for-all, and Kelly is purposeless, and purposely impeding girls in staccato heels, making them break from important streams of telephone chat and acknowledge her, and be made furious by that.

She carries on over the brow of the hill, past hairsprayed matrons heading into the Willow Tearoom, and turns right up Rose Street, which is a proper street with a pavement, so is fine. There's a lovely art deco cinema there. They have film festivals. She's never been to a film festival; it sounds like a glorious, greedy thing. How many films can you eat in one go? Once, she went inside the cinema's foyer, and it was all glossy, brown polished wood, like being inside an ocean-going liner. Not that she's been in one of them either. There are tenements across the road, along Renfrew Street and running down all the wee truncated streets, to where the motorway butchers the city. Until it gets to the motorway, Renfrew Street is a fine, long street. The end near Charing Cross is becoming gentrified – they're building high, glassy apartments – but there are still plenty of solid Glasgow tenements, some fresh-painted and pot-planted, some that are dodgy-looking student lets. A scatter of faded bed-and-breakfasts too. And there, occupying the basement and ground floor of a Victorian sandstone block, is her next destination. The Outreach. Or *Dexy's Midnight Scunners*, as Dexy likes to quip. Quip. That is the very word he uses. It suits him; there's something of a jaunty flourish to it.

Quitter? Naw, I'm a quipper, me. Aye. If you canny laugh, you're deid.

Kelly has destinations the way a cat does: places to call in on, to stop off, groom or nap. Kelly's destinations are howffs and doorways and dosshouses and parks. Sometimes they are the late-night bus, or the subway, where you can go round in circles all day for the price of a single ticket. They are gratings, benches, closes and doorways. Occasionally, they are skips. The Outreach is the best. But, like any stray, you mustn't outstay your welcome. Kelly cannot bear to be tolerated. Toleration feels worse than pity.

The close mouth is open. She goes inside, chaps the front door. There's a bell, but it never works. She rattles the letter box. Then she goes back out of the close, to lean over the railing, and raps her knuckles against window glass. She suspects the soundless bell is a filtering tool. If you're half-hearted about your need, *the way is shut. It was made by those who are homeless.* Only the desperate and the resourceful gain access to the Outreach. Kelly does this a few times, jouking in and out of the close, banging door, then window, to elicit a response. Tries shouting: 'Little pigs, little pigs, let me in!' Eventually, a tired-eyed teenager sees her through the window. A moment later, there is sound and movement behind the front door as the girl flicks the sneck, opens up. She drifts back into the kitchen before Kelly's even shut the door. You're aye assured of a warm welcome at Dexy's.

Music pounds. Or is it Kelly's head, still? No, there's definitely drums, reverberating from under the floorboards. *Boogie in the basement, coffee in the kitchen. And NAE GEAR ANYWHERE!* One of Dexy's many mottos. He's something to do with the council, he says, but Kelly's not sure. It's too confusing, the agencies and charities, the support workers and the social and the dole and the food banks. Would it not just be easier if one group sorted the lot? Then there'd be one big, safe net instead of hundreds of wee, frayed ones, which frequently don't join up.

There's room for twenty folk to sleep at the Outreach, but it's first come first served, and already Kelly knows she's too late. Doors open at three, so you can bag a bed and dump your stuff, then you're papped out till ten at night. Ten to ten to ten to ten. Dexy sings it like the *Doctor Who* tune, so it doesn't feel so bad. *It's no a rule*, he says. *Well, aye, it is, but. But it's no cause I'm a bastirt, know? It's their rules; they'd shut me down like, if I didny. Regulations, know?*

And fair's fair, because Dexy does his best. If it's blowing a gale, or snowing, he'll always try to squeeze a few more folk in. The deal is you've to hide out in the back court if there's ever an inspection.

'As-salāmu alaykum.'

Two shy dark heads bob, two sets of eyes lower to the faded rug. The woman sorts her headscarf, which has slid backwards from her hair. Nobody can pronounce their names. Dexy addresses them collectively, calls them Jesus-Mary-and-Joseph, or the JamJays for short. The lady is very pregnant. She never speaks. It's the man who said hello.

'All right?' Kelly follows the couple into the kitchen. The man eases his wife into a chair, and the simple action pierces Kelly's heart. The lassie who let her in is stirring something on the cooker. She's new. Her belly protrudes through the open folds of her dressing gown. Another ripe with child. The girl's barely sixteen, if she's that. The things folk do to get a bed. Dexy doesn't apply the ten-to-ten rule if you're pregnant. There's the man himself, slicing slabs of bread.

16

Arranging them in a wide dish, his thin fingers gleaming with butter. He looks up. A weasel with kind eyes.

'It's yersel, Kelly. How's things?'

'Shite. How's you?'

'Well, I'm making my famous bread and butter pudding. With marmalade, à la Delia. And I only do that on a good day.' He pours a carton of cream over his creation. Dexy fancies himself as a bit of a foodie. Claims he had a short-lived career as a fishmonger in Morrisons. And it's true, he is pretty nifty with a knife. Kelly imagines Dex could probably fillet anything.

'Wee Shaz at the paper shop was doing a stock-take, and guess who got lucky? I mean, one day past the sell-by?' Dexy sniffs at the open carton. 'Doesny even smell.' He scrapes the residue out with a spoon. 'You, on the other hand . . .'

'Piss off.'

The JamJays pause in their tea-drinking. Kelly has no idea what they do or don't understand. All she knows is they are failed asylum seekers. Imagine failing at that. Just failing at asking for help. Christ, that has to be pretty low. That's why she rarely puts herself in the hands of others. Why let them unskin you more?

'Fell into a bottle, did you?'

Boom.

Just like that, he splinters her. Her fresh-washed face. The hair she thought was flat.

'Canny kid a kidder, doll.'

Dexy reaches for the teapot as Kelly reaches for the door.

'Ho. Hold up. You no wanting a cuppa?'

'Not if it comes with a pile of sanctimonious shite.'

'Ooh, get you.' Wiggling his fingers below his chin. 'Sanctee-moanious? Away and sit down and stop your nonsense. I canny offer you a bed . . .'

'I'm not wanting a bed!'

'. . . but I can offer you tea and nae sympathy. Maybe a daud of marmalade if you fancy?'

Kelly has a sudden craving for sweetness. She sits next to Mrs JamJay. 'When are you due now?' she asks her. But it is the man who holds up one finger. 'Week,' he says.

'One week? Jeez. What'll you do then?'

Mrs JamJay blinks.

'Dexy, what are you going do then? You canny have a baby here.'

Dexy passes Kelly a mug. There are small asterisks tattooed on each one of his knuckles. She's never asked him what they represent. 'Havny a clue. I've been onto the social. Et voilà – one piece and marmalade.'

A chipped plate is placed in front of her. Fat bread, glistening with gold. Oh God, it is so delicious. Sharp, bright citrus. The floury comfort of the doorstop slice, salty butter. Kelly feels the marmalade running down her chin, but she doesn't care.

'Bottom line is, they've already been telt to get tae.'

'Get tae where?' says the girl at the cooker, scratching her bum. Kelly's glad she's not staying for dinner.

'Get tae fuck, get hunted, go back home and get bombed – pick any one of a number of choice phrases, Aleisha darling. They all amount to the same thing. Nae bugger wants to know.'

Aleisha nods vaguely, pours the contents of her pot into a soup bowl. She helps herself to a slice of bread and heads for the door.

'Here, doll,' says Dexy. 'Any chance of you turning your music down? We'd another complaint from next door.'

'It's meant to be good for the wean.'

'I think they mean classical and that. No drum and bass.'

'*Drum and bass*. Aye, right, Grandad.' Aleisha gives them a collective sneer as she exits the kitchen.

'Is that a new telly?' asks Kelly. There's an enormous flat-screen hanging from the wall above the bread bin.

'Aye. They other buggers were hogging the one ben the front room. Know how I've got a women's group meets here on a Tuesday, then there's the rehab, and the men's sheds dudes, and now we've that addiction support group "huddle" an all?'

'I lost three year a ma life to the heroin!' Kelly and Dexy chant in unison. Mr JamJay pats his wife's arm.

'Five, actually.' Dexy rubs his knuckles on his chest. 'But who's counting?'

'Proud of that, are you?'

'Ach, aye. Still staunin, amn't I? Even though I'm here all the bloody time, so I am. Stuck in this kitchen.' Forearm to forehead, he assumes the stance of a tragic heroine. 'Anyroad, I was fed up missing *Homes Under the Hammer*. So I treated masel.'

'Very nice. Very . . . subtle.'

'Well. No quite mine yet. Had to get a wee loan, know?'

Kelly imagines buying things for her house. She thinks she'd put pictures on the wall instead of tellies. She stretches her calves. Magic waves surge. Lovely waves of warmth. She can feel the lull of sugar that is sweeter than the sweetest sugar ever tasted. How it tricks your body into relaxing, how it amplifies your senses. She can hear the tinniness inside her ears, rushing like sea. Can feel the brittle hardness on the backs of her heels split in the comfort of the kitchen. Beads of condensation trickle down the tiles behind the cooker. Long flat tiles, which makes her think of public lavatories. There are toast crumbs scattered on the worktop, there are friendly pots and jars with spoons stuck in, which reminds her of a family, bustling. Aleisha's muted drums are a heartbeat in the womb of this house. Kelly's eyelids relax. If she sits here any longer, she will never get up. Which makes the point at which you have to leave the same as ripping off an Elastoplast, before the scab is healed.

Ach, everything hardens better in open air.

'Dex, you got a minute? I need some advice.'

'Aye, sure.' He raises one dramatic hand. 'Haud up a wee tick.' He goes into the hall, comes back wearing a See-you-Jimmy cap. 'OK, fire away. That's me got my agony uncle hat on.' He giggles away to himself. 'Been waiting for an excuse to wear this for ages.'

'Hilarious. Look, can we maybe go somewhere private?' On her lap, Kelly's hands are trembling. Or maybe it's her knees.

'Ach. The JamJays canny understand a bloody word we say. That no right, Mr J?'

Mr JamJay smiles. 'Yes.'

'See?' Dexy lifts up the teapot. 'More tea, vicar?'

Kelly would rather the JamJays weren't there. The husband watches his wife, who nibbles on an ender of bread. She is like a downy, round bird, and he an oak tree, if an oak tree could be made of love. Kelly has a sugar-rush urge to cut them down. Just for spite. Just for . . .

But she knows that after that wild release, she would be sadder. Smaller. Much like she feels right now. She holds her cup out for a refill, though no tea born of man will quench her raging, mouth-furred thirst. Who needs love like oak trees, but, when you have Dexy with a kettle?

'What do they do all day?'

'The JamJays?' Dexy smiles at them. 'Mostly wait. Now, what can I do you for? Boy trouble, is it? Dr Dexy's sexy surgery is open.' He clasps his hands, head cocked on one side. He is a small, thin man of indeterminate middle age. Sand-coloured hair and chiselled cheekbones, one of which is snaked with a fine white scar. His chin points. His eyes pierce. There is nothing spare about Dexy. Life has tanned his hide, and taken several of his teeth. But he's not a victim. Not of anything. He may be small and wiry, but those wires he's strung with are razor-sharp. He is quite possibly an angel, Kelly thinks. Talks mince, but she would trust him with her life.

He found Kelly one morning after two men had kicked the crap out of her. She had a Sally Army sleeping bag then, kept it rolled up dry beneath an arched bridge. That night, she'd gone to sleep cosy, woken to find someone urinating on her face. Kelly was stupid then. Kelly had not seen the joke. The two men pissing on her made her see the error of her ways.

Dexy didn't work at the Outreach when they met. He was a hobo, same as Kelly. Doing well, though; he'd a regular *Big Issue* patch. Coming off the methadone, on a waiting list for a house. What a neat trajectory. Aye, right. Nothing is that linear. Dexy had had several 'fresh starts', of course he had. Some Kelly had heard about, some she had not (including actual details of his alleged excursion into fishmongery). You don't pry. First rule of the shifting sands of living on the streets. Folk tell you what they want to, and you believe it or you don't. Questions are the devil's work. Because no fucker knows where questions might lead. But Kelly never knew Dex when he was at his lowest, so she'll never know if he always had that capacity inside him to find a space for someone else.

'It's about this,' she says, dumping the bag of money on the table. 'Forty quid. And I don't want it.'

'One: where d'you get it, and two: how no?'

'One: a lassie on her hen night gave me it, and two: because there was another eighteen pounds in it last night. Which I'd a wee party on.'

'Ah.'

'And three . . .'

'There's a three?'

The JamJays' heads are following the conversation, dipping from Kelly to Dexy to the bag of coins.

'Three?' encourages Mr JamJay.

'Three: the lassie also left this behind.' Kelly slides the envelope across the table.

The flap has come unstuck. Limply Dexy shakes the envelope, and the ring, plus some wads of toilet paper, falls out. 'Aye, very secure. Excellent packaging there. Get you a job with FedEx nae bother.' He places the band of diamonds on the top of his pinkie. 'Aw, Kelly. I do, doll. I do.'

'Beautiful, isn't it? Cold and colourless – just like your eyes.'

He blows her a kiss. 'I know someone who'd gie you a good price for this. Plenty bling-bling. Even though it isny real diamonds.'

'No?'

'Naw. Cubics,' he says, with pursed-lipped authority. 'Look – they're no even round. Check out that one in the middle; it's like a wee boat.'

'Well, I feel bad anyroad. It's the lassie's engagement ring, and it's burning a hole in my pocket. It must have fallen off when she was chucking me the money.'

'Please?' Mr JamJay is holding out his cupped hand for the ring. 'Yes, diamond. Marquise.' He nods. 'Like almond, no? Or eye.'

'Marquise? Is that like a cubic?'

'No. Very nice diamond. Is cut, so.' Mr JamJay chops the edge of his hand on the table. 'Cut. Cut.' Mrs JamJay flinches a little. He pats her hand. 'But it is diamond. Very nice.'

'Naw, pal,' says Dexy. 'You canny get a boat-shaped diamond. They don't come like that.'

'My husband was a jeweller,' says Mrs JamJay, quiet as quiet.

'You speak English?' Dexy takes off his stupid gingery cap. Now he's the one playing eyeball ping-pong, his glance moving from the husband to the wife, to the ring, to Kelly, to the wife. 'I thought you couldny . . .'

Mrs JamJay shrugs. 'There is nothing to say.'

There is a long moment when no one speaks, then Dexy goes: 'Fair enough. So, Kelly-ma-love. What's your problem? You don't want to sell the ring, and you don't want the money the lassie gied you either. Toffs are careless, eh?' He rolls his eyes, to include the JamJays in his exasperation. See, even when he's being annoying, he is kind, because he doesn't want the JamJays to feel left out, nor be awkward that they might have revealed more of themselves than they wished. There is sweet and sour in Kelly's mouth. Too much sharing. She licks crumbs from the edges of her lips. Maybe there is a fellowship of all the people who have ever lived with no walls, no door. Here in this kitchen that belongs to none of them. How jealously you guard your own wee piece of privacy.

It is definitely time to leave. Get to the point, Kelly. Get what you need and go. 'No, I don't want to sell it. I want to give it back to her. But I don't know how. They wouldny take it at the post office – I don't even have a right address. I thought, you can maybe get on the web, can't you? See if you put her name in, you might get her on the Facetime thingy.'

Dexy turns the envelope in his hand. 'Dumfries and Galloway. Is that no down near where you're fae? How d'you no just take it there yoursel? It's just a wee place. Sure if you asked around . . .'

'Me, go to Galloway? Aye, right. No way, man.'

'How no?'

Kelly thinks about this. She does, she tries to find some words, and she knows hundreds of good ones, hundreds and thousands. But there is simply no room to organise them into sense. 'Because . . . well. How can I? I've got no—'

Dexy shakes the Tesco bag. 'Money?'

'No. I've—'

'Hunners of prior engagements? Big day at work? Used up all your annual leave?'

'Ach, piss off, Dexy, right? I knew you'd be bugger-all help. Here.' She drops the bag in front of Mrs JamJay. 'You take this. For the wean, all right? All the best and that.'

The kitchen door is heavy, it still has its Victorian finger-plate. As she shoves it, she sees a distorted brassy image: Mrs JamJay is rubbing her eyes. She shouldn't be bloody shouting. See people, Kelly? See you? She's made the woman cry.

'Kelly, wait! Fucksake.' Dexy catches up with her in the hall.

'Dex, I just wanted you to look on your computer. What is it with people? See when I ask for something, how can they no just do what I ask? How come I get a fucking interrogation, or someone deciding they know better than me what I want? I'm not stupid. Do I look like I button up the back?'

'Frankly, ma dear, you look like you've nae buttons at all.' Dexy slips his arm through hers; he is about to pull her back into the cloying warmth of the kitchen. 'Here. You know I've got your back, doll. With or without buttons. What's wrong with folk wanting to help you?'

She bats him away. 'Because how do they know? How do they know what I need to help me? And what do I do when they stop? Eh? What am I meant to do then? I sort me, only me, no other fucker but me, all right?'

'All right. Jesus, doll, keep your lovely' – he actually ruffles her hair; she flinches, ducks: will the man not take no for an answer – 'tousled wig on.'

Why did she not keep ten pounds of the money? Or just a fiver? A fiver would buy a big bottle of White Lightning or a couple of cans. She could take it up the Necropolis. There is something cheering about being surrounded by dead people: they are mouldering while you, for once, are on top. Even the richest ones, in their ornate wedding-cake tombs: they are the ones who are stuck. Not you. You. You can . . .

'I can go anywhere I want,' she yells.

'Good for you.' Dexy is hugging her – how did that happen? Dexy is not that much taller than she is; she's kind of drooping over him, her backside sticking out like a prow, like she is the arse-end of a ship. But she's too knackered and hung-over to move. The trembling is in her legs now too.

'Kelly doll, I will trawl the internet for you, all right? I will try and track your wumman down. And you're absolutely right. Nobody can make you do a fucking thing if you don't want to.' His hand rubs the space between her shoulder blades.

Her face is pressed into his shoulder. 'I think I'm just gonny dreep here all day.'

'Well, darling, at some point I'll need to take a pish.'

Dexy's shirt smells of washing powder. Suds and snow-flakes. A twin tub. Wooden tongs. Her mum tugging on the pulley, cheeks scarlet, blowing bubbles from her hand to land on her daughter's curls. Kelly straightens herself. 'I release you.'

Dexy takes her face in his hands and kisses her forehead. 'Bless you, my child.' It is such an unexpected thing. 'Maybe you should get away fae here, though. Fae Glasgow, I mean. Serious. Doesny matter where. None of my beeswax where you head. But sometimes we get stuck, don't we? In a place, or a thought. Whatever. And that can make us crazy.'

She puts her fingers to her skin, where he kissed it. Her skin is no-man's-land. He is still talking.

25

'See my big pal Abdi? Lovely guy. Beautiful wife, three cracking weans. But see every year? He goes a wee bit mental. Mental good but, know? I mean, if you know you're heading there anyroad, best do it . . . Ach, I'm no explaining it right. Kind of like a controlled explosion, you know? Take yersel off. Radio silence. A great big sky?'

Down in the basement, Aleisha's music throbs and swells. The more Kelly pushes her finger into bone, the harder everything becomes.

'Anyway, every year, that man takes himself off to the sea. You never know when it's coming. Well – you kinda do. Lucky bastirt's a teacher, so he's got all they holidays, know? But he says it's like he gets a smell under his nose, like the wind is calling him. So, off he goes. Packs a wee rucksack, says cheerio to the wife and weans, and away. Off on his own wee walkabout. New man when he comes home.'

Kelly runs her hands though her hair, so that she is the last person to have touched there. Not him. It is her head. Her life. She fastens her greatcoat up to her chin.

'Where's my home, but, Dexy? Where would I come back to?'

'Is that no the point, doll? Why we do it?'

'Do *what*?' She steps into the close, which is colder than the flat, but not as cold as outside. It is a pissy-smelling netherworld, where you pause, shake brollies, turn up collars. Gird your loins to greet or go.

Dexy shakes his head. He looks so disappointed in her.

'You know what?' she shouts as she enters the street. 'You're a really shitey guru.'

Chapter Three

Outside the Gallery of Modern Art can be a dodgy place to sit. The broad stone steps are perfect, mind: prominent, inviting, and topped with a sheltering Greek-style portico, upheld by fluted columns against which you can lean your head. But they go through phases here, like a mad housewife tidying up before visitors. Sometimes they say it's 'for security', but once, the council just went full mental and started blasting classical music to scare off the goths that used to loiter here. Whatever the reason, when she's telt to move, Kelly never argues. She just packs up her stuff and shuffles off. Then comes back a few days later. *Contributes little to class discussions, but has a quiet persistence* (Primary Six school report).

Her paper cup has blown over. It's not even that windy, just the updraught of the passers-by, all passing by. Today, she's claimed the bottom step. Corner right: out of the eyeline of the museum attendants, but in prime position to catch plump businessmen en route to lunch. You'd think they'd be the most generous donors, those men off to partake of some nice oysters or sole with their bulging business accounts, but they're not. Often, it's the wee wifies, or the buskers coming from Buchanan Street, if they've had a good day. This is not a good day. Yesterday was all right.

Kelly was here then too. Sundays are slow in town, but this is always a good spot for tourists. A novice would go for outside a church on a Sunday, but the faithful can be surprisingly mean. *I've already given*: it rests unsaid on their mouths as they trot past. She made six pounds yesterday, with which she bought a Burger King and a can of Tennent's. Tennent's is weak as pish, it doesn't count. Even so, one sip gives you the thirst. Pouring golden, barely touching the sides, and soon as that can was done, she craved another.

This is what happens. You are good, so good, and in place of reward, you get punished. All you have built, brick on painful brick, is for naught. When you stop drinking, your previous tolerance crumbles away, and Mental Kelly Ten-Pints finds herself pished on two. Which might make you a cheap date, but it also makes you slippery as hell. Kelly feels as if she is spinning on the rim of a whirlpool, doggy-paddling like fuck before the sucking takes her down. And she can't go there again.

Your disease is progressive, Kelly. It will always get worse.

Those lassies, though. Those hens. Out on the town. High heels and spangly tutus. The whole gang of them, cooing and dipping like doves. Make you boak. Her, fighting with Dexy. Leaving that kitchen while the others got to stay.

Anyway. That was Sunday, and she got through it. Today is Monday, and her mood suits the day. Whether you're working or not (and Kelly is – she's grafting right now), Mondays are aye depressing. Even the weather is dour. Oppressive cloud lends a pewter light to already grey walls. Opposite, on the other side of the street where there used to be sky, construction workers are building a high tower, which dwarfs the surrounding buildings. The council have tried to compensate by stringing reams of fairy lights on either side of the gallery. They stretch right the way across the square, which is all very pretty at night, but by day it feels like you're under a giant net.

'Right, pal, you'll need to punt yersel.' Big black boots appear in the slab of paving Kelly's been staring at. She stiffens. Lifts her head a little higher, sees green trousers with a fluorescent yellow band. Not the polis then.

'M'on. I've no got all day.' A clunky wooden brush is sweep-sweep-sweeping with impatience. She glowers up at the owner of the broom. Even street sweepers think they're the boss of you. But this one falters. His big sonsie face goes red. 'Och, I'm sorry, hen.'

'For what?'

He goes a deeper red, and she sees it, sees it. Sees herself, reflected in his eyes. 'Here.' He looks down, fumbles in his pocket. Takes out a wallet. 'Ach . . . I've nae . . . Sorry. I thought I had a fiver. Here. Sorry,' he repeats, offering Kelly a pound coin. He actually places the money in her hand, and the tenderness of his gesture reminds her of her dad dispensing pocket money.

'You'll no get up the dancin' wi that, but . . .'

'No, but I can buy masel something nice.' Kelly gives him a smile, to show she is in on the joke.

'You stay where you are, hen. I can work round you.'

'Cheers, mate. I'll work round you too.'

The street sweeper opens his mouth to reply, then doesn't. They both nod, return to being gruff. The coin is a warm, solid circle in her palm. Kelly shifts her buttocks from side to side, redistributing the pins and needles. There is a stickiness to her left bum cheek that suggests chewing gum. Maybe she should call the street sweeper back. She feels a lightness in her chest at the thought of that. She won't, of course.

The Gallery of Modern Art sits on Royal Exchange Square, so there have been plump businessmen here forever. There are expensive leather and designer dress shops and a boutique that sells nothing but *hand-finished gentlemen's shirts*. That sign always makes her laugh. The bad bit in her pictures a row of florid, smart-shirted yet trouserless men being pleasured by the salesman at the till.

Kelly has made a tablecloth out of an old *Metro* newspaper. A lone ten pee lies half in, half out the cup, which is covering the face of an angry politician: a woman with a blue rosette and a vulture face. A snatch of song keeps orbiting Kelly's brain. *My cup's full and running ohhh-ver.* Try as she might, she cannot stop that song from spinning. Lacing underneath is the twist and stab of Dexy going *Is that no the point, is that no the point*, his nebby chin bristling. Kelly thinks that the inside of her head must look like her gran's old mending bag. All different colours, some neat and bundled, but in general, it's one giant mess. Knots, skeins unspooling, wee pointless scraps kept 'just in case'.

You have chosen to have no roots, Kelly. So what keeps you in one place? Could Dexy read her mind? *Stuck.* He used a word out loud that she'd just thought into herself. Though occasionally when she thinks she's just thought it, folk look funny at her. Which suggests Kelly maybe does say things outside her head too. It's really hard to tell the difference when you have no one to talk to, except yourself. Folk don't appreciate that. See when you answer yourself back? When it comes in a different voice and you weren't even expecting it? That's a total mind-warp.

It's worth it, though. To be free to live exactly as you please. There are no restrictions on Kelly's life, no rules except her own. Yes, there is weather, but weather brings sun as well as rain. There are no roofs, but there is boundless sky. The sky reminds her of the sea, and home. She often looks up, here in Glasgow. She heard a guide on one of those open-topped buses, on his microphone to the tourists. *Always look up*. Folk here don't do that enough. You can see saplings grow from gutters, you can see swimming birds and unseen faces. There is an angel on top of Dennistoun Library that she is particularly fond of.

She puts her cup upright, the pound coin joining the ten pee. Blows on her hands. Her fingernails are mawkit, thick with mud. It's not especially chilly, but the gesture is a neat wee trick. You're saying *I'm cold.* You're saying (in the manner of a silent movie) *help me.* A man in a suit, two feet from where she sits, walks by eating a panini. He sees her watching him. Hesitates. Takes one more bite. Wraps the greaseproof paper around the remaining sandwich, and she sits up straight, like a good girl; he is looking past her, fine, but that's fine, folk do. That street sweeper was a rare creature. With most, it's like they canny make eye contact until they're actually handing you the food, or dropping you some coins; as if you must only exist for the split second they have decided to acknowledge you (and they do feel really good about themselves at that point, she imagines). See if you actually did exist for longer than that, if they thought you really were a real person, who still breathed and needed to eat and had nowhere to sleep either side of this transaction, then, well, it would just rip their knitting. For how would they ever escape you? Like patting a stray dog. Jeez, you want to, of course you do, you want to offer it a wee bit comfort in a callous world. But what if it follows you home? So Kelly is ready for Panini Man. She will be a decent dosser, not intimidate him. She will sit up nice for half a sandwich. She senses his shadow cover her. One step, two step. She looks up in time to see him drop the packet in the bin.

Traffic noise stops. Seagulls mime, and the only sound is the inner roar that rises.

Belly.

Breast.

Ears.

'Enough to put you off your food, eh?' She bawls it, grinning like a loon through spitting teeth, because yelling feels better than sobbing. She is up on her feet, and the fucker feints. Does he think she's going to hit him? His elegant tan office shoes clip-clip-clop backwards, like a flustered cockerel crossing the road – *why did the chicken* – but she couldny give a toss. It's the panini she wants, not him.

'Five-second rule,' she says out loud, to the folk not listening. Studious they are, those passers-by, in their not-listening. Her cheeks burn. The bin is one of those closed ones, with a letter-box slot. Gingerly she puts her hand in, praying there is no jaggy glass. The bin is nicely filled; she doesn't have to plunge too far, and the sandwich is still wrapped. Good. It takes a special kind of hunger to flick a fag dowt from a part-chewed pizza, but she's done that too.

Kelly has done it all.

In the distance, she hears a siren, or a screeching. There is a growing, rumbling presence: thunder. But the thunder is overlaid with a high-pitched screaming: a collective swell of the cityscape. Everything shakes, people start running, wailing. Her first thought is that a girder has fallen from the building site, then she sees a double-decker bus careering up the road, except it isn't on the road, it is juddering along the pavement, and there are bodies, human bodies, flying up; flies to a giant hand, just swatted, folding and sprawling as the bus takes everything with it. Splintered groan as a lamp post goes, and the impact sends the bus skiting from the pavement to the road, shooting across towards George Square. Panini spills, Kelly sprints. Out into the road. Stops.

Can't breathe. Can't breathe.

Left and right, it is a scene of Armageddon. Debris and people and pieces of bus and the deep dark spread of blood. A skein of battered cars. The bus has smashed to a stop, overby. Its face into a wall. There is a woman kneeling by a man. She is screaming his name, screaming it, screaming it to the heavens. Another person leans over the woman to give him the kiss of life. Air quivers. Kelly can see the bevel of the sky. Kelly can see glitzy carrier bags strewn like leaves; she sees an upturned pram, an elegant tan office shoe spinning on the tarmac, and everywhere, Glaswegians are running. Towards the fallen folk, crouched on knees, jackets off, pillows made, bandages torn. A girl gets up. Crumples. Someone catches her. There is a traffic light lying on the road, across the junction. Still blinking. Sparkling. Pale head beneath. Unmoving.

'Oh, Jesus Christ, what happened?' cries a woman.

Where do you look? What can she—

'What happened?' shouts a museum attendant, running out of the gallery, stabbing at his mobile. A figure in yellow jacket and green trousers pushes past her, dropping a broom.

The tan office shoe is static. Kelly runs to where it is, scanning the twisted metal and the broken shapes for a foot, a leg. There is a terrible blank weight over her eyes and ears; she is peering down a narrow tunnel, everything shortening. Shoe. Foot. Skin. Finding the man, on his back with his head on the kerb. She can only see one leg, thinks the other is bent beneath him. She can see the hidden pink mouth of his open stomach, leaking blood.

'Do you move him?' she says to the people rushing by. 'Should we move him?' she says to the people standing glaikit. Waiting for someone who knows to take the lead. All around her, people are crying, or being capable. 'Can you move?' she says to the man, removing her greatcoat.

Chalky grey, his lips shift, eyes skittering, trying to make sense of the sky. The air is thick with petrol fumes, and the metal taste of his blood.

'You're all right, mate. It's going to be OK.' She bundles

33

her coat-tails with her fist. Makes a pad, and presses hard into the hole. He moans, teeth chittering like crazy. 'Sorry, sorry. Am I hurting you?' But she has to stop this blood from coming out. 'Somebody help me!' she shouts. 'Over here!'

His eyes are flickering shut, and she's singing at him, like a total nutter.

'*Ca' the yowes*,' she murmurs. '*Tae the knowes*.' She sings softly. Stroking the brown hair off his brow as his eyes close down. The only thing moving is her hand, stroking and shaking. It grows bigger, fills her eyes with trembling pink flesh, and there's a sturdy male voice going, 'OK, pal. We'll take it from here.'

Kelly backs away, still on her knees, from the two cops, who begin working at the man's chest.

'It's too late,' she says, but they ignore her.

She fetches the man's shoe. Puts it on his foot and crawls away.

If. If you hadn't looked at him, he wouldn't have crossed the road.

Her nails are bleeding.

If. If you had been quicker, you could have plugged the hole in his gut.

Kelly scrabbles harder in the dirt.

If. If you hadn't raised your hand, you would never have been here. None of this would ever.

None of it.

None.

The way you hit her, flat of the hand upright into the flesh beneath her jaw. Not her jaw. Her throat. You know it is her throat: the soft give of it, the startled cracking back of gulped breath, of choking break. Of your own dangerous palm, folding in on itself as the body drops. Heavy.

Heavy legs, heavy shoulders. Shouting. Your father, slapping you? You, running from the awful huddle you had made.

Afterwards, huddled in your room. Dark. Cool, until the ringing doorbell and the tread of police boots on feet, in your hall, your hall – and your flatmate, letting them in, letting them all the way up to your cool, dark room, and the light flooding on.

They're coming to take you away ha-ha.

Except he isn't your flatmate, and it isn't your room. It is a borrowed couch, a stained Dralon surfboard that smells of accidental nights.

She is back there again. Why there? Why now? Kelly tugs at her hair, desperate to forget. She can feel gritty earth on her scalp. She takes a long breath, and lets go. Another breath, then she returns to her task. She claws further into the hole she is digging in the mud; she has marked the spot with two big purplish stones. Under her favourite angel, in the overgrown garden next to Dennistoun Library, is a shimmery feather-tree. She thinks it's what they call an acer. The purple stones match the colour of the tree. It's a forgotten garden this; the old house it belongs to is long empty. Not even Dexy knows about it; it's a place she can come and rest and be quiet. A safe place.

Glasgow is in shock. You can feel it permeate the city's walls, turning glittering mica into tears. Her citizens are reeling. They shuffle, catch eyes and have no need of speech. Weeping strangers are consoled. Grown men embrace, and shops give out free coffees to the bastard polis, who are getting pats and claps instead of pelters. It is the saddest kindness. You wish it could always be this gentle here. Night has come to the dear green place. The Gallery of Modern Art has become a starlit scented sea of tea lights and roses, the reams of reporters and camera crews keeping a respectful distance until folk leave the glow of the candles. Then they pounce. She'd seen a blonde woman in a Puffa jacket put her arm round a crying man. Nodding, listening, then letting him go and writing in her notepad. Kelly stayed, hunkered near the columns, until dusk fell.

Heart attack, I heard. Aye – at the wheel.

If. If you hadn't been there.

No sure. Six folk? Maybe seven? Och, here, son. Just you let it out.

Where will the man in the office shoes be lying? Soft rain begins to fall. Kelly had left the city centre in the dark, when the pressing crowds got too much, swelling with people on their way home from work, folk who'd heard it on the news and just wanted *to be there*. Why? Why stand in a place where a few hours earlier you might have been mown down too? They've cordoned off the streets, the actual places where the crumpled shapes Kelly cannot erase were lying. But even so, folk press and throng. Wanting to be present on those precise, dark spots. Why? Could you not just sit at home watching your family chomp dinner, and understand how the loss of them would splinter you, would keep on splintering for years to come? Could you not just stand on a cliff edge instead, or dip your foot out in traffic from the safety of the kerb, and think *how fleeting, how fragile I am*? Feel the ache of all that unfinished business left to do?

Kelly walked straight through the Merchant City, skirting blue lights and flash bulbs. Marched the full length of Duke Street, through the city's old heart, purposeful walking with no direction but out, and it so happened it was east and it so happened it was here, to this garden. Following her feet, because she didn't know what else to do.

Ach, Kelly is a liar. Kelly needed a drink. The rain mists and murmurs, dripping into her eyes. She shoves her hair behind her ears. Feels grime on her face. She'd to dig really

36

deep the first time, when she was burying the engagement ring, finding a space under this nest of roots. Deep as deep, to keep it safe from herself, until she'd worked out what to do. But now, she wants it. Needs it. Needs to lose herself in the burn of numbing alcohol. Too late for a pawnshop, but there will be someone, somewhere, who will give her twenty quid for a diamond. Every place has margins, dark tidelines where flotsam lies.

There is a blue-lit mortuary on the banks of the Clyde. Will the man in the tan shoes be lying there?

Tiny puddles form. She can feel the sting of her torn nails. She scratches deeper into soil. The living, dank smell of earth.

All those strangers, reaching out. There is too much speaking in her city, too much pawing going on. Open mouths, open arms. A desperation to give abounds. People are literally giving of themselves at the blood bank, queuing all the way down St Vincent Street. As if they must bleed too. The city feels like a sombre Hogmanay, when every stranger is a friend and you are forced to link collective arms. *Join in, you know you want to!*

You come to a city for its anonymity. To shroud yourself in crowds. If she had wanted . . .

Yes. The grainy earth rustles. Her thirst intensifies. Behold – an old Burger King bag. She shakes off the dirt, unwraps the bag. There it is: a long, boat-shaped diamond, flanked by two smaller stones. She slips the ring onto her finger; she doesn't know why, but it looks so nice. Oh, it is magpie-bright. Glittery. She sways her hand this way and that, bright eyes winking, and she does not think of the girl who owns it, nor the screams of falling people, nor the man. Nor Dexy. She will not think of him. He could sell the ring for her, she knows that, but if she sees him, she might break down. Be like all those other people, and she's not.

She's not.

Kelly's hands are filthy. The rain hardens; it is a million tiny needles jagging through her jumper. She is suddenly freezing. Remembers that her greatcoat lies with the man. Wherever he's been taken, her greatcoat will be there, sheltering him. Even if they've chucked it in a bin, it did its job and sheltered him, and she wonders about the before, when it wasn't hers, when the coat was a soldier's. When did the soldier wear it? Did it once soak up his blood too?

She shivers. She's never thought about that. Maybe that was always her coat's destiny: to be a winding sheet. Maybe one frost-glazed morning the fabric would have been found stiff with her final breath. Kelly, her coat and the last doorway she ever cooried inside.

It can happen like that. Nobody skippers down for the night expecting not to wake. Especially if you're buzzing, or snug with warm drink. You don't notice then, how your body chills. How the empty slooshing in your tummy infiltrates your brain and your pulse speeds as you become slow. Clumsy-sleepy slow, and then you burrow and you burrow in, all tight and too-hot and chittering. That is when you're glad of the shout-and-shake, a polis or a street worker with soup.

Keep alert. Keep alive.

Keep moving.

The Fruitmarket. Kelly pats down the earth she's disturbed. Up at the Fruitmarket will be a good place to go. Full of people whose work starts at three a.m.: merchants and chefs, fishmongers, florists. A twilight time where things fall off lorries and bruised fruit is punted amongst the fresh. There is bound to be some shady dude happy to buy a diamond in with his beansprouts. She looks up at the old sandstone house in whose garden she squats. *Hopefield* is carved above the door. The house is from the same era as the library next door, a time when Glasgow was the second city of the Empire and names got hewn in stone. Nobody comes here. One final scuff of her boot smooths the earth flat.

As she creeps from the garden, white light falls from a street lamp, a vein of bright across her arm. The ring on her finger glitters. Kelly trembles her knuckles and the diamonds come alive, dancing prisms in the rain, and the moonlight, and the piercing LED. She feels the angel watching her from the roof of the library.

I was going to take it back.

The angel is a clever, proud girl. Copper-green, she stands on a globe and reads a book, forever stuck at the same page.

Look, she's lost the ring now anyway. Far as the lassie's concerned, it's already gone.

Kelly tells herself this all the way up the road. Her knees are stiff again, and her ankles. The joints of both her big toes feel hot and tender. The proof of last night's binge is flaring through, in angry beacons.

Nae doubt, it's gout. She can hear Dexy singing like a demented pixie. *Bloody hell. You're gonny swell.*

She limps onwards, up through the desolate north of the city, where it is all long, bleak roads and high flats. Past a juddering, static taxi where the driver sits with the window down, smoking. Words curl from the radio inside. *Police are appealing for witnesses.*

'All right?' He nods, in another gesture of unwanted solidarity. Kelly feels she has to nod back. It is so strange, this being noticed as a person. Besides the driver and her, there is nothing; it's as though the stillness of snow has fallen over Glasgow. As she moves beyond the reverberations of the taxi, the streets hold silence like a cradle. Walking at night is a thing to do; it's different from skulking in the day. At night, you can own the city, you become legitimate. Kelly knows and pushes at her limits daily, but night is the difference between being in a cage and being in a safari park.

Kelly, tell me. What kind of animal would you be?
Well, Kelly, I'd like to be a cheetah. Or a lion maybe.
Would you? Aye.
Aye, but I'm probably a . . . wee mental stoat.

Where did the man in the tan shoes live? What if he had a pet? What if he lived alone and he had a pet and nobody feeds—

Stop, Kelly. Just stop.

She hugs herself tight, shoves her hands into the heat of her armpits. At last she reaches the sprawl of Blochairn, and the Fruitmarket. Acres of low storage buildings, a recycling plant, and a view of the huge gas storage towers that dominate the horizon. The M8 motorway hums in the background, but there's no tune to it. Behind the gas towers, the dark sky is thinning to pink, and she thinks the rain has stopped. When you're wet, you're wet, so you stop noticing.

Oh man! Look, there is the Budgie. Her heart leaps at the recollection of lost nights in friendly fug. It's been a long time since she's been in there. The building is a simple, windowless block, with serrated buttresses along one wall, like a set of stairs lying on their side. It is marooned in wasteland that used to be houses, and is the place of legend: a market pub with special dispensation to open at the crack of dawn. Pop stars have drunk here after gigs; there are photies behind the bar.

Kelly has a special trick, a philosophy if you will, of forgetting things the instant they are not in front of her. It's her mental equivalent of travelling light. *I've forgot you already*, she tells the man lying swaddled in her greatcoat. All bad things, get to the back of the queue. Cause if you can't remember them, then they haven't happened. It's a thing to be cultivated, this goldfish brain of hers. Alcohol and fitful sleep help. Sober, it is harder. She had actually forgot about the Budgie, though. Soon, it will be serving

40

fried Lorne sausage and pints for the nightshifts coming off. Pints. This is serendipity.

'Sssseh,' she says, enjoying the tickle of sound on her lips. She tries to remember where that word comes from. Serendipity. And how she knows what it means.

Blochairn Fruitmarket is not a pretty place. No Covent Garden, this. The metal gates of the complex are open, lorries filtering through as dawn begins to blink. The recycling plant is also open, in case some all-night reveller gets the urge to bank his bottles responsibly. There's a big green hopper for old clothes out front, and a sign that says: *Please do not leave bags outside the hopper*. There are piles of bags outside the hopper. Kelly hirples in. A security light flashes, and she freezes. Nobody shouts; the car park is empty. Over to the hopper, quick rummage through the bags to find something that will keep her warm; she doesn't care what, because nothing will ever be as good as her great greatcoat.

Even so. She's glad she gave it to the man. That he had the comfort of it.

Comfort, Kelly? He was bleeding . . .

Shut up, Kelly. Please, shut up.

Halfway down the third bag of old jumpers and shoes, she strikes gold. It's a big, checky tweed coat with a furry collar. Is it real? She sniffs at the fur. Bit foosty, but then, that could be her. She tries the coat on. It is cosy and volu-minous. *Madam, that is so you. It will go with everything, you know.*

Kelly's not very tall, and the fabric falls almost to the floor.

Perhaps madam might like a slight heel?

There are plenty of shoes in the discarded bags. *Oh, I couldn't, thanks. No heels. Ma feet are louping.*

She checks the coat for pockets: two nice deep ones, and a silky secret one inside. 'Serendipity,' she says again. Her tongue sticks. Her mouth is so, so dry. Kelly's thirst is furious and suppressed, and it won't be contained much longer. She needs the lull and guile of *glug glug glug*, the upturned glass, the liquid shimmer, coming in tides, in and out and swallowed – in, and you go deep into the bottle where all you can see are reflections.

Quick as her limpy legs allow, she crosses over the road, through the gates of the market complex to where shutters are being flung up, produce packed, and baled, and swung, where cabbages are spilling, foreign spiders running from their banana clusters, vans reversed, trousers hitched, notes thumbed. It's the men thumbing notes she seeks, the single figures lurking, looking this way and that, not the genial, red-cheeked family wholesalers who've been here since forever. Even the market seems strangely muted this morning. There are more head-shaking huddles than business being done. No whistles and shouts. Perhaps that will work to her favour, if sympathy freights the air.

Kelly steps inside a huge, long hangar. On the ceiling, two endless strips of fluorescent lights gleam all the way down, like an upside-down airport runway. Vehicles are parked alongside striped canopies. Every clatter is amplified; voices, even sombre ones, echo, dip and soar. Kelly scans the vast space until she finds a name she recognises. *Lu.* Beside the navy blue lettering of Mr Lu's Cash and Carry, a tired-looking gambler leans against a transit van, counting his winnings. She knows they play some clacking game with tiles here, in the cubbyhole behind the oilcloth. Funny what you remember. You wouldn't know from looking, but the Lulus, as Dexy calls them, specialise in oriental fruit and vegetables – and reset. They have bought stolen gear from her before. Once. Her kidneys shudder. She approaches the gambler. Must not be too desperate . . . but all she can see is the Budgie, and the man wrapped in her greatcoat, and that girl standing

42

and falling, and her going inside the Budgie and the man behind the bar going *what will it be* and her putting down notes and picking up the glass and not stopping, not stopping until she gets that fine quickening sweat on and the colours blur and the tide turns and takes her. Far and forever into blank.

'I need money,' she says. The gambler shrugs. 'Here.' She shows him the ring, winking on her finger. *Don't look at me like that.*

'Real diamond. That one's a marquise.'

The gambler grins. 'Is that right?'

Kelly pulls her new coat around her. Surely she looks smart, a woman with a fur collar? 'Look,' she improvises. 'My car's broken down and I need to get it fixed. Right now.'

'Aye, sure.' He takes her hand, all the better to study the ring. But he must notice her filthy broken nails and the jittering she cannot stop. His black hair flops over one eye. 'Much you looking for?'

'How much'll you give me?'

He releases her hand. Runs his eyes across her body. The gambler has a missing front tooth. His canine. 'Do I know you fae somewhere?'

'Nope.' She doesn't want Dexy to know she was here. It's none of his bloody business, but. His judgement doesn't matter. Nothing, none of this matters, except the cool, crisp cut of the coming drink. Just that drink she is going to have. Just that drink, and then the next one. And the next and the next until no one else exists. Until Glasgow stops weeping up close in Kelly's face, and there is no mangled leg, no man. No blood . . . 'So?' Biting back the urgency. 'How much?'

'Twenty quid?' He uses his thumbnail to pick at the gap between his teeth.

'Fuck off. I need a hundred at least.'

The gambler laughs. 'Cheerio then.'

'OK, fifty.' She says it too fast.

'Twenty,' he repeats, withdrawing one purple note from his trouser pocket. The greasy fabric is bunched there, and bulging at the groin.

I love him. Connor. I mean I really, really love him.

If you hadn't been . . .

'Christ. Thirty, OK?' She goes to pull the ring off. Already gone too far; she can't unfeel the sticky-rimmed counter awaiting in the Budgie, the clear and lucid hardness of the glass, the bitter promise as the drink coats her lips, as it hits, hits, and rinses the screaming from her ears. The skin of her knuckle is stretched shiny and red. 'Thirty, yeah? Take it.' But the ring won't come off. The more she tugs, the deeper the circle digs in, until her finger begins to change colour and even the gambler gets alarmed.

'Forget it, hen. I'm no interested.'

'Please!' She thinks her voice is getting louder, folks' heads jerking.

'Gonny just fuck off,' the gambler says. He pivots towards the oilcloth strung like a backdrop. The ring is really hurting now, her swollen gouty knuckle insistent that it shall not pass. The gold bites, constricting her ability to breathe. 'Please!' She seizes the man's arm. 'Just twenty quid. Please!' Her brain swells too, with desperation, compressing nerve and sinew, bone and purpose into this one shining fact that, through her panic, he is her only saviour and she will do anything, anything, for him to give her that twenty-pound note.

'Please,' she says, lower. She lets her mouth hang open, keeps her tongue up tight against her teeth. Sucks her cheeks in. A cloud rushes behind his eyes. Kelly still has the power. *Ha.* He'd not gambled on this. Shock, and then revulsion. He comes closer, closer, until his chest is pressed into Kelly's furry breast. She doesn't blink. The gambler raises his fist, forcing it slowly into her chin. When he speaks, it comes from his belly, in the softest of growls.

'Piss off right now, you filthy old cow. Or I will end you.'

As the gambler shoves her, Kelly ricochets into someone else. 'Ho! Easy there! You all right, missus?'

Kelly looks up. And up.

'Is this man bothering you?'

The light from the ceiling makes a halo. Kelly squints. He's huge: a big red-haired galoot of a lad, built like a rugby player, with a boxer's nose. The gambler has melted away. Shame heats her skin. The big lad has taken her arm. 'Are you all right?' he asks again.

'My car broke down. I'm stuck. I need to . . .' The lie is faint. She waits for him to mock her. 'I found a scorpion in my lychees!' she shouts at a woman staring at her.

'Just get tae fuck, you old skank!' The gambler reappears in her line of sight; he is pushing again, there is a scuffle, the ginger giant lets go her arm, blocks the gambler with a hefty elbow, more commotion – she hears someone cackle, 'Christ. I wouldny fight over *thon*!' People are laughing, and a woman's voice cries out: 'I'm a person! I'm a person, a person!'

The endless strips of overhead lights move runway-fast, Kelly being pulled or ushered, she isn't sure, away from the gambler and the fuss she has made. Noises rolling, people haggling, their world closing over her brief intrusion. No one noticing. Or caring. A daft auld cow. A Kelly cow.

She is shaking.

'What an arse. Look, are you OK?'

Not sure where the sound is coming from. Pain booms from her swollen finger; she can see the pain surround her, in black, concentric circles.

'Just breathe slowly.' It is the giant red-haired boy,

steadying her arm once more. 'Can I . . . Do you need anything? Here – do you want a coffee? I've got a flask in my rig.'

Kelly's forehead buckles. It hurts, this slab of kindness. As if all the sad love sluicing through Glasgow this morning has welled and broken over her head. If she's not careful, she is going to cry. She flexes her fingers, trying to pump the blood.

Sometimes we get stuck.

Glasgow is . . . Her chest burns. Glasgow is finally drowning her. The city is a ripped-wide belly, and it is liquid seeping dark, and it is Dexy's admonishments and a baby born to nowhere and men pissing on her as she sleeps, and it is *you do not deserve* and streets that will kill and it was a jewel, a maze, a hope destroyed.

Two old guys trundle past with a barrow. 'That's another one died in the hospital.'

Kelly stares at her ugly hand. Where is she? Was she ever here?

'Here. C'mon.' The giant boy leads her outside, to where the sun is now fully up. She blinks through spindles of light. 'Here we are.' He gestures to a metallic-red lorry with a Saltire draped behind the driver's seat. *Grier's Haulage* trails in gold letters, and a ram's skull is lashed high above the bumper.

'I'm Craig, by the way. You sure you're OK?'

She thinks about this a minute. Can't trust herself to speak. 'What's your name?'

She can't stop shaking.

'You said your car had broken down. Can I give you a lift somewhere?'

Lift. It's a funny word, thinks Kelly. She sees it written inside her head. Maybe she has her eyes closed. She used to love crosswords. Puzzles that made you play with your own

46

brain, shepherd it into connections it didn't know it knew. *Lift*. To pick up and move. To steal (colloq.). To elevate. To enlighten. To arrest (colloq.). To raise to a higher level.

She cannot go on like this.

'What do you think?' Craig's massive hand is reaching upwards, touching shiny, metallic red.

It has been a long time since Kelly's been asked what she thinks. It has been a long time since Kelly was inside a vehicle. She suspects the last time was a polis car, but she can't be sure. The thought of wheels, of flight. Of crashing buses and speeding miles. Of Glasgow's cloying maw. Of the gantry in the Budgie and glittering bottles to sluice it all away. Of Dexy's disappointment. Of open roads and open doors.

She can't stop shaking.

'Well, let's start with coffee, eh?' he says.

He opens the door to the cab. Quite a stretch, she'll have to watch her creaking knees. But there is a handy handle to grab onto, to attain this high doorway to somewhere else. Doing this means nothing. Kelly means nothing.

I didn't mean it.

If you were not there.

Kelly doesn't do decisions. Decisions have consequences, and consequences fuck you up. She doesn't have to think; she's simply climbing in a cab. With her puffy red knuckles, she grips. With her aching legs, she bounces, and the fire sparking from the stubborn diamonds on her finger bounces too. The cabin smells masculine. The seat is nice and soft. The lad unscrews a Thermos and pours her a drink. Fragrant coffee under her nose. Sunlight on her cheek. She sips. Sips again. Makes the cup of coffee last as long as she can. Until her hands no longer shake. The boy fiddles with paperwork, but she can sense he's impatient to get on.

'So. Where to? Can I give you a lift anywhere?' he says,

starting the engine. It hums beneath them. She feels warmth rising from the heater. Imagines the city shrinking away. The ring sparkles. She twists her hand to and fro, making rainbows flicker. It really is the prettiest thing. *What do you think?* she asks. Not out loud, obviously – the giant boy already thinks she's crazy. (And with good cause, Kelly.) Even so, she'll let the ring decide.

What would you be going back to?

'Or d'you need me to call someone? You don't look very well.'

She shoogles her hand a wee bit more. The diamonds go blank.

'Where are you going?' she asks.

'Portpatrick,' says Craig. 'You know it? Down in Dumfries and Galloway?'

'Oh aye.' She laughs at this, and it suddenly feels loose and easy, like she is in the breaking sea. Herself, lifted up in the laughter. Laughing at the joke that is her life. Laughing, and a wee bit scared. But fuck it. Aye.

'You utter little bastard.'

'Pardon?'

The ring frowns, and she frowns back. But you have to admire its cheek.

'Fine,' she says, sinking into creaking leather. For a few more hours, she will let herself be carried. 'I'm too tired to argue. Let's go to Portpatrick.'

Kelly will shake the dirt and soreness of Glasgow from her boots. And she'll see what she does when she gets there. It might mean everything, and it might mean nothing at all. She sets her face towards the windscreen as Craig reverses out. The morning sun blazes the gas towers gold.

And her journey begins. Again.

*

—Burn, baby, burn! Kirkcudbright inferno!

Two dervishes chanting. Chucking seaweed at one another and dancing on the beach. Amanda wears her school tie in a bandana, is ripping her blazer badge from its stitches, condemning it to fire. A boat, a book and a lion, going out in a blaze of glory.

It is your last day of school.

You watch the crest of Kirkcudbright Academy flame, add your chemistry notes to the conflagration. Later, the whole gang will come and you'll bake potatoes in the embers and get gloriously drunk on cider, but for now it is just you and her. Writing your names in the sand.

Kelly and Amanda. Kelly 'n' Mandz. Kellnmandz.

Best friends forever, on the last day of term.

She has made you a crown of bladderwrack. You wear it with pride. Look how she leaps and gyrates round the bonfire. Amanda the acrobat, turning cartwheels. Walking on her hands. She is more elegant than you, more lithe, but you don't care. She's also younger, but you are wiser. And that's the way it goes.

—Spin, Carlotta, spin! *you shout. For a second, you are children again, not teenagers, playing one of your endless make-believes. 'Carlotta and Zora' was your circus game. She grins at the name, remembers instantly, because you think the same, you and Mandz. She arches her spine, pretends she is a bareback rider balancing on an imaginary horse.*

Then other pals come, lots of them, and Mandz stops cantering on the beach. You are not done. You are not ready to stop. Momentarily, you continue your dance, but it isn't the same without her. Someone laughs, and you pull the seaweed crown from your head. Then Mandz lets out an almighty whinny. The made-up horse rears, gallops into the sea, and the serious partying commences.

All of the school is your pal tonight. Best friends forever. Your friend Katie's house overlooks this beach. Her folks are away on holiday, and you've told your mum you're staying over, to keep her company . . . We'll have pizzas, yeah . . .

'Let's Go Crazy' blares from a ghetto-blaster, and you do.

Oh, you do. You will always remember the first time. The last day of school. First day you get properly pished. But it is on healthy, appley cider, full of bubbles, fun. You drink until you're sick. A purgatorium behind the spit of rock. A refill. Another refill. The dark reek of 'something stronger' offered by Darren Carruthers – who is Katie's big brother and so should technically not be there. Leavers only, you agreed, but hey, the more the merrier, and, oh, the smack and pucker on your lips. Harsh whisky. Blind haze, white light. A beatbox thumping 'This Is Not A Love Song', and you are wild, wild, wild.

'Cum on feel the noize!' Your fists are all pumping, a primal chant. Darren rips off his shirt and seizes you by the waist – you will never forget that lurch in your belly. It is another first: a pristine, perfect feeling that is clean and dirty all at once. And so you kiss him, there, kiss first the bold glint of his clavicle in the pour of moonlight, with juice and whisky spilling on your lips, and then you flop together on the blood-hot sand.

You think it is the happiest time you ever had. You, on the cusp of everything.

Then you wake, and it is sunrise. You never made it to Katie's house, but the night was warm and you are young. No stiffness then. You and Mandz leave the beach, leave the bodies where they fell. Young, hard bodies, gone soft with drink and sleep. Part of your head feels it's lying there too, cleaved and pounding; you have never been this thirsty. Or ill. Darren sprawls on his belly, snoring.

—Did you two . . .? *Amanda leaves the question hanging.*

—God, Darren Carruthers? No. No way.

You don't think you did, at least.

You grin and squeeze one another. Hold hands like this is Primary One, because you both need to stop weaving as you walk, but also because this is momentous. Just like Primary One. Which was the first time you and she set out alone and into your future. Mandz had a doll then, called Looby-loo. Got it for her fifth birthday, and she took it everywhere, even school. You thought they'd laugh at her, but your classmates loved it. So you decided you loved it too. You craved that doll, you wept for that doll, wept so hard that your mum got you one too. I'll call it Libby, *you said.* Libby-loo and Looby-loo. Best friends forever.*

You and Mandz walk down the Stell, past the posh houses with their private moorings and their waterside view, and into town, where it smells of fish. The scallop boats have all put out to sea. The Harbour Café is quiet. Coffee, doughnuts and you are alive, alive-oh. Your sand-crusted shorts are clean enough, for you were a neat drunk then; you vomited with the accuracy and energy of youth, and it always missed your clothes.

You and Mandz will hitch from here, or get a bus; it doesn't matter. But today, there will be momentum! When your exam results come in, it will be official. You will both go up to uni and share a flat. Those conditional offers will become fact. Those UCAS letters you've hidden. They can't stop you then, not when it's official, even though they'll try. But Glasgow? *your dad will say, shocked.* It's so far away. *Your mum will understand, though, you think. You've seen how her eyes are restless. How this wee toun seems too small to contain her.*

51

Today is the start of the rest of your lives. You and Amanda. Today you are going to Glasgow for a recce. You are going to try it on for size. All through the times you forced her to study – because I can't do this alone – you have promised her this treat. Kept it glinting, tick-tock, in front of her eyes. From the rucksack at her feet which she used as a pillow last night, Mandz produces your long black tunic and some eyeliner.

—Here.

—Wait until we get there, *you tell her. The Cult are playing a gig at Queen Margaret Union! And you have tickets. You grin and squeeze some more. Knock back paracetamol. Then you both shake the sand from your toes.*

Kelly and Mandz.

Chapter Four

The old woman has been asleep for ages. Craig glances sideways, as he's been doing periodically all the way down the road. He loves this stretch, where it hugs the Ayrshire coast. A lot of the drivers hate the fact it isn't dualled, hate the twists and rises of it, the inescapable sluggish progress sandwiched between foreign cars and motorhomes, the closer to the ferry you get. Tedious, but Craig reckons the view makes up for it. On a clear day you can see Ailsa Craig. Every single curling stone in Scotland – in the world maybe – comes from there. Not a lot of people know that. His granda was a keen curler, a bowler too. Wasn't just sport: he loved to impart facts about every aspect of the world, just let them slide out, casually, as he puffed his pipe.

'Take it I'm stuck with you?'

It is the ring the woman is talking to, not him. Even in her sleep, she's been fiddling with it.

'Afternoon,' he says as she begins to stir.

'Is it?'

Blinking like a bush baby. She actually isn't that old when you look past the matted, steely hair. But her skin is roughened and raw, starbursts of veins covering her cheeks.

'No, I'm just kidding. You want a drink?' He nods to the dashboard.

'What?' She jerks, startled, scared almost.

'In that wee shelf under there. There's some bottled water.'

'Oh. Yeah. Cheers.'

Lips barely touching the neck, she chugs it down; he can see the clear spiral of the water as it torques and pours into her mouth.

'Downing it in one, eh? Somebody's thirsty.' He swings the wheel, coasting through the long lope of road that curves down to Ballantrae. Can see a camper van *and* a tractor up ahead. Great. He'll be stuck behind them for ages now.

'What?' She's scowling. 'You taking the piss?' Ice-sharp, yet the way her face protrudes from the fur collar of her coat makes her comical. It is far too big for her. The garish check of the fabric reminds him of his mum. That's why he stopped: some wee old lady getting harassed by a ned. The bright coat is deceptive. Underneath, from what Craig can see, she is pretty rank. Dirty men's trousers. One jumper, possibly two, of indeterminate shade and shape. And each time she shifted in her sleep, a puff of sourness released itself. He's pulled the wee bag on his Magic Tree right down, but the synthetic lemon scent is no match for—

'What's your name?' he asks, just as she goes: 'Who's that?' She indicates the photo taped to the dashboard – Maureen on a night out, hair all big and up, teeth gleaming.

'Oh, that's my girlfriend.'

'She's pretty.'

'Aye.'

Bleary-pink eyes, but quick with it. 'You don't sound too sure.' The woman burps softly. 'Pardon me.'

He doesn't want to think about Maureen right now. One of the joys of long-distance driving is that you get to be away for days at a time, out of sight – and out of mobile range. He's definitely going to sign up for France and all. A whole week abroad, with a trip to a vineyard thrown in at the end? Too right. His boss is always looking for novel ways to recruit volunteers.

'So what's your name?' he asks her again. There is a gap coming up, just enough road that he can jook past the tractor at least, before the next series of bends.

The woman slumps in her seat. Mumbles a couple of syllables he can't make out.

'Sorry?'

'Kelly.' She says it defiantly, with another trademark scowl.

Craig indicates to move out; if you're going, you're going, foot down, pressing hard and heave the wheel and—

'Fuck!' He swerves back in, seconds before a skein of oncoming motorbikes blare past.

'Jesus!' Kelly shouts. 'Jesus, you stupid, stupid bastard! You could've got us both killed.'

Craig grips the wheel, heart skittering. 'Keep your hair on. We're fine.'

'No, we arny. Just let me out here.'

'Here? Don't be daft.' They've already passed through Auchencrosh. 'Look, we'll be at Cairnryan in ten minutes. I don't mind dropping you in Stranraer, though, if that's where you want to go?'

She is wincing as she pulls up her boots. Maybe that's where the smell's been coming from; he hadn't realised she'd unzipped them. A drip splashes on the toecap of her boot. Christ, is she crying? He says nothing, eyes on the road. Occasional glances over. She is chewing at the cushion of flesh below her thumb. The cabin seems filled with fragile glass.

'Kelly, I'm sorry, right? I was an arse. I shouldn't have pulled out there. I'm sorry, OK?'

She nods.

'You want some tunes on?' He'd kept the radio off when she was sleeping. The speed at which she'd conked out made him think she really needed it. And to be honest, once she'd taken him at his word and clambered in, he had no clue what to say to her. Cause folk don't do that, do they? Usually, if you go 'Can I help?' or whatever, folk just smile and say 'No, I'm fine'. That way, nobody gets embarrassed.

She shakes her head. They drive on for a while, listening to engine noise. It's Kelly who breaks the silence. 'I seen the accident yesterday. The one in town.'

'Seriously? Christ. Was it—'

'I don't want to talk about it.'

'Sure, sure. I got you.' He has a million questions he wants to ask. Immediately, she is transformed from bag lady to trauma victim. Witness to the eye of the storm. Everyone is talking about it. Is it true a guy tried to jump into the bus to stop it? Did the people die right away? What was the noise? Did they make a noise? Craig has never seen anyone die. With his gran . . . she's the only person he knows who died, and that was very quiet. Typical Gran – no fuss and nonsense. It was just one day he was at school and she was home, in the kitchen, and then his mum came into the class-room to get him, and that was it. She was gone.

He feels shit that he laughed at Kelly. At her vulnerability. He needs to reset the balance.

'Maureen's pregnant,' he says, nodding at the photo. It is the first time he's said it aloud.

'Is that right? Congratulations.'

'Cheers.'

'You don't sound very happy.'

He glances at his own eyes in the rear-view mirror. Blue, with sandy lashes. Maureen's eyes are green. 'I'm just a bit . . . We weren't planning it, you know? Least, I wasn't.'

'And what does Maureen think?'

What *does* Maureen think? It escalated so fast, her telling him, the pause of shock and awe. Him not saying the right words – did he actually say any words? – while his brain was thinking *fucking hell* and his world was constricting like somebody had sooked it up with a straw. But then it was blossoming too, all the whorls of noise and broken images in his head that were trying to make a picture.

'I don't know,' he says finally. 'We had . . . och, we'd a – it wasn't a fight exactly. But she ended up greeting.' He blows air through his teeth, trying to dispel the memory of Maureen's tears. 'Christ. It's such a massive thing, you know? I don't have the first clue what to do.'

Kelly helps herself to another bottle of water. 'But a baby's such a wee thing. Really. When you think about it. Here.' She's taken the lid off for him.

'Oh. Thanks.'

'Have you spoken to her since you left?'

'No.'

'You should.'

'Aye. Maybe.' He takes a drink. What on earth could he say? *I'm sorry I wasn't happy when you told me. I'm sorry I ran away – because you'll always remember that bit, won't you? I'm sorry I wanted to go and ask my mum what to do, and I'm sorry I freaked when I remembered how my mum got left on her own too.*

No matter what happens, Maureen will know that Craig does not know how to be a good dad. Not being a good dad is in his DNA.

'I'll phone her when I get to Belfast. Maybe. I need to get my head straight first.'

Kelly stretches out her legs. 'Ooh-ooh.'

'You all right?'

'Nope. My joints are made of crystal. And the crystals are made out of wee.'

'Um. OK. If you say so.'

'Gout, Craig,' she says sternly. 'It's a terrible thing.'

'Is that no what Henry the Eighth had? Can you still get that?'

'Apparently.' She wiggles her fingers at him. 'Stay away fae the demon drink, son.' When she smiles, her face crinkles into bright folds and the broken veins blush. 'And, Craig?'

'Yes, Kelly.'

'Phone her now, eh? Don't leave it till it's too late.' She snuggles into the seat. 'Because you never know when too late will be.' She closes her eyes.

It is around eleven when they get to Portpatrick. Craig has to deliver a load of veg to the hotel and the three pubs there, then pick up whatever shellfish has been landed at the port and take it back up to Cairnryan in time for the ferry. There isn't that much turnaround time, but the lorry is refrigerated. If Kelly is in no rush, he could take her for a bite of lunch at the Crown. She's sleeping again, head back, mouth slack. Relaxed. He doesn't know why, but the thought makes him happy.

He pulls into the side entrance of the clifftop hotel. Stops, and stares at the breaking sea. Up here is astounding, surpassing even the view on the road down. Craig jumps from the cab. The air hangs blue above a steel-green ocean, seagulls wheeling and drifting in to feed their squawking young. The tang of salt. His mobile phone. You get a good reception up here. He walks a little bit away from the rig, so there is nothing in his sightline but the green of the grass and the blue of the beyond.

He and Maureen speak until it stops being awkward, and they are them again, and the gap has gone. He allows the bubble of doubt to pop open, finds she was in there too, and then they are laughing, laughing at all the other bubbles that burst like pearly spray. *I love you*, he shouts, over the sound of the sea.

When he returns to his rig, he will thank Kelly. Not too fussy, because he doesn't think she'll like that – more of an *All right, Mrs Smart-Arse. You were right. Come and I'll buy you lunch.* But when he returns to the red lorry with its grinning skull and its static Saltire, Kelly has gone.

Chapter Five

Wow. Just wow. It takes the breath from you.

Full swell of the tumbling ocean. Moon pulling, earth tilting, spinning so that the water sloshes from sea to shining sea. Clifftop gannets cry into the wind, which buffets and salts the dove-white clouds and the rippling, racing grass.

She had forgotten the thrill of the sea.

Up high on the cliff, Kelly sits with her back to the old radar station. She thinks it might have been from the war. Radar or telecommunications, its big dish booming out to sea. Then BT started using it. Now it lies empty: wooden doors padlocked, its thin Crittall windows rusting through flaked blue paint. A lighthouse without the tower. Or light. But once upon a time, it blink-blinked a pulse across continents, trying to communicate its presence. The outpost reminds her of that grand ice cream shop in Largs. Only grubby. Grubby art deco. 'Deco,' Kelly says aloud, cupping her hands.

'DEHHH-COOHHH,' she goes, into the gusts of wind and the glistering light.

'DEHHH- COOOHHH AND CRIIIIII-TAAALL.' Up on her feet. *Crittall*. How does she know that?

She glances behind, but there is no one around. Sit down, you silly cow. She has always loved Portpatrick. It is both pretty and majestic. Stare down on the vast flat yawn of breathing ocean, and you could be at the end of the world. Yet here leads to many places. Over there, beyond the horizon, is the Isle of Man. Then Ireland. Follow this cliff path round to the left and there are smugglers' caves and coves made of the smoothest rose-pink stone, and a rugged golf course clinging to the cliff.

Kelly hugs her knees. She remembers this. Thirty years and she remembers this. It is spooling out in tatters.

Her dad took her to a Burns supper here, at the golf course. One of their few excursions out, after they'd brought her home. *Wee, sleekit, cowrin, tim'rous beastie.* It ended badly. Wine, whisky *and* gin. She's pretty sure she shouted *Rabbie Burns was a dirty old shagger* at the club captain as he was rounding off 'The Immortal Memory'.

Right now, Kelly's thirst for a drink is overwhelming. It's a whispering, roaring, all-erasing blur. If she eases into it, into just feeling the feeling, and fighting it, she can no longer see the humiliation on her dad's face. Nor the arms that supported her across the golf club's tartan carpet, the feet that led her out. She can still see, vividly, the diamond crystal facets of the whisky tumbler, the amber smoke within. She sits on her hands and waits. What a nice boy he was, that Craig. He'll be a good dad. She takes a long breath. Holds onto the rough grass beneath her palms. To her right, you can make out the turrets of the grand white hotel, just the tips of its fairy-tale towers, further back along the clifftop.

After a while, when she's sure Craig must have given up and driven off, she takes out his sandwiches. He could've offered her one. Cheese and pickle, naturally. Plain, straight-forward. Big hunks of bread, ragged edges. She suspects it was Craig who made his own pieces, hastily assembled after his fight with Maureen. Chewing hurts her teeth. Surprising how long they've managed to stay wedged in her gums.

Despite the rest of her bits and bobs, Kelly has endeavoured to keep her teeth clean. Skin you can scour, hair can be unmatted. But teeth – she bares them here – are little pearls of permanence. Toothpaste is a luxury, so she uses liquid soap in public loos, applied with a just-rinsed finger. You can get those wee packets sometimes, from City Mission, full of travel samples of shampoo and doll-size soap and Colgate. These 'sanitary packs' appear sporadically – she reckons one of the Mission's volunteers works in a hotel, and filches supplies when the chambermaids aren't looking.

Sss – sanitary.

What's the one thing you think of when you say that word? And what's the one thing that's never in their sanitary packs? Fanny pads. You can get them at the food bank, but you need to be 'referred'. So stripped are you of your humanity that a more appropriate person than you must decide if your menstrual blood deserves catching. She thinks you can maybe get them free now, in colleges and that. Luckily, Kelly is fast becoming a dried-up old prune, so the Bodyform versus scrunched-up-bog-roll dilemma no longer applies.

She downs another bottle of water – she has relieved big Craig of a six-pack of Strathmore water as well as his sand-wiches. What a cow. Tongue probing: she could do with a wee rub the now; her teeth are quite furry. Ah, but that was a good sleep. Feeling safe with Craig, and the movement and the warmth while you were still and comfortable. Sleep is often a godsend. Sleep and staring. Kelly does a lot of that.

Identify your triggers, Kelly. That's what Shirley says. And says, and says, and says. If Shirley had a catchphrase, that would be it. Delivered in a sing-song voice. Stupit, simpery Shirley-the-addictions-counsellor. God bless Shirley. Shirley the Shirehorse, Kelly calls her (aye well, she's called her worse too). Their sessions were more like jousting.

Identify your triggers, Kelly.

Eh . . . being awake?

Don't forget to reward your progress.

With a cheeky wee glass of—

Perhaps if you tried to take this seriously. Life is full of choices, Kelly.

Seriously? You think I should be serious? Here was me thinking I was having great fun. D'you know I shat myself last week?

You do realise you will die, Kelly?

Well, we all die, Shirley.

Your gout. Your liver. Your palpitations. You only have one body, Kelly.

Kelly tugs at a clump of grass. Poor Shirley will be sad. Sad at the state of her. She pictures catapulting Shirley out to sea. Just firing her by her braces. Yup, she wears red braces on her jeans. Jeans, dungarees and dirndl skirts. That is Shirley's wardrobe. Or maybe she just dresses down to make her clients feel at home. In her Glade-perfumed office, with the calming, abstract colour-block canvases purporting to be art. They make Kelly furious, those 'paintings'. Often, when Shirley is speaking, Kelly is staring over her head into a swirly blue-green whorl and being utterly enraged at the audacity, at the lack of effort that has gone into making, and choosing, those pictures.

She tears the grass she's mangling from its moorings. Wee crumbs of dark earth scatter on her hand. She had been doing so well this time. That time. That last time. But that bloody bride-to-be had to go and give her money. A bagful of shiny money. See if it had just been the usual, a couple of quid in ten and twenty pences? Kelly can handle that. Buy a bag of chips. Eat chips slowly. Walk about. Find a doss. Go to sleep. But how are you meant to deal with a big cash bonus bonanza? Doubtless the lassie thought she

63

was being nice, but you'd be as well giving a suicide a loaded gun. Kelly cannot be trusted. It is a compulsion: there is never *just one drink*, and it is never enjoyed. It is devoured; she flagellates herself with it, purges herself of misery and shame until she is hollow-sick.

The water she's tanned sloshes in her stomach. There's some uncomfortable gurgling occurring down below; actually, she's feeling a bit squeamish. Wolfing giant Craig's giant sandwiches like that. No wonder he's such a big lad. She should have rationed them.

Empty yourself of all desire.

Good call, Shirley. Detach yourself and you will not be reached, not be hurt, not be judged. You will become a void to be avoided. Kelly stares ahead. Despite its movement, the sea is timeless and patient. Up here, you are totally exposed.

She's got the taste. Got the taste. She wants a bloody drink.

What's to be done?

Although she got a few hours' kip in the lorry, Kelly doesn't feel refreshed. Her body is used to half-sleep; it functions on the barest of care. Being rocked to sleep in that cabin has spoiled her. Deep and clean it was. She wants more. She wants to be in a room with a roof. A room that is not shared, where you can sleep until you choose to wake, and never be disturbed. A hidey-hole, just for today. To sleep and sleep until her thirst has melted and the blood-coloured knot and the brown leather shoe at the edge of her vision has gone.

There is nobody else on the clifftop. She gets to her feet. Rattles the mesh fencing that stands all round the radar station. Without complaint, the mesh flaps wide at the base. She wriggles under, goes round the back. Front door is too obvious. Everywhere has a compliant back window, the kind with a hopper that . . . Nope. What about this one? Nope.

The windows are stuck fast. Salt air will do that to metal. Ach well, Kelly. Direct approach it is. She nips back outside the fence, picks up a chunk of rock. Under, round, take aim and—

A lovely shattering crack. Elbowing the shards of glass away – *that's you blooded now, tweed coat. Yes, this is the kind of reprobate you're shackled to*. Her great greatcoat witnessed many misdemeanours; shame upon shame was heaped on that once-proud uniform. So her thinks-it's-posh, new, furry tweed coat had better get used to it too. She hauls herself over the windowsill, and in.

Smells OK. The radar station is not derelict, merely abandoned. There's a noticeboard, with rosters on, and a sink with . . . Huh. No water. Pale yellow walls, surprisingly graffiti-free. Well seen this isny Glasgow. There's a dusty coat hanging and an old yellow jacket on a peg, and . . . She goes into the next room. Ya dancer! A tatty, stained . . . oh yes . . . reasonably comfy couch. Without further ado, Kelly tilts the Venetian blind, drapes the dusty coat over her for a blanket and curls up. Outside, the sea continues to shush. For hours she will focus on this, and on the rainbow sparkles that live inside the ring, until sleep arrives. Before it takes her, one final thought comes, fast like a shooting star: that her greatcoat had an honourable death at least.

Sunlight nudges her awake. It falls in slatted fingers through the blinds. Eyes webbed with sleep, Kelly blinks and waits for the familiar chill of stone to seep. But underneath is soft, spongy. She tests it with her fingers. There is a definite bounce. She didn't dream this peaceful couch. She stretches out, a feline in the shaft of sun, until the pressure in her bladder forces her to sit. She wriggles her toes. Refuses to look down, except she finally has to, because she canny find her boots. When she does peek, the black and bare feet of a hobgoblin greet her. Grey horns, curled and fused into flesh that can no longer feel it. She shakes out her bundled-up socks. Dry skin flies in dandelion spores. Can you tell the passing of time from feet flakes? Like rings on a tree, maybe the layers of callused skin on Kelly's toes narrate her life. Right. Find boots, then out for a pee. But as her bare soles spread on the cool linoleum, she remembers the sink. Not too high, nice and wide. She squats her arse over the lip, sighs her deep relief. There is no water to sluice her piss away, so she takes a long draught from one of the remaining bottles, then rinses the sink clean. Kelly is not an animal.

She checks the cupboards, but of course there is nothing in them. Sits a while on the couch. Another while passes. Then another. Sips the last bottle of water. The pale yellow wall brightens as the sun fires up. Good colour choice, this – cool in summer and cosy in winter. Well done BT's interior decorating department. It would be quite good just to stay here. She could make curtains for either side of the blinds. Get some pot plants.

The ring on her wedding finger chuckles. Kelly wiggles it, and chuckles back. It is probably time for breakfast. Lunch? She stoops to put on her boots. Realises her knees aren't too sore. In fact, she feels ready for a walk.

Out into the clifftop breeze, and again, that green and metallic-blue view. Down past the wall of the white-turreted hotel she goes, where the giant boy dropped her off yesterday, down past memorial benches positioned to face the sun. The path is broad and well paved, becomes wide steps as you near the long sweep of the port. Portpatrick nestles in its landscape. It's not cowed by the cliffs and the height and the sea; it simply relaxes into its curved bay. Portpatrick is white houses with blue doors and welcome mats. It is a clean and smiley town. Unlike Glasgow, its air is bracing and its streets are sparse. Palm trees flourish: proof of the Gulf Stream. Fresh lobster at the Crown Hotel, and acres of creels on the harbour. There are fewer shops than Kelly remembers as a girl. The ones remaining are festooned with ropes of coloured-glass floats and pottery knick-knacks. She eyes the outdoor tables looping from pub to pub. A whole row of pubs. Outside one, a family is enjoying chips in a basket and gleaming barley-sugar pints. Must be lunchtime right enough. Pints for breakfast isn't normal.

Kelly pulls her coat around her, though it's mild. What they call an Indian summer. She's embarrassed by what lies beneath. Fifty miles from home, and that's it started already. The walk of shame.

Kelly. You are being ridiculous. There's barely anyone left to remember you.

Barely.

She looks for a distraction, sees tourists clatter from a minibus. *Pilgrims' Progress*, it says, in curly gilt along the side. They seem like an interesting bunch, all cameras and white sneakers and bobble perms and caps, as they trill past her, towards the Crown, gathering themselves at three adjoining tables. It's a happy jumble: menus tossed and swapped, chairs scraping. There is lots of laughter. The family look annoyed.

'Hi, honey,' says a lady with white sunglasses. 'Thanks for waiting. May I give you one of these?' The lady's just got off the bus too, has the distracted look of an organiser about her, with her clipboard and little satchel. She sounds American. She's offering some kind of leaflet. When Kelly ignores her, the lady raises her sunglasses (it's not even that sunny).

'Oh. My. I'm sorry, ma'am.' The lady snatches the leaflet away, as if Kelly might contaminate it.

'Ho!' Is it her hair sticking up? She pats at the top of her head. Now that the offer is being retracted, Kelly wants this leaflet.

'Pardon me,' says the lady. 'I thought you were one of my pilgrims.'

'No, but I'll take your leaflet.'

The lady lowers her sunnies. 'Um, sure, sweetheart. If you're . . . In fact . . .' A megawatt smile switches on. 'In fact, absolutely. I'm sure if the good Lord put you and me here together on this very spot, then he *meant* for you to have this leaflet. Here, darlin', here. Take two. Say,' she clamps red-nailed mitts onto Kelly's hand, 'would you like a snack? Hey, Marlene!' She is shouting now, waving at a large pink woman who is downing a pint of something pale.

Kelly takes a step back. She's got herself in too deep. They're gonny baptismally plunge her in the sea, or steal a kidney.

'Would you ask the server? Could we get some food to go?' The lady releases her grip, but only so she can panto-mime eating a sandwich to a befuddled Marlene, who shouts back, 'But we just got here, Sooz.'

'It's not for me,' she mouths, pointing ostentatiously at Kelly, who is clearly blind as well as deaf.

'No, you're all right, thanks.'

'Oh, honey. Well, bless you.' She's squirrelling in her satchel. 'Bless you indeed.' Jesus, woman, not the hot hands again. 'And may your progress be a happy one.'

They part, the lady to her pilgrims and the pub, Kelly to across the road, as far and as fast as she can. Oh, people. Her heart flutters; she is reedy with lack of air. Too much interaction for a piece of paper she didny even want. Trouble with you, Kelly, is you're thrawn. Her fingers tingle where the lady clasped them. The pressure of manicured thumbs on begrimed skin. Kelly's hand felt sore when the woman grabbed her, and now it just feels warm.

She fans herself with the leaflets, drifting towards the plash of water. There is nothing on the other side of the street except the railing and then the sea. They used to come here on a Sunday, and the kids would have cream soda with lime. Her mum always had Pimm's, tea and a scone, Dad a lager shandy. They'd sun themselves till their shoulders burned, then go down to the beach to cool off. Orange Crimplene swimsuit, a wee gold buckle pressing on her belly button. She thinks her mum taught them to swim here. Another splinter of memory takes her unawares. Red lips, a flash of dark, wayward hair. Forever in a cloud of perfume. Her mum looked like the Green Lady picture your gran had above the fireplace. Myriad bangles clinking on her wrist. Silver, amber, rose gold. She never took them off – Kelly can hear them clear as anything, even now, wiping seawater from her brow. There is sand on her nose.

Was it here?

She goes down the stairs to Portpatrick beach. There's a couple of dog walkers by the harbour wall. It's cooler here. Breezy. Tide is out. The ground between Kelly and the sea is damp and sheeny. Imagine marking that pristine sand.

Behind her, in the village, a church bell chimes. On and on until it reaches twelve.

More than – she works it out – forty hours. Kelly has been sober through one of the worst days she can remember. What does she do now? Portpatrick isn't the kind of place you beg. She glances at the leaflets the lady gave her. *Pilgrims' Progress*, in the same florid gold. *Travel through Scotland in the footsteps of saints and sinners . . .* Yawn. She notices a ten-pound note has been slipped between the folds. Cheers, doll. She stuffs the note in her pocket. Flexes her fingers. Her joints click and grate, but they move. Do they feel less knotted? She examines her knuckles. Maybe. Tests the ring again. Still stuck.

That was nice of her, though. The lady. Nice, and quiet. She suspects that was out of keeping: someone who wears white sunglasses when it's not even that sunny is bound to favour extravagant gestures. Ten pounds – well, you'd get four pints for that. Or if there's a corner shop that sells White Lightning? Any cider, she'll take any cider, coppery plump bottle vibrating as you chug it down. Two two-litre bottles, big as a baby.

Or.

You could spend your ten pounds on a bus, go straight to Gatehouse and give that lassie her ring.

Be sober, Kelly.

You know you want to.

Ninety meetings in ninety days. That's what they say, but then *they* would be arseholes.

Every day you are in recovery, Kelly.

You know that if you drink again, it will be worse than before you quit?

Aye. You told me that the first time, Shirley Shirehorse. One day at a time, swee-eet Jee-sus. See when you have no home and no watch, time is a difficult concept to grasp. Mainly, you are marking time and wasting time and working terribly hard to not acknowledge time at all. Time measures you. It is a passage. Its purpose is to regulate work or ritual. What if you have neither? What if all time does is magnify the deep and pulsing waste of your life as it drifts before your eyes?

More than forty hours. That's how long the man in the tan shoes will have been dead.

The bridge of her nose tingles, and the skin below her eyes. Kelly makes herself yawn. She tells herself this is not important.

The leaflets are branded the same as the bus. Is it a cult? There's a spectral hand lifting a spectral curtain on a spectral Celtic cross. *South-west Scotland – a cradle of Celtic faith.*

Join us on a journey through the past as we explore the medieval tradition of pilgrimage. Enjoy some of the most beautiful and forgotten corners of this ancient land as we retrace paths where saints were made, kings were humbled and sinners shriven.

Shriven. That's a cracking word. Combining shrivelled and craven. Religions do have lovely words to play with. So what if Kelly does go to Gatehouse? What then? Cut off her finger or cut off the ring? In the sealight, the diamonds laugh. Water, water, all around. And not a drop to drink. Her head is tender with all the bouncing light. Maybe seawater would loosen the ring. Or seaweed? It's pretty slimy. She takes a tentative step with her cloppity boots, off the stones and into sand. The sand is firm; her boots don't sink. You never know on this coastline. It's more dangerous further in – the Solway Firth is a place of diagonal tides and rapid, shifting estuary sands. But Portpatrick isn't sleekit like that. Probably why her mum brought them here to swim. It definitely was here that Kelly did her doggy-paddling – she recognises the jumbled stone of the harbour wall, the stunted lighthouse at the end.

She closes her eyes. Listens. Hears seafoam and gulls. The plutter of a gentle wind. Her boots creaking. Crunching sand. Sand was in their sandwiches! Long-gone laughter from voices no longer there. It was raining, Kelly remembers, it had started raining while they were in the water, that time she was learning to swim, and they were shrieking, and her mum was laughing, going *What's wrong? You're wet anyway!* They had to run all the way up the beach, to where her dad was. They could see him as they were running, scooping up the rug, towels, the picnic. Wrestling with the windbreak, its rainbow stripes flapping. Together they carried the remains of their day back to the car. Sitting damp, with steamed-up windows, as they shoved egg and sand sandwiches into their mouths.

Kelly's eyes water in the sting of salt. She scrubs them with the heel of her hand. Focuses on the rolling sea. The sand sucks as she walks, closer to where fine, lace-white wavelets break onto the shore. Trousers flapping. She bends to roll them up. She hates it when the hems get wet – it's worse, somehow, more horrible than when you're simply soaked right through. *Onwards.* Her boots land wet kisses on wet sand, leaving a puckered trail. She lifts a clod of seaweed. Its pustules are rubber: the skin of a cartoon monster. Pressing its tendrils onto the golden band of the ring, enjoying the pop as the pustules rupture. But the stubborn ring clings on. Maybe if she doesny drink. Maybe if she takes her time and soaks up the sun and pisses a lot and doesny drink anything but water, the crystals will dissolve. Kelly's not sure if that's how gout works, but it seems eminently sensible.

And it will save her from herself.

You have done this before, Kelly. You can do it again.

Satisfied, she decides to have a wee sit-down. There's no rush. Never any rush when your day is a faintly threaded search for stuff to eat and stuff to keep you warm. Kelly checks out the damp sand. Her great greatcoat would have stood up to this no bother, but she's not sure about the tweed. The fibres are quite hairy. She'll be walking about all day with a sandy arse. There's a big line of rock at the water's edge. That'll do. Oh, but you're so close to the water. Splish and splash, and the tide's coming in. She holds the burst seaweed up to the light. She could probably eat that, if she had to. 'I'm a forager,' she tells the seaweed.

How good it felt to let her toes spread on that cool lino-leum in the old radar station. Fucksake, Kelly – you are at the beach! What's the first thing you must do on the beach? It's practically the law. Quick as a zip, her boots are off. Socks too – both pairs. You should never take your boots off in public. One: you canny run; and two: what if you

can't get them on again fast enough? (And three: ohjesus-
christ, the smell.)

There we have it, though. Off they come, and her toes
are very much enjoying the air. (Feet are quite like farts, she
thinks. They never stink in private.) Her heels press on wet
sand. The soft give cradles her ugly toes, covering them with
grains as light as kisses.

There is no such thing as fate. Kelly firmly believes this,
because, dear Christ, what if this life has been waiting for
you all along? Is there such a thing as happenstance? This
ring will not move from her finger. This lorry has taken her
here. An hour's drive from here, that bride is getting married.
One hour from here, and Kelly has . . . she works it out . . .
four days. Four days of not drinking. Finger shrinking.
Tidings bringing. Walking singing.

She looks again at the leaflet. (She's lost the other one
already.) On the back is a handy map, a firm red line joining
Portpatrick to Glenluce, Glenluce to Whithorn, Whithorn to
Wigtown, with triangles and crossed circles and tiny castellated
towers. Four places. Four days. Her own wee walkabout. She
knows this landscape well enough. It is machars and rhins
and moor – huge empty distances of windswept sea and grasses
that bend in unison. She can tramp acres of nothing till she's
heather-purple, while avoiding actual human life (or pubs).
And the best of it is, no one knows she is here. If the ring is
not off by Saturday, it's finders keepers and no harm done.

Does that sound like a plan, Kelly?

Yes, Kelly. That sounds like a plan.

Pop pop-pop pop. Kelly kills off the last few pustules.
Flings the seaweed into the air and the sun flares it into a
stream of green and purple fire.

Well, she isny following those God-botherers, that's for
sure. She'll just sit tight till they're gone and let the sea
gentle her toes.

Chapter Six

Dexy plays with the letter on the table. It's from Moovup, the charity that operates this place on behalf of the council. The charity that pays him.

Dear Mr Dixon, it has come to our attention that . . .

Strange, seeing it written down. Mr Dixon. But that is his name. They don't trade in surnames much at the Outreach. Keep their labels loose and fluid. If you've gone to the bother of reinventing yourself with some elaborate (or absurd) nickname, then who is Dexy to burst your balloon? In fact, he makes a point of creating silly names himself, for anyone who troubles him. Might be their story is too sad, like the JamJays, or when he wants to diminish their power, like this pair here. The Lu brothers. Or Haud It and Daud It Fae LuLu Land, as he likes to call them. (No to their faces, obviously. Fucking flay you with a death star, or whatever it is they call they wee, sharp spinny things.)

But Christ. *Mr Dixon.* That was his da's name. Not his. You've to earn a mister, don't you? By age or endeavour, that's the trick. Names are strange.

'Dex?' Tony Lu raps the table with his big gold ring.

Dexy drops a desultory card down. 'I'm out.' The game moves on. He reads the rest of the letter, then creases it, sharp down the middle. Opens it out again and folds two wee triangles in to meet each other. Your name starts off long, and it doesny feel like it belongs to you. Then you get older and you claim it. Or, if you arny going in the right direction, it claims you.

Paul Michael Dixon. His primary school teachers would utter his name like they were pronouncing sentence. Very prescient of them. Or maybe it wasny prescient at all, but preordained, because they were preordaining it.

Come out here. Mr Donnelly would make him stand in front of the class. You are a stupid boy, you hear me? And a liar. Your eyes are perfectly fine. Of course you can see those numbers right.

Aye, he could see them fine. He just couldny read them.

Paul Michael Ignatius Dixon. Be sealed with the gift of the Holy Spirit – Father Mallen, with his creepy hands. Who would bless you, then belt you. Man, Dex was only wee. Seven, eight at most?

Paul Michael Dixon. You were warned. Out here now. Cross your right hand over your left hand. Palms up.

'Here, Dex.' Tony Lu is snapping his fingers under Dexy's nose. 'You deaf? You got any more beer?'

'Top shelf. Fridge.'

Paul Michael Dixon. I have no option but to suspend you. That was the heidie at secondary school. Dex had his own chair outside the guy's office. Probably put a plaque up to him after he'd went. But fuck you, Mr McBride, because Stow College said Paul Dixon was a boy they could do business with. If he kept his nose clean and took advantage of the additional literacy support on offer and seized this opportunity with both hands. That was what the man at his interview said, leaning forwards to impress upon Dexy the importance of each phrase.

Dear Paul Dixon. We are pleased to offer you a place on . . . What was the course again? Something about mechanics?

Dexy tries to picture the letter, the one his wee maw propped up on her teak display cabinet, next to the fake Lladró angel she'd won at the bingo. She kept it there, showing off to the neighbours. Right up until the citation for breach and assaulting a polis turned up, and the offer was quietly withdrawn. Did he fuck resist arrest. Lying polis bastards. They were trying to take Dexy's cairry-oot off him. What did they expect? He thinks he became Dexy around then.

'Cheers.' Absently he takes one of his own cans from Tony's wee brother Mikey. He loves that pssh-ftt noise when you pop the ring pull. For an addictive personality, the drink doesny really bother him. He can take it or leave it. Drugs, though. Man. Well, they are a whole other delicious, devious ball game. What starts behind the bike sheds with a wee bit of blaw becomes a wee bit of dealing, a wee bit of scoring. A big long tunnel to obliviate your shitty day, until before you know it, there is no day. No night. No wee mammy cause you fucking knocked her purse. Flogged her fake Lladró. Hit her wee pleading face.

No choice.

No, nothing but the itching and the craving and the taking and momentary bliss, but it's a bliss that shrivels in direct proportion to your need of it, and then your whole life is about that one shrinking moment, about affording it, finding it, securing it, grafting for it, robbing for it, fighting for it, fucking . . .

Aye, it's a pure riot, so it is.

He scratches his arm. He hopes wee Kelly's all right. She's not been in for days. She scares him when she goes off on one like that. Losing it. You don't see it very often. Usually, Kelly keeps herself to herself. Likes to be present around the edges only. Of events, life, people. Herself. Drunk or sober, she is a mystery contained. She comes and goes. Does her own thing. Dex has always approached Kelly the way you would a wild animal. No so much a wounded deer, but an auld grey mule who spends her days drifting and chewing the cud, but who may suddenly go mental and kick your head in.

Dex chugs a long, cool draught of lager down his throat. Mules arny even wild, are they? Anyway. The point is, being nice to Kelly, or – God forbid – offering her a space in which to interact, on some level of honesty or truth, turns her into a total flight risk. In all the years he's known her (if you can ever 'know' Kelly), he's only had a handful of what you'd call deep conversations. And even then, she's always holding herself in. From time to time, you get glimpses, brief, rare glimpses of another person she might be. A woman who does not make herself as ugly and smelly and disagreeable as possible. A woman who is not aimless, who has not switched herself off to the world, but who feels and burns and is consumed. Her flashes of temper are what show she's still alive.

Skelly Kelly. That's what Dex calls her when she's in a strop. *You've went all skelly, Kelly,* he'll say, and make her laugh. Occasionally she will actually let Dex make her laugh, but it is only when her guard is down, when she's slipped into maudlin but is not yet full-blown radge. Dex will always try to provide folk with what they need. Within reason. But 'fix' them? Never. Paul Michael Ignatius Dixon has had enough folk try to fix him over the years to know that interventions are more about the giver than the receiver.

'Want a smoke?' says Tony.

'No, you're all right. In fact, Tony,' Dexy does a wee cough, 'would yous mind not smoking in the kitchen? Only I've two pregnant lassies staying the now.'

Tony lights up his cigarette. Blows the smoke in Dexy's face. Dexy owes them money. Not so much that they'll hurt him, but enough that they are enjoying the wait. And it looks like he'll not be winning it back the night.

'Fuck this.' Dexy switches on the telly.

'Ho!' said Tony. 'We're trying to concentrate here.'

'Well, away and concentrate in your ain house then. I'm not even playing any more.'

The Lu brothers ignore him. When he was at his worst, Dexy was feared by all. *Dexy? Pure mental, him. Stitch you soon as look at you. Avoid him like the plague.*

Dexy flicks through the channels on his big new telly. Avoid him like the plague. Dexius Maximus. No. That would be his Roman general name. A plague would need to be . . . some kind of 'itis'. Deximititis?'

'Ach, fuck it,' says Mikey. 'I'm out too. Oh, here. Is that here?'

'What?'

'On there? The news. Is that no here? That bus crash. Gonny turn that up, Dex? Ho, gies the doofer.'

He chucks the remote over. *Deximititis.* Aye, that will do. That's what he has. All his entire life. Deximititis. Dexy refolds the central crease along the length of the Moovup letter, then doubles it back to make wings. Noise complaint, is it? Fucking no allowed to enjoy yourself, or have a wee bit music on now and then? Christ love you for wanting to pretend that this place was a normal house. He flicks his wrist and watches his creation fly. The paper plane soars for all of three seconds, then loops elegantly to the floor, onto the wee rug that lovely woman Samira brought them, because she was so grateful to finally get a floor of her own that she decided she didny need the rug as well.

'That's another one pegged it,' says Mikey. 'Death Alley, eh?'

'Aye,' says Tony. 'That's no where it happened, but.'

'Is it no?' says Mikey.

'Naw. George's Square is bigger.'

'Here, is that not George's Square, Dex? Where that bus crashed?'

Dexy would love to go and smash their faces in, whatever 'good neighbour' grassed them up. He picks at his arm again. This neighbour was anonymous. Didny even have the courage to say it to you straight. That is exactly what Dexy should do, with all the shitey neighbours; he should burst all their noses, then drag them in here. You try spending an evening in this soulless shell of shit, sharing a kitchenette with nineteen other folk, then getting yourself up and out at the crack of dawn to shuffle into the sunrise, because if you don't . . . *It has come to our attention that* . . .

'Dex!' says Mikey.

'What?'

'There, on the telly. Is that no George's Square?'

'George Square?' He glances at the screen. 'Naw. That's Royal Exchange. Look, lads, yous'll need to be heading soon. I need to go shopping for the night shelter.'

'I don't know how you do it. All they dossers.'

'It's just gieing folk a bed, Tony. And making twenty rolls on sausage of a morning. No big deal.'

The news is showing candles flickering round the Gallery of Modern Art – you can barely see the steps for flowers – then it switches to a man in hospital. Propped up on pillows, he is death-warmed-up in bandages. Tubes all coming out his arms, with his wife stroking his hand. But the man is looking at the camera and he is saying, 'I want to thank her. She might be a down-and-out, but she saved my life.'

His wife kind of nips his hand, and the guy lours at her. *What?* The skinny bird interviewing them turns to the camera, all serious like, and lowers her chin and speaks that reverently you'd think the man was already deid. 'With Mr Grey and Police Scotland's permission, we're showing this CCTV still, in case anyone who knows our homeless heroine might want to get in touch.'

And fuck him if they don't show a big splashy photie of

Kelly's physog. Her hair's out her face for once, so you can see her eyes, which are copper with golden flecks. They are eyes that catch you like Velcro. One and a half eyes only; she is partly in profile, her nose and chin strong, as she bears down on what Dexy assumes is the man, although his face is pixellated. 'You've a right witchy face,' he told her once, but he meant it kindly. She reminds him of Patti Smith on a bad day. Through all the grey, shambolic sadness of her, Kelly's chin has remained determined. He sees that as a sign.

He thinks he makes a noise, or maybe starts to say her name, but it is daft Mikey who goes: 'I know her!'

'How come? So do I,' says Dexy.

'Man, I knew it. *Now* I get it.'

'What?'

'You running hoors now, Dex?' Mikey is grinning away, a horrible, leery, tongue-oot grin. 'Is that how you've all they pregnant lassies staying here? Got a wee stable going, is that it? Keep the ripe juicy ones for yersel, and send the auld mingers up the market?'

'Mikey, what in Christ's name are you talking about?' Dexy hasn't considered for one minute that Kelly would have been anywhere near that bus accident, but it's right enough, when you think about it. She often parks herself at the Gallery of Modern Art.

'That auld jakie.' Mikey rewinds and freeze-frames the image. 'Aye. Definitely. That's her. Clatty auld tramp. Tried to sell me a ring the other day. Desperate, she was. Then, when I wouldny buy it, she fucking tries to sell me a blow-job instead.'

'Aw, man,' says his brother. 'That's putrid. Look at the state of her.'

Dexy feels his gut shrivel. 'Bullshit. Kelly wouldny do that.' He grabs the remote, presses *play* so her face disappears.

'Oh, would she not? Fucking aye, mate.'

'Was she OK, though? Ho, Mikey! Was she all right?' Dexy knows how fragile Kelly is, how lightly she clings to the surface of things. Seeing that destruction . . . man, they are showing the final death toll on the telly right now, using people's actual photies, with that slight unfocused blurry haze to denote they've already ceased to be. He scratches at his arm. To see carnage erupt in a place she felt safe. Christ. You'd bolt for sure. Or do some damage of your own. As far as Dexy is concerned, unexpected violence begets unexpected violence, full stop. And if you canny lash out, you turn it inways. Christ. Kelly, hen.

'Naw. Batshit crazy, so she was.' Mikey is crushing his can. 'Ended up bawling the place down, then going off with some boy in his rig.'

'What boy?' says Dexy.

'Did she try it on wi him too?' Tony takes the remote, rewinds it again to the still of Kelly bent over the injured man. 'Look. She could be chuntering away there for all we know. Is she a right gumsy? Has she got her own teeth?'

'What boy?' repeats Dexy slowly. 'What rig? Had she been drinking?'

'How the fuck would I know? A lorry. Blochairn's hoaching with lorry drivers.'

Aleisha sticks her head round the door. 'Here, Dex. Can you tap us a fiver?'

'Well, hello, gorgeous,' says Mikey. 'You legal?'

Aleisha enters the kitchen fully, her pregnant belly nudging the door wide. Mikey goes to say something else, then doesny. Instead, he wipes his nose with the back of his hand. Drains his can.

'Dex?' She stares at them: three men all gazing at the frozen screen. 'What yous watching?'

'You know the rules, hen. I canny. What is it you're needing

81

it for?' He feels damp on the pads of his fingers. Shit. He's making his arm red raw.

'None of your fucking business.' She lifts a cigarette out the packet on the table. 'Here, what's that?'

'We're watching pensioner porn, doll,' says Tony. 'Check out that mad old gobbler.'

'I know her.' Aleisha sparks a light, and Dexy winces. He canny bear the thought of all that poison pouring into the baby's tiny lungs. Aleisha blows a smoke ring. 'Was she no here on pudding day?'

'Pudding day?' says Tony.

'When we had bread and butter pudding.'

'Aye, hen.' Dexy waves the smoke away, as if that will help.

'Aye, that's right. What's her name again? Jeanie?'

'Kelly, Aleisha. It's Kelly,' Dex snaps at her. 'Look, Mikey, would you know the guy she went wi if you seen him again?'

'What guy?' says Aleisha

'Man, I don't know,' says Mikey. 'He was a massive big ginger, so probably. Aye. I think I ken him. He's got a rig with a sheep's heid on the front. A big skull, know?'

'How? What's she done?' Aleisha is really bugging Dexy. He is trying to think.

'She's been kidnapped by fucking aliens,' he says.

'You're joking.'

'Naw. Run away with a lorry driver,' says Mikey.

'How come?'

'Look, Aleisha, love. Gonny gies peace, eh? I've not got any money and I canny help the now, OK?'

'Sake,' she mutters. The door slams.

Kelly was doing all right, this time. She worked her way through that last bout of rehab, kept to her contract, the works. But it is such a thin crust, over a wound that never really leaves you.

'If you see that driver again, will you ask him? Please, Mikey. Ask him what happened. Where she went.'

'Aye, all right, Dex. Chill.' Mikey stares at him. Then his face breaks into a grin. 'Aw, man. You gonny track her down? You think there's a reward?'

'You're an arse,' says Tony. 'It would be her getting the reward anyroad. The guy in the hospital would reward *her*. No the person that finds her. Anyhow,' he slaps his brother hard, on the back of the head, 'what the fuck were you doing letting a clatty dosser gie you a blow-job? Eh? What would Ma say?'

'But, Tony, I didny.'

'Aye, but you thought about it.' Tony hauls his brother to his feet. 'Right. Up the road. We've got work in . . .' he checks his watch, 'six hours. So we need to get some shut-eye. And Dexy . . .'

'Aye?'

Tony gives him a charming, careful smile. 'You've a week to get me my money. Or one of they fingers comes off.'

Chapter Seven

It is the noise of whimpering that draws her. Stupid, stupid. You should never investigate unbidden noises – that is pretty much the second rule after never removing your boots – which was also stupid. Kelly is now walking on the equivalent of sandpaper. No matter how much she scrubs her feet, the stubborn sand has bedded in. Portpatrick beach refuses to let her go. Still, at least it might smooth her corns.

She wiggles her toes. *I'm walking on sunshine. Ooohooh.*

Tell yourself it is a mobile pedicure, and the discomfort becomes pampering. Same as when she tells herself that not eating for a day is her on a diet, or being soaked to the skin is what keeps her skin fresh. (Aye, for fresh insert weather-beaten. But you know what? Kelly never gets spots.) Usually it is best not to think of comfort, not to imagine a time where hand cream was important or you might have plucked your eyebrows before a big night out. Memory is a bastard. Suddenly, you remember the breath of anticipation in the mirror. The sharp and brutal nip, the precise small throb of pain, and before you know it, that wee nip has slid through your ribs, is lodged deep below your breast. It really hurts when it does that, the tenderness opening with it. There's a picture in your head of your bedroom, and the hopeful night ahead. Can take you ages to reclose the wound. So. Yeah. Best not to go there at all.

The whimpering she can hear is animal, not human. As she gets closer, there is a gamey smell, which she doesn't think is her (although you never know). Closer yet, and it is the iron tang of blood.

Four hours Kelly's been walking now, and she's drunk with tiredness. Every fibre aches. But there's a headiness to it that she's quite enjoying; her heart is in overdrive and her breath coming in heaves. She holds onto a dry-stone dyke, in a field ringed by trees. Risked life and limb to get to Dunragit, so she has. Well, not quite. But she has climbed cliffs (on a path, not vertical – she's not Spiderwumman) and skirted hedgerows. She has walked over a curious bridge to nowhere, its grassy verges high above the lorries and caravans of the A75; she has dodged a dodgy-looking water treatment plant with rusty stopcocks and a DANGER sign, then had to vault (clamber) a barred gate to reach a railway track, where a very stern notice informed her she would be fined £1,000 for the privilege of crossing, if she was caught.

And this is it? First stop on the *Pilgrims'* map. Dunragit. Blimey, O'Reilly. It's a bit dour.

Her knees are weak, but not yet defeated. In fact, it's difficult to tell what her knees are doing: they are numb with effort. Once she stops walking, she fears she might never start again. (That thought is not unpleasant either.) The dyke that's supporting her abuts a barn. A barn aquiver with whining air. Dun*ragit*. Name suits this place. It is a raggedy, done-in kind of farm the barn belongs to, facing onto the hamlet's main street. Her hunger nudged her towards the farm; she had a vision of an apple-cheeked wifie who might provide milk and cheese in return for . . . ach, who knows. A smile? Or Kelly could kid on she's a witch and threaten her with a curse.

But there's no apple cheeks or apple trees here. There is a grey pebble-dash house with a Land Rover parked outside, strident with Britannia: two Union Jacks on the bumper and a Help for Heroes sticker in the window. There's this run-down barn, and a sky full of pain.

You can't ignore it. Some pitiful scrap of life is calling. You. The universe. His mum.

What would Jesus do? Kelly consults her pamphlet (on closer inspection, she can't justify calling it a leaflet any longer, since it's four pages long and full of things you never knew you wanted to know). For a scuzzy field, a row of houses and a scatter of farms, this place has got a disproportionate write-up:

Din Rheged, meaning 'Fort of Rheged', refers to the fifth-century Brythonic kingdom of Rheged. Along with Trusty's Hill in Gatehouse of Fleet, it's possible this was one of the royal sites of the forgotten kings of Rheged – and may indeed have been the site of King Arthur's northern court.

Aye, right. And that big mound of earth across the road will be where Merlin's buried. Ah but. No but.

For a long time Droughduil Mote was thought to be the earth mound of a twelfth-century castle. However, excavation has revealed that the fields between the mound and Dunragit village contain one of the most important Stone Age sites in Scotland, housing the remains of three massive concentric timber circles – the outer one six times the size of Stonehenge. Built around 2500 BC, it's believed this huge monument was a ceremonial meeting place for south-west Scotland's early communities: proof that spirituality was ever-present in this holy place!

They probably sacrificed virgins there. A bulge of dual carriageway now rips through the sacred site. My God. She fans her hot face with the pamphlet. The thrill of it. She'll be peeing her pants by the time she gets to Glenluce, if every point on her pilgrim's progress is as exciting as this.

The whines continue.

Kelly pushes the door to the barn. She canny bear it any longer. If a creature is trapped – she looks for a big stone – she will put it out of its misery. There's nothing suitable. Fuck it: she's going in. She can always come back and howk a piece out the wall if needs be. The door creaks. The whimpering stops. At first, she can see nothing. Lazy light drifts through wooden cracks and rusting metal. Her eyes adjust. Stairs reveal themselves as hay bales. The rearing stallion is merely an old motorbike, hanging on the wall.

'Chh-chh.' She crouches, rubs her fingers together. Searching for the source of the noise. A swift rustle, then a thump-thump-thrumming. Demented heartbeat? There is a ripple of black, sweeping past jumbled pitchforks. Feathery black – it's a tail. A puppy is trying to wag its black and white-tipped tail, but it's been tethered so tight it cannot stand. Hobbled by the back legs, a rope biting the blood from its skin and bone. Kelly's heart thins. She is shaking with a damp sweat. The dog and rope are so tangled it's impossible to see where one ends and the other begins.

'Shh now. It's all right, wee yin. Try and lie still.'

The pup is baring his tiny teeth, but his white-tipped tail continues to wave. The more he struggles, the tighter the rope becomes. His whining increases.

'*Jesuschrist*. Please stop it, sweetheart. Stop crying.' But it's useless; she canny get the knots to budge. What kind of fucker does this to a baby? Her joints grind as she pulls herself up and clatters, searching, through the assorted tools: pitchforks, a spade, big pliers – no, they're clipper things.

For sheep? She squeezes them, touches the blade. They're unwieldy, but she's no time to look for anything else; if the pup keeps squirming, he'll cut off the blood supply completely.

'Shh now, darling. Please, please trust me. You've got to stay still.'

His deep brown eyes are terrified. Kelly lays her cheek alongside his, next to the growling, gasping teeth. He will either bite her or understand.

'*Ca' the yowes. Tae the knowes. Ca' them whaur the heather growes.*'

For the second time that week, she whispers a song she has not heard in forty years. Kelly has known her brain a long, long time, but she doesny understand it. Why it sometimes urges her to gulp down poison until her liver swells, and other times it reaches in and unlocks a moment of soft, quiet joy.

'Now, I want you to be a good boy and hold really still, OK?'

They lock eyes. His whole body shudders. She moves her hand to stroke the crown of his head. His nose wrinkles, but he doesn't snap. Kelly steadies herself. Keeps one hand stroking his warm head, while the other opens the shears, slips one scissored blade under the exposed length of rope that runs across his haunch.

'OK now. Good boy. That's it.'

She glides her hand from his head down his trembling backbone, to rest beside the opened shear. Slow, slow, slightly lifting the rope, knowing it will hurt him more as she does so. But she needs to get a clean cut, away from his skin and fur. The pup yelps as she tugs, and she presses down quick, praying the blade is sharp. First cut only makes it halfway through, and now the wee bugger is snapping at her hand, but he's so hamstrung he can't reach her, so she saws and chops again, again, until the vicious rope breaks. The puppy's leg kicks free, but there are still more knots – *I'm so sorry, pal*. She holds him down with her elbow while she snips and tugs, and then his other leg is free and his wee body leaps and twists for joy, and he is upright, panting. Paws proud upon her chest.

'Hello,' says Kelly.

Hello, says Collie, with a massive outpouring of licks. She lets him knock her over, because they both deserve it. Head in the hay – and possibly dog shit. He's nuzzling into her, under her oxter so he can shut the world away. Kelly gets this wee creature instantly. She's feart to look too closely at his legs – they will need cleaned and dressed at least. She doesn't know if there's enough skin on his limbs for stitches.

'Excuse me.' A voice above her. White-hot with rage, but terribly polite. 'Do you mind awfully telling me what's going on?'

Kelly sits up, the pup panting into her chest.

'It was this wee fella. I heard him crying.'

An angry man (is there another type?) looms. His hair is white, his complexion dullish mauve. From down on the floor, where the view is mostly hay bales, she can also see: one yellow tweed jacket, a burgundy tank top, white shirt with a fine brown check, and a green knitted tie. She's pretty sure that when she gets to her feet, there will be cords and green wellies too. If you were playing country-gent bingo (and who doesny like a nice game of that?), Kelly would be yelling *house*.

'And?'

'And I came in to help him.'

'Please get up.'

She obeys, but only because she was going there anyway. She sets the pup on the floor, brushing clumps of straw and loose dog hair from them both.

'You are aware you're trespassing?' The man is holding a walking stick. Not in a feeble, supportive way. He is holding it in both hands, horizontal across the line of his portly belly.

'Eh, well, there's no law of trespass in Scotland. Actually.' She has no clue where she remembers this from, but she says it with authority, while scanning for another way out.

'You are on private property. This barn is my property, this land is my property. And so, may I say, is that animal.'

'He's bleeding. Someone tied him up too tight. By his back legs, for Christsake.' Arms folded. Jaw out.

'I'm well aware of how the dog was tethered.'

'Did you do that to him?' There's a spreading warmth on Kelly's right calf. The pup is relieving himself on her leg. Ungrateful wee shit. But she doesn't react. Instead, she keeps a steady fix on Major Tom. Doesny know who he's up against. Kelly is a super-starer. Kelly will not blink first. Cloistered in this barn with a man who is raging. And has a big stick.

'I've told you already. You're trespassing.'

'Did you do that to him? Why? Why would anybody want to hurt a wee soul like that? That's fucking cruelty is what it is.'

The man's gaze is sweeping round the barn; when he speaks, it is to the middle distance. He refuses to make eye contact with Kelly, despite her very hard stares. This is what it means to be beneath contempt. 'Well. As far as I can see, you haven't actually damaged anything. Judging by the state of you . . .' Ah, now he does it: lasers in with the killer look. 'I'm quite sure you'd prefer me not to call the authorities. So can I suggest you dust yourself down and be on your way?'

'How? So you can tie him up again?' Snailshell spirals of light float behind her eyes. People. Fuck. She canny do this, all this tension in her bones. If he blows on her, she will fall over. 'What gives you the right? Is it cause he canny talk? Bet you've loads of animals on this farm. You treat them all like shite?'

She's in his tractor beams now. The man begins to advance. He has a military bearing, is slapping the bottom of the stick deliberately slow. *Dunt. Dunt.* Into *dunt* the palm *dunt* of his hand. Kelly canny shut up, though. She doesn't know how to get out of this, how to make it right and save that wee dug's skin. 'What do you think all those animals think, eh? If they could talk, what d'you think they'd say? They'd fucking say *please don't hurt me.* Wouldn't they? All they pigs imprisoned on their sides so the babies can suck their teats – I *seen* that on the telly. And see they fucking shears you've got? Fucking useless, so they are. They must *chew* the wool off. D'you no think that hurts? Christ, you've a . . .'

She's been moving further backwards as he gets close; he's got her at the door. Clever. Army tactics. Never corner a rat.

'Now.' His breath is thick with yesterday's brandy. She doesn't flinch. His mauve nostrils open wide. She can see each wiry, steel hair inside. Tiny crumbs cling there. The pores on his nose are a mesh of black dots. Dot to dot. You could join them up. Make a monster. 'I also have a shotgun in the house. Matter of moments for me to pop in and fetch it. Dear.'

'Aye. Very good.' Kelly's brain is singing. One single rising note. Impossible to hear herself above it; she's not clear if the words are outside or in. The puppy is yapping; he senses her fear, and the yapping unites with the singular silent hum and her need to press all the frenzy and brutality into violent words. 'You wouldny fucking shoot me, ya cunt.'

The angry man catches his breath. He is getting off on this. 'No. But I would shoot the dog. Useless little beast.'

His brandy breath. Her unreleased breath. Uncomprehending, then understanding.

'In my book, time is money. And you're interfering in my ability to run my business. So. I'll advise you one more time. You leave me to train my sheepdogs as I see fit, and I'll leave you to . . .' his teeth are the yellow of old piano keys . . . 'be a frankly quite disgusting beggar. You do know you smell of urine?' Teeth still on show, he swings open the door of the barn. 'Off you fuck, then.'

Kelly finds herself outside, in the flat grey sky of Dunragit. She is shaking and crying. What is she doing here, exposed on an open plain? She should be safe, contained. Not raw with people up in her face. She starts to run, out of the field, along the road. Past a decaying brick factory, her breast rasping. Knees on fire, and each fall of her ankles is like shattered glass. Her lungs hurt. Ahead, another road, then open countryside and a tempting winding lane. She has reached the outer limits of Dunragit. No going back. She need never be here again. She grips onto a *Give Way* sign. Slides down to crouch on the verge, but her knees are too sore. So she sits, legs splayed onto the road. Her damp trousers stick to her. Damp with tiny, voiceless fear.

The old man was terrifying – and Kelly reached way past dog height; all the way up to his shoulders. She crawls onto her side. Curls up, face down on the grass. Feels the sharp edges of herself spill over. Fatigue is making her nauseous. And the hunger is too. She bought a cold pie this morning, with that lady's money. Juice, too, plus some toothpaste. But that was ages ago, and you canny eat toothpaste (she's tried). She has five quid left. No shops in Dunragit that she could see, but then she wasn't really looking.

She heaves up phlegm. Spits. Is disgusting. A small, filthy woman, sprawled in earthy dust. You can't lie here, Kelly. How no? Well, for one your legs are on the road, and two.

92

Just gonny no. You can't sleep rough in the country. Not be on show like this. You're not in the brazen city, where they let it all hing oot. See in the countryside? Poverty's private. Even that bastard in his knitted tie might be all tweed coat and nae knickers for all you know.

Country life, it's so pretty. Long, dark fields. Live bodies as your business. Mother cow plucked from child. Stopping your ears and filling your pockets with the cut and crack of earth. Everything below the surface, and you toil in dawn and you toil in dusk. For what? For what? For buttons. But you paint your farmhouse white. Keep your tractor clean. Drink your drink as you sort the accounts. *Pour me another, Kelly-ma-love.* Her uncle was a farmer, when she lived down this way. He had a shotgun too.

Eyes heavy. The road is empty. She's not heard a single vehicle since she's been lying here.

But that puppy.

'Sorry. Sorry,' mumbles Kelly. She rubs and mumbles. One more minute. She will lie here for one more minute, gathering up the courage to walk away. In a day or two, she will forget about the dog.

Forcing one eye open, the one that is not pressed into the verge. Take a look around you, Kelly. There are houses dotted here and there, nestled in the landscape. Each containing people. People and their lives and their cruelties and their needs. Think of all the homes you have ever walked past. Yes, there will be happy ones, of course there will. But there will also be want. There is always want. How many walls conceal beatings or broken wills? Unled lives, worlds of bruised submission? Is that not why you stay mobile? You can be convinced your whole life is an actual journey, if you don't stop long enough to let it swallow you.

In two days, you will be far from here. In six months' time, the pup will be a sheepdog. Or he won't.

Stuff always gets left behind.

Eyes heavy. She lets them close.

'Excuse me. Are you all right?'

'Sorry. Sorry,' mumbles Kelly. The skin on her face feels tight. Her chin sticky with drool. She sees a rubber wheel. Tiny trainers. There's a woman with a pram, and a wee boy tucked behind her. He is chewing on the sleeve of his anorak. They both look horrified. Kelly tries to scramble up.

'Oh! Jesusfuck. Ma knees!'

The woman tuts, puts her knuckles to her mouth. No, to under her nose. She ushers her son away. 'C'mon, Bobby. Quick. Hurry up and we'll get our tea.'

But Bobby is fascinated by this unkempt scarecrow they've found in the hedgerow.

'Bobby!'

Dutifully he turns to follow his mum. 'Why is the bad man sleeping there?'

Kelly's body has seized up, her hips louping. She clings to the *Give Way* sign, watches the little family run from her. She follows the rush of their receding backs until they are out of sight. Tells herself it's not important. In fact, it's a wee victory. How Kelly looks is designed to keep folk away.

She can't work out how long she's slept. Her head is pounding. The wee boy had a school bag. So. It is after school. Teatime. She tries to shake the woolliness from her brain. Ooh. Her bladder twangs. She pulls her trousers down to take a piss. She's not been asleep that long. Twenty minutes, maybe? Half an hour? That's better. She shakes, sorts herself. What they call a power nap.

Power. There is some racing childhood memory. Of *power* and teatime?

Dry your eyes. On your feet.

Eyes right and . . . 'shun. The lane leads onwards. She

fumbles for the pilgrim map. It is hanging from the pocket of her bright, checked coat. Imagine if it had fallen. Imagine if she'd pished on her only map. Her finger glitters. She checks the ring. Still stuck. OK. Next up is . . . Glenluce. *A Cistercian abbey*, blah blah. OK. The lane to her right runs parallel to the A75. If she concentrates, she can hear the low hum of traffic in the distance. She stares ahead, to acres of sweeping grass. The fur of her collar tickles her chin. Onwards. That way is towards Dumfries, and so . . . She turns the map sideways. Yes. That thin lane of small trees and golden fields she can see is roughly in the direction of Glenluce. So she'll follow the lane and keep her fingers crossed it doesn't peter out. It's either that or walk alongside zooming traffic.

But it whispers, still. A memory of *power*. A voice shouting out *power*. Her fork raised, at teatime. The telly on. The dark, oozing mince of Findus Crispy Pancakes.

Once more, Kelly's brain is being unfathomable. It drills her limbs to obey her heart, when her head is, for once, being sensible. *Onwards.*

But imagine going back.

Skeletor! That creepy cartoon they watched after school! 'By the power of Grayskull!'

She lets it rip, the force of her shout and flailing windmill arms far exceeding the strength she thought her legs had. Without thinking, her body birls. *Choices, Kelly.* Half a circle, arms akimbo, and she is barrelling back past the factory, down the street. No doubt past the wee boy's house, as he spoons in his tea and his mum looks horrified. She keeps running, through the gate, the field. The barn. Do. Not. Stop.

What if you're too late?

What is late?

The man's not even bothered to tie it up. The pup cowers in a corner. Half upright, head pressed into his downy chest, he pretends to be asleep, but she knows he's not. Major Tom is sitting on a hay bale. Waiting. With his shotgun on his lap. Like he *knew* she would come back. Like he wanted her to.

Kelly.

Kelly.

Do not blink.

As he raises his shotgun, she grabs one of the pitchforks that lean against the hay. Swings the implement hard and fast to skite his head, whoa, his arm flies up, unseated. He falls, there is a terrible bang, but Kelly is diving for the pup. She scoops it into her arms. Turns around and scrambles for the door. Nobody comes after.

Outside. Where the air is free.

The grey sky turns and the wind breathes. The oak trees sing as you run. Your face in his fur. Skittering heart, skittering heart. You check all his limbs. Skittering heart, skittering heart. Apart from the rope wounds, he is fine. You. You are not fine. But you're here, Kelly. Mental.

Your two heartbeats, echoing with life.

Nobody comes after.

*

The halls of residence echo with life. There are boxes full of life, piled on top of one another, carried in armfuls, laid out on shelves. Your room is at the end of a corridor, next to the boiler room for the whole block. Second year, and you are hanging on. It has been a struggle, but your fingernails are sharp. The buzz and jostle of Glasgow has been so much louder than you thought. Glittery with bright young things, and if you don't sparkle, you fade. What tribe to be in, when there are girls with their own cars and boys who play rugby, when there are wannabe

pop stars with Wet Wet Wet smiles and cropped-in
wedges? There are debaters with tongues of fire and
activists with green hair to match their politics, and the
red braces and badges and donkey jackets of Gehhh-et
your Socialist Worker *here – who often share one pint*
between three in the QMU, *demonstrating communism in*
action.

You have nursed questions and thoughts in tutorials,
kept them into yourself for fear of being found out. You
have stood at the door of the drama studio and swallowed
hard, but never made it in. Kidded on you were reading,
every lunchtime, alone in the union canteen.

You never planned to do this alone. How could you?
I'll be fine, you both said: you off to your brave new
world, Mandz to her job in the Harbour Café. Just to tide
me over. *She was smiling. All brave.* You'll see. Wee stint
at night school and I'll be up there next year.

—Come and visit.

—I will. Promise.

But there are always reasons not to come – and most
of them are yours. You don't want her to see how small
you are, how you flit through the university's cloisters
pretending to be purposeful, when really you are lost.
Grateful for the vaulted Gothic arcs the cloisters cast,
because you are studying architecture, so measuring lines
and shadows is OK.

Second year, and Mandz is still not here, but you are,
and you WILL be different. If you listen any more to the
whisperings of doubt, to the evaporation of the drops of
confidence you thought you possessed, it will cripple you.
So you throw yourself in (what a jolly expression – maybe
you should hang about with the rugger boys?). You want
to be the finest version of you, yourself, that you can, so
you blacken your hair, eyes, clothes. You squander your

grant on Doc Martens and a crimper; you sign up for the
student union committee: Ents! Ents! – not Treebeard, but
a cool job booking bands – go on, take a drink – *and for*
a field trip to Bath where you will study elegant terraces –
go on, take a drink – *and you are the best, most eloquent*
version of yourself, then. Full and comfortable in your
gawky body, while your tongue is silvery and expansive.
You say stuff, and people laugh. Folk save you seats in the
lecture hall. In the pub. Suddenly, you are in a huddle –
go, on, take a drink! *Occasionally, you are at the centre,*
and in those times when you are not, when you are
floating in your quiet, sober space, your reputation buoys
you.

But top it up you must, and you do. Oh, how you do.
You are busy with being the bubbliest, brightest you.

Second year is a blur of joy: unfiltered, raw. A series of
firsts. Love. Sex. Jägerbombs. Drugs. A protest march.
Absinthe. An occupation, a rage, a purpose, a point. A
pill. A fail. You blaze your way through second year,
swallowing everything that is put before you. Sometimes
you think you could swallow the moon. You stay up all
night, all summer. Home becomes the place where you are
small now, not here. And all the while, alcohol is the oil
that lubricates. It is the undiluted bliss singing on your
breath; it is your mistress and you are the master of it. Of
all you survey.

—One resit, yeah, no big deal. Yeah. Tell Mandz I say
hi. Summer school. I know, Mum. But it's important.

Except there is no summer school. There is a squat.
Blacker and blacker, you ink yourself along the veins you
will open later. You have mattresses and vodka, there are
boys who look like girls, girls who look like boys. One
weird hippy called Patrick, who has long hair, round
glasses and a box of delights. He talks earnestly to you of

karma. Bass guitars loll against the walls, you lay your head on studded biker jackets or the groins of the boys who look like boys, and everyone is in a band.

You are singularly you. You rule the world, till third year comes and you get a letter from the uni, and fuck them, you aren't even sure you want to go back, cause you've got a job in Virgin Megastore, where all the trendy kids strut and you can get tickets to every concert and swim in a sea of skinny, back-combed men, and then there are all the pubs you must visit: Hurricane's and the Rock Garden and, here, *is that Clare Grogan there? Her from Altered Images? – I could be haaa-ppee . . . One night you sink five tequilas, don sunglasses to dance with the stuffed bear by the bar, and next thing you are singing in a crappy band.*

YOU RULE THE FUCKING WORLD!

—Kelly, *whispers a familiar voice. You, in your squat. Dreaming of home. Feeling tears splash from the face that is whispering you awake. It feels so real. It sounds like your dad! So weird . . .*

—Kelly.

Opening your eyes to a cobwebbed skylight overhead. Your cheeks, tight with flecks of last night's vomit.

—Oh, Kelly, darling.

It bloody is! It is your dad there, stooping over you in the squat and sobbing. Mandz too. Mandz is there. Her hand in yours, so you know that it is serious.

—You have to come home.

It is your mum. Of course it is.

The last thing you told her was a lie. You'd said that this was important.

Chapter Eight

Christ, she hates her job. Jennifer Patience slams the drawer shut. Slams it again, so that Jimmy, her boss, will notice, but the editor is now draped over another partition, explaining to the online-correspondent-trainee-reporter-unpaid-intern why she will have to rewrite her excoriation of council bus-lane cameras. Jimmy and the Head of Roads are golf buddies, you see.

It is a good piece Jennifer has written. But there is *too much of you in it*, apparently. Bollocks. Jennifer Patience is old-school. Ear to the ground, never forget a face, and she can sniff out a story a mile away. (And yes, she understands cliché too. And irony.) Crisp, incisive copy, written without fear or favour. Jennifer can churn out reams of the stuff before breakfast. What Jimmy means is that there isn't enough of him in it. Or rather of 'the brand'. New owners, new direction. More tabloid, less investigation. 'Um – how can I put this?' Jimmy had scratched his head. 'Wee bit less *red* in tooth and claw?'

'I'm off,' she tells her open-plan colleagues. No one is really listening. She misses being part of a proper team. They are talking about hot-desking: a game of journalistic musical chairs. All that will happen is that nobody will dare leave the office at all once they've bagsied a space. And so the decline will continue. Sharp pencils and shoe leather replaced by legless creatures with pale eyes and giant digits. Creatures who will never see the light.

Of all weeks, this is a week for walking through your city. That bus crash has injured Glasgow itself; there is a palpable sense of . . . Jennifer doesn't know what exactly, but it is what she's been trying to capture. Crafting a story is like wine-tasting. You've to immerse yourself, catch the top notes, the body. Discover what aftertaste remains. On her walks, speaking to folk, what she's been getting is fragility. Tenderness. Weirdly, pride is coming through too. A sense that this sprawling, disputative city has cohered.

One last scroll through the newsfeed as she is putting on her coat. Reading the final death toll of that awful, awful crash: each life with its own face. Its own story. And the survivors . . . they'll all move into recovery phase soon enough. Oh, not the injured, but the journos, winkling out any juicy tales of derring-do. *This*. Now, this one is interesting. Her finger alights on Martin Grey, the guy who was rescued by a tramp. A female tramp, no less. She heard his interview on *Reporting Scotland*, and has tucked it away for future reference. There is a fuzzy still of his saviour from the CCTV, and that's it. Not much to go on. She clicks to enlarge the woman's picture. Frowns.

'Has anyone found that homeless hero?'

Couple of shrugs. 'Nah.' Katya doesn't turn from her screen. Her husband works for the Beeb, so she's the unofficial office guru. 'Bunch of calls, but nothing concrete so far. No one's got the time, you know?'

Jennifer knows. A nice, traditional, human-interest piece, but there are still issues of blame to be attached to the incident, of anger to be directed, and those things are far more interesting. *Get your readers angry* – that seems to be the new 'brand' default. She rolls the cursor over the woman's face. Time enough to track down a hobo when the dust is settling and the story needs fresh legs.

Except.

Except. The woman's mess of hair. It reminds her of something. Last year Jennifer did a piece on this crazy guy in Garnethill. Ex-homeless himself, he'd started running an outreach centre. She'd gone there to interview him, with a snapper in tow. Jennifer keeps meticulous notes. Well, when she moves to the *Washington Post* and wins the Pulitzer, there will need to be an archive . . .

Third drawer down. *Welfare. Society. Social, social housing, housing issues, homeless, homeless stats, homeless services, homeless* . . . Here. Two years' worth of articles. She always clips a few photos to the piece too. *Why, when it's all online?* kids like Junior Miss Intern over there will ask. Because you've got to feel the story in your hands. You can see them frown when she says stuff like that. Look at her oddly.

Jennifer fans out the photographs. That nice Mr Devlin does an excellent line in freezing emotion. He really is a good photographer. Somehow he has this ability to see how the air will shift the instant before he presses the shutter. *There.* There it is. This one, this photo. Here. In the kitchen at the Outreach. Three clients sitting round the table, with the nutter – Dixon? – serving them soup. His head is thrown back, laughing. The ladle is out like he's conducting an orchestra. *Don't make them all look like wasters, right?* She can recall his exact words as he agreed to the photographs being taken. Two of the others are watching him, also laughing. But one, a woman, is looking past him, past the table to something outwith the frame. She has matted grey hair and a prominent nose. Her chin rests on her hand, so it's hard to see her full face. But the nose. It's quite a nose.

Side by side, Jennifer compares the profiles. If they were fingerprints, it would be a match.

She presses print and leaves the newsroom.

The newspaper offices are down by the river. She could walk to Garnethill, but she gets a cab on account. It is a small, remaining perk that will no doubt vanish soon. On the way, she texts her mum. Issy had a sore tummy this morning, which meant no school, and panic, and Gran to the rescue. But Jennifer will pay for it, she'll pay. She also texts Rodge, who won't reply. A lowly sports hack to her senior reporter when they met, now he is *Rodge Around Football!* STV actually had him get his teeth done. Rodge loves it. He has added many veneers since, but he is still her husband. And weekdays he finishes work bang on six.

Can u get Iz from Mumz? X

She gets out of the cab at Rose Street. The Outreach is still here. Paintwork more scruffy. It's a door entry, but a wedge of wood has propped it ajar. Jennifer goes into the tiled close. First on the left, if she recalls? Yes. She is right. Jennifer is always right. Jennifer's memory is like a Rolodex. It just spins and spins until it clicks. Which means that erasing Rodge's blonde netball player of six years ago (*darling, I'm sorry. It's just, you were so distracted with the baby*) or the recent lipstick on the discarded water bottle in his car is not so easy.

Nope.

Up yours, forensic memory. She chaps the door. Wee try of the handle, just in case. It is open.

'Hello?' She ventures inside. The hall smells of curry. 'Hello?' she calls, louder. The smooth soles of her Office boots squelch on the rug. Jesus. It is soaking. She is standing in a big puddle of Christ knows what.

'You fae the social?' A young girl shuffles from one of the rooms into the hall.

People answer your questions so much quicker if they think you're authority. But Jennifer is not that kind of journalist. Not yet.

'Hi there.'

'All right?' The girl is in a dressing gown. Is very definitely pregnant. Oh, there's another story right there; she looks about fourteen, with her colour so high and her long hair in her eyes.

'Sorry.' Jennifer smiles at her. 'What's your name?'

'Aleisha.'

'Hi, Aleisha. I'm Jennifer. I'm a reporter. I'm trying to get in touch with . . . Does Mr Dixon still work here?'

'Who?'

Click-click-click. 'Dexy?'

'Oh aye. He's no here but.'

'That's a shame. You know when he might be back?'

The girl shrugs. 'No idea. He's away up the Royal.'

'Oh dear. Nothing wrong, I hope?'

'One of the lassies has went into labour. Waters burst.' She nods at the carpet. 'Right there. Fucking Niagara Falls. You're standing in it.'

Jennifer steps off the rug.

'Dexy's went up with her man. He canny really speak English.'

The girl is too young to have been here last year, surely, when those pictures were taken. But you should never make assumptions, about anything. This is the kind of place folk must mill through constantly.

'I don't suppose you could help?' Jennifer takes the photo from her handbag, shows it to the girl. 'With this?'

'Oh aye. That's here. That photie's of in here. In our kitchen.'

'Yeah. Yeah, I knew that. I'm actually trying to find out about this lady.' Jennifer taps her pinkie next to the woman's image.

'Her? Aye.' The girl holds the photo up to the light. 'That's Mad Kelly, so it is. Total skank. Oh.' She returns the snap to Jennifer. 'Are you here about her going off with that guy? Fucksake. Did he do her in?'

'What guy's that you're meaning?' Jennifer smiles again, hiding her confusion.

'The guy at Bloch—' The girl stops. 'Much?'

'Pardon?'

'You're a reporter, right? So how much you gonny pay me?'

Jennifer might be quick, but Aleisha is quicker. Jennifer puts the photograph back in her bag.

'Well, Aleisha. That depends on what it is you know. Look. Will we stick the kettle on? Tell me, when is it you're due yourself?'

She takes the girl's bony arm. Leads her though to the kitchen and closes the door.

Chapter Nine

'What have we done? Eh, Collieflower? You think we killed him?'

Kelly looks at the dug. The dug looks at her. Should she even give him a name? It's not as if she's going to keep him. Christ, Kelly can't look after herself. She's hardly mothering material to a six-month pup. Six months? A year? God knows. He is wee, yet gangly. His head is far too big for his body, and his legs haven't caught up with his clodhopping paws. She cups her hand back into the stream of water, pours it over his bloodied hindquarters. Both of them are panting. It is nicely mild. She tries to stop worrying about the man and enjoy the moment. Just this, here.

They are sitting in a lovely spot, in a tree-lined glade by a small river. Dappled light gives an underwater ripple to the scene: grassy bank, clear brown current bubbling over shimmering pebbles. A wounded dog and a demented wumman getting soaked as she tries to hold water in her hands. Collieflower is shaking, although she barely touches him as she leans over and pours. He has had enough human contact for one day. But she's worried the cuts will get infected. Every time she douses him, he has another wee lick at his sore bits. She's sure that dog spit is the cleanest saliva you can get. Or something. Anyroad, the worst of the stickiness is coming off, so between them, they're doing something right.

'Right, pal. That'll do you.' The cuffs of her jumper and the thighs of her trousers are sodden, but she doesn't want him . . .

The pup stands. Shakes himself, then trots straight into the river.

. . . having to stand in the river in case it hurts his cuts. He grins at her, and laps furiously at the water.

Kelly grins too. He has the most beautiful, cheeky face. How could you get angry at that? Fuck it. Old Major Tom deserved all he got. Prick. Guys like him are cockroaches. She hugs her knees in. Feels shivery. She definitely heard a gunshot. She can't unhear that ripping bark of sound. Her ears are full of whining, a continual high-pitched whining, and she doesn't know if it's the memory of the dog's plight, or the keening noise she made as she ran, or the sound that bus made as it skidded, or the fact that her lungs are actually quite furry inside so that breathing can be a problem sometimes. Or if it is the pitch of the gunshot, playing over and over until her eardrums rebel and make their own masking hiss.

Aaaaaahhhh.

Collie cocks one ear.

'Sorry, wee man. Did I give you a fright?'

She will have to learn to regulate herself, and not scream out loud. Regulate – is that the right word? So long as this wee boy is with her, she must work very hard not to scare him. To keep the things inside that need to be kept there.

Kelly. Don't be so fecking stupid. The man won't be shot. The gun was nowhere near him. Was it? If he fell . . . He did fall. Right under the chin. That's how you'd top yourself. Was the gun close to his chin?

No. Nope nope. No. You did nothing wrong. Except for battering him. With his own pitchfork.

If.

If you were not with people.

Collie's had enough of the river. He splashes onto the bank. Comes lolloping straight to Kelly.

But if you were not there, then this wee darling would not be here.

A glorious, exuberant, earth-jolting shake, and Collie showers them both in glistening droplets.

They lie awhile, him snoring, her staring up at the sky. Midgies dance and dive, but Kelly is a pickled old trout. Apart from flying into her eyes, they rarely bother her. *Plegh*. And her mouth. She sits up. She'll need to find Collie some food. Unless he's smart enough to catch a rabbit, then they could cook it on a campfire. If Kelly was smart enough to make a fire. There's a neat ring of stones further along the bank, full of blackened grass and ashes. That's what gave her the idea.

'C'mon, boy. Hup. Time to go time.'

They can't be far now, from Glenluce Abbey. Dusk soon; you can see the haze of shadows, the clouds rimmed with gilt. There might be a shop at the abbey. She kicks at the old campfire as they pass it, for no other reason than to destroy. Aye, the abbey will be closed, but God won't mind. For Kelly and Collie are pilgrims in need. And if they need to jemmy a door to get at the Wall's ice cream and pre-packaged scones, then so be it.

'Here, boy! Collieflower! Here!'

Daft bugger doesn't know his name yet. He's scrabbling away at the campfire ashes. Gives a yelp, then comes cantering over. His ears fly behind, rising and flapping like beating wings. There's a bubble growing inside Kelly's chest, bright and bursting. Such a deep, sweet feeling. She realises what it is. It's happy.

'What you got, you eejit? You got a stick?'

He's proudly carrying some charred remains, which he drops at her feet. She reaches to throw it, but it's not a stick. It's spongy.

'Jesus, dug!' She lets the thing fall from her hands. 'Have you brought me a turd?'

Collie shakes whatever it is, then begins to chew.

'Oh God, no. Dirty! Dirty boy.' Fighting to take it off him, but he thinks this is a game. 'No!' The thing breaks apart, so they have a chunk each. Pink and curdy innards. It's a badly burned sausage. Collie has already devoured his chunk. Is staring intently at hers. Kelly is used to being starving. Kelly eats out of bins. A dog-devoured bit of sausage is not the worst thing she's put in her mouth. The way Kelly deals with hunger is not to think about it. To refuse to notice the empty groan within her stomach until food comes her way. Then the groan becomes irresistible. It becomes a roar. The pink meat looks all right. She sniffs it. Collie watches her holding the sausage.

'Here, boy.' She offers it out to him. And the slapping of his tail as he wolfs it makes her belly full.

Another mile, and they come upon the abbey, tucked in a field to the left of the crossroads at which Kelly and Collie stand. From here, it doesn't look much more than a crumbling gable end.

Man. Is this whole pilgrimage destined to be one big nothing?

The road to either side of the crossroads is broad enough for two cars. The road ahead, however, is very steep and narrow; is barely a road at all. There's an old metal post pointing upwards.

Whithorn – Pilgrim Way.

She checks the pamphlet. Whithorn is indeed the next stop after this.

'It's a sign, Collie.'

109

The pup cocks his leg on a clump of wild flowers.

'A sign. Get it? No? You couldny even give me a single wag?' He is definitely listening, mind. This dug is clever.

Kelly 'n' Collie – Fighting Crime!

Kelly 'n' Collie – Adventures R Us!

The signpost gives no indication of how long it might take to get to Whithorn, but it looks a long way on the map, which seems to be telling her to go round anyway, not up. There are no mileages on the map either. It's beginning to dawn on her that the map is quite vague. More of a sketch, an exercise in joining dots in a pretty pattern. Which would explain why all the pilgrims were being ferried on a minibus.

'What do you think, Collie? It's going to be dark in a wee while. Should we stay put or press on?'

Does it count if they just keek over at the abbey? Is that a proper pilgrimage? Collie sits down, begins to scratch himself. His wee leg buckles, and he topples over.

'Och, pet. You're knackered.'

She picks him up. The pup lays his head over her shoulder and sighs. 'You like it up here, don't you? What can you see, eh? This is different from being on the ground, isn't it?'

The warm weight of him in her arms. Oh, you never felt anything like it. How he moulds to your breast, goes limp with safeness, and your hand underneath. Your hand is all that is holding him up. When you were running with him, before, you didn't think, because there was only the running and the getting away. You could let him go, Kelly. He trusts you, this little scrap, and you could just open your arms and break him.

The air drops. The sky is calming at the end of the day. Great, pale billows of cream and deep, burning peach glow behind Glenluce Abbey. The view opens out; the abbey complex rolls beyond what you first saw. There is a spread of stonework, low falls and foundations. A softening of the light. It shines through the highest wall, the arch and a hint of turret. Tall, stepped gable with empty window spaces. Arched and oblong. *Let's see what's through the arched window.*

Be kind, Kelly. You did that once. You were nice to folk. You remember? She tries to think of when. And of when she didn't have to think of it. Of not actively deciding to be nice instead of hurting.

Collie begins to squirm at some new, exciting smells. Kelly can see donkeys in a distant field. There is a dry-stone dyke around the abbey, with a gate that is locked. No impediment for Kelly 'n' Col. (Col – that's got a ring to it. That might be his name when he grows up.) She lowers the pup over first. He whines, then leaps up at her as she climbs over too. They go down a path, past a clutch of outbuildings – she clocks a ticket office.

'Probably have snacks in there,' she tells Collie. 'We'll come back when we've done a recce.'

They skirt round the outer walls, climb over and into the heart of the place. Cobbled traces of long galleries and rooms. Her family used to visit castles when she was wee, thoosands of them (it was a passion of her mum's), and it's always the built-up bits you gravitate to: the nooks and corners where there might be dens. Or ghosts. It's where the walls rise that you can imagine actual lives. If you can make out the rooms, the line of their fireplaces, then the sound of rustling silk or the vision of a lady bending to poke the flame comes more easily. The tang of incense is stronger if you can touch the actual niche in which a censer might have rested.

Was it monks or nuns who lived here?

She checks her pamphlet. Monks. There's an artist's impression of two white-robed hooded dudes doing some gardening.

111

The Cistercian Abbey of Glenluce was founded in 1191 by Rolland, Lord of Galloway, as a daughter house to Dundrennan Abbey in Kirkcudbrightshire. The gathering point for the approach to Whithorn for centuries past, King Robert the Bruce himself rested here on his final painful pilgrimage to pray at St Ninian's shrine in Whithorn.

'That's where we're going, Collie,' she whispers. 'Whithorn.'
Why is she whispering? These grassy walls are thick with silence; it's dense enough to lay over you, to coat your tongue.

Bruce did not pass this way again, returning via Glentrool – the site of his first victory over the English. Following the Scottish Reformation in 1560, the abbey fell into disuse. The well-preserved south transept gives a sense of the building's scale, while the chapter house, dating from 1500, is still roofed and intact. Close to Laggangairn Standing Stones, with their pilgrim crosses, and a rest stop for the faithful through the centuries, this tranquil spot by the water of Luce remains a rich and enduring devotional waymarker today.

'We're at a devotional waymarker, Collie. Fancy.'
Underneath the screed of writing is a reproduction of a pilgrim's badge – three wee Playmobil men, each wearing a pointy hat, beside an N for Ninian. The men look like a row of birthday candles. According to the pamphlet, this badge identified the wearer as a genuine pilgrim, not a beggar.
'We should definitely get one of those.'
They continue to explore, weaving in and out of the remnants of rooms, and into a wide central space. *The Cloisters*, says a metal sign. Kelly thinks immediately of university, concentrates instead on the smoothness of the

stone. There is a small section of cloister that has been rebuilt: a handful of graceful arches, and a porch roof sheltering a locked wooden door. *The Chapter House*. She dunts the door a few times, but it won't give. She follows Collie on his pee 'n' sniff trail round the side of the building. Here, the sky is turning purple and orange-red. Light spreads like blood, so that the walls and the grass seem to run with it, as if the light is liquid. The horizon is smudged shadow, blending into deeper cloud and thickening hills, until she can no longer see the lines.

The porch facade reveals itself to be an actual four-square structure, the only part of the abbey still intact. There are two mullioned windows on the far side – this must be the wall facing the door that wouldn't let her in. Kelly steps backwards, to get a better view. The windows are beautiful. Twin arches, stone-framed, with a triangular keystone, each with three arched panes at the bottom and a curious scoop-and-circle design at the top. She's not sure if these upper bits are meant to be flowers or clover. Or a sort of curly cross? Four interlocking circles of etched glass, each circle patterned with smaller interlocking circles. In the centre of the four connecting circles is a fifth. On both windows, this central circle is etched with a long diamond. She holds up the diamond ring on her hand, splays her fingers so she is looking through inverted Vs. Long, fingery shadows waver back at her.

The windows are a perfect matching pair. Twins. Identical apart from the way the light hits them. The low sun washes rose gold over bumps and undulations, staining the glass with colour, though it is clear. The windows take her breath away. Kelly presses her face against the glass. She can only see tiny fragments and distortions of the room inside – there is a central fluted pillar. A vaulted ceiling tinged with a hint of sea green, and rust at the corner apex of a curve. It could be traces of a lost mural, or rising damp. Because the space is locked, she wants to be inside, there, where it is sheltered and beautiful, and where she is not allowed. She doesn't believe in prayer, but she would like peace, and it seems to her that a sealed-off holy-of-holies might offer a special kind of quiet. The thought that she can't get in makes her angry. There are rocks galore kicking about; take your pick from loose scree to chunks of old pillar. Those lower glass arched bits, you could fit through them easy enough. Why shouldn't they go inside, her and Collie? They are wayfarers too.

Kelly holds a big smooth stone. It is heavy.

Kelly 'n' Collie. Pilgrim pirates.

Aye. She could smash that window, no bother. It's only glass. No different from breaking the window of the telecoms station in Portpatrick. Collie sits on the grass beside her. Patient. He too is watching the dancing glassy light. His shadow spills before him, a monster dog. Ears pricked towards sounds Kelly will never hear. He is so little, his shadow dwarfs him. She drops the stone and swings him up, so he is high upon her shoulder.

'Hey, wee yin. You all right?' She walks with him draped, kissing the smooth fur on top on his head, and his tail beats frantic against her breast. 'I think we've nearly seen it all . . . Fucksake!' She is falling, stumbling on an open channel half covered by a row of overlaid slabs. As she yelps, Collie barks, wriggles out of her arms, lands awkwardly on the ground.

'Here, it's OK, Collie. It's OK. Shit, I'm sorry, boy. I just got a fright. Are you all right?'

Solemnly Collie peers into the end of the trench, the bit Kelly just tripped on. The row of slabs is broken here, and there's a gap, and a dark drop. Not enough to fall through, but you could break your ankle. 'Bloody sue them, so we could.'

The Reredorter (Latrine), another sign advises. 'Lovely,' she tells the dog. 'It's the monks' old crapper. Och, well. Waste not, want not.' She undoes her trousers, squats over the trench. She's been needing to go for ages. Beyond the latrine is a flat sward. *Monks' Graveyard*. Oh, that's charming. Poor sods live a life of penury and prayer, and what's their reward? An eternal view of the communal toilets. Did the dead monks even get gravestones? It doesn't look like it, though it's hard to see much now, except outlines of grey. Night is definitely upon them; the hills have turned to black masses in the distance, the remaining light becoming colourless. If not the chapter house, where are they going to sleep? There's a skinny tower over at the far wall, but as she moves closer, she sees a light come on, a rectangle of yellow, and the shape of a house just beyond the outer abbey wall.

'Shit! Shit.' She crouches, clicking her fingers at the dog. 'Collie!' she hisses. 'Away! Come over here. *Here.*'

People live here. Living people. How is that possible? It's an empty ruin. Why would you live here? Have they heard her galumphing about? Oh my God. Did they see her take a shit? Prickles under her skin, on her cheekbones. She's having a hot flush. When she is sober, Kelly tries to have standards. Granted, they are not the standards of the normal nine-to-fiver, but baring her arse to spectators? Even in her lost world, defecation is private.

It's growing too dark to move on. Best thing is to huddle in a corner until dawn, then set off before the folk in the house waken. Here. This spot will do. They've come to a long flint-stone arch – almost a tunnel, but high and open at both ends. She'll let Collie nap, but Kelly will keep guard. They might call the police on them. Or that old bastard farmer could be cruising the countryside, seeking them out.

Her skin goes cold.

It is broken. The calm, the pleasure of this place is

shattered, and all Kelly feels is afraid. Life is rushing in through the crack she has made; things will come and get her in the night. She is surrounded by graves. Under her, probably over her. Short puffs of air, that's all her furry lungs are holding. It hurts. Gasping and gasping, cooried in the curve of the rock-hard wall. Collie whines, pawing at her.

Will they have buried the man yet? The man with the tan office shoes. Wrapped his ripped belly in her great greatcoat and laid him in the earth? She doubts it. Unless he was Muslim. *They* do it quick. But he didny look Muslim. He was a posh white man in pinstripes and shiny brown shoes.

If. If you were not there.

'I'm all right, boy.' She finds the breath to reassure the pup, and it's not so bad. Her lungs are stronger than she thinks. Takes a bigger, slower pull of air. Collie settles, curling into her lap. He will get heavy, but for now, it feels wonderful. Other folk. Folk like her, folk on the streets. Some of them keep dogs for company. She'd never thought about how a dog must keep you warm as well. It always seemed too big a hassle. Another mouth to feed – though dugs are amazing at encouraging the sympathy vote. But plenty hostels won't let you in if you've a pet. And Kelly hates the way the animals shiver on the pavement. How beaten-down their eyes are. She couldn't do that to Collie.

'We'll find you a proper home, wee yin.' Stroking his velvet ears. 'Somewhere you deserve.'

For tonight, they are Kelly and Collie. A duo far superior to Kelly 'n' Malki. Or to Kelly 'n' Joe, 'n' Carl, 'n' Big Wilson, 'n' Symie, or any other person she's socialised with, shagged, shacked up with, stolen from . . .

Kelly 'n' Mandz. The original twosome.

She misses being the other half.

If you were not there.

Kelly opens out her coat, pulls a piece of the fabric over Collie's haunches.

'So. Is it up that big hill tomorrow, or do we take the main road?'

The pup whickers in his sleep.

Kelly. If the man had stopped to help you, if he'd just given you his sandwich, he would not have been on the road.

The final streaked light of day is slipping; the moon is yet to rise. The diamond ring transmits faint beams as she strokes her dog.

'Well. We shall defer that decision until the morning, Collieflower.' Kelly rests her hand on his spine. Stares into the coming night.

*

Defer, defer, defer. Defer to your elders. Defer to the doctor. Defer to Mandz's gentle admonishments and bright encouragements to 'come and see the gang'. Defer one uni term, two uni terms, the rest of your life. Defer gratification until you are in your room, enjoying each wee glorious gasp of beer as the ring pull pops and the can breathes open – have they bastards hidden the gin? – defer going into your mother's bedroom, for that is what it will forever remain; your dad can't sleep there, on the cold of a deathbed, and neither can you. You cannot sleep at all, the silence of the countryside is deafening. It smothers you at night and kills you in the day, until there is only the soft pant of your throat and the narrowing of your life and the blueness of your rattling veins and the clinging sadness of your family.

Your mum is dead. That is why they came to get you.

Clifftop walking does not bring release. Brave trips out with your father end in torrid scenes on golf-club floors.

117

*The Harbour Café only harbours left-behinds: sad Jessie
and Billy the fisherman and Mandz and Darren Carruthers
sharing a chair;* she on his lap, his hands resting lightly
between her knees, and two becomes one, *but it is not you.
None of this is you. Your home aches with loss. The loss of
your mother. The loss of you. You, you. It is all about you.*

*Your dad catches you making breakfast. Tea with
vodka, and you see him blink at your shame. He footers
in the doorway. Tries to say . . . what? That you remind
him of someone? That you used to be his daughter? You
want to say,* I know, Dad. You don't have to try and find
the words. You have lost your wife, but I promise you
won't lose me. *But it is too hard, and you will do it, you
will. Once you are fortified, swig one, swig two, and then
you find yourself instead on a bus with your luggage –
how did that happen? You have no idea if they put you
there. Or did you leave a note? Check your bag: it is
neatly packed. Under clean pants and socks, someone has
tucked in Libby-loo.*

Back to uni, see a counsellor. Yes, yes. We understand.
*So you get your grant and you get your stash, of Bud and
Pils and Midori and whatever. Even Bezique is drinkable
with lemonade.* Let's have fancy cocktails, *and you miss
your rent but you* FIGHT *for your right to* PAARTY! *And
there is another squat and there is another guy, there is
always a guy. Thin and beautiful. This one has peroxide-
blonde spikes, wears shades inside the house. Cool as.
You've seen him look at the cover of* London Calling *and
try to emulate Paul Simonon's pose. But his name is Malki,
not Paul, and he cannot play a note. You spend your time
fucking and getting fucked and staring at the moving
ceiling while you pass the bottle and take a draw, and
buzzing fingers take you further than the furthest stars.*

In come the pills and the tabs to take you further yet,

the Eccies the jellies and smiley faces that make you forget. Forget the mess, the mourning, the mistakes. Forget Mandz tracking you down and turning up and you taking the piss. You and Malki, the whole squat laughing at her, because she's dressed for the occasion. Trying so hard to fit in that your heart aches and your heart breaks as the laughter crashes down. She has borrowed Darren Carruthers' leather jacket, has tried to spike her hair in a facsimile of yours, backcombed country-mouse hair, black-winged ringed eyes – she looks ridiculous.

—Oh, look! *you say. You are mortified. A Kelly clone!*

They all find this hilarious. But she stands her ground and speaks her mind. Gives up, quickly, trying to play along. God, the girl starts begging, and you mock her more. Malki's pretending he's Kate Bush, he's flapping his arms, falsetto-singing Ooh, Kel-lee, it's mee, oooh pleeze, come home now! *And the room is in hysterics. But you will not leave the safety of the herd, not even to give her the courtesy of some privacy as she talks and talks and cries and tries to hold your hand, Jeez, the cheek of her, and you, your ice-cool cracking, screaming at her just to* fucking go!

She left you twenty quid. That's what she was stuffing into your hand. But you always need more money. Malki gets you and him jobs in McDonald's, so you can get a place together, just the two of you, and you can definitely afford the rent if he deals a wee bit too. He says he'll work as well, of course, except he never turns up and you do. You flip burgers for eight-hour stretches and try not to cry. Because your life is fucking marvellous. Uni slips below the horizon. You wave it on its way, glad to be unencumbered. Honestly. Because now you can get on with your proper life – though you don't tell them at home. Not that uni is officially done. You cannot bear the thought of all that fortitude. Of your wee dad's confusion. His awful hurt.

One day, you come home to Malki sleeping with a skank called Diva. You smash his stereo and he smashes your jaw. But it is only dislocated, and he is really, really *sorry. You embrace his weakness as love as he is sobbing at your breast. Make friends.* Take a drink. *Bite your lip.* Take a drink. *Take it out on the punters at work, rude, ignorant consumers of pap, who chew with their mouths open and speak as if* you *are the moron. One day, you just have enough, and gob in a fat kid's milkshake. You do it in full view of the queue of people, after the kid calls you a stupit cow, then you tell him to enjoy his drink.*

They make you hand back your uniform, your name tag and *your hairnet. Who are you, Kelly, without your hairnet? Technically, it is assault, but the police let you off with a warning, until that evening, when you are celebrating your (moral) victory with one bottle of Glen's Vodka, some sherry (you don't know why) and a chaser of Special Brew. Malki arrives home with a team – company is always welcome; you've not really been getting on, so the more the merrier, more people, more drink, crank up the music, Malki is war-dancing in the kitchen, he's impaled your Libby-loo doll on a skewer and is torching her in the sink –* what a laugh, what a fucking riot, man *– and in flow more folk, and then Diva the skank appears with her skanky, dreadlocked hair, which is begging to be tugged, to be ripped from her dirty, skanky head,* that is my doll, not yours, *well, it all kicks off, you and a bottle* fuckin come ahead, *you are out, fighting in the street,* I'll swing for you, ya hoor, *the polis haven't even finished their backshift, and it's the same ones who warned you earlier that come back to jail you now! Oh,* *the laugh you all have, back at the station. The cells smell of pish and they give you a plastic mattress.*

Who is it comes to get you? Not your darling Malki, the traitorous, shagging bastard. No. It is the good angel to your bad. Mandz. Mandz is standing there, all clean amidst the filth.

—I'm taking you home, Kelly. This has to stop.

On the way, there are no recriminations. Just you, exhausted, and Mandz's arm around you. Then, as the train is coming into Dumfries, she tells you she's got engaged.

Chapter Ten

'Hello? Hi there. I thought you might like some breakfast.'

What a grand dream Kelly is having. Diamond shimmers through her lashes and some beatific face inside a cloud of sun-ripened hair is hovering above. Beyond? Is just a heid and hair. Big pink mouth; the mouth is asking if she would like some breakfast. Behind the bobbing head there is a tunnel or a castle and a circle of clear blue sky. Shortly, a topless man will offer Kelly his muscular tanned hand, will pull her up to snog the face off her. In her dream, she is wearing a fur coat, which moves of its own accord. Very disconcerting, to open your eyes and see your fur coat leaping towards the beatific, looming face.

Dreaming that you are in a place you're not. It's an occupational hazard.

'Hello,' says the face. It comes with a hand, which is touching Kelly's shoulder. The face is on haunches; no, there is a body too, concealed behind a dancing Collie.

'Sorry to disturb. It's just, the warden will be here to open up soon. And I thought you might like some breakfast.'

Kelly sits up. Her neck is cricked from the way she's been lying, and she's a mouth like a badger's arse. The voice speaking to her is frightfully posh.

'Sorry,' says Kelly. 'Sorry.' She reaches for her coat, which has slipped off and become a dog bed in the night. The tip of the fur collar is all soggy. 'We weren't doing anything wrong.' She starts to shrug it on; with her coat on, she'll look respectable.

'No, of course not. I wasn't suggesting . . . Look.' The pink mouth smiles. It's not that big; now that Kelly's come to, she can see all the bits of face are in normal proportion. The lady smiles again. Wrinkles fan from the sides of her eyes, like extra-long, happy eyelashes. Pastel. That's what she is. Lemon-grey hair. Turquoise jumper and pearls, and there is a smudge of pink lipstick on her teeth.

'I'm Clara. I live in the old manse. Over there.'

'I'm really sorry.' Kelly starts to button herself.

'Don't be silly. You've nothing to apologise for. You were tired, I presume, and you had a rest. That's exactly what this place was built for. Did you know that hospital and hostel are from the same root? And hospitality, of course. A place of rest. Et voilà, L'Hôtel-Dieu.' Clara extends her arm, saluting the abbey. The slack skin of her neck quivers.

She's clearly not stayed in some of the hostels Kelly has. Why is this woman not kicking her butt? Perhaps Kelly's still inside her dream. Best to go with the flow, anyroad. 'Just give me a second and we'll be on our way.'

'It's not me. I don't bother about these things in the slightest. But the warden can be a bit . . . proprietorial. Historic environment and all that. Sorry, dear. What was your name?'

'Kelly,' she mutters. Names are private, you don't just give them away, but she's still half asleep, and fuzzy with it.

'Well. Good morning, Kelly.' Unasked, Clara helps Kelly to her feet. Very uncomfortable, to have a stranger seize her. But the lady makes no fuss, simply holds her wrist, then drops it when the job is done. 'And who is this delightful little chap?'

'He's Collie.'

'Yes.' She's chucking him under the chin. The wee traitor is loving it, rolling onto his back and flashing his bits. 'But what's his name?'

'Eh, Collie. As in Collieflower, cause his face is all whiskery. It made me think of a flower. Like a dog rose?'

You're burbling, Kelly. Nerves. None of that makes sense.

'The name of the rose, eh? Very fitting.'

Neither does that.

'Chop chop then, campers. Step this way.'

'Look, I promise we're moving on. I just,' Kelly lowers her voice, 'if you live over there, could I possibly use your toilet, please? And would you maybe have a biscuit or something for the dog?'

'Oh, I think we can do better than that.'

The dew glistens on the grass, rims Kelly's trousers, her boots. Those cobbles were hard to sleep on, but at least they were dry. Being wet and waking is the worst. Collie runs ahead, keeping up with the lady. Kelly listens. Faint birdsong, rolling gurgle of the river. The *phut* of her boots, compressing damp grass. Those are the only noises. She'd forgotten the deep silence you get in the countryside. You wake to cacophony in the city, always.

Clara is standing by the dry-stone wall. 'We're just through this gate. In you go.'

Kelly tries to keep her coat from flapping. The stench of her will be crawling out her clothes.

'Fry-up suit you?'

'I'm sorry?'

She's taking them to the front of the house Kelly saw last night. It's a handsome old manse, built in the same stone as the abbey. Probably *of* the same stone, when you think about it. Clara holds the front door open.

'You're not one of those vegans, are you?'

124

'No.'

Kelly steps into a tiled hall, the pattern of mustard and blue repeating in neat squares and diamonds all the way through to the kitchen, which is where they're being led.

'Good-oh. Thought you might have been one of those crusty bods. We get a few of them about here, dancing and dowsing for ley lines.'

'No. I'm not a crusty. Not a vegan either.'

'Glad to hear it. Lot of nonsense. I can't abide all that sentiment. As long as the animal is treated well, nose to tail, that's what I say! Eat the bloody lot of it, eh, boy?' She ruffles Collie's back so vigorously, he is forced to stop bouncing and sits in the middle of the floor. Or maybe that was Clara's plan all along.

Unsurprisingly, her kitchen is pastel too. There's a pale blue range cooker, cream units, scrubbed oak. And a collection of novelty teapots colonising a broad dresser by the window. On one shelf alone, Kelly can see a Chinese pagoda teapot, a frog one, a smiling ginger cat, some kind of gnome or leprechaun and a jowly, beaming moon, replete with spout and handle.

'Now.' Clara picks up a spatula. 'Leave your coat there.' There is the most glorious aroma of sausages coming from the range. Kelly canny believe the dog isn't climbing up the cooker. But he sits intently. Eyes on Clara and her wandering spatula. 'Cloakroom is through the lobby. It's just the gardener's toilet . . . Oh. Are you wanting a bath?'

Am I wanting a bath? Kelly would die for a bath. The thought of warm suds lapping her parched skin. She can feel the knots in her joints twitch at the mere suggestion that they might unravel. Clean. Not smelling of her own body, but of Clara's unguents and lotions – which will be ranged in pastel bottles along the edge of the bath. The bath will be a cast-iron one, Kelly reckons, the kind with claws. But the pleasure of going in would be too painful, for she will only have to get out again. And she doesny know this woman from Adam. Kind, eccentric. Axe murderer? You just don't know.

Never take your boots off, Kelly. Far less your pants. (Aye, if only she'd listened to that gem of advice over the years.)

'No, cheers. Loo's fine.'

In the small, functional (pastel) room, she pees and washes her hands and face. Ach, fuck it. She'll do her oxters too – who knows when she'll get another chance. She wheechs off her two jumpers and her vest. Bras are a long-forgotten luxury, but hey, when your tits are hinging, just let 'em swing. Avoiding the mirror on the front of the door (easy enough when you screw up your eyes), she has a nosy in the bathroom cabinet. Amid the cotton wool and Optrex, there's a row of wee shampoos and moisturisers, the sort you get in hotels, and a pack of two toothbrushes. Two? That's just greedy, so it is. She pops the pack, slips one into her trouser pocket. She'll do her teeth later, in private. Kelly can make an awful retching sound when she brushes. She likes to get right round in about her molars.

Forgetful, she swings the cabinet door shut. Catches a face in the mirror. It is her grandmother's face, on her sickbed. Gaunt. Grey and tangled shock of hair. Hollow eyes and reddened cheeks. But Kelly's cheeks are not red from the flush of fever. Her skin is crazed in broken veins. She touches below her eye. A white fingerprint appears, disappears as the blood flows and the white is engulfed by red. Repeats the action. Red. White. Red. Horrible, bluish brick-red. Spilled and drifting blood, inside her. Where does it go, if it's not in its proper place? She pretends the face is not hers, so it's easier to bear. Weatherbeaten. Would a person call her that? But the spread of the vessels across her nose, and splaying purple at the sides, suggest a different descriptor.

Alky.

A is for alky. Aged. Atrophied. Ancient. Absurd. A is for

architect. Kelly might have been an architect. Kelly might have built bridges and towers.

She tries to flatten her hair into her head. The tugs are too tight for her fingers to comb. So she wets it. Lays the towel over her face, inhaling the flowery scent of washing powder.

'All right in there?' Clara is on the other side of the door. 'Breakfast ready when you are. Scrambled eggs OK?'

'Aye. Fine. Thank you.'

Kelly waits a minute, though she doesn't know what she's composing herself for. It's only a hot meal. She gets them twice a week at the Wayside Club. No biggie.

In the kitchen, Clara has laid the table, made a pile of toast, and Collie is tucking into his own mini fry-up: sausage, bacon and scrambled eggs by the looks of it. Kelly is so hungry she would actually eat straight out his bowl.

'Here we go. Have a seat.' In Clara swings. Over Kelly's shoulder, onto the table, a laden plateful of sausage (square and links), two potato scones, bacon, mushrooms, fried tomato and eggs. 'Help yourself to tea and juice.'

There is no cutlery. Kelly doesn't care. She picks up a sausage and tears into it, grease running down her wrist. Crams it in, takes another. Hasny a clue how she'll tackle the eggs.

Clara goes to sit opposite.

'Oh God. I'm so sorry. Forgot cutlery! Honestly. Donald says I'm away with the fairies half the time.'

'Donald your husband?' Kelly licks her fingers. Embarrassed, yes, but mostly starving. She sooks on a tomato until the cutlery cavalry arrive. On a trolley in the corner of the kitchen she notices some sherry glasses. Tiny fluted vases for the containment of fudgy goodness. Indeed, a bottle of Croft sits alongside.

'No, dear. My son. Here we are. Oh, shall I get napkins too?'

A square of embroidered cloth, far too pretty to use, is laid before her.

'No, alas. My husband and I are . . . parted.'

'I'm sorry. When did he die?' Kelly shovels in the scrambled egg. It is too delicious. She is eating a cloud of golden fluff. Maybe she pegged it in the night, and she's in heaven. Concentrate on what you do have, Kelly. The food. Not the drink. Collie stretches in front of the range, paws twitching. She has an urge to press her face into his belly. Blow raspberries on the mottled pink.

'Oh, he's not dead, dear. We're div*orced*.' Clara utters the word like it's an STD. 'Man was a total arsehole. Good riddance, I say. But I see you must have a significant other. When's the big day?'

Kelly has just put an entire triangle of potato scone in her mouth. Slightly over-crisp, a corner stabs the roof of her palate as she tries to chew and swallow.

'Your ring. It's lovely. Quite . . . showy, isn't it?'

Clara's smile spreads to her eyes. Kelly has learned to be a rapid judge of character. If you hitch or doss or beg, you develop a second skin, or sense . . . ach, she doesny know how to explain, but there is an energy that comes off people. It tells you when to dodge, when to embrace. Not literally. Kelly doesny do embrace. Except Collie, obviously.

'It's not real diamonds.'

'Ah.' Clara pours them both tea, from a sleeping field mouse curled round a haystack.

'Clara. This is really kind of you. But I don't have any money, you know. I can't pay you.'

'I didn't imagine you could, dear. Rich people tend not to spend the night on cobbles.'

'Why are you doing this?'

'Why would I not? You were hungry, weren't you? Sugar?'

'No. Ta. It's just, most people don't.' This tea is nectar.

Every home should make tea in a ceramic haystack. Kelly and Clara sit and sip. A clock ticks. Collie licks his balls.

'Is that right?' says Clara, when enough time has passed. 'Well, I'm glad I'm not most people. Finished?'

'Yes. That was magic.'

'Can I get you anything else?'

That bottle of Croft, please? Such a lovely shape to hold in your hand. Bottle green is my favourite colour.

'No, thank you.' Kelly begins to stack the plates. The trolley's quite close to the sink.

'Och, leave that. I'll sort it later. Well, if you don't want more to eat, could I offer you two a lift anywhere? Where's next on your travels?'

Kelly considers this. Her legs ache; the entire length of her legs, mind – the pain is not focused on the joints. In fact, they seem to hurt less than usual. She prods one knee under the table. There is no corresponding shaft of pain.

'It's OK, thanks. I know what way we're going. We're doing the Pilgrim Way.'

'Oh, how lovely! I thought you might be. Shall I pack you a little food for the way?'

Pressure building in her sinuses. Kelly scratches the side of her nose, tender where the purple veins shame her. 'Thank you.' Her voice sounds hoarse.

'My pleasure. Wish I was as adventurous as you two. Give me two ticks. Help yourself to more toast.'

Kelly hears Clara bustling, but her eyes are shut. A contented woman, enjoying her bulging belly and the comfort of her chair. And not crying. Concentrating every fibre on not crying. Imprinted on her eyelids are the lines of the trolley. The sinuous bottle on top. Door opening. Clara's footsteps, diminishing down the hall. *Get it. Don't get it. Get it. Don't get it. I'm going to get—*

Clara returns with a small backpack. 'I hope you don't

mind. It's my grandson's old thing. But it's waterproof. Very light. Save you cramming everything in your pockets.' On the back of the bag is a speeding Tardis, birling through space below the legend: *I Am the Doctor.* 'Now, I've popped in a couple of spare pullovers too, in case it gets chilly. Red sky this morning, you know – shepherd's warning!'

'Clara, I can't—'

'No such word as can't. You'll be doing me a favour, honestly. They're really rather ugly. My husband's old golfing gear. The new squeeze doesn't like him playing golf. Now,' she stoops to pet Collie, 'I haven't forgotten you, Dogrose.'

'Collieflower.'

'Ah yes, Collieflower. Sorry. I noticed Collieflower doesn't have a collar.'

'So? It's no against the law. I havny stolen him, if that's what you're suggesting.'

'I'm not suggesting anything. It's just, if you're doing the pilgrim route, there's parts where you'll have to walk along the A75, or cross it at least. He's a beautiful boy – yes, you are, Collie Dog, you really are – but he's still very young. And, I suspect, a teeny bit naughty? So would this be of any use?' She unhooks a leather collar and lead from a hook by the kitchen door. 'The collar's probably a little large, but we can make an extra hole or two with a knife.' Clara kneels to try it round the pup's neck. 'Yes, a wee bit loose. I'll make one here. Can you pass me that chopping board, please?'

'Won't your dog need it?'

Clara is stabbing at the collar with a kitchen knife. 'Not my dog. No. Prince went off with my husband.' Stab. 'Seems the squeeze hates golf, loves dogs.'

'Why don't you take him?' It is a spontaneous eruption; it is sense and serendipity. Collie needs a proper home. Kelly will only harm him. She will try, really hard, not to, but she will.

'Who, Jeremy? I've told you, I don't want him. You have no idea what a relief it is not to wash his bloody—' Stab.

'No. Collie, I mean.'

'Take your dog? There we go. Perfect. That is a perfect fit. Yes it is, clever boy.' Clara fastens the collar.

Kelly waits in a soundless bubble – she can hear Clara, but she also can't? She is in a dwam of her own making, she's said *Take Collie*, so it is said, and hinging there; you can't unsay words, oh, you can never bloody unsay words . . . Who's the man with the cat? Clanging a cymbal in her brain. *Wake up, neurons. You used to be smart.* Schrodinger. That's it. Kelly 'n' Col are in a box, neither together nor apart. She does not know how she feels.

'Why would I want to do that?' Clara asks.

Collie shakes himself, comes over to press into Kelly's leg. She runs her finger under the collar, checking it's not too tight. She's not at all sure he likes it. Who'd want a noose round their neck? When they get outside, she'll take it off. Where's your head at, Kelly? He is not your dog.

'He's not—'

'He clearly loves you. Look at him.'

Kelly doesn't want to look. She nudges him away. 'Yeah, but. It was daft to bring him. He's got wee legs. I don't want to knacker him.'

'Take your time, then. There's no deadline for doing the Pilgrim Way.'

'I've only got three days left. I've got to be somewhere . . .' She is twisting the ring on her finger. It's definitely getting slacker. If it wasn't for her swollen knuckle, she could probably yank it free.

'Meeting someone special?' Clara clocks Kelly footering with her fingers.

'No. Aye. Kind of.'

'You know, dogs are more resilient than you realise. Border

131

collies especially. Working dogs can walk up to twenty miles a day. Look at him.'

Collie is standing, expectant, by the door. Raring to go.

'Don't you miss your dog?' says Kelly.

'Of course I do. But dogs are a tie. And he was a Lab – very smelly.'

'But are you not lonely here, on your own?'

'Och, there's always folk about. Interesting people come to visit the abbey. People like you.'

Kelly snorts. Clearly the woman is cracked with loneliness if she thinks Kelly is interesting. Dragging in strangers to give them free B&B. What's that all about?

'Collie could keep you company, but.'

At his name, Collie circles round Kelly. Returns to the door.

'Proper sheepdog, that. I think he's decided for you. And it's a very sweet thought, and I do appreciate it. I really do. But, Kelly, I'm having a wonderful time. Thirty-eight years, trapped with the one man. You've no idea the freedom. I can eat cornflakes and read all day. Chat to whomever I fancy. No ironing – ever! I'm off to Malta next week with the girls.' Clara hands Kelly the *Doctor Who* backpack. 'I helped you because you needed help. That's it. Why complicate things? I think if we all put something in the kindness bank, it's an investment, isn't it? Maybe it will be there when we need it. We all need kindness.'

Kelly accepts her help to squeeze her arms through the straps of the bag.

'Hmm. It's a wee big snug. Let me . . . That's as much as they'll go. Och, that's fine, eh?'

Kelly waves her arms, which can only go so far, restricted by the tightness of the shoulder straps. Must be how a turtle feels when it's turned the wrong way.

'Aye, aye, that's great. Thanks.'

'Well. Good luck, Kelly. It was lovely meeting you.'

'I . . . You too.' Words are inadequate. The pit of her stomach is glowing. Briefly, Kelly pats Clara's arm, staying far enough back that she won't try to grab her.

'Can I just say . . .' She feels her face go hot. She looks at the floor. 'I'm really glad you're not most people.'

Clara doesn't wave them off – that would be twee, and neither of them is that kind of wumman. Kelly and Collie leave the manse and cross over the road. It is dry out, but the blue sky of yesterday is muted; it can't decide yet what it wants to be. It is the colour of washed-out denim, turning grey above the hills. Kelly has no hood. She lost her bunnet in the skip. 'Just as well I've not been at the hairdresser, eh, Collie? Wish they still made Rain Mates.'

Having a dog. Stops you talking to yourself for one thing. But Kelly is glad Clara didn't take him. Relieved, and oh so very glad. Kelly 'n' Collie. For now, that's what they are. They are still in their box, and this walk is not spiritual. It is functional. To increase her blood flow and reduce her swelling. At the end of it, decisions will be made, and Collie will be a decision. She is not sentencing him to a life on the streets. She tweaks his ear. 'Ready?'

The pup leaps and grins, with no idea what he's so happy about. He just is.

Whithorn – Pilgrim Way.

She touches the wooden sign, for luck. They put their heads down, commence their ascent. At first, the road is tree-lined. Tall birches that shimmer and droop, leaves touching above your head. On a scale of steepness it is would-go-on-your-arse-if-icy steep, but not crawl-on-your-hands-and-knees.

They climb for what must be miles, the air growing warmer and duller. Kelly sweats. She cracks a long branch off a tree, to use as a walking pole. Collie thinks this is a game, keeps snapping at the base of it, tugging and growling until she's forced to break the top off and give it to him. 'Right. That's your stick. This is mine.' He holds it in his mouth, gallops forwards, charges back. Delirious with joy. She hasn't taken his collar off, but he doesn't seem to care. The road's very narrow; it bends and winds so it's hard to see what's coming next. If a car were to speed down here, you'd have to jump into the hedgerow. Country lanes are the scene of Kelly's childhood; she knows fine to walk closer to the right so you are facing oncoming traffic, how to walk smartly with your shoulder to the middle round a bend. Collie knows none of these things. He is a baby.

Kelly is responsible for him. Jesus.

'Collie!' she calls. 'Wait for me. Don't go too far.'

Amazingly, he stops.

'Good boy. You don't need a lead, do you?'

Past a row of neat white houses, with lupins and red-hot pokers in the gardens. The road begins to widen. Still rising, but straighter. Eventually the incline decreases, levels out, and they walk a while on the straight. Kelly's legs are jelly-weak. Her heart is powerful; she can feel it pounding in tides. *Boosh*. *Boosh*. Your heart is a miracle, really.

The trees have thinned to moorland. Grey clouds clamp down low. The hills are fuzzy with mist. It's an austere landscape. Empty. It is beautiful and sad and it makes her ache. Once, these hills were full and fertile. Nobody talks about the Lowland Clearances. Kelly only knows about them because there was a band called the Levellers that she liked. A punky folk band, before those things were popular. Kelly got all the music papers as a teenager – *NME*, *Melody Maker*, though you drew the line at *Smash Hits*. The group's name was something to do with the English Civil War.

She loved knowing origins. Song lyrics, band lore, all that underpinning and unpicking was precious then. You'd to seek it out – if there were no sleeve notes, you'd have to listen and listen again to a particular track, lifting and dropping the needle to make out the words your heroes sang. Living in a wee toun in south-west Scotland, opportunities to go to actual gigs were non-existent. So when Kelly and Mandz saw a poster advertising *The Levellers* in Gatehouse Mill, they were delirious. So delirious they didny read the small print. Turns out it was a *talk* on the Levellers, not a concert. And the Levellers in question were the Galloway Levellers, brave eighteenth-century dyke-breakers who rose in protest at landowners dividing their common land with walls. After the girls' initial shock (they should have guessed when they saw the audience going in – all tweeds and woolly jumpers), Kelly and Mandz had stayed to listen. Might as well – they'd got the bus over and the next one wasn't for two hours. She'd not learned much of her own history in school, not the local stuff anyway, but Kelly had learned a wee bit of it that night, and though they laughed after, and took the piss on the bus on the way home, it stayed with her. The beginnings of a seam; that there were stories untold. And just because they were untold, it didn't make them untrue.

'Collie! Here, boy. Wait.'

Kelly climbs over one of the low stone walls that flank the road, to stand in the middle of the nothing. No homes. No beasts. Acres of undulating moorland, peat and pounded stone that were ancient trees once, and mountains. Collie scrambles over the wall after her. Together they walk on wiry yellow grass. Seeing nothing. Listening to nothing. Tenant farmers and cottars, families swept from here, quietly as you would brush off dust, to make room for cows and sheep. But for a while there, they'd stood their ground, massing, working together to topple these old stone dykes when they were new.

Far above Kelly, a black bird wheels. Dipping, dropping, it's big enough to be an eagle. Another joins it and they dance, circling round and down. One drifts low and straight overhead. Kelly can make out the russet belly and white fishtail as it passes. A red kite, riding the updraught, elegant as a Chinese dragon. Or a phoenix – because she's pretty sure the kites were made extinct here as well.

'OK, boy. Hup.' She guides Collie over the wall, further up where the stones have fallen and it's lower, then climbs it herself. Collie looks disappointed to be on the road again. 'Is there not enough sniffs for you here?' Then she worries it's his paws – is tarmac too hard for puppy pads? 'Here. Give me your foot a wee minute.' She checks one front paw, then the other. They are pink and black and firm to the touch. Like roughened leather. 'No, you're fine. You hungry? Will we walk a wee bit more then find a nice spot for a picnic? I wonder what your Auntie Clara's packed us.'

Having an Auntie Clara would be a fine thing. Kelly does have aunties, though. There's her mother's sister, whose husband was the farmer who shot himself, and Auntie Joan on her dad's side. Or she might not. They'll both be in their eighties now. Yeah, Kelly might not have aunties at all. She thinks of the tightness of her family unit when she was young, the New Year parties in orange-and-green-painted living rooms, Advocaat on G Plan sideboards, a bundle of cousins. Playing proper party games – that was Auntie Joan's speciality. There was one where she blindfolded you, made you stick your finger in half an orange and told you it was Admiral Nelson's eye.

No wonder Kelly's scarred. Are those normal games to play with weans? She sucks in a lungful of air. The silence up here is profound. It's difficult for her to remember her family. She struggles when one memory bangs up against another, because then they start to push and force, and you can't filter them. They all just pile in en masse, a total stramash of memories, each carrying its own suitcase, and it's you, you who are in each suitcase when they open. You spring out at whatever age you were: eight when you did the Nelson game, your finger squirting, you peeking below the blindfold, seeing the cuff of your blouse – a green blouse under a red velvet pinafore (your mum had nae taste) – and Mandz was there too, squealing, and now you are both squealing your heads off on the dodgems at the carnival, and there's your mum, oh, my wee lovely mum in her sheepskin coat. To hold her, because you can almost feel it, the plump give of her flesh as you press in, talcum powder kisses, you would never feel sad again if you could only hold her . . .

But. Then she'd see you, Kelly. See the fecking state of you, and she'd want to die all over again.

If she listens hard, Kelly can hear variations of wind, and the hush of long grass – a hollow, husky rattle. It's nice. A bit like wind chimes. Up ahead, Collie has come to a halt. The road splits in two, making a Y shape round an old cottage surrounded by trees. There are no indications to say which road goes where. Kelly pulls out the pilgrim pamphlet, which is getting totally creased. She wipes her forehead with the back of her fist. It's too warm. Though the sky is leaden, she's got her coat tied round her waist (which has made her *Doctor Who* backpack far more comfy). Once they've eaten, she'll shove her jumpers in the bag too.

She studies the pathways indicated on the leaflet. No proper directions, it's all just wee lines. Unless you're a crow, the map is pretty useless.

'Aye, very good, Collie. So Glenluce is here and Whithorn's there. But how do we *get* there?'

The breathing wind becomes louder, becomes the throaty sound of an engine. 'Collie, here!' She gets him on the verge. Grips his collar, head down so she can check she's definitely got her fingers right through, but he sits anyway, like the perfect wee puppy he is. They are in amidst the belt of oak trees that skirt the cottage. She knows they are oaks because of the leaves – kind of like wavy fingers, or seaweed. The vehicle chugs past, taking the left-hand fork. It's a green Land Rover. With two Union Jack stickers on the bumper.

Kelly drops to her knees, cuddling the dog into her breast. She makes them both shrunken and still, but he will hear her heartbeat, the man will hear, the whole world will hear her manic heartbeat, too fast, too fast ohGodplease-don'ttakehim. *Shh, baby. Shh.* Her mouth is on her baby's head, *shhing* through his fur, *shhing* into his brain. Collie is smart. He will understand.

The Land Rover disappears over the crest of the ridge. Kelly is virtually lying on her dog, and in that moment, she knows she would protect him. If there was a gun or a fist, she would put her body between Collie and the danger. You just would. Underneath, Collie is being squashed flat, but the wee soul doesny whimper. Good as gold. Do dogs read minds? Daft cow, Kelly, of course they don't. But they might read people.

That old bastard is seeking them out. With his waistcoat and his shotgun, he is hunting prey. Kelly 'n' Collie lie in the grass, because she doesny know what to do. But if he comes back, if he comes back. That will be worse: they are lying splayed. Two fish on a hook. She jumps up. Collie shakes himself.

'Let's go, kiddo.'

Kelly jog-trots along the right fork; right, ha, it seems like the right road, it's slightly broader than the road Major Tom took anyway, so it's probably the pilgrim path. They should keep off the road. Christ, this whole journey, she needs to keep off the road.

Fucking, fucking people. Fucking leave me alone.

There's a gate, across the other side, not padlocked. Open it, through. Keep to the fields that edge the road, at least till the danger's past.

When, Kelly?

When is the danger ever past?

Over cowpats and tussocks, Kelly marches and Collie trots. He is in his element, tasting unmentionables under hedges and on the wind. Kelly keeps tight to the edges of the fields they cross, alert for the sound of vehicles or the movement of beasts. She has no idea what Collie will do if confronted by a sheep, but she suspects it won't be pretty. Farmers shoot dogs who interfere with their stock; don't even need to bite, just the chasing is enough to merit execution. She's saved Collie from that fate already. A ghost walks over her grave. What if it's the same as her greatcoat? What if each end is destined from the beginning? Taking you there, always, the current drifting and playing with you, but always pulling you there.

A clutter of stones by grassed-over furrows. That will do for a seat. She calls the dog to her, wanting to feel his warmth. Obedient, he sits. Kelly puts her arms round his sloping back. He presses his head into her breast. Pushing with all his might, while his body remains still. It's as if he is taking comfort from her pulse. Kelly swallows an entire bottle of water, not caring where the next one's coming from, and they eat a few of the sandwiches Clara packed. She's done them proud. Cheese and pickle. Ham and tomato. Pork pies, apples, crisps and the remains of a packet of Bonio. Kelly rations the food; it will last them two days if she's careful.

Good. Maximum avoidance of folk. Clara was – is – wonderful, but a morning of human engagement has left Kelly spent.

Begging is exhausting. Say that to a housebound dweller and they will laugh. Or rant, if they're of the why-should-I-work-just-so's-you-can-sit-on-your-arse-all-day persuasion.

Safe in their hoose with their telly and their walls, they have no concept of a soul's fragility. Nobody does, until they are made vulnerable themselves. Strip away your trappings, rip off your shell and let's see how hard you are. When you beg, you have to think of everything. How you look, how you sit. Where you sit. In what manner do you hold out your hand? Cupped (greedy)? Outstretched (pathetic)? Do you speak or stay silent? Raise your head? Write a sign, have bare feet? Stay alert, take drugs to numb the pain, slur and shiver, look clean, or drink and drink so you are never sober.

In your head, you are always somewhere else.

But that's just you. That does not take account of all the interactions you will have that day. With your potential saviours. You will be laughed at, mocked, ignored. You will be spat on, kicked, offered half a cup of someone's latte. Folk will give you a tenner and touch your cheek. Folk will pretend to put money in your cup, then body-swerve away, or spill your cup over, on purpose. Occasionally they will stamp on it, and they might as well be crushing you. You will close your eyes to make it go away. You will smell burning – a lit fag has been laid against your cardboard. You will wrap tin foil round your ankles and wrists to keep the cold out, and stare stoically ahead while a bunch of workies jeer, 'Ho! Tin Man! Where's Dorothy?' Over and fecking over. You'll hear a noise to the side, flinch, and find a hand laying a whole meatball Subway beside you. You will cramp and freeze, scared to lose your spot. Bursting for a pee. You are always scared; it is a bright vein that twists through you in knots and pulses. It never rests.

And you will know the whole world is scared. The suits and the stilettos, they're all scared too. It is why you embarrass them. You are their fears made flesh. Like is calling unto like – and they don't like it.

Kelly and Collie let their food digest. Her pent-up panic

wants to go free range, but she makes herself try to relax. Major Tom is cruising the back roads. He is not yomping fields. Chill, Kelly. Or pace your panic at least, for fecksake. She chews on an apple. Has no clue when she last ate fruit, is surprised by how much she enjoys its sharp bite cleaning her gullet.

She lies back along one of the stone ridges, gazing at the thickening sky.

Once you properly stop moving, it's as if your body slips a gear. It lets its guard down, is more sensitive to the pain that's been drumming you for miles. Her heels nip like buggery. Balls of her feet too; they will be full of blisters when she takes her boots off. Pop-pop, same as the seaweed. Below her knees is weak, as if someone has milked her legs. Fluid-filled flesh above her tender joints. She flexes her fingers, and the ring glitters. She feels the glitter travel beneath her skin.

Time drifts like sips of wine. Pewter clouds, shiny smirr that coats you in soft, damp mist. It falls in cobwebs, silent through the stillness of the moor. Sweat cools to shivers, Kelly too slow to get her coat on before the fine rain creeps into her T-shirt. She is sandwiched in moist unpleasantness. The rain begins to talk to her. It runnels over the stones on which she rests, painting them dark to show their pattern. Then it passes into the quiet, for it is only part of the silence. If she concentrates, the silence up here is overpowering. It is as heavy as a mountain on her. There's been no traffic on this road the whole time they've sat here.

Collie does a massive dump, which definitely signals it's time to move. Kelly knows when she looks back what she'll see. The stones she was resting on are the remnants of an old steading. They've been lying on the foundations of someone else's life.

She walks to the far end of the field, where there's a

five-bar gate. Locked. Up and over. Shoogles it at the base, encouraging the dog to belly-creep beneath. From here, the land begins to dip. Wonder of wonders! Kelly can see the sea! Way below, a low grey vista after a patchwork of fields. She can make out houses, a spire. A proper town. Whithorn! It must be. St Ninian came ashore at Whithorn, she's pretty sure. This'll be the juicy bit. At last, *Pilgrims' Progress* will reveal its secrets, with tales of saints and sinners. Couple of statues, maybe a wee museum? Thank God, they've been walking for . . . she hasny a clue, but ages. In the city, there's always clocks or bells to mark your hours. If not, people's habits will give you clues – office workers eating lunch. Shops open or shut. Folk high on after-work drinks. The country-side is more difficult, but she's learning to read the sky. Relearning. Out here, nature rules. It is weathering her deeper than it ever did in Glasgow.

She can do this. It is literally all downhill from here. The idea of pilgrimage is daft; Kelly is merely walking from place to place. It's what she does in Glasgow every single day. But her wee map is bringing a semblance of order and purpose. She is beginning to enjoy the satisfaction of ticking things off. Of accomplishment. It is reminding her of how she used to study. Kelly was never a mind-map type of gal. What worked for her was lists of facts, learning said lists of facts, repeating and ticking off the remembered lists. Nothing wrong with learning by rote. Just look at where it gets you.

They walk down the widening road. Rain spritzing, but it stays light. Occasionally Collie will yap at the droplets, trying to bite them. When she tells him he's a daft boy, he laughs with puppy teeth, and she laughs too. Houses begin to dot the landscape, bungalows and new-builds scattered either side of the road. One has a Saltire fluttering in the back garden. That makes her smile too. Where Major Tom's flags seem oppressive, this one makes her feel brave. It probably wasn't even him in that stupid jeep. Could've been anyone – Galloway is hoaching with crusty old Tories. She finds Collie a stick to hold in his mouth, but he uses it as a battering ram, dipping behind her, then clattering it into her calves. He thinks this is a great game, as is the chase to yank the stick off him again.

As they enter the town proper, the buildings get older: white-harled or solid sandstone. The main street sheers steeply left, then right. Surrounded by windows, Kelly feels exposed. She scans the parked cars, but there is no Land Rover. Major Tom is long gone. He will never find them, now they're so far off. Her shoulders unclench. Collie barks at a passing tractor, and she puts him on the lead. 'Just for a wee while, pet. It might get busy.'

Kelly came here with the Sunday School, and it was full of tourists. She's sure she did. But she doesn't remember Whithorn being on such a slope. Then she sees the big brown sign.

Welcome to Glenluce – the Valley of Light. Historic Glenluce Abbey 1½ miles.

They have walked in a giant circle.

*

The very last time you walk through Galloway, before you leave for good, is the night of Amanda's engagement party. She doesn't like being called Mandz any more, because that was for kids, and we're not kids now, are we, Kelly? No, *you say dutifully, and all the while you are thinking of how best to smuggle in a quarter-bottle, because she is watching you like a bloody hawk.*

—You have to be able to do this, Kelly. To go to places with other folk, and just have fun, and not get stocious. Don't you see?

—Yes, *you agree. I do.*

I do.

Her ring is a modest twist of gold, binding two discreet and perfect diamonds. You have not drunk for five full days. If you can do five days, you can do six, then that will be a week. No problem. You would like a wee smoke, just to take the edge off, but it's not a craving. Not like this. Alcohol is your drug of choice. Was.

And you are not craving. Christ, you're not an alky. You've just been sad. And now you are happy. Playing nice. Amanda has lent you a dress, although you are no longer the same build. Where she has filled out, you've become shrunken. It takes a while to find an outfit that does not show your concave breasts and conceals your tattooed forearm (special request from your dad), but there you are, the pair of you. You grin and squeeze. Hold hands like it is Primary One.

—Pretty as a picture, *says your dad, blowing his nose.*

—I can't believe you're getting married.

—I want you to be my bridesmaid.

You start to cry. Ach, what are you two like? *says your dad, and you think he's greeting too.*

Town hall. The party is upstairs, in a vaulted hall with disco lights. From tots to octogenarians, the full spectrum of Kirkcudbright's denizens are represented. Kirkcudbright is an odd little place. Traditionally beautiful, with yawning skies and hidden wynds to house fisherfolk and farmers, it has bustled along for centuries. Full of lambent light and picturesque charm, it has always attracted artists.

However, as folk do like to be beside the seaside, it has also become home to two distinct types of incomers: eco-warrior artists and retired expats. (You reckon these are the folk who couldn't afford France and are happiest playing bridge with like-minded chaps.) There are entire

144

shops in Kirkcudbright devoted to the sale of red corduroy trousers, plus bijoux studios and galleries galore. You want to dislike these folk, but you don't, and you can't, for they all choose to come to Kirkcudbright. And usually they are pretty decent. This place you have discarded, they have opted to make their home. And with them, and by them, and for them, your wee toun flourishes. There's Ms Addison, your old art teacher, channelling her inner flapper girl and having a chinwag with Admiral Smyth (RN). The admiral gives you a cheery wave – he is chairman of the horticultural society and a leading light in local history – a history that is not his, but which he has studied nonetheless, until he knows it better than you. He helped you write your personal statement for uni. So you don't stop to say hello.

You choose a corner, stand in the half-dark. Observing and concealed. You have a headache that begins in your heels, travels the length of your crumbling spine, to explode in bright blooms on the back curve of your skull. To the outside world, you are the shy girl in a corner.

Ach.

You know your place in this tableau. You know you are the talk of the steamie, the subject of sidelong glances and shaken heads. Without a slick of liquid lustre, you know you are absurd. Exposed. What are they doing, dragging you out into the light? You are damaged goods a motherless child a disgrace to your name a crushing disappointment. Voices in the shadows hiss, insisting this is true. That there is no warmth for you in this place, no matter how hard you pretend. You are beyond hope, have moved from an object of pity to being barely tolerated.

So who are you trying to impress, Kelly?

One of your hands is pecking at the other, or your knee is jerking. You can't be sure, but it is impossible to stay as *still as you need to be. When your dad isn't looking and Man— sorry, Amanda, is surrounded by cooing girls all craning for a swatch at her finger, you hit the bar. Sweet God of unbridled bubbles – well, that would be Bacchus, wouldn't it? – for the first hour, it is free. You indulge, freely, in this generosity, never loitering for too long, moving round the outskirts of the room as you sip. You make sure it is always cola-coloured, or in a long Ribena-esque glass, which you raise wryly and dutifully as your dad catches your eye. Look, Daddy. I'm being good.*

Gradually the night becomes light, and full of sparkles. There is a lovely, sleek window of time where you fit your own skin. Loquacious and golden, holding court and charming hearts. Oh – I never saw you there? How are you? *If only that could always be your frame, that quick, sharp window before you are mellow. Then maudlin. Then full of bile. Sting of alcohol burning your throat, or is it your voice rising? My doll. Mine.* Darren Carruthers. Well, pal. Congratulations. I am so, so happy for . . . here. How about a wee dance for the bridesmaid . . . I'm gonny be your bridesmaid, didyouknowtha, Darren . . . Oh, c'mon. A wee slow dance. You know you want to. Yeah, that's better. Oops! Better hold me up. Ah, Darren. Darren. You smell so good. Shh. C'mere. Remember that night at the bonfire? Our leavers' do? Mind how we were gonna . . . *and you lift your chin, deliberately. And the long, dark slide of your tongue and of your downfall comes, you are Lucifer tumbling as you lick his lip, and, half thunderstruck, he half parts his own lips and your other half, no, his other half, is bearing down and you are wrestling with the angel. Hair and teeth. A caterwaul. Catfight.* I FUCKING HATE YOU.

Oh, Mandz.

The way you hit her, flat of the hand upright into the

flesh beneath her jaw. Not her jaw. Her throat. You know it is her throat: the soft give of it, the startled cracking-back of gulped breath, of choking break. Of your own, dangerous palm, folding in on itself as the body drops. Heavy.

Heavy legs, heavy shoulders. Shouting. Your father, seizing you? You, running from the awful huddle you have made.

Afterwards, walking. You walk for miles across fields so they cannot find you. At one point, you maybe hitch? There is a blur of light and warmth and speed. You have lost your shoes. You are not sure how, but somehow you make the late-night bus to Glasgow. One small miracle in a night so dark. Pressing a payphone, pressing all the numbers, crying for help, with no replies. You don't know who you call. Maybe no one at all. All you can remember is a seeping blur of black, black fields and filaments of tearful light. The city looming. Feet bleeding. Finding your room. Dark. Cool, until the ringing doorbell and the tread of boots on polis feet, into your hall, your hall – and your flatmate, letting them in, letting them all the way up to your cool, dark room, and the light flooding on.

They're coming to take you away, ha-ha.

Except he isn't your flatmate, and it isn't your room. It is a borrowed couch, a stained Dralon surfboard that smells of accidental nights. So you must have called someone, right? Someone who has let you in, and is now letting in these policemen. When they tell you to get up and gather your things to come to the station, the only thing you have in the world is the borrowed party dress in which you stand.

Chapter Eleven

Colonel Alasdair Charteris bangs his stick against the window. That bloody postman is back again, and he is parking on Alasdair's lawn.

'On the drive, you imbecile,' he shouts, but the postman just waves. He is wearing shorts. Alasdair had noticed that earlier as he lay parched and in agony on the floor of the barn. Despite the humiliation of having urinated himself a hundred yards from his own front door, despite having lain there all night in the filth because no matter how gritted his teeth were he simply could not stand, despite having crawled and dragged himself like a slug through the straw, being unable to reach the door latch, summoning all his strength of will to bally well GET UP, MAN and then passing out, at the actual point Alasdair was finally being delivered from his nightmare, he had noticed that his rescuer was possessed of a very fine pair of tanned, blonde-haired legs.

The front door to Chateau Charteris swings wide. 'It's only me. That's Fiona home safe. I brought you a few things.'

The postman waltzes straight into Alasdair's home. Doubtless it's a familiarity born from helping Alasdair to the bathroom, then into the shower, but he cannot bear the presumption. Ye gods, that shower. Amidst his distress,

Alasdair had insisted on wearing his soiled underpants throughout, then shimmying from them under a towel once he was washed. But even so. Another man's hand on his naked wet arm. Holding him, and the man being soaked with it, and laughing through the spray. That was an entirely different nightmare. Alasdair had focused on the smart beige tiles in his shower stall. On the fact that it was not a damp wooden cubicle like the type they'd had at school.

'Don't you knock?'

'Didn't want to disturb you.' The postman's eyes are clearest green. They gleam behind his spectacles. 'How you feeling now?'

'Bloody sore.'

'Yeah. Fiona says you need to keep the ice on it. Fresh ice every hour for the next twenty-four hours, or until the swelling goes down. So I got you this.' He unveils a huge bag of ready-made ice cubes. 'You got a freezer, Al?'

'It's Alasdair. The freezer's in the outhouse. And that's all very well, but how am I meant to hobble out there every five minutes if I've to keep this bloody ankle elevated?'

The postman thinks for a minute. Alasdair can see the small muscle in his jaw flexing. Moving in dimples below his cheekbone. Odd, angled planes the man has. Almost Slavic. Alasdair met a fellow once, in Macedonia, just after the conflict. With the UN peacekeepers—

'Got an ice box?'

'Pardon?'

'In your fridge?'

'Yes, but it's too small.'

'Ah, but what I'll do is decant as much as I can into the ice box, then put the rest out in the freezer. That'll keep you going till I finish my rounds tomorrow. Then I'll come and top you up.'

Is there a hint of double entendre there? Alasdair never

knows how these things work. He imagines some would see his life as a series of missed opportunities, a branching spine of paths not trodden. Not Alasdair. His life is one of discipline and focus. Weakness is never an attractive quality. That is the most valuable lesson he was ever taught in school. If you cry when being thrashed, they merely speed up and thrash you harder.

'Cheers for letting me use your jeep, Al.'

'It's not a jeep. It's a Land Rover.'

'Aye, it's just the insurance – when I had to run and get Fiona. I'm not allowed to carry passengers in the post van, see. Not even if it's life and death.' At this, the postman nudges him, but gently. 'Could have been death, eh? If I hadn't found you in time. Just as well I'm a nosy bugger. And that I've access to an angel of mercy, of course.'

'Yes.' Alasdair uses his walking stick to scratch his leg. The pain is radiating, spiking pins and needles from the ankle bone. 'Yes, it was very kind of you to fetch her. Fiona. Very decent.'

'Told you she'd know what to do. Feels better when it's properly strapped, doesn't it?'

'Mm.' The postman's wife is a nurse, apparently. Retired nurse, but nursing is like soldiering, Alasdair imagines. You never really lose the knack.

You do lose the camaraderie, however. But that's entirely different. It isn't a loss. It is a misplacement. Or perhaps a revelation. Camaraderie is a facade, really. A superficial gloss to oil the wheels. None of it means much. Each time you transfer units, every promotion stage you climb, you leave chaps behind. Just the way of it.

'Can I get you a cup of tea, Al? Wee bite to eat? Fiona says you can't have ibuprofen on an empty stomach.'

Initially, when the postman had found him earlier this morning – the postman whistling and Alasdair yelling –

he was adamant he was taking Alasdair to hospital. Alasdair was equally adamant he was not.

'Thirty-eight years in the army, man. I know when something's bloody broken.'

He'd begun to wish he'd never shouted for help. All he wanted was to be ensconced in his recliner chair, within easy reach of the telephone. A small and comfortable command centre from which he would direct operations. He would tell Jim Clarke at Lowgarth to see to the sheep, he could order Tesco to deliver, and, when business and sustenance were taken care of, he would plan his attack. Police first. Police for the thief, then veterinary surgeon for the dog.

Alasdair will not be taken advantage of. That is the Charteris code. Good God, the family crest is a hand holding a dagger aloft.

That bloody animal. A dog more unlike its mother you couldn't find. Alasdair is surprised by how much he misses Bess. This last litter was too much for the old girl. Should probably not have bred her again. Pedigree bitch, mind. Pups at four hundred pounds a pop.

Biting him like that. The little shit has to learn obedience. Of course he was never going to shoot it. He is not an executioner. How dare that female, that demented, filthy female, think she can come onto his property and tell him how to run his team? The woman looked as if she couldn't run a bloody bath.

Will the police want to inspect the crime scene? He doubts the local constabulary will be especially thorough, but then he's only lived here a few years. Has no real experience of rural bobbies. He certainly hasn't bothered to subject himself to their rigmarole of inspections and licensing for firearms. He is a military man of four decades' standing, for God's sake.

Might that be a problem, though? Firearm discharged, evidence of gunshot? Would they even notice?

Will Alasdair simply be inviting more fuss and drama if he telephones the police? Fuss he does not want. No, he is perfectly capable of sorting things himself. You do not retire to a rural sheep farm for fuss and nonsense. Early rises, early nights. The discipline of honest toil. A rigorous, heartfelt day. A door to lock, and . . . peace.

It is not a lonely life.

'Al.' The postman touches his arm. 'Are you hungry?'

'I . . . No. No, I'm not.'

He sits himself on the chaise adjacent to Alasdair's recliner. Tanned legs stretching to infinity. Impressive calves. Chap did say he rode a bike when the weather was fine.

'Here. I brought you a paper.'

There is a red-topped tabloid nestled in the man's lap.

'Thank you. But I only take *The Times*.'

'Fair enough. I'm Tony, by the way,' says the postman.

Did anyone ask for introductions? Anthony. Anthony and Alasdair. All the As.

'You're not married, Al?'

'I beg your pardon?'

'It's just, your post. It's always addressed to you. No Mrs Charteris.'

'And how is that your concern? Do you examine everyone's mail?'

'No. I just wondered who you've got to look after you.'

'I don't need looked after. Take care of myself perfectly well. This is . . . this accident was just an aberration.'

'You never said what you were doing out there. How come you fell so hard?' The postman is flicking through Alasdair's bookshelf, through the board games section at the bottom. It is hard to bear. Mauling his possessions. Presumptuous. Alasdair's fingers grip his stick. He has an urge to strike the man's hands as they carefully slip one green box from the rest.

152

'I fell. Knocked over a bucket and slipped on the water. Wet hay. It's an occupational hazard.'

Alasdair has been humiliated enough. *A banshee woman attacked me and stole my dog.* Not a soul need know. Once he is able to put weight on his ankle (which according to Fiona should be in a day or so), he will seek the woman out. She had no vehicle. Was a sight to behold: scarecrow hair and a fur-trimmed travel rug for a coat. He is a trained military searcher. If she's remained in the locale, he will find her. Actually, he will enjoy finding her.

'I could pop in, if you like,' the postman is saying. 'After work. Just for the next couple of evenings.'

'Why would you do that?'

'I could make you your dinner. Have a game of Scrabble.' He taps the box he has withdrawn. The games are stacked in a certain order; now it is all disturbed. 'I'm good with letters, me.' He smiles. There are amber sparks inside his eyes. 'Get it?'

'I'm sure your wife would prefer you to eat at home.'

'My wife?'

'Yes. Fiona. You said "I'll away home and get my Fiona". I distinctly heard you.'

'Oh, Fiona's not my wife. She's my sister.' The postman shuffles forward in his seat. His bare knees are virtually touching Alasdair's elevated leg. He repeats it, as if this fact is important. 'Al. I've never been married. I live with my sister.'

Anthony and Alasdair.

A chime to it. A warning bell.

Alasdair wants to say: *I know your game.*

He wants to say: *You are lovely.*

He wants to say: *I am so lonely. I will never make you happy. I haven't really been happy at all. Don't let that happen to you.*

153

Instead, he says, 'I'm rather tired now, Anthony. Thank you for all your help, but I'm fine. I really am.'

'Ah. OK then. I'll be off.' The postman gets up to leave. As he walks behind him, he settles his hand, briefly, on Alasdair's shoulder. Alasdair swallows. 'If you change your mind . . .'

'I won't. Don't forget your paper.'

The postman leans over to pick up his red-top. Alasdair feels the brush of the man's shirt rubbing on his hair. His scalp responds.

'Close the door, would you, when you go out? Make sure the snib's off first.'

'I . . . OK. Look, there's some good crosswords in this paper. I'll leave it, just in case. You might get bored. I can pop one in with your post tomorrow too.'

'As you wish. But in future, Anthony . . .'

'Yes?'

'Just leave the letters in the box. The one at the foot of the drive. '

Alasdair Charteris opens up yesterday's *Times*. He stares at the old news jumping on the page until he hears the click of his front door closing.

Chapter Twelve

A pompom fashioned into a furry globe of the world is bouncing in the windscreen. It's suspended from the rear-view mirror, along with some miniature Tibetan wind chimes and a flat disc in the shape of a cannabis leaf. Which says *Weed My Lips.*

'You all right now? Em – vous êtes OK?'

'Oui.' Kelly keeps her eyes on the snotty rag of hankie she's contorting in her lap. It is turning crispy. Doubt the guy will want it back in this state, but she'll offer.

'Vous voulez . . .' She gestures at him with the limp and crinkled handkerchief.

'No. Merci. You're fine. You keep it.'

She sees him glance at his wife. The man has a straggly ponytail and round glasses, which turn opaque as he moves his head. The couple driving her are a pair of ageing New Agers. The woman has hair similar to Kelly's albeit cleaner, the same static, defiant grey. A statement against the patriarchy, against dyeing and plucking and all those hairy norms. (Or in Kelly's case, a statement that she doesny possess a hairbrush.)

The man looks at Kelly in the mirror. 'Em – vous avez . . . been here long? Depuis longtemps?'

Kelly, Kelly. You are such an arse. The man speaks better

French than you. Why did she think this was a good idea?

When Marie and Donnie (yes, seriously, that is their names – and they have a guitar) found her snivelling by the road-side – when they were the one vehicle actually decent enough to stop and see if this greeting madwoman was all right – Kelly had got all flustered. She wasn't prepared. It was as if she'd taken off her armour and laid it down at the side of the verge for a rest. On and off, she must have been crying for a good hour when they stopped. Even Collie had got bored with her by then. He'd given up licking her face and was lying down, alternately yawning and licking himself instead.

She couldn't handle the raging despair that kept washing over her. It would ebb and flow, then flow again. Out of all proportion. Kelly had got lost on a walk she didn't even need to be doing. So what? Big deal. *You're an arsehole, Kelly*. Well, you knew that already. *You're a fucking loon!* She had tried shouting at herself, to see if that slapped her back to reality. (It was probably why no one else had stopped.) But the relentless bubble of tears kept on coming: her, scrunched on a scrubby bit of grass facing the junction of the A75, on the way out of Glenluce. Hot, wet Kelly. A clapped-out auld banger, gushing steam. Could your break-down be any more public? She'd had a whole empty moor to roar and greet on if she'd wanted it, but no, she chose to flip out on a traffic island instead.

She abhors it, this strange adolescent fury she feels. And this sharp recall of past events that keeps bowfing out on her – she doesny want that either. What is her mind playing at, opening doors and shaking out corners?

Just leave it well alone, Kelly.

Well, I'm trying, Kelly, I really am, but it seems we are running away with ourselves.

Indeed, it seems that the walking is calling up ghosts, is capturing and framing flickers of time she thought she'd cast off. Is it because she's getting old? Might it be the opposite of puberty – her dried-up body raging? She has nobody to ask. She hasn't been to a doctor since a touch of pneumonia last Christmas took her to A&E. But Kelly doesny need doctors. She needs bugger all, except left alone.

It's only the weak who fear solitude. Weaklings fear being cut free from all those lies, of being untethered from the rules and bullshit that tell you being cared for makes you whole. If you only care about you, then nobody gets let down. Quid pro quo. You don't hurt them, and they don't hurt you. She doesn't get why more folk don't understand that. Because it's quite liberating when you do.

Today is Thursday. The wedding of the girl-whose-ring-she-wears is on Saturday, and Kelly has spent half a day fannying about. Been as well running on the spot. She has still to do Whithorn and Wigtown before she gets to Gatehouse, and there's some standing stones, and a holy well. According to the pamphlet, there's a torrent of holy wells. She's already missed Purgatory Burn, and that sounded a right laugh.

The name derives from when lepers were given the last rites at Glenluce Abbey, before journeying over the moors to the colony at Liberland. Once the lepers had crossed the Purgatory Burn, they could not return.

Well, that was that, she'd thought, snivelling on her traffic island. She'd never make Whithorn by tonight. Canny even do a pilgrimage right. You waste of. Fucking. Space. Deliberately she had pressed the boat-shaped diamond into her finger, indenting the flesh below her knuckle. It no longer chuckled to her, the ring. It was disappointed in her efforts too.

157

Just at the point the gold mount was piercing her skin, but before actual blood spilled, Marie and Donnie's camper van had pulled up. Under normal circumstances, Kelly would have legged it. Orange VW, turquoise flowery curtains, the works. Peace signs and rainbows ahoy. *Hey, check us! We're crazy happenin whale-savin love warriors, a-comin to rescue the world!* (Best delivered in a Cliff Richard accent.) Do-gooders. Givers. They are the most demanding of all people. But they caught her off-guard. It was that sneaky wee Collieflower, wagging his tail and sniffing at Marie's hand hinging out the window.

'Hi there, puppy-dog. What a sweetie. You OK? Can we give you a lift? We're headed towards Port William.'

The shifting landscape of people's expressions: Kelly is such an expert, when she has the guts to look folk in the face. Most days, though, her world is only feet. Maybe up to knee height, depending how brave she is feeling, but generally her field of vision is much truncated. When she is being humble/moved on/shouted at/reviled/admonished, eyes-down is usually the best stance to take. Sometimes you can have a wee game with it, though – like, see when she and her paper cup are out grafting, she'll try to recognise any regular benefactors (or regular troublemaking dicks), plus assess how generous random passers-by might be, all from their footwear. It isn't an exact science. For one thing, people (i.e., not *you*, Kelly) tend to have more than one pair of shoes. But there are some days, days like today, when you just canny be arsed, you are so spent and weary with being good, or invisible, or not scaring the horses, that something breaks, and your head jerks up and you just eyeball the bastards. Raw, like they are your equal, and they should fucking suck it up. If you detach yourself from the fact that it's *you* they are slowly responding to, it can be quite funny to watch. Take this pair, Donnie and Marie's initial expressions. Open. Friendly (goofy teeth). Sincere to slightly shocked, to guilty, to really, really trying to stay sincere, to eyes spinning with the effort of thinking *how do we retreat?* But Kelly was weakening her stern glare even as she was glaring it. They had such a comfy camper van.

So she panicked. She wanted a lift, and she wanted to be left alone. She wanted to spare everyone's blushes. Somehow, this translated into being French.

'Je ne comprends pas.'

Being foreign would turn her instantly exotic, make her eccentricities quirky. Plus she'd have an excuse to not really speak.

'Ah! Vous êtes française! Très bien! The Auld Alliance, eh? Vive la France.'

'Oui. Vive.'

Crap. Of course these globetrotters would speak French.

Anyway, by the magic of mime and nodding, Kelly and Collie have secured a seat in the rear of the camper van. It is a long vinyl-clad bench, side-on to Marie and Donnie, involving quite a bit of effort in staying put. You have to brace yourself and turn into the bends.

'Longtemps? Uh . . . for deux – eh, two weeks?'

The road towards Port William runs like a steel river, slicing and skimming the contours of the land. Poor Collie keeps sliding across the floor, but he doesn't seem to mind.

'So how come you've got the dog?' says Donnie. He is driving with one hand on the wheel. His other shoulder is jiggling about – he's rolling down the window.

Buggery bums. She hasny thought this through. Four huge white wind turbines dip their wings almost into the road.

'Um . . . He has the passeport?'

'For a dog?'

'She means the pet passport – to say he hasn't got rabies? Rabies, eh?'

159

'Oui, oui. No rabies. Pas de rabies.' Kelly seizes the opportunity to do what she does best. Diminish herself. 'Je m'excuse. He is ming . . . le chien does not smell so good.'

'Ach, it's fine. Countryside reeks of all sorts.'

When she is alone, Kelly exists only within her head. Being with people forces you to be weighed and measured. A horrible thought enters her brain. Was Clara's lovely offer of a bath an admonishment? Nice eggs-over-easy Clara? Was it an indication that she actually couldny bear the reek of Kelly in her house? Well, fuck her. Fuck their benchmarks and their standards. *Reek*. The word is gallus. Has swagger and heft. Kelly is Kelly. Being Kelly is fine.

The couple tell her they are going for a week's stargazing.

'Do you like Scotland then?' asks Marie. 'This your first time?'

'Oui. Is beautiful.'

'Where else have you been?'

'Uh . . .' *Feck*. Her heid is nipping; she canny keep this up. But how to get out of it? Kelly is trapped in a web of Francophile deceit.

'Où êtes vouz allez?' Loud and slow, just the way the furreners like it.

'I go to Whithorn? I 'itch.' Port William is about halfway there, Kelly estimates. She will escape while they set up camp, head for the hills.

'Oh, Whithorn's nice. There's a wee museum . . . Here.' Marie lays her hand on Donnie's bare knee. Cut-off combats for a peace warrior. 'Why don't we take her, Donnie, eh? It's a nice drive.'

'Mais non. Is fine. Merci. I like to walk.'

'No offence, but you look done in, Raquel.' Donnie half turns so he can see her for confirmation. Raquel. It was the first French name she thought of. 'So does the wee man. No, it's settled. We're in no rush. We'll take you right there.'

Is this cheating? Kelly wonders. To not do your pilgrimage on foot. But she has been walking for hours already – just not in the right direction. Does that balance it? Plus, those Americans were in a bus, and she's pretty sure Robert the Bruce would've got to ride a horse. Is it the journey or the means that's more important? All she knows is that she has to complete it. She has to visit each place, and she has to do it by Saturday.

Or.

Or what, Kelly?

OK, then. Not *Or*. And.

And then, Kelly?

Aye well, then, is then.

She is still sober and her joints feel all right. Kelly starfishes her fingers. Gives them a wee shake. The ring moves slightly. She clocks Donnie watching her in the rear-view mirror. They both look away.

Kelly and the eco-warriors (now *that* is a good name for a band) drive on through hamlets of new bungalows and old farms, past stacks of hay wrapped in pink plastic with funny faces painted on, past a converted schoolhouse with two alabaster mermaids in the back yard. On and on runs the road; it has become arrow-straight, runs straight and straight for miles until it dips and you can see the sudden, glistening spread of the sea. It fills the horizon. On the journey, Donnie and Marie do that thing all Scots do. Be proud of Scotland. They tell her their nation's story – *have you seen?* and *did you know?* They talk of Bruce and the Ettrick shepherd. Of Devorgilla, who carried her husband's heart in an ivory casket (he was dead first). They move beyond Galloway, to speak of Wallace, Burns, and beyond and along and up, extolling Glasgow and Loch Ness, St Andrews, the Kelpies, the canals, the castles – *not that Eilean Donan one, though. Too touristy.* They insist she go to the palm-fringed shores of Plockton, to

Mull, Iona and lonely Barra – *where the plane lands on the beach*. Loch Maree, Deeside – *oh, and Colonsay is gorgeous. They even make their own gin!*

Kelly claps Collie's head, says a lot of *oui*s. Guilt sweats from her pores, and she doesn't know what to do.

Closer and closer looms the sea; it waiting patiently and you spilling towards it, closer, closer, until you will surely cascade off the rim of the earth. To end your days at the place where the sea becomes a giant waterfall. Which the ancients knew all along. But then, just when you think you must collide with the ocean, the road banks sharply to the left – you've just been in a game of chicken, the road blinks first, and the van is bumping along, hugging the coast, just as you are hugging this bench. On Kelly's right, the wide vista of sea shines, petrol blue and rippled glass. To her left, soft hills hold scattered caravan parks. Donnie says they haven't booked. It's out of season, they'll be fine. He's a gardener and she's a nurse. 'What is it you do yourself, Raquel?'

'Pardon?' A cover story, she needs a cover story. The road's becoming twisted as it climbs, zigging and zagging. Donnie brakes suddenly for a tour bus coming the other way.

'Travail? Vous?' says Marie.

Ach, well. In for a penny. She has gone too far to recover this. 'I am actress? In film?' *Inspirational, Kelly.*

'An actress! Wow.'

'Oui.' Kelly nods, quite excited by this development. 'Oui. This is for the research? I travel for the research.'

'Oh my God. Did we interrupt . . .?' Marie's hands cover her mouth. 'Was the *crying* . . .?'

'Ah, oui, oui. Je suis the methode actrice, non?'

'Och, that's such a relief. I was that worried when I saw you, wasn't I, Donnie? I said to him—'

'What's the film, Raquel?' Donnie sounds more doubtful. 'Is the dog part of the story?'

'Je regrette. I cannot say.'

'Och, that's a shame. What was that film we saw, Donnie? The one about the hitchhiker who picked up men? Mind, she was right weird.'

'That one where she was an alien? That whole film was weird.'

They talk for a while about films, and Kelly relaxes into her fantasy. Yes, her film is about a dying woman who must make one last trip to – naw. Why would a French woman be coming to Scotland? Does the dog need to be in it? No, Collie, sorry. She chucks him under the chin, and he sighs with contentment. Och, but that wee face is so beautiful. No, don't complicate stuff. OK, the film is about a French woman whose father is – no, mother is dying. *Write about what you know, doll.* And on her deathbed she tells the woman her dad isny her dad. No, her dad's a big hairy-arsed Scotsman she met as a student, and—

'Raquel?' The camper van is slowing. 'We're just going to stop here and get a few provisions. You need anything?'

Yes, thank you. Yes, I do – in this order: alcohol, food, confession. Some Pedigree Chum too, please, as she thinks Collie is getting sick of sandwiches. But a French actress would be laden with le cash, n'est-ce pas? And Kelly is not. She will hoard the few notes she has left until Auntie Clara's goodies run out completely.

'Non, merci.'

They're coming into Port William. *Calor Gas Scottish Village 2008*, the brown sign informs them. Donnie pulls up in a wee square, goes into the shop. She considers getting out and running off, but bloody Marie decides to climb in the back and fuss over Collie, so Kelly's stuck.

'Och, he's just gorgeous. Yes, you are, baby. What's his name?'

'Chou-fleur.'

'Chauffeur? Well, Chauffeur, you're a wee cracker, so you are. Oh.' She stops patting him. 'What happened to his legs?'

Collie's wounds have scabbed over; you only see them when you ruffle the fur.

'Uh . . . the bushes? Avec the berries noir?'

C'mon, girl. Hold it together. Berries noir?

'Aw, wee pet. Did the nasty brambles get you?'

Collie writhes in paroxysms of delight at all this attention, legs splayed, head rolling. Kelly pats him too, just so he remembers who's boss.

'Here, that's quite a ring, Raquel. When's the big day? What's his name?'

Think, damn you. Think. 'Uh . . . Jacques.' (Cousteau. He's a diver.) Kelly withdraws her hand. 'We don' know. Après le film, peut-être.'

'Me and Donnie had a long engagement too. I was never very sure about the ponytail . . . Och, OK, you.' Collie whines and paws at Marie for more fuss. 'Mr Impatient.'

The camper van is just a grown-up doll's house. Opposite the bench Kelly's sitting on is a miniature sink and a two-ring cooker. Neat cupboards flank the window, a row of small cups and saucers line a shelf, and there's an embroidered panel above, of garlanded leaves and tendrils. Kelly extends her legs. The vinyl seat has moulded to her arse cheeks. Ach, there are worse places to be trapped.

Donnie returns with two carrier bags, a jumbo Bonio for Collie and a tray of three coffees. He hands one to Kelly. 'Here you go. There's wee sachets of sugar in the cupboard if you need.'

'Cheers. Tha—' She is about to go 'thanks very much', in the same clipped and guttural tones with which she has just said cheers, but collects herself. 'Chee-*eers*. That is what you say, non?'

'That's a very good accent, Raquel. You been practising?'

164

'Mm. I try.' Kelly stares into her coffee cup, the hot liquid burning her lips.

Donnie and Marie swap places, to give him a rest from the driving. He takes a newspaper from one of the bags before dumping the rest of the shopping in beside Kelly. 'Just stick the messages down behind the seat. Yeah, that's fine.'

Kelly notices a bottle of Bell's whisky poking from one of the bags. She shuts her eyes. Marie is quieter when she drives, more cautious, and Donnie is reading his paper, so she doesny feel rude. She didn't force them to ferry her to Whithorn; they offered.

'I'll just pop on some music, will I?' Marie says. 'You'll like this. It's called *Scotland the Brave*.'

Oh, Christ. Bagpipe music. See, this is where you lose the tourists. Aye, the pipes can be stirring, in the right setting, like a rampart or a battlefield. But when they blare it out in knitwear shops . . .

An insistent electro beat begins. Then the haunting, melodic wail of wee Jimmy as Bronski Beat booms out. It catches her in the throat. 'Smalltown Boy'. She listens in silence, her head tight. Next up is the Waterboys, then Aztec Camera, Big Country, Simple Minds, and on, on through a pantheon of Caledonia's finest. The CD is a compilation of Scottish bands, and it is glorious. Through half-opened eyelids, Kelly watches her country speed by, hears the sounds of her youth, before the music moves up an octave into pleasures unknown. A sliding guitar twang, you can hear the guy's fingers move on the fret; it pings low into her navel.

'Who – qu'est-ce que c'est?'

'Oh, that's Biffy Clyro,' says Marie. 'Bit heavy for us, but this one's quite nice. It was on *The X Factor*?'

Kelly has no clue what *The X Factor* is, and does not ask. She lets the music transport her. It fills her chest, makes her heart speed. It feels a little like getting drunk. The CD lasts all the way to Whithorn; at least until they come to a cross-roads close by the town. Which gives them choices.

Your choice, you know. You drink to escape, Kelly. Instead of facing your issues, you drink to ameliorate them.

Is that right, Shirley? Bet you say that to all the pissheads.

Shirley-the-counsellor used to do that: slip into a more sophisticated register when she spoke with Kelly. Only in the one-to-ones; she didny do it in group. Kelly knew what she was up to; she'd have done it herself, had she been of a mind to play mind games with Shirehorse Shirley. An alcohol and substance misuse counsellor whose shtick is to remind the client that the client (patient? Mandatory, court-assigned, ne'er-do-well serial rehabber? Kelly has an array of monikers) used to be smart. It will either shame you into paying attention, or – in just the same way as Shirley deliberately not sitting behind her desk does – remove the barriers between you. Aye. As if saying a few fancy words and sitting on a couch would *ameliorate* the fact that Shirley had power to crush or cure Kelly on a whim. Rehab was extortionate – if they didny think you were properly engaged, you were out on your ear. (Extortionate to the state, not Kelly, but you still get reminded of the costs. Another wee guilt-trip technique to keep you honest.)

'Raquel?'

She can hear Marie's distant voice. 'We were just saying, we were thinking about getting some dinner.'

Kelly opens her eyes again. Her hands are folded in her lap. The ring twinkles, all coy.

Well, I am properly engaged now, Shirley. So there. She wonders what Jacques will be having for his dinner. Brie probably.

They are at a crossroads. Choices on the menu are: Whithorn (2½ miles), Isle of Whithorn (3½ miles), St Ninian's Cave (1½ miles).

'There's a nice chippy at the Isle,' says Marie. 'We were thinking of heading there. Fancy it?'

Chips. Kelly's mouth waters. Big, greasy chips, a slab of cod, crisp and golden. Would they serve it with a lemon wedge? More important, are Donnie and Marie buying? Donnie is staring at her. He has gone very quiet, and he is chewing her up with his eyes, like she has become a Gorgon. Was she snoring? Bedhead? She touches her hair. It feels no worse than usual. Donnie's round glasses dip down at his paper, the discs flashing mirror-bright, then he dips up and stares and fleetingly swivels his chin so he is taking in the line of her nose.

Instinctively, she shields it with her hand. She knows her nose is bigger than it need be, she doesny need reminded of the fact. She makes herself eyeball him, because there's an odd frisson going on, some kind of power struggle where he's forcing her to shrink away. Has he only just noticed she's disgusting? Then she sees him look at Collie, and her stomach drops through the floor of the van.

In the paper. There's something about Collie in the paper. About Kelly stealing him. The rounded walls of the camper van press in; you could choke in a place this poky; canny even stand up, she needs to get out. They are dithering at the crossroads, and that is fine, perfect. She takes hold of her *Doctor Who* rucksack. Clicks her fingers at Collie. It's a command she's never taught him, but he'll know it's code for *RUN*. Collie yawns. Licks his paw.

'Ici,' she says brightly. 'I will depart ici.'

'What, you want out here?' Marie swivels round so her elbow rests on the back of the driver's seat. 'In the middle of nowhere?'

The road splits three ways. There's a dark tree-tunnel of a lane, leading in the direction of St Ninian's Cave. She'll go that way – primarily because it says it's not suitable for cars.

167

'Ah, oui. For le film. I see a place is good for le film. You understand? Mais, merci. Merci beaucoup pour votre . . . help.'

'Raquel.' Donnie is fiddling with his phone. 'I forgot I'd this great app. For translating stuff. Can I just try it on you. Quick like.'

'Je m'excuse.' She shuffles over to the back door, goes to slide it. *Please don't be locked. Please.* Grating, grudgingly, it slides across.

'Raquel.' Donnie clears his throat. 'Je ne pense pas que vous êtes française.'

Kelly gets one foot on the ground. 'Allez,' she says to Collie, who finally shifts his arse. She clicks her fingers, brings her other leg down, and Collie jumps after.

'Au revoir,' she calls through the rear door.

'Cheerio then, Raquel.' Marie scooches her head down so she can wave to her. 'Good luck with the film.'

'Un moment!' Donnie's reading from the screen. 'En fait, je pense que vous parlez dehors de votre derrière. Et que vous êtes aussi écossais que moi!' He rushes it out in a torrent, because Kelly is slamming the door back over. 'Au revoir,' she says again, waving and smiling as she takes her leave.

'Right, Collie. Leg it.' She marches towards the lane. *Merde.* You could get a car down here easy enough; that sign is bullshit. *Don't run, don't run*, she tells herself, moving briskly down the long, thin road. Faint noise of an engine; she stiffens, gets ready to dive between the trees, but the noise fades away, and she quickens her pace. Round the bend, she breaks into a run, Collie chasing, barking at her, circling her feet as she throws her chin to the sky and laughs. Tall beeches and limes sway, clasped together overhead, their feathery branches dwarfing her.

She shouts at the treetops: 'Je m'appelle Raquel! Je t'aime, Jacques Cousteau!'

Hands on knees, wheezing with laughter. Collie sniffs her hair, no, he's trying to chew it.

'Get off, you wee galoot.'

But this is not at all funny. She pushes Collie off. Donnie was comparing her with something in the paper. He was definitely, methodically checking her out. Or was it Collie? Was there a photo of Collie in the news? Kelly's shoulders loosen slightly. Must have been. For how the hell would Major Tom have got a photo of her?

There are thoosands of collies out there. They couldny prove a thing. She begins to jog-walk. Regulates her breathing. Maybe there was a description of her as well, though, and Donnie was reading what she looked like. That could be a problem. Ditch the coat? Man, she should've knocked a jacket from the camper van. How she wishes she'd stolen that whisky. Golden, healing, ignite your bones forty per cent proof uisge beatha. The water of life.

You drink to escape, Kelly.

What sane person wouldn't? Imagine, Shirley, you are presented with two choices: 1) Being catapulted into a screaming room filled with backwards mirrors and jaggy spikes and fire and being forced to bang your skull against the walls again and again and again. Or 2) Being invited by thon nice Mr Bell to partake of a bottle of his magic juice, and subsequently chill for a while in a padded castle where you can bounce and flop and go over your wilkies, lightly colliding with the softness, and giggling as you go.

Surely, Shirley, it's a no-brainer? Whatever door you choose there will be a headache at the end. But at least, for that brief respite, in the bouncy castle you are happy. Happiness only works if it's fleeting and tinged with sadness.

The tree-lined track they're on opens out into a farmyard. To one side is a rough car park and a latched gate. *St Ninian's Cave (1 mile). No vehicular access.*

169

'Well, that doesny tell us much. Let's see what our trusty pamphlet says, shall we, Col?'

Collie pisses on the gatepost.

St Ninian was the first church missionary to bring Christianity to Scotland. He built a church at nearby Whithorn, and was bishop there, dying in 431. Reputedly used as a place for personal prayer by Ninian, pilgrims have been attracted to St Ninian's Cave for centuries, many to give thanks for journeys by land or sea, others to seek the spiritual and physical healing for which Ninian was renowned.

'Right. Come on, dog.' She lifts the latch. 'Let's see if we can get us some spiritual healing. And then we'll eat, I promise. You hungry? Din-dins?'

Collie leaps and twists like a salmon, and Kelly blows him fish kisses, waggling her hands for gills. The pleasure radiating in her as he canters is vivid. It's beyond the limits of being captured in words, but it is there. Dense and indescribable. A kind of stretching inside her soul.

Feeling that this is possible. That it's allowed.

There is a soft whirr as they pass the farm buildings: long, dark prisons for cows. Kelly averts her eyes. The Galloway of her childhood had rolling fields and fattening herds, milk cows that swung their udders as they grazed. But these fields are cropped and empty. The whirring noise comes again, a mechanical breath. She sees movement: a small grey camera on the top of one of the sheds. It's following her. And then it slaps her, cold. CCTV. Major Tom is exactly the sort of paranoid old prick who'd protect his farm with cameras. He will have a picture of her.

Christ.

She tugs her hair over her face, hurries on down the track.

170

Change of plan. The map says there's a cliff path all the way to the Isle of Whithorn. She's not doing it in the dark, though. If they rest up here tonight, set off first thing tomorrow, she can tick off . . . she checks . . . St Ninian's Chapel without setting foot on any road.

Or you could just give up and go home, Kelly.

Nobody will notice. Nobody will care.

If you hadn't been there.

Nobody will care.

Yet here you are. Walking because you must. It is your penance. You have legs that can flex and bend and run; you use those squat (hairy) legs because you can. You must. Carry yourself out and see the world – wasn't that always what you were going to do? You and her.

Kelly 'n' Mandz.

And then you stopped wanting to see any of the world, didn't you? Nothing beyond the limits of the rim of a bottle, and your own greying fringe.

Collie waits patiently as you have another wee crisis. He cocks his head as you shove your hair from your face. First chance you get, you will chop it off. Find a new coat, and be transformed.

'We can dye your hair too, Collie Dog. Eh? What colour would you like to be? I'm thinking pink, cause that won't draw attention to us.'

There's a lassie getting married on Saturday who will care if you give up. Think of her face, Kelly, as you get down on bended knee . . .

All right. As you sidle up shy-like and go *remember me*?

Kelly spins the ring on her finger. It's fairly slack now. Her gouty flare-up has abated. Come on, Kelly. Who are you kidding? She *knows* that if she were just to wrench and twist and gie it a bit of welly – pop. Off the ring would fly.

The end.

171

Except she's not ready for the end. Kelly has a map and a plan. Kelly has acquired a dog and a *Doctor Who* bag. For the first time in ravaged, spilling years, Kelly is going to see this through.

She crouches, rattles her hands on her thighs, and Collie prances his approval. Kelly prolongs the pantomime of bounce and pounce, trying to reboot that feeling of happiness. Terrified she's burst it. Feeling stuff is messy. It hurts. But, oh, the rush when you hit a high.

Daft.

Collie decides for them, birling on his tail and shooting after an unseen creature. She follows. 'Gaun yersel, wee man. Rabbit stew for tea!'

Kelly, you are daft and blind. It's still there, that feeling. It's locked inside you. *Focus.*

The light slips and the grass shimmers, and Kelly can feel it, really feel the rattle of the grass, as if her skin has slipped with it, and whatever she is made of is what each green blade is made of, and each worm she knows is churning underneath. And that she could be the light and the sea too.

They walk through a pretty woodland, and everything is bright-alive. She can hear the feathers of the birds as they dance on twigs, smell the tang of ocean before they reach it. A burn splashes and chatters, breathless that it's so near the sea, and for a second, Kelly thinks she's hearing voices in the water, low as a radio murmuring in another room. A web of precious threads, infinitely complex, but so simple, so obvious; they run right through you too, through the air and through the lush green-beyond-green cliffs swathed in honeysuckle and brambles that rise either side, making a neon U-shaped frame to contain the sea as you approach.

They emerge onto a lunar landscape, and the intensity drains away. There is calmness here. Soft greys. Blues. St Ninian's beach is wide and shingled. Flat pink-grey skimming stones and a line of green seaweed, then black-toothed rocks, then the sea. She has never been here. You don't *do* touristy stuff when you live in a place. It's breezy. Kelly gulps in lungfuls of salt-wild air. The stones slide and crunch as she walks, a hollow sound, as if they merely skim an echoey vault below. Laboursome to walk on; even sure-footed Collie struggles. Way over to her right, the cliffs roll sloping to the sea. And then she sees it – the fabled cave. How can you not? It emerges from the cliff like a piece of theatre, or an Egyptian temple carved in rock. A soaring, shattered, towering cleft, all square-blocked shards and slices where the rock has sheared and fallen to form steps up to the cave mouth.

As they get nearer, she spots tiny cairns of stone. A moon-scape forest of them, dotted everywhere: on top of boulders, by rock pools. Simple towers of flat pebbles, five or seven stones high, the biggest on the bottom – although some have built theirs with the biggest pebbles in the middle, so the shape blooms out like a petrified snowman. Folk have scaled sheer cliff faces to place them on ledges: it's serious stuff. It's as if Kelly has entered a miniature-cairn-building compe-tition. She picks up her own pure white pebble from the beach. She doesny know why. The cairns sit alien and mannered beside the natural rock. When she looks more closely, there are other unnatural impositions too. Crosses. The pebble beach is spiked with lashed crosses. Formed from driftwood, bound with orange and blue fisherman's twine. Crude tree trunks and fragile twigs, big and small, they litter the beach, transform it into an eerie graveyard.

Kelly shivers. Wind is picking up. Sky is fading. Collie shoots off again, chasing a white scut into the tangled under-growth clinging to the cliffs. She lets him run, carries on, clambering up the natural steps and stairs to reach the cave.

Well.

Kelly scratches her chin.

It's barely a cave at all. All the bold, slashing angles of jutting rock above, the great fissure, the wrought-iron cross driven into stone, all zigging darkly down to . . . this.

A slim niche, which goes back twenty feet at most.

St Ninian, you might have been a great guy, but your cave's all mouth and nae trousers.

She goes in anyway, because that's what you do, but there really is nothing more. No hidden chamber round the back. Inside, it is claustrophobic and dank. Folk have graffitied names and crosses on the walls. Tender messages, which she doesn't want to read. Kelly doesn't like it, doesn't like how the cave narrows in and bevels above her head; she starts to get breathless. Why would you shut yourself in here, Ninian, when you had all that stark beauty outside?

'Collie!' she yells from the cave mouth, cupping her hands against the wind. She moves further out, and her hair lifts, fluttering. 'Collie!'

No trace.

She sits outside the entrance to the cave, watching swifts dart and play. Takes out the remains of Clara's picnic. They are down to their last Scotch egg.

'Collie! Here, boy! Dinner!'

The sun is beginning to tinge the water pink. Dark soon. Up on green cliffs on the other side of the bay a prism of light glints momentarily, then is gone. It's getting chilly. Would be good to make a fire, but she doesn't have a lighter any more. Nor matches. Nor tin foil, string, loo roll or any of the other useful things her great greatcoat used to carry. Kelly has a fur-trimmed coat and a donated packed lunch. She has become soft.

'*Caaaw*llieflower!'

Eventually Collie bounds towards her, his white-tipped tail flying high. There is something bounding with him, a grey thing, hinging from his mouth. It flaps in time with his ears. Grotesque. He drops it at her feet. Her dog has found a rotting seagull.

'Get that to fuck! Away, Collie! Jesus, get away!'

Confused, Collie's tail slinks down. Porpoise grin, pink tongue panting, his dance becomes more urgent. He picks up the body, shakes it, and Kelly screams.

'Right. That's it. You are honking, dug! Get in the sea.' She chases him down to the water's edge, but he will not be parted from his seagull. They feint and weave, over sea foam and slippery rock. Four legs (and a pair of tattered wings) are no match for two. Knackered, Kelly is forced to give up, watch from afar as Collie crunches through his putrid feast.

Despite the falling temperature, she's sweating like a pig. She refuses to be as clatty as her dog. She fetches her *Doctor Who* bag from the cave, goes to brush her teeth over a salty rock pool. Crouches to pee, then, before she decides it's much cosier not to, she wheechs off her bottom half so she can rinse out her knickers too. Drapes them over one of the bigger crosses, in the hope they'll be dry by morning. The harsh sea wind scours her bare arse. Quickly, Kelly puts her coat back on.

She makes camp in the lee of the stepped rocks that lead up to the cave. Holds her bag against a smoothish boulder, draws her coat round her knees, then rests her head on the spinning Tardis. The cave is not what she thought it would be. She doesny want to go back in there. It feels too much like a prison. She munches on the final packet of crisps. That's fine. She doesn't have to. There is what you want and what there is, she thinks.

Seagull digested, Collie slinks over to join her.

'I'm not talking to you. You are vile.'

He flops against her legs.

The setting sun sends up a crimson distress flare as it melts into the sea. Maybe hope is the horizon, all teasing and glinting sea-glitter and out of reach. Life is the road that waits for you to choose it. She takes the white pebble from her pocket and rests it on top of the nearest cairn. Impossible not to be near a cairn on St Ninian's beach; there are four within her arm's reach alone. The pebble can be her candle, she thinks, for the man with the tan office shoes.

*

Prison changes you, but not in the way they want. You don't emerge reformed and contrite – you come out fighting. Maybe you are battling yourself: your demons, your vices. Fears. Under the pain you pretend is not there (because I'm haa-ppee! *You do an actual wee jig as you emerge from the jail*), *there is also bite. Compulsion snaps at your heels, a very ugly dog that wants to lash out and wreak revenge. An explosion is how it feels. One where you ricochet from the doors of Cornton Vale jail. You try so hard to walk straight, but there is no one there to meet you.*

A specially trained adviser will work with you before you leave prison, not only to address housing issues but to connect you to other kinds of specialist support if needed.

Aye, right. Throughcare, they call it. At the Homehub. Home. Yes. You could go home.
This is positively encouraged, because you have a local connection, see. You will be someone else's problem. And if you don't . . . if you can't go home, yet fail to provide a reason that fits their box, the response remains the same: But it's where you're from, yes? Dumfries and Galloway?

You may be homeless, but you will be a homeless Gallovidian.

What if your 'specially trained adviser' is on long-term sick and her replacement is pregnant and has a double caseload and is covering another jail because they are short-staffed too? All this to see if you might – just might – be eligible for temporary accommodation? You aren't gonny hang around an extra month to get a bed found, are you? So you clatter out, you and your pent-up energy, glistening and alive, you are good, you are good, aye, aye, sure you'll make that appointment with Shelter or the Housing or whatever it is they are chuntering on about, and – oh – here is the pavement and here is the open sky and an actual bus if you want. Jump on, hen! *Here is life unwrapped. You recall that?! So what if it is unwrapped, and if it is revealing itself, all voluptuous and oozy-good. Man, this is good, isn't it? You smile your newly released smile at a wee lassie on a bike who gives you the finger. Weans, eh? Life is good. And all the while you are looking round for someone to share it, share your good, great fortune, and where will you go now, now you can go anywhere? Well, where is the best and happiest place?*

You could always go home.

Yes, but where is it that you could slip in quick, Kelly, and fit? Fit and sit and sip and slip: slip your skin. Just for a wee minute. Just till you catch your breath, then you will be off, off, on this big adventure that is life, your new life. Your worthwhile life, said the social worker with the stern square glasses.

You are flooded with uncertainty. You stand in the street where the bus has dropped you, overwhelmed with choice. How do you enter this new life? You have learned typing and sewing. You have been equipped

with 'mindfulness techniques' and are used to your
mouth being dry.

So very dry.

You have steps, steps to follow.

You know you have AUD, yes?

Hi. I'm Kelly and I have Alcohol Use Disorder.

If you know your use is disordered, that means you can
reorder it, right? And clearly, then, some degree of 'use'
must be OK, because it is not 'abuse', is it? They have
cleverly tweaked that, to be non-judgemental. Och, you
are a chancer, aren't you, Kelly? Aren't you? You're a
light-fingered, sleekit, murderous hoor, who always sees
your chance, the main chance. That's the story they made.
About you. You are legend.

Choices. There is Guido's wine bar. You could go in
there, for some pasta. Obviously, just for the food. And a
think. Or that old man's pub that does pie and peas. They
announce this proudly on a blackboard. The Stirling
Arms. *If it is Tuesday, you can get bingo too. It tells you,*
on the board. Is it Tuesday? The Stirling Arms. *Is this*
Stirling, then? Yes, you think it is – there is the castle up
on its crag, where Mary, Queen of Scots was crowned.
You think. You're sure you learned that on a school trip.
At the foot of the cobbled road that leads to the castle is
a phone box, with an actual phone. You look up again,
admire the pub's craw-stepped gables – is there any other
kind? Whoa, you feel dizzy. Put out your hand for
balance. Creaking phone-box door. Public lavatory too, of
course; inside is vile, but still. The phone has a gentle,
insistent buzz when you lift it up.

You could go home.

Daddy, *you'll say. Just the one word, and he'll know.*
Just one word. That's all you need to get out.

You dial the number. You wait, your coin ready in the

slot. *A woman answers who is not your mum. Can never be your mum.*

Choices. You always have choices.

—Is my dad there? *Your voice is small.*

—Who is this? *says the woman, and you hang up.*

The Stirling Arms. Wide open. You have to be more brave. Your head drifting. Slapping it back. And fluid, you have to be fluid. Warm and yeasty. Knock it back. Arms wide open to the universal fug. Come, traveller, rest your head. One ruby-red kiss to make it better. Ruby, rose, claret, all the wine reds you could ever wish. Lined up. Twinkling. One merciful kiss. Then onward. You promise them all. It will be onward.

Step one.

In you go, to your brave new world.

Chapter Thirteen

Two nights in a row, Jennifer Patience has come to Blochairn Market. It is a brash, noisy place, full of odd characters and with a dedicated pub serving alcohol round the clock. Reminds her of a newsroom. She sits, wrapped in her trusty Puffa jacket, at a vinyl-covered table in the café. Strip lighting shrilling through her eyeballs. She tries the two-fingered shiatsu pressure-point massage she's read about in *Woman & Home*, but the dull ache won't shift. Last night she hung about here till three a.m., which went down like a lead balloon with Rodge. Especially as she was back in the office again by seven.

Christ, Jennifer. Are you getting paid for this?

Of course I am.

Of course she isn't.

Gone are the glory days of investigative journalism, where you could devote entire shifts to chasing a single story. Quantity, throughput, quotas of column inches to be filled – that's what drives them now. If you can't crib a story from the wires or a council committee paper, turn it round in twenty, then move onto the next on the conveyor belt, you're just not doing your job. No room for deviation.

Ping. An original thought. Unexpected item in bagging area.

That girl at the Outreach shelter, Aleisha, tried to convince

Jennifer that the disappearance of the elusive 'homeless heroine' might be a murder inquiry – with potentially a bit of sex trafficking thrown into the mix. Jennifer has done her homework, though, and she suspects it is more mundane. If she's not still in Glasgow, the woman has probably just hitched to somewhere else. Which isn't really a story.

To where, though, and why? That. That there is the story.

Jennifer already has the headline: *Homeless Heroine Flees Terror Site.* But there are two ways she can write the hook. Around your facts, you make a frame. That frame will dictate your story. And your story will dictate the news.

Overwhelmed and heartbroken, Glasgow heroine aims to escape the spotlight

Or: *Down-and-out drifter vanishes, concealing her shady past*

There was that homeless guy down in Manchester, after the concert bombing. Lauded as a hero, it turned out he was stealing purses off the victims. For now, Jennifer is still mulling. What will play better with their readership? People have been sad about the accident; now people are being angry. At who? Is it the bus driver, who's still in intensive care? The bus manufacturers? The council, because of the roads? The scaffolding nearby, the weather? There must always be fault. Fault, and explanations, and then somebody must pay. Jennifer needs to craft it all with care, because it is not the job of the press to report random things, randomly.

Ideally, Jennifer would like to speak to 'Glasgow's homeless heroine' before she decides which way the story will go.

Aleisha gibbered a lot of nonsense for her hundred pounds, including a lurid tale about the Fruitmarket and bone-bedecked lorries, but she did provide one very useful fact: the woman's name. *Kelly.* With a photograph and a partial name, good contacts in the polis and the click-click-click of her excellent memory, Jennifer Patience can dig for gold.

And gold it has been.

So, actually, she has plenty of 'whys' to choose from. All she really needs is the where. Where has our wumman gone?

Hence two nights freezing her ladyballs off at Blochairn Market, waiting for a red lorry with a sheep's skull on the fender to roll on in. Jennifer believes in having many irons in the fire at once. And a scoop is a scoop is a scoop. Someone else will get a name for the heroine soon enough. There are times to be patient, and there are times to publish and be damned.

She smooths out page five of today's edition.

WHO'S THAT GIRL?

As Glasgow wakes to another day of grief and confusion following the city centre bus crash, we have uncovered the identity of one of the quiet heroes of the hour. Seen here is a new image of the homeless heroine. We can reveal that the woman's name is Kelly McCallum, and her last known address was Grovepark Street in Maryhill. But we believe she's been sleeping rough on and off in the city for several years, and we really need your help to find out where she is now. There's a big reward waiting for Kelly – and for the person who can help us reunite her with the man whose life she saved.

Said accountant Martin Grey (41) from his hospital bed: 'I just want to shake her hand and say thank you.'

So, being the big-hearted family newspaper we are, we've set up a special Heroine Hotline – and we're waiting for your call!

The phone number is pasted in bold, below Jennifer's byline. Good layout: it is a nice double column, with a decent-sized pic. (She got them to blow up a section of the old photograph in the Outreach kitchen. The newspaper owns the copyright, so no hassle there.) Plus, she likes how the reward is big and vague in equal measure. Martin Grey's family want to help 'get the homeless woman on her feet', as they put it, and his wife didn't say no when Jennifer suggested a public appeal might help – and could they maybe offer a little something there too? The guy runs his own company, for Godsake; they are clearly loaded.

There is no record of Kelly McCallum being a sex worker, so it's unlikely she climbed into the cab for a bit of business. And she's not a habitual traveller – any encounters Kelly has had with the authorities over the last decade that Jennifer can find have all been in Glasgow. Which takes you back to the: why leave now? Why and to where? Without that, there is no story.

Jennifer gets up to stretch her legs, takes another wee turn round the car park. She's asked loads of punters already about the sheep's-skull lorry, but no dice. She supposes folk don't pay much attention to vehicles at the market. It is the produce they are carrying that's of interest. Amazing the amount of fruit-and-veg fondling that goes on here. It is almost continental. Well, she's not lurking in Blochairn for a third night. She has done her best, but sometimes you have to let a story go. Her husband's right – she doesn't get paid enough for this. Anyway, Issy has her school show tomorrow evening, and Jennifer has promised her a trip to Bella Napoli afterwards.

One final desultory circle of the loading bays beside that low hangar overby, one last try of the (frankly mental) pub called the Budgie, then that will be her. Done. But tonight, as she wanders off to do her exit check on the loading bays, Jennifer realises she won't need to brave the Budgie again. Parked on the diagonal are two articulated lorries. One is very dark, possibly black. Hard to tell. The other is paler. Rust-coloured under the wash of the security light. She gives a discreet wee air-punch. Tethered to the front is a grubby skull with horns.

The driver is climbing down from his cabin. She waits until he is on the ground, hitching up his trousers. There is a lot of them to hitch.

'Hi there. How you doing?' Her fingers rest lightly on his arm. 'My name's Jennifer. I've been looking for you.'

The man – boy really, but my goodness he is tall – looks flustered. OK, so not a flirter, then. She removes her hand. 'I was hoping you could help me. I've been trying to find a friend of mine, and I think you might have seen her? This is her. She's called Kelly.' Jennifer shows him the original photograph, of Kelly at the Outreach. 'I took that a wee while ago, but she's not really changed. One of the guys told me she was up here the other day. Thought you might have given her a lift?'

The man holds the photo up to the light. His reddish hair glows. Jennifer watches his pupils dilate. Big dumb lad. Come to Mama.

'One of what guys?' he asks.

'Sorry,' she says. 'What was your name?'

'Sorry,' he says. 'Who are you? Did you say you were a friend of Kelly's?'

'Yeah, I've been trying to find her for a while.'

'Jennifer, did you say?'

'Uh-huh. Maybe she's mentioned me?' *You are a bare-faced liar, Jennifer Patience.*

'No.' He extracts a rolled-up newspaper from his back pocket. 'It's just, I recognise that picture from today's paper. You wouldny be Jennifer Patience, would you?'

'Ah.' She raises her palms. 'Guilty, m'lud. Can't blame a girl for trying.' She risks the arm pat again. 'It's just, it's really hard sometimes, you know? To get folk to talk if they think you're a journalist.'

'How come you think I know her?'

'I was told the vehicle she got into had a sheep's skull on the front. You're very distinctive, you see.' She gives him a lovely, clear smile. The man's face closes over. Shutter coming down. Shit. Does he think she's taking the piss?

'There's a reward, you know.'

'Is she in trouble?'

'No, not at all. In fact, people want to help her.'

'Uh-huh.' He rolls up his paper again. Stares at his fingers, concentrating as if he is constructing a massive joint. God. Jennifer could really do with a glass of wine and a warm bath.

'Look. If you know where Kelly is, just tell me. You'll be doing her a favour.'

'What if she doesny want helped?'

'Well, that's just . . .' Jennifer frowns, trying to think of an appropriate response.

'Anyroad, Mrs Patience—'

'It's Ms.'

'Anyroad. I've never seen the woman before. There's loads of us truckers, you know. With skulls and bones and that on the front.'

'Is that right? Only this is the second night I've been here, and your lorry is the only one I've seen like that.'

'Och, aye. Big gang of us. Hunners. We collect roadkill. Call ourselves the Skullcrushers.'

'Really?' She sighs out, deliberate and slow. Big ginger prick. 'Right.'

'Aye. Sorry I canny be of more help. I need to get on . . .'

'Sure.' Jennifer Patience knows when to admit defeat. 'Have a good night, Mr . . .?'

She can see his teeth, smiling at her in the shadows. 'Goodnight, Mrs Patience.'

Chapter Fourteen

Kelly is keen to leave St Ninian's Cave behind. She's barely slept. Despite the isolation, she couldn't relax. Maybe because of the isolation. Her mouth is dry, and her head feels very delicate. Although she isn't rested, she feels like she is still asleep: detached from her actions, observing herself from above. Small flashes burst at the side of her eyes as she stands, slithering and sclaffing on the stones. Her spine, her calves, her bum all ache. Note to self: a pebble beach is agony to recline on. There is nothing left in the backpack for breakfast. Her sea-washed knickers flutter on their holy flagpole. She tests them. Dry. Ish. Hings on to the crucifix as she steps into them. White arse to the world.

'Total eclipse, Collie!'

He is not helping, jumping round her ankles as she tries to hoick her trousers over her boots. They came off fine, so why won't they go back on? At last she wriggles into them, though the insides of her thighs are chafed raw with sand. St Ninian's Cave broods behind them as she and Collie cross the beach, towards where the cliffs straddle the other side of the bay. Salt air is giving her an awful drouth. They pass the path that brought them to the beach yesterday. She stops by the stream so Collie can have a drink. Takes handfuls of the sandy water herself. More grit than fluid in her mouth;

all of her is sticky, parched with salt. There's an incongruous street sign sticking from the shingle, which informs beach-goers to follow another path up the cliff, to take them to the Isle of Whithorn. Kelly can see the sign fine, but she canny find the path. There are only vague rabbit tracks, wending vertically through the grass. They keep trying, searching for some sensible cobbles, but rabbit track it is.

Collie bounds ahead, barking encouragingly. Kelly thought he'd have the runs this morning, but it appears his seagull supper has gone down well. She sets off after him, doubtful she can make it. The cliff is not that high, but it is steep. Scrabbling her way up, the rock is almost sheer at times. She feels safer on her knees. Her empty belly bows and crests like a sail, filled by the fear of falling. Without knowing exactly what Donnie saw in his newspaper, though, her fear of the open road is greater. Just don't look down, Kelly, and you'll be fine. The path zigzags on, and she follows, face pressed into rock. As she reaches the crest of the cliff, she can hear Collie up ahead, barking. She's learning he has several barks, and this is not the happy *c'mon, Mum* one. It is shrill. Urgent. Puffing, she gets beyond the overhanging tufts of grass, to the broad opening-out of the clifftop. Where a shirtless man is waiting to greet her.

Kelly overbalances. She swoons away and out, feels her belly clutch. The man grabs her arm to steady her. Burning, burning in her bladder. She needs, desperately, suddenly, to pee.

'Whoa there! You all right?' The man is about forty. He keeps smiling. Sun-baked and wrinkled with muscle. He wears leather laced boots and khaki shorts. But he's bare-chested, and it's bloody Baltic with the wind up here. Her weirdo-detector goes from nought to sixty. His dark hair and beard stream in the sea breeze. Teeth slightly yellow. She feels Collie licking through the fabric of her trousers, licking and nudging into her. Feels the vibration of a puppy-growl growing in his throat.

'Shh boy. I'm all right.'

'Sorry. Didn't mean to give you a fright.' The man releases her. Smiles harder. 'D'you think he'd bite me?'

'Pardon?'

He gestures at Collie. A small khaki tent is pegged on the plateau behind him. 'Your dog. I saw him with that seagull.'

'You saw us? Last night?'

'Aye. It's really hard to sleep on that beach. Couldn't get comfy. Could you?' It is all said in a personable, friendly voice. The casual tone. The innocuous comment. The fact he is wearing binoculars round his neck.

Deep, slow fear. Like a caul it comes, up and over. Her tongue too thick to move. Words. She needs to push out words.

The man busies himself with his camping stove. It is the picture of loveliness. A metal coffee pot bubbles. Collie presses himself into her leg. 'Aye. I thought to myself, that dug's fucking mental. Got yourselves into a right fankle this morning too, both of you. With your clothes.'

He has watched her. All night he has watched her. Kelly has been here before, with this caul of fear, creeping. At the back of a dead-end lane. A rattle, a bin lid falling. Drunk lad with his dick out, having a piss. Her, not moving. His two pals, spying her. She was young then. Quite pretty. Kelly has felt this caul in prison too, where a door is closed and demands are made; she has felt it when a shadow looms in the dark and she is not sure if she's asleep; she has felt it when she hears the crunch of boots, the laugh as the boots come again, when they keep coming to sink into her foetal form and kick so hard that her kidney bursts. She has felt it when she speaks up, she has felt it when she's silent.

One single chance to get this right. Bluster, or careful

unpicking? She has her puppy quivering at her side. Anger coils through the fear. You always have choices.

'D'you know, I think I've left my camera down in the cave. Will we go and see, Collie?'

The man stops poking at the stove. Doesny look at her. 'Or you could stay up here.'

'Aye, but I've loads of stuff on my camera. I'm mapping stuff for the Ordnance Survey. Cliff paths. Work stuff, you know.' She smiles and makes herself humble.

The man returns her smile. 'Aye. But I really think you should stay up here. I told myself that if you came up, I'd do you an egg. They're seagull.'

'Sorry, pal. No can do.' Kelly turns away. Her legs are rippling forwards. Under the blade of her cheekbone, she can see one leg strolling, one leg is moving in front of the other, but she cannot feel them.

'Did you not hear me right?' There is a sudden movement, and he is there, his fingers circling her wrist.

'Get tae fuck!' She jerks her elbow backwards, connects with some part of him – temple? Chin? Enough to cause him to loosen his grip and for her to snatch her arm away, Collie snapping, her shoving Collie in front, and they lunge and they scrabble their way back down the cliff path. Sliding on her arse, stone and scree tumbles past Kelly's boots; she slips and skids, maintains a steady, skiting pace, but inside she is liquid. Waiting to hear the man behind her. What will she do? Neck hairs bristle; she and Collie each have hackles.

The path is far too steep and narrow; she cannot run. Collie whines, keeps turning back to check she's there. Would his teeth be sharp enough to inflict damage? What if the man goes for him? Fuck. She will break his neck first, before he touches her dog. She slithers the last few yards, and they are on the shingle and pebbles of the beach, which slip away as she steps onto them. The stones make eddies and little pitfalls Kelly striding purposefully across the beach, never straying from the grassy no-man's-land between beach and cliffs. She doesn't think he's followed them. Imagines she can feel the heat of his gaze, the burn of two glass discs reflecting on the bones of her shoulders. Does he know another, quicker way down? There are a couple of hikers cutting diagonally over the beach to make their way to the cave. He will be expecting her to sheer off to the left, to catch them up, or call for help.

She does not deviate. Instinct tells her not to run, that he is the sort of person who would enjoy the chase. Deliberately calm, she simply turns right at the path that will return her to the car park. Collie hesitates as the man shouts after them, up from where he watches on the cliff. At least, he sounds far away. The only thing Kelly can make out is *HO!* The rushing noise of the burn is pushing inside her ears; she cannot turn round to call for Collie, she's too scared. But Collie is the cleverest boy in the world, and comes streaking past her legs. He circles, running behind and in front of her in a figure of eight until they are well into the woods. If Kelly was sentimental, she would think the dog was guarding her. Trees whisper, they open and close; at some point Kelly and Collie recross the stream they drank from on the beach. It is golden brown here, and clear, but they don't stop.

A trapped bird, fluttering in her breast. All night the man has watched her. He could have done anything. That eeriness, prickling her to stay awake; way down on the beach, she had felt unease. Had attributed it to weird crosses and a desolate cave.

There's a single car parked when they reach the car park; she's no idea if it's the hikers' car or his, or if he's a dosser like Kelly and dwells permanently on cliffs, or some lonely fuck who likes birdwatching. Doesny matter. He has freaked her out.

190

'Good elbow action, mind.' She grins at Collie. Breathless. 'Dinny fash yersel, doggie. Your maw will keep you safe.'

It's an old trick; Kelly does it all the time. Talks a good game. Go mental, swear, break a bottle, screech *come ahead*, if you have to. But never let anyone see you're scared. The moment you do, it's over.

She hopes that man never saw she was scared. Or Collie, for that matter. Kelly thinks she's quite good at hiding things.

Her heart is still going like the clappers. Whithorn's about an hour's walk away. She will not stop until they get there. She desires people round her. If needs be, she'll take her chances with Major Tom. Or even the polis. Isle of Whithorn, St Ninian's Chapel – she turns the map in the pamphlet so it's sideways on. Naw. She decides the chapel is a detour, not officially part of the pilgrimage. All roads lead to Whithorn anyway.

It's a good straight road into the town. Hands jittering, she puts Collie on the lead. He does not like it.

'I know, I know. But there might be cars, and it's too narrow.'

That man has made Kelly feel afraid of everything. Collie tugs. Collie sits down. Collie snaps his head round and grabs the lead in his teeth, pulling and wrestling with it like he's trying to land a fish. Against her will, Collie makes her laugh. A few cars go past, and she braces herself each time, but they never stop. Fields stretch in a patchwork of dark greens. Almost treeless here. Low clouds fill the wide, flat sky, colouring everything dull. Despite the grey day, the landscape feels foreign, like paintings she has seen of countryside in France – by thon dude who cut his ear off.

In her time, Kelly has met many weirdos. Folk who carry their baggage on the outside. She knows it is chance, random, that there is no rhyme nor reason why that man picked on her. She was just there. And maybe he was simply lonely and desperate and sad. But then, who is not? Would he have behaved like that if she was a man? Impinge on her? Would he insist his type of loneliness was more important than hers?

Fucking people. They are too complex, too diverse. Yet she finds she craves them now – if only in the background.

Kelly and Collie enter Whithorn – sacred site of the ancient St Ninian pilgrimage – through a street of council houses. Turn a corner, though, and you're in a sleepy old market town, neat stone cottages and houses flanking a broad main street. A few have geraniums in pots and hanging baskets. One has a sheet up instead of curtains. Right, Whithorn, what are you all about, then? You're sending mixed messages. She consults *Pilgrims' Progress*:

> Whithorn largely retains its medieval layout, where it resembles the skeleton of a long fish.

Does it?

> The main street is the spine, with the houses and their long rear gardens running off in ribs.

The person who wrote this crap is blessed with a fine imagination.

> Here it was that Ninian founded his Candida Casa (White or Shining House), sadly long gone. The lime-washed chapel would have shone from the hilltop where the current church and priory ruins now stand – and it is from both the Anglo-Saxon translation, Hwit Ærn, and the Gallovidian Gaelic, Futarna, that Whithorn gets its name.

Kelly tries to picture the shining white temple, but she canny even find the hill. Whithorn is douce and flat.

A cultural melting pot influenced by Romans, Britons, Angles, Scandinavians and Scots, Whithorn faces south and west, and is enmeshed in a network of seaways. In centuries past, it was an important centre for international commerce – such as German leatherwork and French wine – as well as faith. Kings and commoners alike sought sanctuary and cures at the shrine of St Ninian.

So where is it then? This shrine that will cure you of every ill, the reason for this booklet, for all these dusty feet that have ever tramped here? She checks the picture of a medieval pilgrim (not to scale). Dusty bare feet.

'Should I take off my boots, Col?'

Aye, cause you don't look alarming enough. A fifty-year-old fright wig, stinking to buggery, clad in a travel-blanket coat and a *Doctor Who* bag.

A late-medieval gateway crowned with the arms of the King of Scots will lead you into the site of the priory. Access to the vaults is via the museum.

Kelly really cannot be arsed with more information boards. But she wants to see the shrine. To come all this way then miss it would be . . . She considers. Daft? Defiant? Cutting your nose off to spite your face?

They go through the archway, the stone frame of its structure stark against the white harling. The central keystone is paler than the rest. One wedged stone at the apex, locking the whole into place. She remembers laughing in Archi-Lab at uni as teams of students battled to demonstrate this theory.

193

The professor made them use wooden blocks and blindfolds. Unconventional perhaps, but his lesson has stuck.

Through the pend, they take a dauner up the street towards the church. This is it? It's just a wee slope, hardly a shining hill. There's a scatter of ruins where the priory must once have stood, and a gable wall of the church that came after. The site doesn't have the grandeur of the abbey at Glenluce. The town has nibbled away at its precincts. Set a little further back, Kelly sees the current church, and a poster offering *New for this Year! Iron Age Roundhouse* Tours (*reconstruction). Details at the museum*. She and Collie have a mooch through the churchyard, seeking anything approximating a shrine, until Collie cocks his leg on an ancient gravestone, and she shoos him out. Kelly feels a bit of anticlimax, or maybe it's just the greyness of the day, or the fact that her fight-or-flight adrenaline has long abated. They really need to get some food.

She checks her pockets. She has five pounds and twenty pence. She is not going to beg in Whithorn; she's going to buy breakfast like a normal person.

Along the main street she passes a newsagent's, a charity shop, Priory Antiques and a hairdresser. Beyond the hairdresser, the scent of coffee curls in a beckoning finger, oh, and there's some other smell that makes her salivate. Fresh-baked scones. It's coming from over there – she's found the museum: the Whithorn Story. There is a café out front, but the pavement tables are full. She canny take Collie inside. There's a wheen of postcard-writing and guide-book-reading going on, bobbing tight white curls and baseball caps. Everyone is in coats and sunglasses. Then she hears a lilt of American accent, sees the bus parked across the road.

Pilgrims' Progress.

They have finally caught up with one another.

Kelly doesn't want to draw attention to herself, mindful that her own progress has probably been more eventful, or at least grubbier, than theirs. She retreats, waits on a bench across the road until she hears a pilgrim ask for *the check*. The voice does not belong to the head lady who gave Kelly the leaflet; there's no sign of her. En masse, the group get up, chattering and camera-snapping their way towards the priory ruins. Kelly goes to bag a table. She is unbelievably thirsty; it feels like the drouth of an almighty hangover, without the pleasure of having been pished.

If this is sober, perhaps she doesn't want it.

Hand in her pocket, she crumples her five-pound note. That fiver could buy – four cans. Three litres of Frosty Jack's . . .

It could buy a week's worth of dog food. Collie's had nothing to eat since he caught his own (albeit already deid) seagull. As she pulls out a chair, though, the gods are smiling. There is a ten-pound tip, stuffed beneath a saucer. Push the saucer a little, and lo, 'tis twenty, no thirty of your Scottish pounds! The dafties have left their whole payment on the table. Her breath quickens, her automatic thieving hand coming out to grab and pocket the lot.

See at heart, you are not a nice person. The bad bit's in you, Kelly.

I'm an urban fucking warrior is what I am.

Casual glance at the menu, casual strolling away. She thinks of clever riffs on the theme of urban warriorhood: this is a jungle, survival of the fittest, etc. She pretends she is French Raquel, scoping out a film. But she's just mental Kelly the dosser, who has stolen an old man's money. Or rather, stolen the Whithorn Story's money – a friendly, hopeful establishment that is doing its best to brighten the town.

Starving Mental Kelly. She ties Collie up outside the news-agent's further down the street, goes in and buys two rolls, a packet of ham and a big bottle of water. The man behind the counter actually recoils as she hands him her five-pound note.

Not a word until she's leaving the shop, then Kelly casually goes, 'Wiped my arse with that fiver this morning.' Just loud enough for him to hear.

Do they not get poor people in Whithorn? Did St Ninian not suffer the poor, the dispossessed to come unto him? (Naw, Kelly. That was the Statue of Liberty.) Fair enough, but beyond the flower boxes she can see those council houses too, and the boarded-up shops. There is rural poverty across Galloway – it was present before Kelly left, and she can't imagine it's got better since. The lack of adequate heating – whole settlements where there are no power lines laid, where canisters of Calor gas or storage heaters are your only options, and where your water comes from a borehole instead of pipes. That's poverty. Regions where the major towns are connected by one scenic single-lane road – that's poverty. Petrol, food, leisure – less choice, more expense – that's all poverty. How many times did Kelly and her pals hang about the bus stop? That was it, your evening's entertainment. Not to go somewhere interesting, because there were no buses after six. No buses, no cinemas, no ice rinks, no clothes shops or supermarkets, your nearest train station one hour's drive away, your nearest university or chance of a decent job being in Glasgow or beyond – that's poverty too. And there was grinding poverty on her uncle's farm. In the end, his herd cost him more to feed than they made him. But see, rural poverty is scattered. Quiet. The countryside is for rosy cheeks and healthy hills. Folk don't like their poor bastards to wear it on their sleeves. It is bad for tourism.

Behind Whithorn's net curtains, she can feel the natives observing her. And they are tutting. Folk in small touns are always tutting.

Fuck it. Skin-shedding time.

Outside, she stuffs the ham into the rolls, lays one in front of her tethered dog. 'Right. Eat that. Now stay and be a good boy. I won't be long.'

She takes a bite of the other roll, and in the time that bite is bitten, Collie has swallowed his entire sandwich. 'Christ. You're like an anaconda. Here.' She puts the rest of her own roll on the pavement. 'Now. Stay, Collie. OK? Sit and stay.'

She can keep an eye on him from the hairdresser's window.

'Excuse me,' she says to the stiffly blonde woman clipping her nails over a sink. 'Any chance of a cut and blow-dry?'

The beige and pink salon is devoid of custom. The woman looks startled. Then suspicious.

'How much is it?' asks Kelly. There's a pyramid of Elnett hairspray displayed on a shelf behind the woman's head. A black and moody poster of a girl with a Purdey bob (circa 1972).

The hairdresser shakes her head. Her hair doesny move. 'We've no appointments. Sorry.' *Clip.*

'But there's nobody here.'

She stops clipping. Two red spots in her cheeks. 'I'm just about to close.'

'Half-day, is it?'

'Something like that.'

Kelly has had no breakfast. Kelly has a splitting headache. Kelly feels belligerent.

'Is there some kind of problem?' She waves her notes about. 'Twenty quid cover it?'

No way she'd pay twenty pounds for a haircut, but this is a matter of principle. *Go on, helmet-heid. Say it.*

'I'm sorry. I don't want to serve you.'

'How come?' Lips tight, rolling the segments of flesh softly between her teeth. As though she is about to snarl.

'Honestly? Because you stink. No offence, but I can't have

197

you coming in here – and I wouldn't want to touch your hair either.' The woman shrugs. Returns to her nails.

Kelly can feel her heartbeat pulsing in her wrist. Mute, she leaves the shop, the torrent of words she wants to say pushing behind her teeth, rising under her tongue, except there are no actual words she can sieve off to say aloud. Only a solid crash of hurt. Shame too, but that is a given. Kelly cannot remember what it's like to live her life without shame.

She walks past Collie, who stands, tail helicoptering, then dipping when she does not release him. 'Two minutes, boy.'

Returns to the newsagent's. 'You're barred,' says the man.

'Fair enough. But can I get these first, please?'

'No. Out.'

She ignores him. Picks up soap, shampoo and a pair of kitchen scissors.

'Did you not hear me? Out, or I'm calling the police.'

How's your keeping-a-low-profile project going, Kelly?

She swithers over today's newspaper. But what you don't know doesny hurt you. Lifts a packet of raw mince instead. Can dogs eat raw stuff? Well, they don't fecking cook it in the wild, do they? She lays her items on the counter. 'Please?'

The newsagent has his phone up at his ear. He glances at her purchases.

'Please?'

Something in him unzips, and she gets a glimpse of the decent person he probably was all along. 'No toilet paper?' he says, ringing through her messages.

Kelly smiles. Rueful. 'I apologise.'

The newsagent sniffs. Folk never apologise in return, if there is an outburst, or an altercation. They will accept your contrition – sometimes graciously, sometimes in a huff – but it will not precipitate theirs, because their bad behaviour always comes with entitlement. It is you, the shambling hobo, who is clearly in the wrong. My God, you parade irrefutable evidence of that. Not them. It is never them.

She puts the shopping in her *Doctor Who* bag. Takes her change from off the counter, where he has dropped it.

'Thank you.'

Another sniff.

There is one other thing Kelly needs to do. She returns outside. Down the street, outside the museum/café, there is a commotion. *How can you let fifteen old Americans do a runner? You better find them – or it's coming out of your wages.*

Kelly ignores the sound of shouting and crying. She ignores a clearly disgruntled Collie and takes herself into the charity shop. A wee bell rings (yay! Kelly has saved a fairy). A snowy-curled old lady goes: 'Hello.' Every charity shop she has ever frequented comes complete with a snowy old lady. Kelly browses. There are the usual ornaments and cut-glass gewgaws, there are strange necklaces and granny handbags, and there are several rails of *ladies' fashion*. Hmm. She selects a plain black raincoat, though she really wants the old sheepskin/astrakhan thing. But it already has a funky smell of its own.

'Excuse me,' she asks the lady. 'Do you know where St Ninian's shrine is?'

'Well, they're not a hundred per cent sure, dear. It's probably where he was buried.'

'Where's that?' A pair of jeans, size 10. *Bootcut*. Is she a 10 still? God knows. She holds them against her waist.

'They think it's in the vault. There's a wee changing room, you know, dear. Behind the curtain.'

Charity shop people are generally nice. There is an acceptance of folk like Kelly, in amongst the world's unwanted stuff. Except for the shops who pour water into their rubbish bags. They are total bastards. Deliberately soaking the old unmentionables they've put outside for the bin men, to stop you rummaging and 'making a mess'. They may not want second-hand underwear. But you might.

'No, I'm fine, thanks. In the vault, you said?'

'Yes. So they say. But there's not much to see. No bones or anything. Just a stone cellar.'

Even so. You have come all this way.

'So, do I get in from the church?' Ooh! Kelly spots a pair of cowboy boots. Quite big, but she could stuff them with socks.

'No, dear. You need a ticket to get in.'

A ticket? To see the holy healing shrine that every pilgrim has travelled to from down the centuries?

'You can get one at the museum – it covers you for both. And the roundhouse too, I think. You know, it's great what they've done, reconstructing that roundhouse – really given a heart to the place again.'

'But I only want to see the shrine.' Beforehand, Kelly wasn't that bothered. But now she's aware that the shrine has been privileged, fenced off? Seeing St Ninian's shrine is her damn birthright. Oh, look – there's socks! Actual hand-knitted, will-fall-around-your-ankles socks. *All money raised from the sale of Sarah's Socks will go to a water project in Malawi.* She'll take the purple and green ones, ta.

The lady shrugs. 'Well, they have to make their money somehow. Now, do you need a bag? It's five pee.'

Kelly has bought quite a lot. 'Aye, go on.' This cash is found money; it unfolds, redolent with the pleasure of shopping for your birthday, when both your grans have put twenty pounds in your card.

'That will be twenty-five pounds and five pence then, please.'

Man. That's quite a splurge, Kelly. What will that leave you? She tries to calculate.

It will leave you happy.

She carries her Next carrier bag proudly from Whithorn Cares. Kelly is not a bag lady. Kelly is a person who has shopping. She transfers her messages from the *Doctor Who* bag (which is, after all, the size of a kid's satchel) into the roomy Next one. Unties Collie's lead. 'Hey, boy. What's wrong?' He's shivering. Coories his head into her shins. 'Och, pet. It's OK. I wasn't away for long.'

There's an altercation across from the coffee shop. The pilgrims are trying to get back on their bus, but the waitress is having none of it.

Now, just you haud your horses. I'm telling you – there was no money on the table!

Well, I can assure you, ma'am, I left it right there.

Swiftly, Kelly about-turns, goes back through the arch and into the graveyard. There has to be a way to get into the vaults from here. A lot of dying has been done in Whithorn. There are several fields of gravestones. She can see a high stone wall, which seems to run from the priory ruins, and what looks like the roof of a church hall beyond. That must be it. She and Collie wend their way through the churchyard. Place is empty (apart from the multitude of bodies). There's a gate in the wall, but it's locked. Tantalisingly close, Kelly can see the open door of the vault, see steps leading down. The gate isny as high as the wall; it's wrought iron, the sort of thing you'd get at a side entry in a garden. Wee flex of her knees, which are feeling pretty limber, considering. There is a tug. Collie is chewing through her Next bag.

'Ho! Quit that, you.'

He ignores her, intent on getting intae her mince. She saves him the bother, peeling off the cellophane from the packet. As her baby is gorging himself on bloodied flesh, she hooks his lead and the bag over a spike on the gate, wedges one foot in, near the handle, and *hup-two, you can do this, doll,* punts herself over. Collie barks as her boots go past his ears, but it's a cursory effort. The mince is far more interesting. Her knees jar as she lands. Side-to-side check. Coast is clear. Raquel is starring in a film set in war-torn Brittany. No. In medieval Carcassonne. The Cathars are holed up in . . .

Kelly enters the vault. It is cool and dark, a chain of rooms. The first one has some display cases, which she bypasses. Second is entirely empty, just the simple room and the arched flint stone above. Third is . . .

She doesny bother with the third, because she reckons it's here, in this second, simple void. Her instincts tell her so. Kelly has good instincts. This vault holds silence like a presence. Kelly does not know what happens to the air we breathe, and then stop breathing. Or what happens when the present becomes the past. But she'd like to believe this second chamber is where St Ninian was laid to rest. Just because. Because it is plain and unassuming. And unassuming does not get celebrated enough.

She takes a wee moment in the hush, then returns to the sultry day. Clouds are pressing, wind has dropped. Heat is rising. At some point, there will be a reckoning. The return scaling of the gate is easier, less of a stretch, with the ground higher on this side.

Oof.

She stumbles, but keeps her footing. Collie doesny even glance up; his head is buried in the empty packet, engaged in licking every millimetre, chasing it as it skites round.

'Onward, Collieflower. I think we're done.' She retrieves the packet, unties the dog. Puts her head down when they pass the café, but the bus has gone. All is calm.

Kelly bins the mince wrappings. Swings her masticated carrier bag as they take the rocky road out of Whithorn. At the outer reaches of the town there's a garage, with a petrol station and a forecourt, which has been built into the face of another old church. It is bizarre, and probably a metaphor for something. Collie yips and snuffles at a bunch of new smells where the pavement reverts to grass verge. She won't put on her new clothes until she's had a proper wash.

Maybe Whithorn will cleanse her after all.

*

Been a rocky six months. That's what you tell them at the meeting. Your allocated key worker nods. Key worker is a good cover-all. Social worker. Probation officer. Housing officer. You're never quite sure who all these various folk assigned to you are, at these various meetings and appointments. Lots of meetings, some of which you attend, some you don't. It is quid pro quo: you go to the ones you need something from. They give you reminders at the end. Like dental check-ups. Wee chitties to make sure you don't forget your next appointment. Then there are the phone calls, if you had a phone, and the letters, if you were to have a fixed address. Fixed addresses are places where you can be found. And why would you want that? Why, when you have maximised every opportunity you can to be unfixed?

Unhinged. When you have worked so hard, so viciously, to stay in jail – extending your sentence not once, but twice. When you have cultivated the chilly insouciance of Mental Kelly. Cornton Vale may look like a well-tended housing estate full of not-unattractive bungalows, but there is barbed wire within and without. You found you could make stabby, jaggy stuff from (in no particular order) fingernails, hairbrushes, assorted kitchen implements (even plastic cutlery can be sharpened). And then there was your voice, of course. You could start a riot in an empty room, Kelly. That's what your mum used to tell

203

you. Who knew you could make an incredible-extending prison career out of it as well?

But all good things must come to an end, and they papped you out eventually. From prison. From the one place you were safe. Put you on this hamster wheel of support and services and supervision and supported services and all these people, who make actual jobs out of dealing with you. You pay their mortgages.

You don't deserve them, all this faff. The attention. The frowning, studied, patient effort of them. And, man, that's before you encounter Shirehorse Shirley. But you have not met her yet. She is a delight still to come. For now, you are in this too-hot room, with this key worker and some other woman. Your teeth are throbbing.

—But why did you not come to Turning Point like you were told? *the key worker's saying.* We could have got you a bed. Access to addiction services.

You shrug. You want to say, 'Because I'm not like them.' You want to say, 'Everything up to now has been an accident. Those alkies in the jail, the lassies in joggers with track marks up their arms? Those hardened criminals in the revolving, revolting in-and-out-of-jail door. That's not me. I made a mistake. Several mistakes. I'm not going into another institution.'

You were mental after all, Kelly. Not wanting to get out. That was one mistake: thinking prison walls protected you. All they did was stymie and stifle your inner goddess. Stultify you into thinking that not-thinking is the answer. That living in limbo in your own seven square metres and being told when to put out the lights is the only way to endure. Well, there are far better methods of mind-numbing than that. Plus. You can keep moving on the outside. When things catch up. If you don't like the scenery, you can just change the view.

They start speaking at you in a chorus, your key worker and this other woman.

—It's not too late, Kelly.

—We want to help you, Kelly. To start making some positive decisions about your future.

—He hit me! *you shout.* Malki hit me. I havny done anything wrong.

This is your . . . *Your key worker checks her notes.* This is your boyfriend, yes?

—Kind of. Was.

Another arsehole, another squat. All your Glasgow friends are wankers, you've decided. They are glib and superficial. Your friends in Kirkcudbright were wankers too, but they didn't have this vicious edge. In the city, folk use you soon as look at you. Who was there for Kelly when she got out the jail?

—Now that you've been discharged from hospital . . .

You regard the long white scars on your wrists. Remember how you steeled yourself, holding your breath before the steel point of the knife popped through blue vein and you sliced and you sliced and you stung, so you poured on the whisky to make the hurting stop, you soused yourself inside and out and you slashed at the other wrist even as the blood was pouring down the shaft of the knife.

Who was there for you then, Kelly?

—. . . chance to revisit some of those areas. *The key worker keeps wittering on. You have to go through this charade, to show that you are sane. Ha. Ha.* Peer support, for example.

You look up, through the thick fringe of hair you hide behind. What?

—At Mungo's? You got on OK there, didn't you? At the hostel?

*You drunk your way through Stirling when they let
you out of Cornton Vale, then limped your way to
Glasgow to drink it dry as well. You chapped the door
of every fucker you knew. Away. Not in. Not answering.
Not wanting to know. Not recognising . . . Oh, it's you.
No room. You even tried Peroxide Malki, and you
thought he might have taken you in but for that cow
Diva nipping his ear. Nobody wanted you. You, the
jailbird. The nutter.*

*The violent, dangerous, no-longer-harmless drunk. Fair
enough. Because you didn't want yourself.*

—Kelly. Remember the Mungo Foundation? The first
time you presented as homeless?

Do you remember the first time?

*Out the back of Malki's close was a wee outhouse – the
old wash house probably. The steamie. You went to see a
musical once, about a steamie. You and your mum and
Auntie Mags. And Mand . . . No, no, no. You stuck your
fingers in your ears, though the voices were all inside. You
were so tired and weepy. So you took your half-bottle and
hunkered down there, in Malki's outhouse. The outhouse
had a roof, so technically you weren't skippering. And the
half-bottle was to keep warm, so technically you weren't
drinking.*

*You can hear the two women, there with you in the
room, echo one another. Blah blah blah. Their questions
are making you think, and you don't want to think about
Malki and what you did. Who you allowed yourself to be.
So you focus only on the women's murmurings. Blah blah
blah. You pretend it is the sound of swishing leaves. Blah
blah blah.*

—And substance abuse. *Man, your key worker is
harsh.*

—I'm not a junkie! *you shout.* I never inject.

206

—Kelly, *says the key worker.* Self-medicating orally is—

—Would yous shut the fuck up?

Orally. You hate that word. You let the women pause to be shocked. There is a nice wee silence in the room, there, where they are pausing and being affronted, but the silence swallows you up, and takes you back to Malki's outhouse. That first day of your new life. What would they call it, if they were making a documentary?
Kellywatch? Kelly in the Wild? Unchained Kello-dee? Kelly Diz Glasgae? Kelly Does Tricks? *Technically you weren't prostituting yourself either, in the morning as you watched Skanky Diva go to work in her mauve care worker's overalls. As you sneaked back into the close. Malki and you had a history, see, so it didn't count. And you got a wash and a sleep afterwards, to make yourself clean.*

Once was enough, and never again. You mouthed this mantra as you walked down the stairs from Malki's flat. And you used the money he had given you to buy chips.

—You are not entitled, *the woman who's not your key worker is saying,* to speak to us like that.

—What? *You pull your fringe down until you can see nothing but hair and the bottom of the calendar that hangs behind your key worker's desk.* Catz do the Craziest Things, *it's called, and this month's centrefold is a Siamese wearing sunglasses, looking at itself in a mirror. Trades Description. You hardly think that the cat has put on its own sunglasses.*

They told you that at the DSS too. You are not entitled.

You'd gone there after the Malki incident. There was just enough money left after the chips for a bus fare. Aye, you were a cheap date.

—You are not entitled to continue receiving housing

207

benefit, because you were sentenced to more than thirteen weeks, *the man in the DSS told you. The DSS or the buroo or the job centre; their names bleed interchangeably.* Even if you have an existing tenancy, you will have to make a new claim.

You'd got confused. You thought they'd sorted it out at Cornton Vale, before you left. You were sure someone said they would sort it.

—Can I do that here?

—Claims are administered via your local authority.

—What if I'm homeless?

—Are you presenting as homeless?

—I don't know.

—If you're presenting as homeless, you will need to go to the housing office.

—Will they help me?

—I doubt you'll be classed as a priority need. Housing are only obliged to offer you advice and assistance. Many providers prefer not to accept ex-prisoners.

—Jesus.

—Please don't swear in here.

—I wasn't . . . Sorry. What about the dole?

—I can begin processing your claim for—

—Aye. But can I get the money now? Like, today?

—Did you not have a throughcare session? You can begin the process to claim for unemployment benefit today, yes. But it won't be immediate. It might take several weeks.

—How am I meant to live?

—That's why you would have been given a liberation grant. Did you receive a liberation grant?

—It's fucking buttons! You're telling me I'm meant to survive on that? For how many weeks?

But you could see the funny side, even then, as you

*were shouting at the DSS mannie. So that's what it was
called. A liberation grant. And there was you thinking it
was a libation grant. Silly Kelly.*

—If you're going to continue to be abusive . . . *The
DSS mannie had stood up at this point. Young, wiry guy.
She could've taken him on, no bother.* I'll have to ask you
to leave. And I'm advising you, when you do sign on,
you'll be sanctioned.

—For fucking what?

—Alice. Get Security.

*But you'd still thought they would help you. Those
people. They had made a whole industry of it, a
burgeoning one. Thousands of jobs for people with jobs
to help thousands of people without jobs to find jobs.
And if they couldn't find jobs, find solutions, surely? Was
that not their job – to help you?*

*Where could you find to go? You'd thought there might
have been somewhere. A party maybe. Someone's couch.
That day was special, though, because there was
absolutely nowhere left. You'd used up all your options.
And Malki had made it plain you would not be welcomed
with open legs again.*

*So you spent the night in a lane at the rear of a
multistorey car park, where the prostitutes took their
punters. Seeking sleep in a johnny-strewn doorway,
huddled by a grating that puffed the occasional gout of
warm air.*

*You hear a funny whimpering sound. You look up,
realise you're still in this too-warm office. Can see your
key worker frowning at you.*

—Kelly. Do you still have suicidal thoughts?

You have a sudden, violent urge to brush your teeth.

—Can you please give me some money for a
toothbrush?

—Kelly. If you're not going to engage with the programme, how can we help?

You stare at your shoes to avoid their prying eyes. Drilling through, picking you clean. You only want a toothbrush.

Chapter Fifteen

DAY TWO OF OUR CAMPAIGN!
HOMELESS HEROINE UPDATE

by Jennifer Patience

A huge thanks to our tireless readers, who have been phoning our Heroine Hotline in their droves. So far, we've had reports of down-and-out Kelly McCallum being spotted in Glasgow, Aberdeen, Livingstone, Rothesay and all the way down in bonnie Galloway. We know she's a heroine, but we don't think she can fly! What's most important is that you, our readers, get the chance to reunite Kelly with the man she rescued – so rest assured, we'll be checking out each one of these sightings. In the meantime, here's that number again. Keep your eyes peeled, and keep calling!

For the second day running, Dexy has felt compelled to buy an actual paper at the paper shop. Odd that he, a proud ex-*Big Issue* seller, has dyked the purchase of a daily newspaper since forever. The news is aye bullshit. Far as he can see, it is full of the same old same old. Blaming folk and being angry. Even the anger doesny seem constructive; it is all shallow, finger-pointing stuff. He still buys a *Big Issue*, mind, every week. He isn't sure folk can ever grasp what a lifeline it is, just to chuck a few quid into a vendor's hand. Say *cheers* or *howzitgaun*. How it tethers them to a wee bit hope.

'Can I get a fag?' Aleisha has her feet up on the dashboard.

'No. You canny smoke in the van. Anyway, I've telt you. It's no good for the wean.'

'Sake. You're no my da.' She flops her hands across her bump. Dexy folds the newspaper. He's read it three times, and the story is still there. Christsake. He couldny believe it when he saw that first article yesterday. Who the hell is this Jennifer Patience, that's what he'd like to know. Big photie, the works. Tony Lu had phoned and telt him, but he'd still gone out and bought a paper to read it for hisself. Wasn't even the photie off the telly either – they'd used one taken at the fucking Outreach. He recognised his own kitchen tiles behind Kelly's head. Arseholes. Who gave them permission for that? What do these people think they're doing? Fucking hounding a person. Stalking them like an animal. He finishes his coffee, starts the engine. Poor Kelly will be stoating about, or more likely holed up somewhere, feeling like utter shit, because she's seen a whole streetful of folk get killed, and it will have totally freaked her, course it will, it'd freak anyone, but see her? Kelly is fragile. Porcelain-thin, she is. Almost translucent when you seen her in a certain light; then in an instant she can harden, something mercurial shifting under her skin. He loves that about her.

'Thank fuck,' Aleisha mumbles.

'What was that, hen?' But he heard her fine. The indicator ticks as he waits to turn out of the service station.

'Can we stop off at Gretna, then? There's a massive shopping centre there – you can get really cheap trainers.'

'We're no going to Gretna, Aleisha. That's nowhere near

212

where we're going. And this isny a road trip.' Leaning forward in his seat. He's not used to driving a van. Windaes are too high up.

'Eh, excuse me, Einstein. But are we no in a fucking motor? And are we no on a fucking road? Aye? Well, it's a road trip.' She stabs at the radio, turning up whatever shite she is forcing them to listen to now.

Dexy pulls onto the motorway. The lassie is nipping his heid. He only agreed to her coming because . . . well. He isny a hundred per cent sure. This morning is all a bit of a guddle. Soon as he saw Galloway mentioned in that bloody woman's article, it clicked. Dexy knows exactly where Kelly is headed.

'Aye, all right, bawheid.' He gives the finger to the guy behind him, who is blasting his horn as Mr Lu's Cash and Carry judders into the inside lane. 'Fucking three lanes, pal,' he shouts.

'Dexy,' says Aleisha. 'Anger's really not good for the wean.'

'Naw, but sleep is, doll. So why don't you get a wee bit shut-eye, eh?'

Once he'd squared it with Tony to give him a loan of the van (luckily, Mr Lu's empire stretches to two vans, and Mikey had went on holiday to Blackpool, so the spare van was just sitting there, smelling of exotic vegetables) and made sure the relief warden for the Outreach was available (he was), Dexy was ready for the open road. But Aleisha went and sidewinded him.

'Can I come?' she said.

'You don't know where I'm going.'

'You're away to get that Kelly wumman. I heard you on the phone.'

'Naw.'

'Please, Dexy. I get scared here on my own.'

'You arny on your own.'

'You know what I mean. That relief guy's all right. But . . .'

'But what?'

'He isny you.'

Wee boot went for the heartstrings. Aleisha had grown up in care. This pregnancy is her way of creating a family of her own – hopefully sans the da, who is a wee fud.

'Please, Dexy. What if something happens . . . to the baby when you're gone.'

'Aleisha, you're five months pregnant. And fuck knows how, but you're as healthy as an ox.'

'M'on, Dex. I can help . . . navigate. And keep the tunes going. *Please*. I've never went out of Glasgow. And I don't want you going on your own.'

She had looked genuinely feart. Christ, a moment of weakness, him clocking her wee face, and checking he'd enough cash for petrol, googling *Gatehouse of Fleet* and *weddings*, going, *Aye, right, all right, Aleisha* before he'd thought it through.

So here they are, the odd couple, hot-footing it down to Galloway. Dexy isn't sure what he'll do when he gets there, but . . . he just knows he should go. There should be some kind of barrier between Kelly and the arseholes of the world. As soon as that reporter susses where Kelly grew up, she'll be headed there too. Bet your life on it. And he doesn't know how he knows it, but he knows that Kelly will just want left alone. Even if there is some big juicy reward on offer. She needs to be by herself. Why else would she jump into a strange guy's lorry and disappear off the grid? Aye, cause she totally keeps such regular hours otherwise, doesn't she? But this is different. He is certain. This is not Kelly being Kelly. This is Kelly running. And now being hunted.

He feels guilty too. Part of this is his fault. He put the idea into her head. Saying she should piss off out of Glasgow.

He meant it as a positive thing, but what if Kelly took it different? And then something really shite goes and happens to her, seeing all they people mown down, and her, shaky, fragile, hinging-by-a-thread wee Kelly trying to stop some man fae dying, and wanting desperately to talk to Dex about it afterwards. The prick who told her to bugger off. But that's not the worst of it. Because he is well aware that when something really shitey happens to you, it throws up other really shite stuff with it. See folk like Dex and Kelly? See all those fragmented jigsaw pieces that have made you who you are, instead of how you might have been? Well, they are only ever a skin's breadth from breaking through the surface. Cutting you up from the inside.

'Brilliant about Mrs JamJay, eh?' Aleisha shouts over the noise of the radio. She'll need to turn it down, he canny take the noise. 'Isn't he pretty, the wean?' She's beaming at her phone, and then at Dexy. He knows exactly what she's looking at, since it was him who sent her the picture.

'Aleisha, he is gorgeous.' Dexy risks moving into the middle lane, to overtake a lorry full of logs. Dark pink and startled in the bright of the hospital, the JamJays' baby had waved his wee limbs at him – a newborn sea anemone, fronding and feeling his way into being. There had been talk, once, of a son of his own, over in Garthamlock. Claims – well, more like rumours – that Dex was the father. The lassie was gorgeous, a big blonde, totally out Dexy's league, but he was too full of the junk then to know, or care. Full of all kinds of nonsense. It had given him the gift of the gab, aye, when he was away with it. Speeding and fleeing. Ducking and dicking about. Oh yes, he floated and shimmied on the drugs. Effervescent. Brave with it, squaring up to the guys, chatting up the dolls. Then sinking like water down a drain. And when your whole fucking life runs down the drain, taking many long, sore years to do so, man, by that time it's too late. Way too late to do anything about it. So maybe there was a boy – a man now, he supposes. A boy over in Garthamlock who is hopefully as tall and good-looking as his mum, and way smarter than his dad. If there is, Dexy will never know. But he can imagine. How it might have felt.

Oh, but the untouched smell of that JamJay wean, when Dex held him in the hospital. He was the first person in to see the baby after he was born. Possibly the only one, for who did the JamJays have here? He will never forget the smell of the baby's head. If pure has a scent, that talcy, biscuity sweet warmth was it. Overcome, Dexy had bent to kiss him, then kissed Mrs JamJay, which was utterly taboo, Christ, he leapt away as if he was scalded, apologising to her, her husband, the wean, but the woman was grace personified. She simply held Dexy's hand and said, *thank you.*

'I canny believe it, mind,' he says to Aleisha, slipping back into the safety of the nearside. All they juggernauts are giving him the heebie-jeebies.

'Believe what?'

'What? Gonny turn that down, eh?'

Aleisha sighs, but obliges.

'Cheers, doll. Aye, they've went and called the wean Joseph. Here's me thinking I was kidding them on, and they've actually called him Joseph. I mean, they're saying Yousuf, but it's the same thing.'

'But that doesny make sense. Mr JamJay is Joseph, sure? So they should've called the baby Jesus.'

'Aleisha, away and don't be daft. You canny call a wean Jesus.'

'How no? Ma cousin called her wean Chanterelle, and that's a fucking mushroom.'

Dexy can't help it; he starts laughing.

'What? What's so funny? I'm serious.'

'Aye, I know you are, hen.' He glances at her wee pouty face. At her neat ponytail and careful make-up. Feels a surge of affection. She's just a child, the soul. He shouldny take the piss. A child having a child.

'This is all serious stuff, pal. No a joke. None of this is. I mean, what's gonny happen to the JamJays now? That reporter woman wanted to do a story on them too, when I told her. Said it might help—'

'What reporter woman?' Dexy's fingers. Hoicking into the wheel. He is sandwiched between two massive lorries, but it isny them causing the cold spikes in his belly. Or this building, disbelieving rage. 'Aleisha.' He speaks quietly. 'What the fuck. Have you done?'

As per usual, she starts greeting.

'Aleisha. Fucksake. Was it you that told that reporter Kelly's name?' Wanting to shake the teeth from her, but he can't risk taking his eyes from the road, nor his hands from the wheel.

'I'm sorry, Dex. Don't shout at me,' she wails. 'I done it for you.'

'What?' White fury, blinding him. *Don't bloody turn this onto me.*

'Aye. She went on and on, hassling me. Said she'd gie me money.'

'How much money, Aleisha? How many fucking pieces of silver?'

'A ton.'

'A hundred pound? To sell Kelly down the river?'

'Dex, I was feart they boys were gonny cut you.'

'Who? What the fuck are you on about?' A lorry behind him is flashing its lights. 'What?' he shouts in the mirror. 'Fucking what?' Realises the motorway is climbing up here, and he is slowing. Doing thirty and losing traction. 'Shite.' He puts his foot down, the van lurching as Aleisha starts waving her hand under his nose.

'Fucksake, Aleisha. Quit it. I canny see what I'm doing.'

'See? Here. I've got the money here. I brung it with me. You can give it to them.'

'To who?'

'They Chinese gangsters. They said they were gonny chop your hands off.'

'Who? Tony Lu?' She isn't lying; there is a wad of cash in her fist.

'Aye. That day in the kitchen when yous were playing cards. Then today, I heard you on the phone to them. You were going, *Christ, I know I owe yous already*.'

'Jesus wept. I was asking them for a loan of their van. What kindy films have you been watching? It's twenty quid I owe him. It was a joke. I owe Tony Lu twenty quid. How the hell d'you think they let me borrow their motor?'

'I don't know.' She sniffs. 'I panicked. But I didny know when was the right time to give you the money.'

'Christsake, Aleisha.' Softer. 'Christsake.' He reaches across and pats her knee. 'I thought you were acting weird when we were up at the cash-and-carry. Right, calm down, all right? Roaring and greeting isny good for the wean.'

'*I'm* no good for the wean.'

'Enough of that, you. Stop talking pish. You're gonny be a great wee mammy.' *God help us.*

'I'm really sorry, Dex. I didny tell that reporter much.'

'That's cause you don't know much. Nobody knows much about Kelly.'

'I might have mentioned, but . . . that I'd heard she'd been in the jail? For murder?'

'Jesusfuckingchrist, Aleisha. What is *wrang* with you?' Blood pressure away, his eyes are nipping, smarting. Fuck, he is gonny have a heart attack at the wheel, he cannot deal with all this fucking emotion. 'Who telt you that?'

Oh for a wee toke. Dexy has been clean for years, but this *idiot* child is sending him down the slippery slope.

'Folk talk, Dex. Wee Carol Ann from the Tuesday women's group said she knew Kelly in the jail. That she'd broke someone's neck.'

'And you told that to the reporter?'

'She wouldny of paid me otherwise.'

'Christ on a bike. One of these days I'm gonny break *your* neck, Aleisha Holmes. Swear it. I'll fucking swing for you.'

'Did she no do it then?'

'Gonny shut it? I'm no talking to you. I need to think.'

'Dex?'

'What?'

'Can I get a fag now?'

'Aye, go on.' He stares at the road ahead. Brain trying to shift gear. 'Fuck it. Gie me one too.'

Chapter Sixteen

It is a carnival of books she has chanced upon, and Kelly was not expecting this. Her feet may be louping, but this unfolding scene is urging her to dance. Wigtown bustles with marquees and market stalls. Banners fly from the Gothic County Buildings (which would not look out of place in Venice), green stylised trees on white silk, and flapping Saltires and pennants proclaiming: *Scotland's National Book Town*. The streets teem with studious-looking folk. Twice Kelly has been bumped into by people reading as they walk. It is not normal behaviour, yet all you get is a smile and a shrug.

This is not the Wigtown she remembers from her childhood. That was a faded, end-of-the-pier place. Desolate. But not today. The town has a similar layout to Whithorn; the heart of it is two long streets flanking a central space – Scots Vernacular. That's it! That is the phrase she's been trying to remember. First year: History of Architecture; she can see the page now, as if she is cram-reading it before class. *The Scottish Vernacular*. These medieval burghs shared a pattern and a purpose: long gardens so the locals could plant their own land; a courthouse and a tollbooth for visible law and order; central enclosures for cattle markets and sheep fairs and trade; and there would've been a tron somewhere too for public weighing, so no one got ripped off. Plus a church and church-run school for all your moral and educational needs.

Pretty sussed as far as town planning goes.

Today, Wigtown seems to be replicating its glory days. The air is festive; it is electric with books. The crisp white crack of them, their bold and glossy hardness, the soft, dry whisper-touch that can set your teeth on edge. Bookshops spill open, trestles outside to display their wares – there are five, six shops Kelly can count from here. People throng between the marquees on the central green, carrying armfuls of books, browsing books, discussing books – *I think it's his best yet.*

'Excuse me,' she asks the third person to jostle her – Kelly blocks the flow like an inconvenient rock as Wigtown swirls around her. 'What is this?'

The wee lady who has just dunted her blinks behind her specs. 'It's the book festival.' She's wearing a round, vaguely Arabian pillbox hat, studded with mirrors and embroidery. Kelly must still be looking a bit glaikit. 'Wigtown Book Festival?' she elaborates (though Kelly could have worked that bit out for herself).

'When did it start?'

'Yesterday, I think.'

'No, I mean like, how long ago?'

'Ooh, not sure now. Been going for a while. Nineteen nineties maybe?'

'It's amazing.'

A loudspeaker somewhere announces that a BBC war correspondent is about to commence his talk on 'Afghanistan – My Journey in a Burkha'.

Wigtown reborn. That someone had the gumption to take a dying town by the scruff of the neck and reinvent it. Amazing. Kelly would have loved to come to a festival of books when she was young. To publicly celebrate words and learning instead of hiding away doing it in your room. Like Jane Austen was a porny mag. She likes the sense of pride with which Wigtown is disporting itself. The painted houses gleam brightly though the day is dull. If you don't stand too close to Kelly, here, she reckons, she is not so out of place. There is a fine range of eccentrics stoating through Wigtown. Plenty normal folk – lots of middle-aged couples in nicely pressed slacks, and older folk, mostly ladies in pastel cardigans, clutching programmes and chattering as they go – aye, but there's a fair oddball count too. Kelly has never been at a book festival, so she's no idea if this is peculiar to Wigtown, or specific to all such affairs. Will she follow the willowy girl in chiffon and chunky boots, or the brace of stout men wearing kilts, who ride unicycles and are insisting (while they wobble and dart) that you come and try out the Circus of Words, starting in the Beltie Tent RIGHT NOW! *Juggle with your nouns, throw flames with your verbs, let your adjecti—*

Kelly misses the end of this enticement, because a wee yappy dog leaps from the arms of its mistress and comes running over to see Collie. Unfortunately, it charges directly in front of one of the unicyclists, who wavers, judders . . . and *DISMOUNT!* he cries, to a rousing cheer. The lad lands like a proper gymnast, taking his rightful bow and maintaining his dignity throughout.

Is this thing a dog, or a wee rat? The miniature creature bounds round Collie's feet. Collie sniffs, pulling his snout away every time the tiny thing bounces up. A group of three women follow. Not one of them acknowledges the unseated unicyclist.

'Hey. Cute baby you got.' The accent is clipped, brisk. A very glamorous woman in dark sunglasses bends to retrieve her dog. 'Kom då Axel, hopp upp.'

She flings open her scarlet wrap, revealing a very glamorous cleavage in the process. The woman's hair is wild with curls, and dyed the same matching scarlet as her wrap. Kelly can see a thin line of white at the parting on her crown.

'Busiga gubbe! So, so naughty.' She kisses her dog's puggy nose, the dug giving it big licks. Collie and Kelly look at one another. Roll their eyes.

'Say hello, Axel.' The woman holds her dog's paw, which is the size of a walnut. Makes it wave at Collie. 'Hey. What is your dog's name?' Pinned above her left breast is a diamond skull, which sparkles, quivering, as she and Axel wave.

'Collieflower.' In the face of all this showiness, Collie deserves his Sunday name.

'I like him. Good . . .' She slaps her hand on her arse. 'What is these?'

'Haunches,' says the girl accompanying her. She is chewing her lip, keeps glancing at her clipboard. 'Miss Karlsson, we really need to be getting to your event. We need to do the sound check.'

'Ha. You'll come? Axel likes your Collieflower. She can bring, yes?'

'The dog? Well, it's not really our policy, Miss Karlsson. Health and safety—'

'You people! Why does this country have so many rules? Not to smoke, not to bring your baby. Are you saying I cannot bring Axel?' She bundles him inside her wrap, so he is held in a doggy-papoose.

'No, of course not.'

'Well, so. Isabella. Give the lady the . . .' She snaps her fingers at the third woman, a whip-thin blonde dressed entirely in black.

'Ticket?'

'Yes. The compliment ones.'

Kelly reads the ticket she's been handed. Jesus, that blonde's fingers are like ice.

Unearthing the Bones. A macabre afternoon with Swedish crime-writing sensation Märta Karlsson. Main Marquee, 4 p.m. (sponsored by Bladnoch Distilleries).

'No, no. Give me. Please.'

Märta takes the ticket straight off her again, scribbles on it in biro. 'There. Nice to meet you, lady. Now, come on, Isabella. I think you will make us late.'

The trio sashay off. Strange people. Kelly eases her *Doctor Who* bag from her shoulder. There's a food market in a long tent over there called the Kist, with some mighty fine smells emanating from its flaps. She wants to check the money situation again, count every penny. She fears this pilgrimage has unleashed a monster. On the streets, her stomach knew no ambition; it had learned to doze and grumble, to make itself very small. But it has become quite demanding in the countryside air. She reads Märta's handwriting.

Guest of Märta Karlsson. This dog to be admitted.

Very nice of the woman, but she's never heard of her, and doesny really fancy a macabre afternoon. Would someone buy it off her? she wonders. Before she can identify a willing victim, some soul perhaps who looks in need of having their bones unearthed, the ticket is removed from her hand. It is the lassie with the clipboard. She wields her biro, carefully scratches through Märta's specific instructions regarding canine admittance.

'Like I said, you can't take dogs inside the tent.' She stares at Collie as if it is his fault.

'Fine,' says Kelly, snatching the ticket back. 'We weren't going to anyroad. Come, Collieflower.'

And Kelly is positive that Collie tips his nose towards the sky. A definite flounce to the pair of them as they walk towards the Main Marquee (sponsored by Bladnoch Distilleries). Kelly hovers at the back of the queue, just to see what Clipboard Lassie is going to do. The couple in front of her start murmuring. Then they stop murmuring, cough discreetly instead. The man turns; only a half-swivel, but it is sufficient to catch the widening of his nostrils, his fingers coming up to cover his nose as he stares at Kelly.

Kelly shrivels. Removes herself immediately from the queue, away from the happy tents and the clean, good grass, from the people who have money in their pocket and a right – *a right, I tell you!* – to enjoy themselves. Kelly and Collie: she drags him by the lead, the wee pet doesny know what he's done – *it's not you, baby, it's me* – up the street, the County Buildings and all the fun of the fair behind them. She will go straight to Gatehouse this minute, fucking walk all night if she has to, for the wedding is tomorrow, and she has no clue where or what time, or where. There are three churches in Gatehouse, plus the swanky Cally Palais, and folk have a tendency to be wacky nowadays, don't they – could be getting married on a zip wire or the bloody beach, or maybe up at Cairn Holy where . . . Shit, she never did go to any of those wells or standing stones, did she, but the pilgrimage is finished, done. It ended with Whithorn. This, all this Wigtown crap – this is her just going up the wrong way. There's bugger-all pilgrimy about Wigtown, is there, well she hasny read that bit of the pamphlet, but fuck it, she just wants away. Away from all that it is not hers to own.

You are not entitled.

'Jackie! Ja— Oops. Sorry.'

An arm in a blue and purple anorak blocks Kelly's way. The hand of the arm is still shutting the front door of the Wigtown Hotel, while the remainder of the person is about to step off the pavement. Fucking fourth person to crash into her – and Kelly's clearly not invisible. She stops while the woman sorts herself.

'Jackie, do we take the key with us?' The woman flaps a

key attached to a six-inch wooden thistle. She's calling to another woman over the road. 'It's awfy big.'

'No. Mind they said, Morag – put it on the hook in reception.'

'OK. Two minutes. Sorry,' she says again to Kelly.

'Don't mind me. I'm an aberration.'

But anorak lady has gone, inside the foyer of the hotel, holding the front door open, doing that thing folk do when they are in a hurry: keeping a foot in both camps between the where she is meant to be and the place where she is. Kelly can see her in the mirror of the hallstand, reaching up to a cabinet behind reception and hooking her key under *Number 4*. There is nobody in reception.

Kelly walks two, three paces further on, waits until Jackie and Morag have linked arms and scuttled over to . . . yes, they are indeed off for a macabre afternoon, then pivots on her heel and enters the Wigtown Hotel. Dark-panelled hallway, very nice. Without pause she reaches over for the key to number four, clicks her fingers to Collie, and together they take the stairs. Fervently she hopes there are no ground-floor rooms, and that this single corridor will be a simple . . . Yes. Thank you very much. One: *The Sayers Suite*. Two: *The Burns Boudoir*. Three: *Crockett Chambers*. Here we are. Room Four: *The Hannay Hideaway*.

Unlocking the door. Entering another person's private space. The smell is sequestered, dense with sweat and body spray. Kelly sniffs. Detects a hint of toothpaste. There is an opened sponge bag on the bed, spilling tubes of mascara, Colgate, a hairbrush, Vicks Sinex. Even hotel rooms can become private when you lay your things about you. Even bridge arches or an underpass; you can make them private with your sleeping bag. Just lay it down, put your bits and bobs around you, and voilà. Your ain wee hoose.

Kelly locks the bedroom door from the inside, keeps the

key in the lock. Feels a frisson of trespass, which speeds her movements, makes her flustered as she peels off her clothes. Collie circles, suspicious of the carpet. Major Tom probably never let him in the house.

'It's OK, Collie.' She pats the floor. 'You lie down. Go on, lie down. Good boy.' Jackie and Morag haven't yet been into the shortbread fingers. She breaks the cellophane, puts the biscuits down in front of Collie. In the buff, her tits hang, dangling before her. Kelly is an embarrassment to womankind. She jiggles them, as if she might wake them up. Discovers a sore under her left breast. All that bra-less walking has chafed her bloody. She is the bearer of pilgrim stigmata. She goes to sit on the bed to remove her boots. Stops, and fetches a towel from the bathroom on which to sit. Her feet sting as she pulls off boots, then socks. One sock sticks. She tugs, and a piece of dark skin comes with it. Her feet, which were bad enough before, are in a hellish state. Blistered and throbbing, a bruised toenail she daren't touch, lest it fall off altogether.

In the bathroom, she turns on the shower. Clouds form, misting up the cubicle. She leaves the wee shampoos and soaps alone; she has brought her own, carried in her Next bag. She is only borrowing their water. She takes a breath, hand under the spray to test the temperature, then steps inside the steam. It is bliss. Hot jets pummel her neck, her shoulders. Pouring shampoo into her hands, rub-a-dub-dub. Rub. Rub. *RUB*. Her smarting feet tense and claw, tense and claw, then consign themselves to the healing nip of pooling suds. She soaps her oxters and her groin, all the stinking bits of her, then soaps them again. Do they think folk *want* to live like this? Crusted with their own filth? Cold and old and hungry? Wanting to be seen, and be unseen. Wanting to be present, even in their self-appointed margins. Do they think it's a choice to be scared and lonely? For life to beat you up so fucking hard that you welcome the beatings, because it's all you're good for? Soap and shampoo, running in her eyes, her, squeezing and rubbing; you can't remember touch, to be tender and naked. The mellow water drenches her, Kelly, leeching into tiles and steam, she can't calm her hands, tears coming in wet heaves, then the rinsing, the beautiful, clear rinsing, over and over she lets it pour, chittering in the steam.

When she is as clean as clean can be, Kelly turns off the shower. Wraps herself in snowy towels (sorry, Jackie and Morag, but she is borrowing them too). She checks on Collie. He is sound. Lying on his side, wee paws pedalling in air as he chases dreams. From *Doctor Who*, she retrieves the scissors she bought in Whithorn. Then she forces herself to confront the bathroom mirror.

It is not a thing she wants to do – oh, Kelly, for fucksake. Look at the mess you've made in here. Pools of water on the floor, the mirror misted grey. Poor Jackie and Morag'll have a fit. (Kelly doll, they are far more likely to have a fit at the fact that a wet, naked wild woman is gieing it laldy in their room.)

That's the sort of thing Dexy would say. She misses him. They share a similar sense of humour, like a pal would. Is he her pal? She supposes he is, but it's hard to judge, when your friends are folk that help you. It is the exact opposite and yet the same as if she were Beyoncé or Madonna – is it me they love or my fame? Kelly exhales. The mist increases. Back of her hand on the mirror. Rub-a-dub-dub.

And there she is.

It's the very same face she observed at Clara's house, only more extreme. *Extreme Kelly*. No fringes of wiry grey to be her mask; her wet hair is darkened and slick. She eases it from her face entirely, tucking the strands behind her ears. The broken veins are less prominent, but only because her whole face is garnet-red with heat. And there are traces of another, youthful, lovely face too, which you miss so very much. She stretches the loose skin by her jowls, pulling it into a smile. Does not linger on her naked, ruined body, because every scar tells a story, and what she can't remember can fucking stay that way. Slowly she slides finger and thumb through the scissors. Begins to snip.

At first, she's not sure how short she'll take it. But as the layers and tufts drop away, her face seems to lighten. There is still the memory of cheekbones lingering, and her big nose is more proportionate now it is not sticking from a mop of hair. Joey Ramone! Oh my God. Is that who she looked like? Periodically she scoops out hanks of hair from the basin, puts them in an array of sanitary bags. She tried to flush the first batch down the loo, but the hair remains, floating reproachfully in the bowl, no matter how many times she yanks the plug. Evidence. She stabs at it with a loo brush. They can get her DNA off that. Manages to wedge it into the U-bend, holds it long enough at bay with the loo brush that she can flush and push, and *finally* the bastard disappears.

A chap at the door. 'Hello?'

Collie barks.

'Hello. Housekeeping.' The door handle rattles. 'Is everything OK in there? Is there a problem with the plumbing?'

'No!' Kelly holds her hand over Collie's muzzle.

'It's just—'

'I just had an upset tummy. Do you mind? This is really quite embarrassing.'

'Oh. I'm terribly sorry.'

Collie is snuffling and rummaging. '*Shut up.*'

'Sorry?'

'It's my stomach again.'

'I'll just leave you, shall I?'

'Probably best.'

Kelly lies on the floor beside Collie, one fist at his mouth, the other at her own, to stop from laughing. She has been fannying about in here the best part of half an hour. How long do macabre afternoons usually last? Quickly she mops the bathroom floor, dusts the hair off the counter as best she can. Although she hates herself for doing it, Kelly's body is so clean that she cannot bear to put her sea-washed underwear back on. She rummages through the chest of drawers. Takes two pairs of pants (each one from a different drawer, to make it as fair as possible. She presumes they keep their knickers separate). Climbs into unfamiliar scants, then her new bootcut jeans, which are a wee bit loose, but they'll do. A damn sight more stylish than her men's breeks. She bundles those into *Doctor Who*, along with her old pants and socks. From the shopping bag she gets her new knitted socks (very snuggly) and the cowboy boots.

Wow. What is it about girls and heels? She clicks and stamps, blisters forgotten. Selects her cleanest jumper, then dons the black raincoat. One last look in the bathroom mirror.

Not bad, Kelly. Her cropped grey hair is striking. It sits in little spikes – who was the dame who sang that song? The breathy, electronic *doop-doop* . . . 'O Superman'. Laurie Anderson. Yes. She is a much less delicate version of her. She considers scavenging for some make-up, but the thought only lasts until she blinks and gets a grip.

You are what you are, Kelly.

It is what it is.

She folds the damp towels, places them in the bath. Should she write a note? Apology or appeal? Both will make you feeble, and you are *doop-ooh-doo-doo*. O Superman.

Kelly and Collie walk down the stairs. Her neck is

elongated, slender as . . . Fuck. There is a young lad at reception. *OK. This is going to be rocky. But you can do it. Breenge, baby. Breenge.*

'Hello.' Big smile, straight at him. 'Could you pop this on the hook? Room Four.'

'No bother. See you later. Oh. Is that a dog? Dogs aren't—'

Laurie Anderson (pop star) shuts the door on him, and takes her dog for a walk.

*

A rocky six months? When did you stop counting? When months became years or swooped back to no time at all? Time is fluid now; it loops and vanishes. But you are through the other side, you know you are. It's hard to get a job when you've a record. No, you're not a pop star. With a little help, though, you manage. Sacro has schemes for the care and resettlement of offenders. They want you resettled. The council has schemes – Routes Out, Hands Up, Start Afresh – and you are grateful for their small mercies. You have a job and a home. It is not much, but it is yours, and you never want to sleep in a B&B again. Nor a hostel. You think hostels are more frightening than being on the street. You lie awake in hostels, hearing strangers fight or cry. Your flimsy door keeps you trapped yet unprotected. Pillow lumpy with your possessions underneath, your neck darting at shadows. And when you finally succumb, take just one wee drink to block out the terrors, turn the volume down, the bastards go and boot you out.

But to have your own front door. Finally, to have that. For a person in authority to decide that you are worthy, that you have passed their test – be it endurance or longevity or character or final, final straw. You neither know nor care what hoop you have finally jumped through. Your own front door is a precious gift, and you guard it fiercely. You live a quiet life. When you get the subway to the factory where you help make gloves, you get off a stop early, avoiding Hillhead. You find it hard to bear the students jostling and leaping as they alight for uni. High on life and learning. You used to make that same journey, and however quiet you are, you are not a martyr. During the day, your hand does not shake. In the evening, in your little flat, it does, but only until the first pour, and you tell yourself it is simple anticipation. You deserve this drink; it has been a long day.

Every day is.

Dry white wine, it is only social. By yourself, so who can count? You are such a good girl, no more pills, no smokes. And you wake night-sweated and dull, heart battering to escape, and you swallow it down, drink your litre bottle of water, which you fill each night for these moments. Have a pee. Watch the walls encroach on your tiny room. When you blink, they move a little closer, until you are terrified to close your eyes. In the dark, you talk to Mandz. You tell her about your day and how much you miss her. In the dark, you say all the words you've held inside. You miss your mum and dad. You thought being lonely was what would save you, but no woman is an island.

—Do you ever think about reconnecting? *The nice key worker, Carla, was forever asking you that or variations on the theme. As if she wanted to tick you off her mind before she ticked you off her list.*

—I see your dad came to visit you?

Many, many times. Or he tried to, at least. Funny thing is, in prison, they can tell you when to eat, when to watch TV, when to put the lights out. But they can't make you accept visits you do not wish to take.

You miss your key workers. Christ, you are so low that you miss contact with the people who are paid to care about you. But, Kelly, you are a success. Signed off, cured!

It is only in the dark, alone, that you can talk about what you did. In the waking day, when you have agency to effect change, you do nothing. You are not brave, Kelly. You cling to each day, limp from one small shard to the next. How could you make things bigger? How could you smash through the walls in which you are cocooned, invite a blizzard and face it?

I am sorry, you whisper at night. And you hope it will drift to wherever they are.

You have no family, you tell the new pattern cutter at work. He is older than you, with pitted skin on his face. Has eczema on his elbows; you see it flake when he rolls up his sleeves. He admires your tattoo, and you blush. The glove factory in which you both work has clung on for over a century. Soaking and stretching leather, snipping with tong-shaped shears. Posh hand-finished gloves that are still popular in the type of department stores where they do haberdashery. You love that word. Haberdashery. It makes you think of Miss Havisham, an elegantly wasted rag doll trailing lace ribbons and brocade. Still, hand-finished glovery does not pay the rent, and so the factory has diversified. Where banks of machinists once sat, porcelain formers now drip with latex. This is the section for surgical gloves. For hours every day, you watch eerie white hands wave from a suspended conveyor belt. One of your jobs is to dip-sample. You get to blow up rubber gloves and fill them with water.

You wear white overalls and a paper mob cap on your head. You got six As in your Highers.

The pattern cutter is nice. Divorced, no kids. His name is Garry, Harmless Garry, so you go for a coffee after work. It will be fine, you think. You do not trust yourself to drink in front of him. You are surprised that he asked you, and not a little . . . flattered? No, actually, you feel sorry for him. Sorry that he is patently nervous about having a coffee with someone like you.

You can function like this. It is fine.

He is fine. Garry's fine. You eat lunch together. Talk about nothing much, and that is all you need. Being with him feels like being in a hammock. He invites you to dinner, but that is evening, and your wine, your wine. Ach, fuck it. Life is short. So you play a game, turning wine into water. Every second glass – and you do it, you actually manage it. Restraint. You take this as a sign. With Garry at your side, you can do anything. Kelly, you could rule the world!

He moves in, and your tiny flat feels a little bigger. You are inventive and quick. A litre bottle of water at your bedside can be clear with vodka, if you want it to be.

You drink because seeing people happy makes you sad. But this is the happy house, and you are happy here.

You watch telly, sit and sip together with Garry in a way that is warm. You have limits that are not breached, even when you know you have only just begun, when the third or fourth drink takes flight, and you with it, soaring nice, not high, but buzzing and the pulse of the buzz hitting your teeth like rain. You are giggling and sharp and dark. My God, he likes it. And you love the sensation that you are holding back, that there is so much deeper you could take him, and the feeling turns powerful, turns to slivers of lightning in your veins, your head wrapped in thunder, your legs wrapped round his spine.

Mornings, you are shy. Showers are for shaking and weeping, the fall of the water wiping each day fresh.

You and flaky Garry. Making gloves and making love.

Kelly 'n' Gaz 4EVR.

Chapter Seventeen

'Did you manage to get parked?'

'No, I'm still going round in circles, dear. And me a professional driver too.'

Maureen laughs. They have been calling each other *Mummy dear* and *Daddy dear* since Craig got home. Cocooned in sweet, lovely fibres, the two of them nesting in candyfloss. He brings her cups of tea and extra pillows – *here, take mine. Is your back sore?* – and she preens, and he surges with virility. Craig has asked his boss to take him off the Ireland run, just for a week or two. Just till his brain catches up with the miracle of Maureen's body.

Fourteen weeks she waited to tell him she was pregnant. Alone and yet not, sensing her breasts and belly swell, the cells within her multiply, and him on the outside. Oblivious. It hurts his heart that she knows him so well. Makes him glad too, that she knows him and loves him still. It is Maureen's faith in their togetherness that will carry them. When she looks at Craig, she doesn't see a shitebag lorry driver who does a runner when things get scary. She sees a different man – one who is braver, with a bigger heart. And maybe that's why it hurts, his actual heart hurts. Because Maureen is swelling it with life too.

Nearly halfway through her pregnancy, and she's been on

the journey alone. You shouldn't have to travel alone. That is Craig's work, and now he wishes it wasn't. To be distant, longing to get back – he doesn't think he can handle that again, not now he knows, not when her bump quickens, or later, when she might be scared and breathless, or after, when it – no, she (he is sure it is a she; everything he sees is coloured pink), when she is here, this small life they have created.

Oh God.

He can't get his head above the tumult, it is wash-wash, constant, this ocean of emotions that stops him from sleeping, then jerks him awake. Craig is proud of Maureen yet still a wee bit angry. He is jealous that she has guarded their secret, and deeply ashamed and deeply scared. Each paving stone or moving car bristles with incipient threat. He shields her as they walk through the hospital's sliding doors, arms out to protect her eggshell skin. What if the doors malfunction, slide in when they're meant to be sliding wide?

'Why are you walking like a big ape?'

'Me Tarzan, you Jane.'

She takes his arm. 'You crazy.'

Swallowing down the hospital reek, that melange of the chemical and the human. People are milling at the threshold; there's a shop with cuddly toys and helium balloons. Craig glowers at two women in dressing gowns, opening up their fag packets in readiness for the great beyond.

'Stop it, you. Stop frowning at folk.'

He loves it when Maureen whispers up at him, how her lips brush his ear, and how she has to reach up first, yank him down to her height. That he might have lost all this because of stubbornness and panic. They take the lift to Level Two.

'From here to Maternity,' he says, nuzzling into her. Maureen pats his cheek, a mother already. Out of the lift, they follow the signs.

Please use the hand sanitiser.

Piles. Don't suffer in silence.

NCT Early Birds. Labour suite tour. Meet in Room 2.

'That's us,' says Maureen. 'Room Two.'

NCT, not NHS. At some stage, Craig is going to need a prompt list. Natural . . . no, National Childbirth Trust. He and Maureen are going to have extra lessons, as well as the NHS ones. Fine by Craig. He could study being a good dad for a hundred years and still not be sure what it entails. If there's somebody running classes for the first five years of parenthood, he'll sign up for that too.

Maureen takes his hand.

'What? You OK?'

'Mm-hmm.' She is staring straight ahead.

'Nervous?'

'Bricking it.'

They press a buzzer, pass through double doors. Other couples are assembling, gauche and tender. A young girl is there, with her mum, he guesses. Another lady on her own, studying all the posters on the corridor wall. Room Two is locked, a man says. 'The woman's away for the key.'

The Early Birds stand patiently. Hospitals make folk docile. Quiet like animals waiting in a pen. Craig can't stand at peace, though. He paces, trying to get a feel for the place, though why that is important he does not know; it's not as if he can influence the environment in any way. From here on in, other people will be in charge. But not at the end. Once their baby is born, it will be them: a wee circle of three. Keeping them safe and fed and cared for. That will be down to him.

He can see into one of the wards, through glazed doors. Four beds – och, that isn't too bad. Maureen can't sleep if it is noisy. A nurse comes through the door and a brittle, grating wail comes with her. She is pushing a clear plastic cradle, which contains the source of all that wail. He can't believe the size of the wean. It's totey. Are babies meant to be that purple? Craig rubs his nose. Well, he supposes they'll get used to the bawling. Through another glazed panel he spies a single room. That's more like it. They'll ask for one of those. He watches the couple inside. Middle Eastern or something: the woman is wearing one of those headscarves. Face rapt, cradling a wee scrap with a mass of black hair; her pinkie is crooked, stroking the baby's face. Her man is perched on the bed beside her, like he can't get close enough, gazing, fierce – but it is her, his wife, that he is drinking in. Craig presses his fingers against the glass, his cheek too. He wonders where they are from, what has brought them here.

They don't look like native Glaswegians. He doesny mean that bad-like, because his city is multicoloured and multi-layered and all the richer for it. But this pair are too . . . quiet? He knows that's stupid, because he is watching them through glass – and he canny hear them anyroad. Maybe he imagines it, but there is a subdued hunger to them, an edginess that whispers, *we do not fit*. It's in how the man holds himself alert; it's how the woman keeps checking and rechecking the empty air around them. They make him think of that lady he took to Portpatrick. She didn't fit either, shifting, restless, like she was haunting her own life. He's glad he told that reporter nothing. Where Kelly is from and where she was headed is her business. No one else's. And good on her for trying to help that man. He'd read the woman's article in the paper. Way too gushy and chirpy, considering it was about carnage, but the heart of it was that Kelly was a good person who'd done a good thing. So why couldn't people leave it at that?

He continues to watch the new family, but stepping back a bit, so he's not intruding. When he asked his boss for a break from long-haul trips, seeing if he could just do the local runs for a while, Gerry said it was fine. *Pity, mind. I thought you were gonny volunteer for the camps this year.*

I was. It's just . . .

On the far side of the glass, the man who has just become a father leans over, lifts his child aloft. The wean doesn't even have a babygro, just one of those hospital gowns with the flaps. The man carries him to the window, to show him Glasgow, and Craig feels a tightness either side of his nose. *Gie them peace, man.* He walks back to Room Two, where the NCT Early Birds are starting to file in. Maureen has her arms folded, crabbit.

'Where have you been?'

'Sorry. I was wandering. Wait.' He stops her from going into the room. 'See at work? You know how Gerry does that Caring City thing?'

'Aye. But I'm not wanting hand-me-downs from there, Craig. We'll manage, you know.'

'No, I know we will.' Of course they will; he is going to work every hour to feed and clothe his child, and of course he'll have to work long-haul. That's where the money is. 'But Gerry's been looking for help to take sleeping bags and shoes and that over to Europe. For the refugees.'

'And you want to do it?'

'I want *us* to do it. Before it's too late and we canny . . . Look. I promise you it's safe. Gerry doesny go to the big camps. It's a wee one in the north of France, and you don't even need to get out the rig if you don't want, but it means we'll get to help out a wee bit before . . . you know, and we can travel together in the rig, so you'll know what it's like for me. When I'm away.'

'Miss Carson?' A woman with dangly earrings sticks her head out of Room Two. 'If you and your partner would like to come through?'

'Two seconds,' says Craig. 'I'm no making sense, am I,

Mo? When I'm away, working. I want you to know what it's like for me. And I want—'

Maureen reaches up and pulls his lugs, forcing his face down to hers. 'I would love to go with you to France, Craig Wilson. But on one condition.'

'What?'

'Marry me.'

Chapter Eighteen

New, improved Kelly, wandering still in Wigtown. Why tarry, when there is an open road and the final stage of the pilgrimage to come? Aye, you might chop the hair off her, but Kelly remains an aimless waif. She returns to the bench under which she'd stashed her Next bag. The tweed coat is a bugger to carry, but it's too bulky to fold. She has rolled and stuffed it into submission, she has taken to wearing her second jumper around her waist and putting one of her old boots inside *Doctor Who* to make room, but no matter how she packs it, the fur collar protrudes above the line of the carrier bag's handles, making it impossible to get a decent grip. She looks like she's carrying some dead creature's tail – and the tail is trying to escape.

She really should set off now, get to Gatehouse and give that poor bride peace. It is the night before the lassie's wedding. Kelly sits on the bench. It's green-shaded, mossy, at the end of the tree-lined path along which they have just strolled. She and Collie have each had a gourmet hot dog, and explored Wigtown harbour, such as it is. There's no money left for a bus, even if she wanted one.

It will take her eight hours to walk to Gatehouse from here, she reckons. Eight solid hours. So she needs to shift her arse. They will have to walk through the dark as it is.

That might be nice, mind. Night-walking. Get there by dawn, yes, there will be something fitting in arriving with the rising of the sun. Gandalf and Shadowfax. The boat-shaped diamond circles her finger. Idly spinning the ring – she has been doing that a lot. She's used to the feel of it; its weight is comforting. The smooth birl of gold as the empty ring finger of her other hand nudges the mounted jewels, the slight tug of the marquise where its points catch her skin. The ring has become familiar.

Once she gets to Gatehouse, it's over. From there, Kelly has no purpose. Or every purpose you could think of. From Gatehouse, there will be no excuses. Only choices. In no particular order, she will have to decide: where she goes next; *Collie*; back to Glasgow; back to drink (as if that is a conscious choice. It is your medicine, your fucking design for life); *Collie*; if she really will go to Kirkcudbright and stand there, in that place. In the place that you came from. That's been waiting in your head for nearly thirty years and is the whole, entire reason that you travelled all the way here. No, it's not. Shut up, Kelly. *Collie*. What is best for Collie? To not go there and open up your head, your heart? Your hurt.

Your hurt, Kelly?

Collie licks her hand. Collie and Kelly, going somewhere new. Maybe they could stay in Wigtown, open a bookshop.

No. Too close, too close.

Too much.

She reads the Wigtown entry again, in her pilgrim pamphlet. It is the very last section. After today, even her pamphlet will become superfluous.

Home to Scotland's National Book Town, Wigtown is an unassuming market town with a chequered history. Since the Reformation of 1560, Protestantism reigned in

Scotland, with pilgrimages banned and the monasteries dissolved. However, Protestantism was also riven with division. In 1638, following the Union of the Crowns, the Stuart monarchs tried to impose episcopacy on Scotland. The country, being staunchly Presbyterian, believed in no head of the Church save Christ alone, and rebelled against the notion of the divine right of kings – with thousands of Scots signing the National Covenant in defiance. So began a fifty-year struggle for Scotland's spiritual soul – a dark period known as the Killing Times. Scots took to the hills to worship in open-air conventicles, and were hunted by the authorities. Punishments included fines, banishment, torture and execution. It was here in Wigtown that two such Covenanting women were sentenced to death. You can find their graves at the pretty seventeenth-century Wigtown Kirk. Then, from the church, take the path down towards the River Bladnoch to find the Martyrs' Stake and learn more.

Which is where they are. Behind Kelly's bench is a wooden board, erected *In Memoriam*. The martyrs' story is terrible, and sad. One of the girls they killed, here, in this douce wee toun, was only eighteen. Margaret Wilson. She died with Margaret McLachlan, an elderly widow. They drowned them. Staked old Margaret first, further into the channel, so that when the tide rose, young Margaret would see her friend drown before her eyes. The board Kelly is reading says they did this as a kindness, in order that the teenager would repent. Instead, she quoted the Bible. They've written her words on the board.

For thy sake we are killed all the day long; we are accounted as sheep for the slaughter.

Kelly cannot begin to fathom what she might do, or say, at the moment of her own death. She does not want to see

243

the place where the martyring happened, but she is here nonetheless. She feels she should. Godsake, Kelly, be brave enough to go and see it. They were brave enough to stand there. And they are the first women to be mentioned on the pilgrimage: here, right at the end.

She puts her *Doctor Who* bag under the bench too, beside her Next bag (a profusion of luggage – Kelly, you are quite literally a multi-bag lady now), then she and Collie take the wooden duckboard leading through the merse, into a scudding estuary sky. Tall green reeds and grasses ripple, pierced with bright flowers of purple-pink. Merse is the word she has always used; she doesn't know what else to call this flat, alluvial marshland that borders the river as it opens its jaws to the sea. The wooden slats of the duckboard echo in a drumbeat as Kelly walks above the marsh. She unlatches a little gate, onwards to a granite stake. It's not the original stake, of course; that would've been long-rotted, slimy wood. The Solway Firth salts the mud beneath her feet and smells of home.

The stake is taller than Kelly. She lays her hand on the surface of the granite. It is warm and rough. Surrounding her on every side is wide-open merse. Blue sea widens too, shimmering out on the horizon past the merse. The sky is huge. Domed. Utterly silent. No sound, save her and Collie – and yet there is. Here is echo and pause, as if you are held inside one vast breath. Kelly turns in a circle of blue and green, and Collie prances with her, in a 360-degree panorama of flat, green dancing sward and whispering breeze and distant hills and far blue sea. An unmalevolent place. The sea is the sea. It comes and it goes. They've rerouted the river since. It used to cut a deep channel here. The old town harbour was up by the bench under which Kelly's worldly goods are stashed.

She stops spinning. Dizzy. Which way did they face, those

women? Did the ropes bind them loose enough to choose? What rose at their backs – water or fear? Did they see the sea coming in or lift their eyes to the hills? Could they make out the spire of the churchyard in which their bones would be laid?

To make you wait. To feel the water rise like flame. She thinks of the cruelty of witch-burning. Scotland excelled in that too. She thinks of all the women who are shunned for being wrong. For being dangerous or having opinions. For dressing and living the way they choose.

Collie peers over the edge of the duckboard. Tail gyrating. Kelly breathes deep, clearing her lungs of the silt, gathering in more air than she expels. Good air. She doesn't feel scared at all. Here, this, is actually the most peaceful and beautiful of all the places she has been. It feels more holy too. Celebrating defiance, not obedience.

Suddenly Collie leaps overboard, barking and splashing into the merse. A duck flies into the sky, squawking – oh fuck, is that wee baby ducks?

'Collie! Bad dog! Get out of there, now!'

The dog flounders and flaps, grinning at her. All chuffed with himself. Wee bugger. 'Get out!' But it is not a grin, it is a rictus of fear. The mud here is bottomless, and shifting; he is getting tangled in the reeds.

'Och, you stupid dog. Here!' Kelly kneels on the duckboard, wrestling water and Collie, trying to grab him under the belly. Thick oozing sand and matted fur. She seizes onto any part of him she can, Collie yelping, her yanking, a squelching, plugging tug, and, presto – one uncorked dog.

'You.' She bundles him, filthy, onto her knee. 'You are a bloody menace, so you are.' Collie licks and wriggles as she scolds. Mud splatters, her second jumper absorbing the worst of it. Och, she might as well use it as a towel then. She rubs her stupid dog, can feel his frenzied heart beneath her fingers.

One hollow knock on wood. Kelly halts mid-rub. One sleekit, silt-slick engagement ring stuttering towards its freed—

Not so fast.

Kelly slams her hand on the ring a second before it teeters through the duckboard slats. The marquise diamond bites into her skin. Her fist closing. Rising.

And there it is, in the palm of her hand. Susan from Gatehouse's ring, pert and twinkling. There is a fleck of bloodspot where the sharp point has stabbed her; she'll need to warn Susan about that, when she hands it over. If . . .

When.

Because it's not your ring, Kelly. It never was. And it's time to take it home.

Unburdening. That is what a pilgrimage is for. First Kelly will divest herself of the bulky tweed coat. She has her smart (mud-and-dug-splattered) raincoat. It is light and serviceable. Wipe-clean too (she hopes). The tweed is too heavy – why worry about the weather to come? Back at the bench, she shakes the tweed coat from the Next bag, which means she can carry both boots in there together. Much comfier – plus the Tardis on the front of *Doctor Who* is no longer distorted. There is a wee coin pocket under the flap of the rucksack. Kelly zips the ring inside. Sprawled out, the coat looks like an empty body. She folds it neatly and sets it on the ground. It's there, if someone wants it.

Kelly and Collie return to the main street of Wigtown. The festival events are finished for the day, the kist of delicious foods all zipped up. Evening tingles. Heavy clouds compress the clammy day; this one is not filtering gently to dusk. There is a fat, electric tension, and people buzzing with it. Cafés and restaurants are full, laughter wafting through propped-open doors. Outside the pub, there are tables packed with drinkers, the smokers straddling benches

246

on the perimeter of the fun, beneath strings of coloured lights.

A bald man with a goatee beard stands half in, half out of the pub door. 'Did you guys hear that?' he calls to the folk outside.

'No!' they shout in unison.

'OK. Stop talking, everyone! For the benefit of the deafie smokers outside, that is your interval *over*. Literary Pub Quiz, Round Three. The Tricky One! Question One.'

It is a bookish fairground.

Kelly doesn't want to leave.

'Right,' says the quizmaster. 'Are you listening? Question One. What is the full title of Marjorie Pope's award-winning novel The *Something* Pillar.'

'Marjorie who?' says a young man at a table near where Kelly stands. Watching like a kid through a sweetshop window.

'The Australian, Marjorie *Pope*. She's dead now.'

'Oh yeah. Her.'

'Ironic!' says a woman in a knitted cloak.

'Wheesht! They'll hear you. Write it down!'

'Aye, but am I right? Is it not *The Ironic Pillar*?'

'No, no. It's something like that, though. Oh God, it's on the tip of my tongue.'

'That's what he said!' The young man winks lasciviously, then laughs at his own joke.

'Can we get a clue, please?'

'Can I have a pee, please, Bob?'

A gust of hilarity. The bald man has his head inside the doorway of the pub, and doesn't hear. Must be hard, to quizmaster a bunch of drunks in two different spaces. But smokers will be smokers. It's the one vice Kelly has barely enjoyed.

'What's that? A clue? Och, fine . . . Em. Sheep. Think of sheep. Big boy sheep.'

'Oh, that's helpful. Not. Hey.' Collie has wandered over to the young man, who is offering him a chip. 'Hello, you.'

'Ionic,' Kelly says.

'Sorry?'

She moves closer to the table. 'The answer. I think it's Ionic. There's three main orders of classical Greek columns: Doric, Ionic and Corinthian. Ionic is the one where the capital has scrolled volutes.' She corkscrews her finger in the air. 'Like rams' horns.'

'Oh. My. God.' The young man clamps his hands either side of his face, in an imitation of *The Scream*. 'You sit yourself right down here, my love. You are so in our team!'

'That's it!' says the woman in the cape. 'She's right. Quick, write it down.'

'OK, folks. Question Two . . .'

Kelly smiles vaguely at the group, clicks her fingers at Collie. 'C'mon, you. Leave these folk alone.'

'No way. I'm serious.' The young man pulls out a chair. 'This lot are sooo crap. Please! You've got to help us.'

'Och, I don't know that much about literature.'

'Well, you know more than Jonathon, and he's a bloody writer!'

A bray of heeing and hawing. Question Two is lost in the uproar. The next table along is glowering. 'Gonny keep it down?'

'Sorry. What was Two?'

'It's fine,' says the guy scribing. 'I got it.'

'Question Three.'

The young man pats the vacant seat. 'I'm Pete. I love your dog, by the way. Chip?'

There is a bowl of chips and mayonnaise, another of olives and sun-dried tomatoes. Collie is away being petted by various folk round the table. Kelly's breast swells at all the attention he's getting. Ten minutes. Where's the harm in that?

The quiz rolls on. Kelly gets a few right, but is no great asset to the group. It doesn't seem to matter; they have an easy, collegiate approach to answers – and food. Platters of tempura prawns arrive. Kelly declines.

'Go on,' says Pete. 'They're gorgeous. I ate my body weight in them last night.'

'It's a bit embarrassing,' Kelly whispers. 'I came out without my purse. I was just nipping round the block with the dog.' She kicks her bags beneath the table, hoping he won't notice.

'Oh God, don't be daft!' Pete makes one of the prawns dance over to her. Wiggles it. 'Eat me. Eeeat . . . Oh my God. Is that why you're on the tap water too?'

'No, no.' She takes the prawn as a distraction technique. 'I'm not really a drinker . . .'

'Miranda! Kelly here says she's not a drinker! Remember when you tried that?'

Miranda raises her fluted glass. 'Lasted one and a half days, darling. I am *so* much nicer when I have a glass of fizz.'

'She is, you know. Total bitch without. Oh, Kelly, sweetie. I feel so baaad. Let me get you something.'

'No, I'm fine. Honestly.'

Hanging-on-by-her-fingernails fine. But she was managing, until Pete drew attention to it. She was sitting here, on the periphery of a pub, surrounded by strangers who made her nervous, and glasses of fine liquid dark and brightest sparkles, the blood pounding in her ears, and she was, she is, fucking *doing* it. She has to do this. Forever and ever amen.

'A lemonade, then? Mm? Let me get you a lemonade, please? I honestly think we're going to win this year – and it'll be down to you and your Dorics!'

'Ionics.'

'Gin and tonics!' whoops Miranda. She has long gold hair,

which she tosses, frequently. Collie barks, wanting to be excited too. Kelly calls him over, before he starts to annoy folk. He is believing his own press, thinks he is a rock star. Nobody likes a pushy dog.

'Whatever. Oh, hello, poochy-poo. Oh, Collieflower. I soo want to put you in my pocket. Honestly, petal.' Pete pats her arm. 'I would pay to spend time with your puppy dog. Please let me get you a drink.'

'Lemonade then. Thanks.'

It takes two lemonades for them to finish the quiz, another while they add up the scores. It is Miranda who goes for the third drink; she sets it at Kelly's right hand as Kelly is listening to their scribe (Harry, an archaeologist who is also a poet) tell the story of how he once met Alasdair Gray in a lift. Collie is snoring under the table. Not looking, Kelly takes a glug. Not thinking, she takes another. Not knowing, she knocks it back.

Sheknowsyouknowyouknowsheknows.

Of course she does. A beautiful harshness at Kelly's throat. Heat filling up her fingertips. Vodka. She can feel her jugular vein clench. Unclench. Looks over at Miranda, who blows her a kiss. A scarlet kiss. 'Enjoy,' she mouths.

She already has.

A deep green evening unfurls. More drinks come, clear and innocent, drinks, real drinks, vodka- and gin-tinted drinks, drinks to tingle your tongue and lift your spirits.

Lift your spirits. Ha. *Cheers* and *sláinte*. A *bottoms-up* from Pete, another wink, Miranda winking, and sitting by Kelly and pressing on her knee. Kelly finds she doesn't mind; she is in love with these people, in love with the world. Their world, this world. A bottle is brought over, so now there is no concealing it, and how she likes to conceal it, Kelly, but there it is. Evidence. Sheens of coloured light play upon the surface of the glass; watch how it bobs and dips and pours. Spirits. Such spirits. Unleash the spirits! Glittering there, in the thickening dark with her pals, her bestest pals, Kelly holding court, remembering the good old days; she is *such* a pet, says a man sitting to her left – yes, you are, aren't you, Kelly – and it, this, is so easy, this slip from here to there. There is no road left to travel; there is barely a door, but there is an opening, inside her. No, it is a gnawing-through, it is a bursting, glorious hatching of the black seed at her core. Fuck, she is up for this, she is up for anything. The feeling rides like sex, how your body pulses, Kelly. Can you feel it happening? Unbidden pulsing, forbidden pleasures, why? Why is anything forbidden that feels this good? Another glass? Don't mind if you do, and now you are dancing, properly dancing in the street, and, man, you are invincible, wild.

You are gor-jus! Did you say that, or him? Her? Don't care, anyone will do; you will shag anyone, right here, in this doorway if they offer, because you are waking up inside, you, this, it's all amazing, and you've found the key, the magic keys, and you cannot, will not stop.

Slow down!

Fuck off! All the coloured lights are birling fast, and you will lash out at any obstacle to your pleasure, your need. You snatch up the bottle, it's fucking empty, fucksake, the loss is ravaging, like a series of heavy water balloons bursting, you are drenched, Kelly, you are *soaking*! Ha, oh no, God, it is raining! It is pouring, chucking it down. You find this hilarious, whooo, holding your face up as it pours. The sultry, growling sky has had enough, but you have not; no, no way, and at some point you move inside, not all your pals, but a select few. There is Kelly and Miranda linking arms, then another man joins you, not Pete, you're not sure who, but you are skipping like you're Dorothy and you're all away to Oz. Inside the pub, where it is

251

technicolour bright and you are drookit. The rain lashes on the window panes and the dancing continues indoors, raindrops falling as you gyrate and more bottles appear. Ha ha, look! Steam is rising from your wet clothes; you are literally steaming.

You can handle your drink, of course you can, Kelly. Kelly's dizzy from the dancing, that's all. Feels a wee bit sick. Fingers knotting, you are knotting your fingers through another human hand, and it is terribly funny as your fingers are so fat, there are twenty of them, you have twenty fingers at least, all tumbling over themselves to tie this knotting knot and you are going shh-shh, then Miranda has you by the arm, leading you to the ladies', and her fingers brush your nipple and lightning flashes in your groin. You lean forward to kiss her, and she kisses you in return. Then the man is before you, and he wants kissing too. It feels so natural to kiss another person's mouth. When did you last touch another person's mouth? You are stumbling into warmth and bubbles, Kelly. Memory working like a muscle, it is muscle memory, your ability to consume, and not pause to . . .

Not pause.

Oh, what a night. It is your best in centuries, for this is a GOOD tribe, you are cultured, clever Kelly, and there is a man's mouth on you, then a woman's. Your spine against a marble slab, a tap spurting at your back, laughing like a drain, oh no, that's you, Kelly. There is warm flesh under your hand; there is soft against your fingers, green bottles high above your face, and they are pouring, clapping as you catch the liquid in your lips, and you burst and you starburst, infinite. Time and distance blur. A ceiling burns with bonfires, bright stars with flaming tails, and the tiles are spinning with them.

Oh.

You are.
Oh.

Kelly wakes with the lights going out. *SNAP*. Alone. Shivering cold, why is her . . . Where? Touching herself, her breast. Exposed. She has the blinding imprint of a flash behind her eyes. Sits up, pain thumping in her ears. There is a mineral, bleachy odour. Eyes focusing on unfamiliar shapes. Looming long doors . . . she can see a row of cubicles. A line of shadowy ceramic sinks above her. She follows the grey pipes, using them for leverage, hand over fist, on her knees, to the wall, feeling her way up through the roaring sea in her skull, head tender with noise. A blade of lightning crackles. High window, blazing white. A storm howls beyond the window.

Kelly is alone in the toilet of the pub. Her brain rushes, full tilt like a train. She cannot think above the sound of thunder and the greasy wash of shame. She heaves, and heaves again. Drags herself to the bowl of a toilet, retching, retching.

Wretched. She leans her head on the coolness of the pan. Smells the stink of other people's urine; she can taste it on her tongue.

Head dead. She is utterly empty.

Another heave. Rolling, pivoting from hip to knee, head deeper in; she's sweating now, sweating and shivering, her cracked lips sting with sweat and bile. A second streak of lightning tears the sky outside. It brings a split-second illumination, which is too bright. Too harsh.

Weepy, she curls back on the floor. Fastens up her trousers, which are undone.

Kelly, lying on the toilet floor. Fumbling through nocturnal memories, a flickering movie reel of jump cuts. Blackouts. Leaps of shock as the pictures focus. Gouts of cringing and

253

dull thudding dread that she is here again. She has come all this way and she is here again.

Then there is one stark, specific snapshot of her, outside. Bright as lightning. Tying a knot in Collie's lead.

She jumps to her feet. Tugs the toilet door, out into the unlit, deathly pub. She rattles on the outer doors, which swung so cheerfully to let her in, and they do not fucking budge.

'Collie!' she shouts, trying to make a gap in ungiving wood. 'Collie, I'm here, baby. I'm right here.'

Outside, the thunderstorm rages. She batters her fists on the door, but no one comes. Searching for a light switch, a way to . . . Here. Metal bar. A fire escape. She wrenches the lever and a siren wails, but she is out, out to where the rain is shining the street, beating in rods that bounce on impact. Round to the front, she is sprinting on the slippery pavement; tables, benches, they wait like wooden sentinels; she tied her baby to the leg of a table. Didn't she? Didn't she? Drifts of rain shudder. Strobe-lit sky ignites the road, walls flare in livid monochrome. Racing depths of barely there, fucking *think*, Kelly, but here are her bags: the Next carrier bag and *Doctor Who*, all tucked up under the table, this is where she was, it was. Where she left him.

'Collie!' she yells, fighting the pub's alarm bell, the erupting, roaring sky. 'Collieflower!'

Vicious fork of lightning snakes in a whip-crack tail, blasts the table legs in silver. Collie's lead and Collie's collar, coiled there. Holding nothing but a flattened patch of fear.

Where would he go, where would he go, her wee boy terrified of the storm? She is running and darting, overturning chairs, smothered with the panic of what she has done. How can your body bear you, Kelly? You are a filthy piece of shite, YOU ARE.

'Collie! Collie Dog!'

She runs to the crossroads. Stops outside the County Buildings. Forcing her breathing to be quiet.

Lights have come on at the pub. The alarm stops. Would he run into trees? What if someone has taken him? Christ, what if Major Tom—

Hush. Shut your stupid brain up and think. If you can only do one thing for him, Kelly, then it is to find him. You left him, alone, in a fucking storm.

'Here!' A figure is shouting at her. Waving arms. It is the bald quizmaster, getting closer. 'Did you see anyone at the pub? The alarm's off, but I can't— Oh.' He stops walking. 'It's you.'

Which of the many *you*s is he disgusted with? Doesny matter one snivelling jot.

'Have you seen my dog?' she says. 'I've lost my dog.'

'Was that wee soul *yours*? Jesus, that makes sense.' The man shakes his head. 'Unbelievable. A wee collie pup?'

'Yes!' she cries, the rain lashing down her face. 'Have you seen him? Where is he?'

'Poor thing was running up and down here, demented. While you were . . . People like you shouldn't have pets.'

'I know, I know. But where is he? Please, do you know where he is?' Her hands are pawing on his jacket, pulling the fabric in and out.

'I don't want anything to do with you.' He detaches her fingers from him. 'Are those your bags under my table?'

'Yes.'

'Well, go and get them. Then get the hell out my sight. I've called the police, you know. If it was you set off my alarm, they'll know.'

He strides away from her back to his pub, and she runs after. 'What about my dog? What the fuck have you done with my dog?'

255

'I haven't touched your bloody dog,' he shouts into her face. 'Here.' Thrusting her bags at her.

'Please. Help me. Why are you so angry? What did I do to you?'

'What did you do? You urinated on my bar. On the counter of my fucking bar.'

Hazy, but she remembers now. A literal pissing contest, her saying girls could pee upright as good as men, that she had developed a technique called fast and dirty pissing, it was hilarious, all her new pals thought she was hysterical, and she is, Kelly is hysterical. 'Please,' she begs. 'Please, please.' She reaches out but does not touch him. 'Did someone take my dog?'

'No. We tried, but nobody could catch hold of him. He was too scared.'

One final blow of lightning. It fractures black sky like shattered pearls. Kelly blinks. Defeated. Staring at the sodden ground. The man's feet move away.

'He ran up there,' she hears him say. She looks up. He's pointing past the County Buildings. 'Up by the side of the church.'

'Thank you.'

Kelly gathers her bags and runs. Her saturated clothes cling to her body. The space between her legs hurts. Methodically she searches the churchyard. There are gravestones and trees and tombs; all the flat, table-like ones, she checks them first, working in circles as the storm churns away. Collie is not there. The two Margarets are, though, lying under a slab of white. The Martyrs' Grave. She leans over the fencing that surrounds their tomb, and yes, it is so she can check underneath, but it's also so she can touch the stone. Daft, it is as purposeless as those folk who came to stand at the place where the bus crashed and light their candles. But maybe you are simply saying, 'There you are. And here I am. Noticing.'

Out of the churchyard she goes. Tiny grains of blue and yellow stars pinpoint the ragged sky. The thunder is more distant. The rain is drifting: less urgent, a fine, cooling drizzle. Think, Kelly. Retrace your steps. She shifts the weight of the Next bag into her other hand. Would Collie try to find you? Where would he go?

He would. He might. Dogs follow scent.

Oh, Kelly. He will be long gone.

She crosses the road diagonally, down towards the site of the old harbour. In through the trees, along the track towards the bench beside the path to the Martyrs' Stake. If she could pray, she is praying, chanting out *please. Please, please*, her nails piercing the palms of her hands, *oh pleaseplsplzz* until it ceases to make sense and is just noise. There is the squat wood bench they sat on earlier. There is the bundle at its side, where she left her coat, a dark, shape-shifting shape, soft bundle and the violet glow of after-storm. A splash of brightness, of mobile, whimpering brightness.

Collie is buried, burrowed there, half inside her coat.

His faith is more than you deserve.

*

You'd think the glove factory would be long gone, but, like you, it has gone from strength to strength. In times of austerity, it seems luxury is precious. A wee treat to keep life sweet. And you, you have been promoted. You are in the design team. Yes, the girl who would have built cities now draws gloves. You know your fourchettes from your quirks and tranks. These are the component parts of finger-making, but you can make them sound saucy as you chat about your job with friends. Kelly, you have friends. You and Garry have joined a badminton club and there are drinks after, but you always say you'll drive.

You can drive a car. You have been eight years, three weeks and four days sober. Enough was enough, Garry told you, when it stopped being fun for him and you were no longer dark but destructive. Pockmarked, balding Garry, whom you push and push to see how far he lets you go. When you hit him, he cries. And you are sorry, always sorry, after, for he is a gentle man.

When you are alive with the drink, you despise him. Coursing with liquid glitter, you want to spill the real you; it thrills you that you could.

Do you know what I have done? I am Kelly, destroyer of worlds.

Fear stays your tongue. That grain of self-preservation round which you thought you could spin a pearl.

So you try. You dutifully go to where he leads you. A cold church hall. A circle of sorry. My name is Kelly and I'm an—

Steps and a sponsor for forever saying no. You can do this, you did, you do. Every day you do. You do not drink. You do not speak, not about you, about who you truly are. Not about anything important. And so you have a life. You have reasons to be cheerful. This life is stable. This life is flat.

You think Garry feels the flatness too.

—Let's have a baby, *he says, all chuffed that he has rescued you. And puzzled that your light has snuffed out.*

If you were not there. It would not have happened.

Oh, Mandz, my Mandz.

You do not.

Deserve.

He thinks a baby will be motivation, give you purpose. It doesny work.

Several years pass of doesny working and Garry wanting fertility tests and you wanting left alone and

258

the bottles whispering and your head down, making
gloves. And him all cock-a-hoop because they've
changed the rules and you can get one free cycle now,
on the NHS.

At your age.

Your penance never stops.

Needles and pins and tubes and latex bloody gloves,
you are intimate with latex bloody gloves, inside and out.

Ah.

Still. You are fine. You have a quiet and decent life.

Garry is dull.

Garry is harmless.

Turns out Garry is shagging the new girl at work.

You have seen Garry's paramour. Ellen. She's been
brought into the factory to do marketing and sales. And
she sells herself well: red hair, high heels, short skirt, the
clichéd works. You had a fleeting thought of Skanky Diva.
Maybe it was instinct. Years of waste, that's all you can
think about. For you, for Garry.

For Mandz.

You don't talk to her any more, in your head. It helped
for a wee while, and then it hurt too much again.

But Garry? That you let it go this far?

All those years of waste.

Was your childlessness caused by the sluggish, pickled
fat in your veins? Did your drinking bring the fibres that
bloomed and skeined in your wasted womb? Or was it
simply serendipity? You and Garry were never real. A
child would not have cemented you.

Even so, it was your life. It is the life you have made,
and now Garry is taking it away. Stone-cold sober, you
make a scene. At work, when you find them talking
quietly. You have seen her, seen them. You've suspected for
a while, have observed them like this before. Deep in

*conversation. Jumping apart when you come in. But
today? Today?*

*She is all over him like a rash, and his arm too, today
Garry's arm is all over her. Draped on Ellen's shoulders,
their heads pressed. When you enter Ellen's office, they do
not jump apart. It's like have they planned it. As if they
want you to know their truth. That his patience has
stretched and broken. He has chosen her, and she's chosen
him: the PR girl and your balding, pockmarked Garry.*

Christ.

All that waste.

—You shouldn't have lashed out like that, Kelly. *The
manager of the glove factory is disappointed in you. He
takes you to his office. Uncontrollable it is. Your sobbing.
You don't even know what you're crying for. The manager
is the son of the man who hired you, all those years ago.
Who was generous enough to open his door to miscreants.*

—We have made allowances, Kelly. We know how
hard—

*You sob harder, until the manager passes you a hankie.
Garry and Ellen are huddled outside; she is having her
nose attended to. There is talk of the police.*

—My dad always said folk need a second chance.

All those years, this boy has known your secret.

—We think it's best that you go . . .

Home.

Go to hell.

Go to jail.

*Your fate is in their hands. The manager doesn't want a
fuss. Bad for business, that. They are a luxury brand.*

The police don't come.

*Garry is a gentle man. He talks her down, the PR
bitch. It isn't even broken.*

Nose.

260

Trust.

Love.

They put you in a taxi. You get out at the shops near your house. You want to walk. You want to rewind the day. This life. What it can do.

Hand.

Neck.

Heart.

Your other half.

You are so good at breaking things.

You turn the key in your lock. You have never forgotten the privilege of this – this brief and elegant click. Gold teeth that fit, and tumble barriers. A key is a miracle, its teeth so minuscule yet specific. A key is a solution.

Garry is a gentle man. He says he will move out, so you can stay.

But there is no solution, Kelly. Not to you.

Only this.

You pick the bag up and put it down. You can do this. Delicate paper.

Brown paper bag, from the shop near your house.

Crinkle. Can you hear that crinkle?

Bottle-shaped inside.

You take your head and you hold it, hard. Sit and let time engulf you. Great drifts of time pass like shadow, leap and jolt when you are aware, then, whoosh, a whole evening has escaped you. You are sitting in the dark. Only the street light is lit. The brown paper bag is on the table.

You've had a good run, Kelly.

Garry is gone. That chance is gone.

Only.

This.

You crack the silver seal. Twist it, so metal grates deliciously on metal, you, unclipping oblivion, the genie out, oh, Christ, you quiver and breathe, breathe the crisp astringency of gin, fresh green like a snapped stalk of lettuce or cucumber, your sucking breath clean inside you, oh, Christ you can feel it pour, you want to hurt Garry, this will hurt him most and fill you up. Fill me beautiful again. *Clear and good, you savour what was lost, you slide, present and vital, to where it takes you past the shame.*

Thirst that cannot be slaked. Tears that cannot be dammed.

Only.

Ever.

This.

You realise you are not weeping for Garry at all.

You are weeping for the children you will never have. You are weeping for Mandz. For your dad, for your wee mum.

You are weeping because you know, with the cold certainty of the tide closing over your head, that you have lost your job and you are going to lose your home.

Chapter Nineteen

From the flat in Grovepark Street, Jennifer Patience has worked backwards. Grovepark Street in Maryhill is Kelly's last registered address with a GP. It is the last address on her credit score and her social security records. Daresay some young buck with clever fingers could have discovered all this online. Hey, perhaps hacks will never die after all. They will retain the name, and the honour, of Jennifer's once-proud profession, simply by using their pale eyes and giant digits to hack into all the information a journalist would ever need. No requirement for human contact what-soever. But Jennifer retains, and relishes, her contacts. Cultivates them as precious plants. Real contacts. The beat cop who used to come in for the early edition and is now a chief inspector. The civilian cleaner in another police station, who used to work for Jennifer's auntie, and has quick eyes for reading noticeboards and open files. The medical student her sister dated who is now something in the health board. The home help Jennifer did a feature on when she saved an old lady from choking, who's also a union rep – she thinks you're the bee's knees, and trustworthy with it. Then there's the piece she did on sex offenders, and the criminal justice social worker at Barlinnie she interviewed for that. Nice guy, so you've kept in touch. Lots of rich pickings there. The chairman of the allotment association. The knackered, frustrated sister in A&E. Shopkeepers, teachers, ministers and priests. Travel on public transport. Visit your local. Listen to gossip, conferences, committee meetings. Get involved. Get chatting to the woman on the PTA, and you might discover she's a justice of the peace too. Then there's the disgruntled council officer who will spill anything for a pint and a sympathetic ear – though it's getting much harder to get any alcoholic purchases through on expenses now. God, how Jennifer misses the Press Bar. Yearns to return to that easy-drinking culture, those inky-fingered vultures, pissed as farts, yet always meeting deadlines. They were her people, not these shiny, non-stop-posting, values-shifting, vapid, grammarless . . .

But she digresses. Deadlines, Jennifer. Get to the point.

The point is, she's still not sure. She would have liked a little longer, but the editor's getting bored. Her story needs new juice; it needs to stop being speculative and broad, and start honing in. So she's squeezed a bit harder, and my, there is juice aplenty. Jennifer has even broken out a new notebook to catch all these delicious drops.

She parks her car beside an unassuming building on an unassuming street. Modern yellow-brick houses, some new-build flats with brightly coloured panels on the gable ends. Across the street are older tenements, with shops and lawyers' offices, estate agents and a dry cleaner's along the bottom. There is a first-floor tenement window above the dry cleaner's, a bay. Tucked discreetly in the corner of the window is a sign which says *Addiction Services* in green block type. An NHS logo and a Glasgow City Council logo sit either side. This is the place.

Grovepark Street is many years ago, but it's a fixed point on the map. From there, Jennifer can journey forwards or back. She has been busy and done both. Kelly McCallum is way more interesting than you might think. This clinic above the dry cleaner's seems to be another, if not fixed, point, certainly a recurring one. Jennifer imagines she'll get short shrift here – social workery/therapy types are always the worst for having ethics. But it's worth a try. Even a quote from an unnamed source; there are ways of wording these tricky hiccups, ways you can polish and elide to say so much with so little actual fact. Ideally, she'd like to get the starkness of the contrast, a quote to flank the rise and fall of it, for she's already got a great quote from a former friend at university. Uni-bloody-versity, dear reader!!! Yup. Move backwards, check Glasgow school records – nada. Check Glasgow college records – nada. But check Glasgow Uni records as a total long shot – because you have a friend in their press office who used to be a trainee at the paper, so why not try, God knows you're a trier, Jennifer, and God loves a trier – and voilà, there are several Kellys. Several fewer Kelly McCallums. Knowing her age (thank you, police records and court records and all those good people who keep meticulous records), you can narrow down the years when she would have been seventeen, eighteen, nineteen – and there she is. Kelly McCallum. B.Eng. Civil Engineering with Architecture.

Smart cookie was Kelly McCallum. Once upon a time.

But not as smart as Jennifer.

Jennifer checks her notebook. Kirsty James (51) of AlteredImages Architectural Practice said: 'Well, I didn't really know her that well, she was on our course, but she never said much in class. Looked like a goth, you know? Black eyes, spiky hair. One of those "tortured souls", you know? Bit of a pisshead. She sort of dropped out around second or third year, I think. I heard someone in her family had maybe died? But I'm really not sure. You'd be better off trying to find someone who was pals with her.'

Underneath, Jennifer has written: *Always dressed in black, Kelly cut an imposing if distant figure around Glasgow University. 'Kelly was a tortured soul,' said her friend Kirsty James, a successful architect now living in Lenzie. The pair lost touch after second year, when Kelly mysteriously disappeared.*

Pivot forward into Kelly's future, and there is indeed death. And more records. Indeed, there is one tremendous, juice-pouring-down-your-chin record that Jennifer will keep safe in her notebook until the time is right. Because this fact, if released, might scare the horses, and will certainly cause their readership to lose all sympathy for the chase. Jennifer has to weigh this fact carefully. One: she has no personal animosity towards the Homeless Heroine. Two: it will kill all the enthusiasm for this hopeful, happy story she's been crafting, will turn it into something warped and dark. Which could be brilliant, but not yet, not yet. She wants, desperately, to talk to Kelly first, to bring her out into the open, not send her deeper underground. But three: any other decent journo will be able to find exactly the same juicy record Jennifer has found, if they bother to look. And there is no way they are stealing a march on Jennifer Patience.

So. What to do, what to do? She needs a good quote from the clinic, and then there is one other visit she might have to make. She'd really rather not: she'll have to take the day off for a start, and there's no way the editor will sanction a trip that far south (but fuck it, she'll still claim the mileage). Anyhoo. That's for later. The final instalment. Maybe a showdown? Some good old-fashioned doorstepping. Jesus, after her second day in the job, when her boss made her chap the door of a grieving mother so she could get an old school photo of her just-slain son, Jennifer Patience can doorstep anyone.

She goes into the close next to the dry cleaner's. Takes

the one flight of stairs up. Jennifer never fails to be impressed by the beauty of Glasgow's tenements. The polished mahogany banisters, the gleaming glassy-green tiles. Panes of stained glass bathing the landings with underwater light. Heavy folding storm doors like these. Great, they're open. Lights on inside. She rings the bell for Addiction Services. Is buzzed in.

'Hi,' she says to the young receptionist. 'I'm here to see Shirley James?' She makes it sound slightly like a question, a little uptick of inflection that has served her well. It sounds authoritative, but unthreatening. It sounds like the sort of person you'd automatically want to help.

'Do you have an appointment?' asks the receptionist.

Jennifer flashes her teeth and her NUJ ID. 'It's about a personal matter.'

Another useful phrase. This one has currency. A wee bit scandal, wee bit urgency required? What secrets lie in Shirley's cupboard? *Wouldn't you like to know, Miss Receptionist?*

'Um.' The girl half stands up. 'I'll see if she's available.' Looks at her phone. Thinks better of it and gets properly to her feet. Unbidden, Jennifer follows her through to the inner sanctum. The receptionist is unaware, until she taps the open door of the first office to her right, begins to say, 'There's someone here to . . .' and Jennifer takes over, smooth as smooth.

'Ms James? Jennifer Patience. I'm so sorry to disturb you, but I just need a few minutes. It's about one of your clients.' She lowers her voice, lowers her head a tiny bit towards the receptionist, as if it's this young girl who's the interloper, not Jennifer.

A woman with thick blonde-grey hair looks up. Her fringe falls over her eyes in a manner Jennifer would find annoying. She wears corduroy dungarees over a rust-coloured T-shirt, like an out-of-time kids' TV presenter. On the wall behind her are abstract paintings, blocks of blue and green much like the gable ends of the flats Jennifer passed outside.

'It's fine, Tanya.' The woman – Shirley – signals for the girl to go.

'She says she's a journalist. Will I phone—'

'No. I said it's fine.' Shirley stands up. 'Come in,' she says to Jennifer. 'Take a seat.' She walks them over to a lime-green couch. 'Sit.'

Jennifer obliges. Does Shirley think she's going to therapise her?

Shirley sits in the chair opposite. 'So, tell me. Who's the client, and what do you want?'

'Kelly McCallum? I'm just trying to get a handle on her.'

Shirley nods.

'So you know her? She is your client?'

'I have many clients, Ms Patience. And all of them confidential.'

'I do appreciate that.' Jennifer lays her Dictaphone on the coffee table between them. 'It's just, I'm worried Kelly might be in trouble. I mean, you'll have read all about that terrible bus crash in town.'

'I have.' Shirley's legs are crossed. The toe of her burgundy Doc Marten is tick-tick-ticking furiously away.

'And you've maybe read my paper's coverage? The *Journal*? Seen our little appeal to try and help Kelly get . . . well, get the respect she's due, I guess?' *Inspired, Jennifer.* 'I thought, maybe between us . . . Oh, do you mind?' She smiles as she says this, her finger poised above the Dictaphone's red record button. She always thinks it looks more professional than just recording on her phone.

'I do,' says Shirley.

'Oh. Sure, fine.' Jennifer indicates her notebook. 'OK if I take notes, then?'

'I'd prefer not.'

'Fair enough.' They are sword-fighting now. Jennifer will just cut to the chase. 'Look. I'm hoping that, with your help, we could let the public know what Kelly's life has really been like. Maybe help her turn it around too? But first, I want to build as rounded a picture of her as possible. I realise she's had some . . . difficulties in her past, but you know, that makes what she did all the more remarkable. To run to the rescue of a complete stranger like that.'

Shirley raises one eyebrow, or at least Jennifer thinks she does. It's hard to tell through the clotted fringe. 'You think so?'

'Don't you?'

Shirley smiles, clasps her hands on her knees. But the toecap of her boot is still making minuscule, steady jerks. There is a strong smell of artificial air freshener in the office, one of those plug-in things. It's giving Jennifer another of her headaches.

'Look. We're both busy women. Can I just be straightforward here? Would you like to talk to me about Kelly or not?'

The boot stops jerking. 'Not.'

'So why did you agree to see me?'

'I was interested.' Shirley uncrosses her legs, as if she's finally ready for a chat. 'I'm endlessly interested in people.'

'So am I.' Here's one final chance to bond.

'I'm sure you are. Yours would be a hard job to do if you weren't.'

'Well . . . yes.'

'But what is it about them that interests you? People?'

'I'm sorry?'

Shirley does not repeat herself. She simply smiles again. A gentle, measured smile that is really quite frustrating. She is like a cat. An ungroomed Persian cat. Or maybe a Shetland pony, with all that hair going on.

Jennifer shrugs. 'I like to know their stories. You?' *Straight back at ya, pussycat.*

'I suppose I'm interested in their value, their inherent worth.' Shirley moves forward in her seat. 'In our ability to change and grow and heal. Especially when we're stripped of our pretensions. Oh,' she raises her hand as Jennifer goes to speak, 'don't misunderstand me. I don't mean "brought down to size", not in the tabloid sense. I mean when life pulls the carpet from under us. We like to think there's sense and order in the world – a formula, almost, for how to get by. But you and I both know that's . . .' She scratches her head, lifting and dropping a hank of hair. Jennifer is startled to see a swallow tattooed on her neck. 'Ach . . . well, it's absurd, isn't it? The people who visit me here: Shirley pauses. 'I'm not in the business of "transforming" people, Ms Patience. The people who visit me here: the energy you and I might expend on pushing out into the world, into our plans and hopes and possibilities, they direct inside. Into hurt and anxiety and worry and pain. Into ways of blocking the corrosion it causes. I guess my job is to redirect that energy outwards.'

She stands up. Takes Jennifer by surprise. 'I think what I'm really interested in is our ability to contain multiple versions of ourselves.' She extends her hand. 'Goodbye, Ms Patience. I'm sure you'll do the right thing.'

Blindsided, Jennifer finds herself being ushered from the office, out the door and onto the stairs before she has even gathered her thoughts. She gives her Puffa jacket a vicious zipping-up. Unsure if she is discombobulated or impressed. Either way, it doesn't matter. She takes a moment, leaning against the cool green tiles of the close. All that talk of energies has left her very tired. And not a little confused. But Jennifer Patience has a story to file, and there's nothing else for it. Her mate at Glasgow Uni was very generous with her help. As well as Kelly's brief student history, Jennifer is now in possession of her old family address. A small town on the Solway Firth, famous for its sea-lit open skies, and haunt of the Glasgow Boys. The Artists' Toun – a pretty wee place she's always meant to visit but never has. It seems all roads must lead to Galloway after all.

Chapter Twenty

Kelly keeps touching her dog. They plod, chins tucked against the sheeting rain, Kelly continually reaching down to fondle Collie's ears, or stroke his spine. And he lets her. She walks slightly hunched, Quasimodo-style, her hand trailing as if she's on a boat and the air around Collie is sea. Dipping in, fingers splayed, until she finds his fur again. And again. For the first few hundred metres, she carried him in her arms, but Collie is a ton weight, and wriggly with it. They were both glad when she put him down.

He was quivering when she found him. Quivering and pressing and driving his head into her breast, like he was the one who had done something wrong.

Animals humble you with their goodness.

Kelly does not know how to apologise. She has never been able to find the right words, words that are sufficient to articulate the mess of pain and contrition. Never. For how would 'sorry' contain her deep and shining regret, the wish to turn back time, the futility and self-pity, the furious rage and unbearable

unbearable

sadness.

She has carried her loss for almost thirty years.

Oh, Kelly, the selfishness of you, feeling a loss when it's not your loss to bear.

Collie doesn't understand any of this, and even if she did discover a casket of gleaming, jewelled words with which she could craft the perfect sentence, he wouldn't care.

What he cares about is Kelly's lips mouthing sounds over the soft wisps of his head, or her heartbeat matching his as they embrace. Dogs do embrace, you know. Collie put his paws on her shoulder as she knelt there, by the bench, his head under the crook of her chin. Later, when the pressing-in was too intense to sustain, he had placed his paw in her hand. His vulnerable, unsheathed paw, curled lightly into hers.

The stars come out overhead as they tramp the long road from Wigtown in the night. The rain has abated, revealing these fabulous spirals of dense, diamond-studded sky. Kelly stares up, breathing in moist countryside and the swirling air as it recedes into endless whorls. There are no street lights here to blot the view. The Milky Way ripples, soundless, unbroken.

You could fold this silence like cloth. There is a gentle plop, just a pebble of noise. It's Collie, squatting on the road. She watches him strain. It is not a pleasant sight. Kelly has been feeding him crap, so no wonder. She looks back down the road they have travelled. Pure blue starlight, running over fields and trees, over a still pool of water, a lonely farmhouse. Deep silence. It is lovely.

She kicks the jobby with the side of her cowboy boot, into the verge. She should probably change back into her old, clumpy ones, which do not click so satisfyingly but are sensible for the long walk still to come. And her teeth, she needs to brush her teeth. The taste in her mouth is vile. She will not think, will never think, of that pub and those people again.

You slipped, that's all. Sometimes Shirehorse Shirley will say the nicest things. Maybe she'll say that, if Kelly goes back.

If. Oh, the going back. That is a whole other journey.

The silence rises from the land like smoke. There is a purity about it, something rare and unintelligible, which you never get in town. As if it is speaking to you, murmuring as it moves through those still pools and sleeping trees. So incredibly peaceful.

Constant exposure to sound. What does that do to folk? Kelly recalls when she first came to Glasgow. Could not sleep for weeks. There was nowhere she could go where there wasn't noise and intrusion. Aye, the countryside is *so bloody boring*, she'd say, keen to forget that there were moments of actual joy. You and Mandz on the beach, working in silence to build castles from fine-grained sand.

You have to be careful in the silence, though. If you let it seep beyond its limits you start to lose it. You lose stuff you can't get back and then the whole world is beyond your limits and it gets confusing. Scary till it hurts.

Kelly, Kelly. When did your life conspire against you? When did you start to pretend that drinking hair lacquer mixed with milk was fine?

She and Collie continue, walking north towards Newton Stewart, which is not a pilgrim place at all. The clue is in the name. New Town. To her right, the horizon begins to catch fire. They stop to watch a family of hares play in a field, lit golden by the dawn. Hares are magical. Collie thinks they are delicious. She has to shove his haunches to the ground.

'I said sit, you.'

He refuses, legs four-square, his white-bibbed chest cresting with desire. Luckily, a gate and hedge protects Mr and Mrs Hare and their weans. The bright air grows sharp, freshly scoured from the night before. *Please don't rain on her wedding day.* Kelly wants to promise that she will never drink again. Her rusty knees grind on, her indefatigable dog trots and sniffs and weaves a protective helix between her steps. Around her, old pilgrim routes converge. Behind is the Isle of Man and Ireland. Ahead are glowing emerald hills and the River Cree. And the A75, which they'll have to walk alongside.

She's left Collie's lead in Wigtown. Tied to the table where he slipped his collar.

'I'm sorry, boy.'

There. She's said it. Now say it again.

'I'm sorry, Mandz. I'm so sorry.'

Say it to her face.

Kelly never meant to hurt her. Not like that. She dreams, often, that she is falling. That it is her, not Mandz, who is tumbling backwards and away. That it is her who is gripped by the lurch of horror in her stomach, just at the instant when ground becomes air and you realise there is no more purchase for your flailing feet, simply the weightless, dreadful plunge to come.

A couple of hours' brisk and mindless walking, and Kelly and Collie are at the roundabout on the A75.

'Most haunted road in Scotland, Collie. That's what they say.' If it is, and 'they' are right, Kelly's never noticed. Plenty of times in her youth she has walked along this road, seen nothing that would give you cause for the heebie-jeebies. Fair enough, most times she'll have been guttered and weaving as she walked, but still. Although it's true she might just have missed them, for they are not dramatic ghosts. No headless horsemen or wailing banshees harbingering death. Nope, the most frequent sighting is of an old man at a bus stop. 'Woooo!' she says to Collie, who is cocking his leg against a signpost.

Newton Stewart, straight ahead, the sign informs them. Gatehouse, right, 17 miles.

'Last leg, boy. You up for this?'

He pants at her. Grinning.

It's early morning. Weddings don't happen before lunch, do they? Wedding breakfasts – that's an English thing. Scots pace themselves, for the toasts and ceilidh and buffet after the sit-down meal to come. Then there'll be some sobbing in the ladies' bogs, a small fight and a rousing medley of Proclaimers songs to finish. She and Garry went to a few weddings – his sister, folk from work. Kelly the designated driver. She was everyone's pal then.

I'd love to meet your folks one day, Garry used to say.

I have no contact with my family.

The A75 awaits. They cross at the narrowest point, once they're past the roundabout. Her hand hovers above the scruff of Collie's neck, but he's very good, just trots across. You're supposed to face oncoming traffic, but the verge is wider here on the other side, and they would have to have crossed at some point anyway, to reach Gatehouse. Kelly can just about recall the time before the A75 was built, when the road ran through Castle Douglas and Gatehouse and Creetown instead of bypassing them like it does now. Journeys took forever, and there was always someone being sick from the twisty roads. Now you get a straight run through, from Dumfries down to Stranraer. As main roads go, though, it's still pretty rubbish. One carriageway either side, so tough shit if you've a ferry to catch and you're stuck behind a tractor. That's when the arseholes rev and overtake, misjudging space and distance and time. Maybe that's why the A75 is the most haunted road in Scotland. Now that would make sense. She can think of several cautionary tales told to kids about to take their driving tests. Some that she properly remembers too. Billy the fisherman, for one. Kissed the world goodbye on his twenty-first birthday, racing a soft-top round a blind corner.

Why is Kelly coming back here? You don't disturb ghosts.

Obedient as Collie is, she worries about the road. It's quiet for miles, and then a lorry will roar past. You can hear the traffic coming way off, but even though you step high up on the verge, the gust of a passing artic near knocks you over. And it's a stop-start way to walk. Slow and hesitant when she finds she wants to stride. There is a magnetic pull along this last, short way that will not be resisted.

A car horn beeps at them – no, a van, a wee white one, the driver shaking his fist.

'Fuck you!' she shouts. 'It's a public road. Build us a bloody pavement then!'

What a state she must look. Hung-over Kelly no longer feels nauseous, but the thirst on her is terrible. At least the rain has washed most of the puke from her face and clothes. Up ahead, the white van slows. Stops at an inshot, to turn into Creetown Caravan Park (mini golf included). It has a sign as big as a motorway gantry, and multicoloured bunting. Kelly and Collie march on. When they reach the entrance to the caravan park, the transit is coming back out. Close-up, she can see it's modelled on a black-and-white cow, with ink-blot splodges and the invitation to *Try Our Free Range Milk. Udderly Delicious!* A bright pink udder is painted underneath, in case you didny get the joke. The driver opens the window, and Kelly tenses herself for an onslaught.

'Hiya.' The driver is a teenage girl. 'Did you not see me waving at you?'

'Um . . . no. Not really.'

'I was seeing if you wanted a lift? I've only one more stop after this one.'

'Oh. Yes, sure. That's very kind.'

Folk don't do this in the city. She'd forgotten about the

common code of stopping for a neighbour you do not know. A small, consistent kindness that keeps the countryside moving.

'Climb aboard then.'

Kelly goes round the other side, lifts Collie into the cabin. 'Can you take him? Ta.' Collie's feet catch her skin as he flails.

'Hello, gorgeous. Black and white – you match my van, mister dog. What's your name?'

'That's Collie.' Kelly hauls herself in, flumps down in the seat. Creaking leather cradles her parched, aching head. Bliss.

'Oh dear. Your mummy didn't spend a lot of time on that name, did she, boy? Where are you guys off to?'

'Gatehouse.' Kelly feels Collie settle in the footwell. She draws her feet away to give him room.

'That's no bother. I can take you nearly all the way. OK if I drop you at Cardoness?'

'The beach?'

'No, the castle.'

'Sure, yeah. That would be great.' She makes herself sit upright. 'Sorry. I'm Kelly.'

'Hiya. I'm Laura. I'd take you all the way in, but I'm running a wee bit late.'

'Cardoness is virtually in Gatehouse. Honestly, that would be perfect. Thank you.'

'Yeah, we're a driver short today, so Dad's got me out doing the rounds.'

'Like a proper milkman? I thought you didny get them any more.'

'That's why we're doing it.' Laura manoeuvres her van back onto the main road. 'Gap in the market and all that. Plus none of the supermarkets have taken us on yet.'

'How come?' The last of Creetown disappears from the window. Ferrytown of Cree – that's what they used to call

278

it, long ago, when boats took pilgrims across the firth. Won't be long now. Kelly shivers a wee bit. Bites down on her teeth to stop them chittering. She thought her clothes had dried out, but they must still be damp.

'Free-range milk? It's like organic was a few years ago. They tell you there's no demand. You tell them how do they know if they don't stock it? They tell you they don't stock it cause there's no demand. But we'll get there.'

'Does free range mean you don't use those massive big sheds?'

'Yup. Our cows get to see the sun and eat the grass. Just as nature intended. And we let the calves stay with their mums way longer too.'

'Good on you. I'd buy that.'

'Well, I've still got some left.' Laura gestures to the crates in the back of the van. Gallons of gleaming white milk. Kelly is so very thirsty.

'Nah.' She feels the dryness in her mouth get drier. She's wet on the outside, and desiccated in her bones. 'I'd love to, but I don't have any money on me. I . . . I'll need to get cash out when I get to Gatehouse.'

'Och, just take one anyway.'

'You sure?'

'Yeah. Free sample. Got to catch the customers somehow. You on holiday? Hitching?'

Kelly reaches behind her seat to the crates. It would be polite to take the one-litre bottle. She takes a two. 'I'm actually heading to a wedding. Susan – you know her?' Opens it, greedy for the . . .

Ooh.

Cool.

Thick.

Sweet.

That is so good.

'Oh, you mean Susan Carson? Yeah, she was in my cousin's year at school. Och, Susan's lovely. So how d'you know her?'

The milk coats Kelly's gullet. A little spills onto her chin. Collie watches, keen for his turn – but how do you feed milk to a dog? She can hardly pour it into her hand. 'We met in Glasgow.' She dips her fingers inside the bottleneck, lets him lick them.

'She's dead funny, isn't she? Connor's great too.'

'Yes. Yes, he is.'

A sideways glance. 'So it's definitely going ahead, then?'

'The wedding?'

'Oh, did you not hear? Sorry.'

'Hear what?'

'Och, nothing.' Laura shakes her head. 'My cousin was probably joking. She says Susan's got very superstitious. After the hen night. She said, "For God's sake, don't let her see a magpie or she'll call the whole thing off." But we don't get magpies down here, so it's probably fine. Were you at the hen night? You'd've met her then? My cousin Amy?'

'No. I couldn't make it.'

'So, you're not from Glasgow then?'

'I am, kind of. Thereabouts.'

'I cannot wait to get up there. Get away from this dump.'

'It's not a dump. It's beautiful.' From the window, Kelly can see the Machars across the bay, the purple strut of land where Wigtown is, and down towards the Mull of Galloway. The sea that drowned Margaret Wilson sparkles.

'Well, if you live here it is, believe me. Up to my oxters in cowshite.'

'What age are you, Laura?' Kelly downs another draught of milk.

'Eighteen.'

'Will you take a wee bit advice from an old woman?'

'You're not old.'

Kelly's heart lifts.

'Look how thin you are. And your hair's fantastic. My mum could never carry that off.'

Embarrassed, she touches the crown of her head. 'Away. I havny even brushed it this morning. To tell you the truth, I've been up all night.'

'Exactly,' says Laura. 'I thought that, when I saw you. A party animal.'

'Well, I'm not sure about that.'

Laura shrugs. Kelly senses she's offended her, not taken the compliment in the way it was meant.

'Just don't be in such a hurry to get away from here, all right?'

'How not?'

How to explain it? The always-yearning that feathers through Kelly's veins. That persistent tug. Did you know your heart comes with strings?

'Because you can't recapture it once it's gone.' She keeps looking out the window at Wigtown Bay. A horseshoe of mudflats and salt marsh, a wide mouth into which pours a triumvirate of rivers: the Cree and the Bladnoch and the Fleet. All the rivers of her childhood gulping into the Irish Sea. Fleet Bay lies to the east; they are coming round that glorious curve of road now, where the oval hump of Ardwall Island floats atop the sea. At low tide, you can walk there.

'Aye, right. There's like *nothing* I'd want to capture here.'

The girl's colour is high; Kelly can sense she is annoying her. But her milk-filled belly is fluting. She feels skittish.

'You know all that stuff you think is boring, all those folk you've known forever? The ones that do your head in? You think they'll be there forever too. Like the sea. Just dull, sloshing in the background. And you canny wait to shake it all off. But see when you've been away from a place for a long time, and you come back and you *see* it – actually see it so it catches your breath. Then you love it again. And you'll admit that you missed it all along, because it kind of . . . well, it made you, I suppose. Do you see?'

Laura stares at her. Kelly has gone too far. The indicator ticks. Cardoness Castle perches on its little hill, and they are here, sweeping into the gravel strip that serves as car park to the castle.

'Not really,' says Laura eventually. 'You've a milk moustache, by the way.'

Kelly wipes her mouth. 'Better?'

Laura nods. She looks a wee bit teary. 'Are you saying that this is the best it'll ever get? Me, here, shovelling shite?'

'No!' Kelly takes the girl's hands. 'No, not at all. Your life is there, waiting to roll out in front of you. I'm just saying . . .' She sighs. 'I don't know what I'm saying, right? Ignore me. My name is Kelly, and I talk utter pish. You go to Glasgow, Laura. It's a brilliant city. You go there and you have a ball.' She jumps down from the van, claps her hands for Collie, who leaps without looking, trusting that Kelly will know where she's going.

'Thank you for the lift. Can you hand me those bags down? And the milk? Cheers.'

She didn't mean to upset the lassie. Hopefully Laura will be watching Kelly's skinny arse walk away and thinking, *Stupid old bag. What does she know?*

Nothing, Laura. Absolutely zip.

She raises one hand in farewell to Laura and her cow-mobile. Her tummy is still doing cartwheels. Christ, is she really nervous of being here? Why? Gatehouse has not changed. It is a model village, literally, built to service the big hoose and the mills that came after, with their great waterwheels and man-made lathes. Slim runnels of water stream behind gardens and under walls here, channelled from the ponds further up the hill. Dark secrets of water: Kelly and Mandz used to paddle in them, though they weren't allowed.

The town – and the locals insist it is a town, because it once had a burgh hall – has one main street and three churches. It won't be hard to find a wedding here, though she'll have to factor in the hotel, and maybe the Masonic Arms too, if they still have that nice conservatory. You could probably have a wedding in there. She drags her bags and Collie up Fleet Street, over the bridge, past a wee farmers' market which is setting up in the Spar car park. There is a butcher, a baker and . . . a fruit and veg stall. Plus a man selling smoked fish. When did the dug last eat? What can she do to get him some food? Is she gonny beg? Here, a stone's throw from where her dad might be?

He won't be, Kelly. You know that.

He used to send her letters. Not often, or maybe there were others he wrote and they just never found their way to her. But some did. He was resourceful, her dad. He sent her letters in the jail, of course, after she refused his visits. She never opened them. Rage and reproach. Kindness. Either way, they would have been too much to bear. He sent her letters when she got out of jail, to her probation officer, various rehab places, wherever he could think of. Her old doctor once, the GP she'd had at uni, which was pretty clever. Her dad *is* clever. She guessed the professionals used to talk, have wee case conferences without her, because Dad even found her when she first went to Turning Point. Well, *somebody* must have told him about bloody Shirley, winner of the most annoying counsellor in the world award, because at their second meeting she was sitting there, all smug, with Dad's letter in her lap, going, *Do you want me to open it, Kelly? If you feel you're not strong enough?*

Must've been, what, seven, eight years ago? Oh, yes. Kelly

and Shirley go way back. Only they don't, not really. They are not friends. Shirley the Shirehorse is in the system, and every so often, the system casts Kelly back up on Shirley's shore. Often, it is after a run-in with the police. They don't bother to lift Kelly any more, the polis, not really. Used to be if you were D&I (drunk and incapable in a public place to give you your full accolade), you'd get a cosy night in the cells at Stewart Street, sleep it off, have an all-right breakfast and be on your way. Add a breach and assaulting the polis too, and you'd probably get conveyed to court. Once they discovered all your unpaid fines from the last time(s), you might even get rewarded with a wee stay in Cornton Vale – kind of a school reunion.

Those days were simple days, like jumping on and off a kiddies' roundabout as it kept moving. On and off. On and off. Just a game. But then they go and take this whole spinning idea and develop it – Turning Point, Turnaround. So the criminal justice system wheechs you off the merry-go-round and saddles you with supervision and community payback orders instead, fucking putting you on your best behaviour. Two years! That's how long Kelly's first supervision was (or would have been, if she'd completed it). She managed six months of weekly appointments and agreed care plans, because *we need to address the underlying issues that lead to your offending behaviours.*

Just check out my file, doll.

Referrals to Alcoholics Anonymous, one-to-one support from a social worker, a Turnaround worker, addictions worker (*hey, Shirley, pleased to meet you. I'm going to be your nemesis for several weary years*). On you go to the ECHO programme. *Do you hear an echo in here, Shirley? Shurely you do?* Empowerment. Choice. Hope. Opportunity. Kelly and Shirley got to discuss her triggers, emotions, her alcohol awareness. And best of all, relapse prevention. Plus

Shirley wanted to refer her for trauma and loss support – hence the stage prop of her dad's letter at their second session. Kelly soon put her right on that. Took the letter from her, ripped it into pieces, right there in her office with the infuriating abstract prints.

Fuck you, Shirley. It was Kelly's choice. She chose not to, never to go there. *Choices, Shirley.* One day, her dad's letters stopped. Shirley, alas, has not. Kelly is/was back in her clutches again/before.

Before the bus crash and the bag of money and the bride with no ring.

Triggers, Kelly. Know your triggers. *Well, I didny see that mad parade coming, now did I?*

Her pace is slowing. Now Kelly is in Gatehouse, she doesn't really know what to do. She can't breenge in on the actual wedding. But how will she find the bride's house? Just hing about churches all morning, waiting for a florist to appear? She didn't want to arrive like this, drookit and dishevelled. Each time her legs part to take another step, a faint vegetable odour wafts. She wishes she could feel the way she did yesterday, when she'd cut her hair and had a shower. Maybe if she cleans her cowboy boots?

Aye, Kelly. Gaun yersel. Click your heels. That'll sort it.

She'll be methodical, start with the Church of Scotland at the top of the town. It's tucked down a side street; you can only see its steeple when you reach the clock tower, which dominates the main street. Time trumps faith in Gatehouse. Which came first, she wonders – the clock tower or the church? Both are equally strange. Not quite a matching pair, but there are similarities. The clock tower is square, but flat on top, with weird rounded crenulations that splay like plumes. It stands alone, unsupported by any other building. Just a startled, lonely tower. The church has an oddly castellated turret, which is also square but with a small apex spire coming out the top. It's like they couldn't decide what to do with it – flat or pointy? *Ach, I know, Jimmy – let's dae both*. Kelly thinks each tower is the product of a rich man's fancy.

She turns down the side street to the church. It's surrounded by a high dry-stone wall. There are no yellow ribbons or white roses garlanding it, and the church gate is shut. She goes up the wee path anyway, to try the door, which is also shut. Collie looks at her, head on one side, ears up.

'What? I don't know. Let's just wait and see if someone goes in, eh? Then we can ask. Or, I don't know, we'll go and ask at the market. And if there's no joy there, we'll try the Episcopalian one.' She opens the gate onto the pavement. 'Or follow someone with a buttonhole. Are you thirsty?' She puts her Next bag on the ground. Yes, she'll clean her shoes – somehow – and give Collie some milk. That's a plan. Though what can she put the milk in? Could she just pour it straight in his mouth?

A disgusting flash. Last night in the pub. Liquid poured, pouring from on high, and her knickers at her ankles, oh God you are vile, not fit to be in charge of him. You feel your skin burn – do you feel it?

'Nice arse,' a man's voice drawls. 'But, Kelly, doll. Whit the fuck have you done to your hair?'

'Dex?' She spins round. A skinny wee guy in a baseball cap leans against the dry-stone wall. Skip of his cap, tipping, tipping up. It is as well! 'Dexy!' Arms flinging round necks, some lassie looking on, Collie barking like a mad dog, pleasure popping fast as champagne, and everything is blurred. Is unbelievable.

'Paul Michael Dixon.' She shakes him. 'What the bloody, bloody hell are you doing here?'

'Looking for you, my little alcopoppet.' He holds her face

in tender hands. 'You honk like a fucking brewery, by the way.'

She has no response to give. It is true. She lays her cheek on his shoulder. He doesn't mean to hurt her. Kelly can do that all by herself.

'Here. Shh, you. C'mon now. Don't cry.'

She can't help it; it's sluicing from her in open-mouthed gouts. She doesny think there is much noise; her chin, driving into the bone of him, her mouth working; all she can see is the silky white of his trackie jacket, blotting grey, she sees the damp stain she is making spread and mottle, her roar is silent, and endlessly on, chewing on his shoulder, and Dexy stands and takes it. Solid as a rock. He braces his arms, criss-cross, and holds her, and lets her weep. Collie has wedged himself between them – he cannot stop them converging over his head, but is doing his damnedest to protect Kelly's feet. She is so very tired.

'Right, doll.' Dexy pats her back, as if he's burping her. 'Enough.'

'I canny . . .' Dribbling, heaving. What a state you are, Kelly McCallum. 'I've snottered on your shoulder.'

'Ach, I've cleaned blood and vomit fae your hair, doll. What's a wee bit snot between friends? Oh, here, no, check that out. Bogeys an all.'

'Piss off, Dex. You're horrible.' She snuggles back into the crease of his neck, where it is cosy. A smell of aftershave lingers.

'M'on, you. Bath, then bed. Aleisha and me have got this covered. You mind Aleisha? Yous met at the Outreach.'

'Hi, Aleisha,' Kelly peers over Dexy's shoulder, raises a limp hand at the girl.

'All right, Kelly? How's it going? What's your dug called?'

'Collie.'

'All right, Collie? Does he do paws?'

They take her to the B&B in which they have both apparently spent the night. *But no like that*, Aleisha is quick to advise. *It's got two beds.* When Kelly tries to explain about Susan and the wedding, Dexy lifts his hand. 'I know. That's how we came. Mind you asked me to help you? And I didny? Well, I'm sorry, doll. I should have. Anyway, we're here now, and I can reliably inform you that Miss Susan Carson is getting merrit the day at three p.m. On the beach.'

'Classy. But . . . how d'you know?'

Dex taps the side of his nose. 'I have my methods.'

Aleisha yawns. 'He asked in the newsagent's.'

'Oh.' *Duh, Kelly.* Her head feels twice its weight and size. 'What beach?'

'Cardoness Shore? Some wee chapel?'

'Oh yeah,' Her throat aches. 'I know that. It's lovely. Gey wee wedding, but. You'd be lucky if you could get six folk inside.'

Dexy shrugs. 'Ours not to reason why. Anyhow. That means you've plenty time to get a wee lie-down and then make yourself presentable. Right, cross over the road here. We're staying in that blue hoose over by.'

'Presentable? How—'

'Don't even fucking start me. Christ knows how the hedge turned out, but by the look of you, you've went backwards, forwards and sideys through it. Now git.'

He actually slaps her arse.

Kelly cannot begin to get her brain round how or why he's here. But he is, and he came for her. The inside of her glows. She would like to say thank you, to reach over and take his hand, but now that they are untangled and separate again, she finds she can't. Her limbs feel clumsy.

Dexy uses his key to let them into the B&B makes them all tiptoe up the stairs. He's booked for two nights – *cause I didny know when the hell we'd find you, to be honest*

– but he doesn't think they take dogs. The room is wallpapered in flock, clean, with one double and one single bed. He tells Kelly to take off her swanky boots and lie down on the big bed.

'That's mine!' says Aleisha, and Dexy tells her to shut it. The two of them mutter away; Kelly thinks she sees money pass from Dexy to the girl, but she is so, so tired she could be dreaming. Is definitely . . . She makes her mouth push out words.

'Gonny gimme some dog food . . .'

'Christ, doll, times arny that hard. We can get you a roll on sausage at least.'

'For the . . .'

'Dug,' says Dexy. She thinks he has come over to stroke her hair, but she is on a tightrope; no, it is piano keys, a ginormous great piano, where each step she puts her foot on is a note, a coherent tuneful narrative that fills the room and fills the void and she dances. St Ninian puts his crook down and takes her hand and they are doing that daft toe-tap, not the hokey-cokey, one elephant went out to . . .

Ca' the yowes.

Tae the knowes.

They are dancing in soap suds with Amanda and her mum.

You are lying in your bed, with the covers pulled tight. Tight, because when you were wee, if everything up to your head and neck was swaddled, then the monsters wouldn't get you. Or if you had your back to the door, then the blankets had to be wound right across your back, up past your ears, and you would never turn around, even though you could feel its eyes on you in the dark, this thing, this goblin or the shadow on the picture on the wall; the open gaping mouth, the eyes of bright black coal.

So. You are in your bed, and it is comfy. Truly comfy;

You are silk-rolled in a quilt cocoon. Your head is cradled in pillowy down, your body is squint across the bed. Warm as toast, just the right type of toastiness, and instinct tells you to enjoy it. To not open your eyes to track that elusive sweetness of bacon, because then the cold will start and the bacon smells will stop and the softness disappear. You try to ignore the dry-mouth drouth, the milky-sour coating on your teeth. Oh, but it was lovely. Fine and lovely, the loveliest thing that has happened to you in months.

Warmth.

'Ho! Kelly! Fucking burning my hands here.'

Kelly is woken with a cup of tea and a bacon roll. Delivered by Aleisha, who is looking very pleased with herself.

'Cheers, pal. Thank you.'

'Here. Take it. Cup's roasting. I got something else too. A present.'

'*We* got you a present.' Kelly hears Dexy, at the other side of her. He is sitting on a chair, Collie Dog curled at his feet. Has he been watching her sleep? See, that would normally creep her out, oh man, like that beardy dude up on . . .

She eyeballs Dex. Properly looks at him. Puts the cup on the bedside table, sits up on her elbows, close and closer, coming into focus. Dexy's eyes are green, ringed with brown. They blink calmly at her, all the while she is staring. Not creepy.

'It's something to wear.' Aleisha is virtually bouncing on the bed. 'For the wedding.'

'Oh, thanks. Can I see it?'

'Can *I* see it?' says Dexy. 'Seen as I paid for it.'

'Right. Wait for it . . .' Aleisha delves into a poly bag. Extracts a long peacock feather. 'Right, that's for your hair . . . and this . . . this is your dress. Ta da!' She pulls out a cloud of white. Pulls it and pulls it, an endless magician's scarf of floaty cheesecloth, reaming through her hands. It is a floor-length sleeveless white smock, embroidered with ghostly flowers and silver beading. It is the size of a small marquee.

'Jesus Christ! It's a tent!'

'Were you gonny wear it or sleep in it, Kels?'

She and Dexy speak in unison, their responses pleating one over the other. They start to laugh.

'Fucksake. Yous are a pair of ungrateful bastards. There's just the one place in Gatehouse that sells clothes, all right? And it's a pure mad hippy shop. So it was either one of these or a pair of tie-dyed pantaloons. And there's no flower shops, so I thought the feather—'

'Aleisha, it's great. Honestly. Thank you. Give me it over and I'll try it on.'

Maybe it won't fit her. Dexy winks at Kelly, waiting until Aleisha has turned her head away.

'Nope. No way,' he says. 'You're no putting on your glad rags till you're all washed and brushed. I've ran you a bath.'

'Have I got time?' Kelly bites into the roll, to the most perfect mouthful of bacon. Oh God. Imagine a bath in bacon. 'I mean, we're not actually going to the wedding, are we? I was gonny head early, try and catch . . . I dunno . . . her mum or an usher or that.'

'No,' says Dexy. 'I reckon the later we leave it the better.'

'Why?'

'Just in case.' He scratches his head. His hair's indented all the way round, from where his baseball cap was sitting.

'You look like your halo's slipped.'

Dexy frowns. For a wee moment, she thought they were travelling alongside each other's thoughts. In tune.

'See, because of your hat, I mean? The line of your hat has squashed your hair.'

'Right.'

Why is he not twinkling at her? He's gone serious.

'I knew a lassie once,' says Aleisha, 'that shagged with her swimming goggles on.'

'Why?'

'So they'd leave goggle marks. Telt her boyfriend she was away at the baths – but she was actually jumping his brother.'

'Nice.' Kelly is watching Dexy. There is a furtiveness about the way he fidgets. 'Why "just in case", Dex?'

'In case there's more than one wedding crasher. Let's just get in and get out. Kelly, look. There's good news and there's bad news. What would you like first?'

His face is serious with concern. Does he mean to make her so uneasy?

'Is it about Collie?'

'No. It's no the dog. Aleisha, gonny give me that paper over, hen? Ta.'

He sets the newspaper on the counterpane beside her. 'Right. Thing is, we're no the only folk looking for you. There's a woman – a reporter fae this paper – and she's been running a wee campaign to try and track you down.'

'Because of Collie! I fucking knew it. Dex, see that old bastard—'

'Kelly. This is not about the frigging dug, all right? Just listen. She's been after you for days, getting folk to phone in if they know your whereabouts. Well, see the day . . .' he opens the newspaper, 'the day she's written . . . where is it . . . aye. She says: "We've now narrowed down the search to Galloway – and we think Kelly may be headed home!" Excla-fucking-mation mark. "We believe her last known address when she lived there as a youngster was the Castledykes area of Kirkcudbright. So if anyone out—'

'Stop!' There is a shrill noise in Kelly's head, a single note that plays and plays. *Da. Da. Da. Ca-sil-dykes.* 'How does she know that?'

Why do people know that? How? It is frightening Kelly, the thought of her being spread out on a page. Kelly is private: no address, no phone. She has slipped below the surface, is just feet and a bag and somewhere not to look when you're on your lunch break and in a hurry. But that's on purpose. How dare someone unpeel her past and put it down, write it down in a place for folk to find it? How dare they? She is standing up, though she doesny remember moving. Standing with her fists clenched. 'Why are people looking for me?'

'Well – and this is the good news, Kels – seems you've went and saved some guy's life. The man from the bus crash. Near George's Square? You were there, doll, weren't you? He said you stayed with him and stopped the blood.'

'How?' Her brain is struggling to keep up. 'You've spoke to him?'

'No. Look. It's been in the papers. Him and his wife. And the telly.'

'Jesusgod.'

'There's been a Heroin Hotline and everything,' says Aleisha.

'Hero*ine*. So, if you want to meet this reporter or your man, fine. But it's up to you, no her. And you do it in your own time. I don't want you getting bullied into doing something, Kelly, or coming out into the limelight if you don't want to. Or if you're no ready. They had no right . . .'

She takes Dexy's hand. She really does want to take his hand, does it without even thinking. 'They don't, do they? They've got no right at all. But he's honestly alive? The guy with the office shoes?' Her skin is prickling, like it is goose pimples, but she's not remotely cold. Her great, great great-coat saved that man?

Because you were there.

The goose pimples feel silvery, fine silvery bubbles that

293

are running in a line from the bottom of her neck to the top of her head, pulling her long and tall.

'Is that kindy like karma, then?' says Aleisha. 'Like how you went and killed that one person, but then you saved this person, so it cancels them out?'

'What?'

'That lassie? When you broke their neck—'

'Aleisha,' says Dexy, 'you shut the fuck right up.'

Pop-pop go the bubbles. Acid bubbles, splashing through Kelly's skin. She shakes her head.

'Kelly, doll, just fucking ignore her. I telt her she was talking bollocks.'

Kelly sits on the edge of the bed. The bathroom door is ajar. She can smell soap and see the rim of a turquoise bath with a white and blue shower curtain. The pattern is hexagons. Kelly picks a hexagon, draws it with her eyes and puts herself inside it. Folding and folding, dead, dead wee, while they are talking.

While she is talking.

'No, Dex. She's not.' The hexagon is throbbing. Mutating.

'See?' says Aleisha.

The hexagon swells out, its points dissolving, stretching into the shape of an eye. To the shape of a marquise diamond.

'I didn't kill anyone.'

'Of course you didny, doll. I bloody telt her that. You wouldny.'

'So how come you were in the jail? Carol Ann *told* me—'

'I broke my sister's neck, Aleisha.'

Kelly gazes down her long neb, into her past. One cervical fracture, chipping off a fragment of bone. Did you know you have twelve thoracic vertebrae in your chest area, Kelly? *Yes, yes, I do, thanks.* Well, they are measured T1 to T12. *I know. I've looked at diagrams.* So if, due to a catastrophic fall in which you send your sister swallow-diving backwards onto a long flight of stone steps, a wee fragment of bone splinters down the spinal canal and lodges at your T12 (saws and stabs at it actually, rather than simply lodging), the resulting spinal cord injury means that while you will probably have fully functional muscles in the top half of your body, there may be little or no function in your lower limbs. Add in some compression damage to the nerves and you will most likely be sentenced to a lifetime of chronic pain too.

You and her both.

'Holy Christ,' says Aleisha. 'Aw, man, Kelly. That's bad, bad shit. Heavy shit.'

'It is, isn't it? Really bad shit. I put my sister in a wheelchair.'

'Kelly,' says Dex. 'I don't think you need to do this.'

All the hexagons on the shower curtain are dancing.

'No. I do.' She presses two fingers into the side of her nose, at the bone curve of her eye socket. 'It was an accident. I meant to . . . I was pushing her, we were fighting, like. And I was pished. Really pished.'

You did assault Amanda McCallum to her severe injury and permanent disfigurement. How do you plead?

Guilty.

She forces herself to look at Dexy, to see his reaction and not imagine the flinch, nor the coldness in his voice when it comes. His eyes are wet.

'We were in a big hall, at a party. My sister's engagement party, actually. I was . . . I was trying to get off with her fiancé.'

'Christ, hen.'

'But there were stone stairs, and she fell right down, or I pushed her. Fuck knows. But I did it. I did it, Aleisha. I broke my wee sister's neck.'

She curls on her side. It is only her, and her heartbeat,

and then Aleisha curls behind her. Collie, pushing his wet nose into her palm. She can feel Aleisha's baby, knocking quietly against her spine.

'Baby doll.' Dexy gentles her head. Kelly can see hexagons, flat and static. She can feel rough, callused thumbs knead her temples and the whisper of a kiss at her ear.

Chapter Twenty-One

'Darling.' Susan's mum kisses her, then immediately thumb-rubs her cheek. At least she didn't spit on her hankie to do it. 'You look so beautiful.' The feathers from her mum's hat tickle Susan's nose. She is going to sneeze. The inside of the chapel is damp and cold, which doesn't help. It was Connor's idea.

That isn't fair. It was Connor's idea because she brought him here. First time Susan took him home to meet her folks; she had wanted to show him the most gorgeous view in the world.

'I'll see you down there, sweetie,' says her mum. 'I love you.'

Susan nods. 'Love you too.' She looks outside. On a sunny day, you could be anywhere. The tiny chapel has two open pointed-arch windows. There is no glass in them, just wooden shutters that passers-by are trusted to close when the weather gets really bad. Each window has ornamental black-iron gratings, wrought into patterns and fused across the window frames. But they don't serve any purpose. The bars don't protect the chapel from the elements or from intruders. The chapel door is always kept unlocked. So what is the point of them?

One of the windows faces out to sea. The other, Susan's

favourite, looks back along the beach to tree-fringed rocks and the dark green sweep of Gatehouse Bay. On this window, the iron grating is in the shape of half a shining sun. So clever how it all joins up. The semicircle in the top right corner, the beams radiating diagonally across the window, down to the bottom left, where curly iron waves rise to twine with the sun.

Her friends and family are waiting there, on the beach beyond the metal waves. She has to stoop slightly to see out. A wee dais has been built from decking boards, on which the bride and groom are to stand. They will become their own cake-topping decoration. White chairs are ranged on bleached biscuit sand so fine it could be dust. And on those chairs sit aunties and uncles, mates from work, school friends, cousins. Connor. Everyone who loves her, really.

They are so lucky. After the storms of yesterday, Susan was prepared to cancel the whole thing (again). But today has woken fresh. Bright sky. A timid, palish blue certainly, but it is more blue than grey, and the shafts of sunlight, when they fall, are 'quite celestial', according to Dennis the photographer. He is bugging the life out of her; has been at their house since breakfast, recording Susan getting her hair done, Susan getting her dress on, Susan going to the bathroom – she slammed the door on him then. Stayed in the bath for over an hour, till the entire house was panicking.

Soaping and shaving. Not staring at the third finger of her left hand, because when she did, she would start crying again. And then her mum or her sister would go, 'Oh, for God's sake, Susan. You can get another ring.'

It is not the end of the world.

When she emerged from the bathroom, her eyes all pink, she told them it was just the steam. Alison tutted and fetched some cucumber. Mum sent out for Optrex – *just in case.*

She hates this. She has become an ugly Bridezilla, in the

happiest moments of her life. She wants to look back and remember this heavenly view, not the pain in her head because her veil is tugging. Her desire for every aspect of this day to be perfect is ruining it. Might ruin her and Connor too. He is patient, he is lovely. But he no longer finds her fears and superstitions a source of gentle fun. It's because it matters so much. How she feels about Connor, that fierce surge where she thinks the breath will just leave her body whenever she sees him, and the knowledge that if it did, she wouldn't mind. That he would have been worth it.

The minister steps inside the chapel. The hem of his cassock is rimmed in sand. 'Ready?'

Is she? What if this fierceness burns out? What if the storm yesterday was a warning? What if it is a sign?

Amy nudges her in the back. The flower girls lift their baskets. Shells and sea holly. A wash of eau de Nil and pale turquoise, her bridesmaids shimmering in homage to the sea. They descend the stone steps to the beach, her sister holding her elbow in case she slips. Dad is waiting at the bottom, whisky-scented breath as he takes her arm.

The wedding party begins processing across the sand. At the same time, through the haze of her veil, Susan notices that a bizarre alternative procession is taking place, coming towards them, mirroring them step for step. At the head is a crop-haired woman. Her long nose gives her an air of elegance, all swan-neck glide until you look below the neck. White sailcloth billows around her; she wears a kaftan over cowboy boots. Look closer, and there is a small peacock feather behind her ear. The woman bears something silver cupped in her hand, but Susan cannot yet see what it is that she conveys. Beside the woman, a young collie jumps. He is incapable of travelling more than two steps without plunging forwards and digging up a bowl of sand. The dog has made molehills all the way down the beach; *that will look awful in the photos*, Susan thinks. Is she in a dream? A man follows after the woman and the dog, a skinny ned in a baseball cap, come to rob them blind. Is her wedding being hijacked? Bringing up the rear is a pregnant teenager. She is loving the attention, waving like the Queen of Sheba as the congregation mutters and squirms.

Susan wants to die. This is not the dream she dreamed of. The crop-haired woman is almost upon them; it is a flat oyster shell that she carries in her hands, grey and thick silver and baby blue and ice. Sand kicking up as she walks, a glimpse of hairy shin. She sways her hips and bears her load with grace and a wicked smile. Breasts loose and bouncing. God, she is bonny; they are all thinking it, everyone on that beach.

'I brought you your ring,' the woman says, offering the salver-shell. Susan feels faint, giddy. But it's true. Her engagement ring is there: there is Connor's grandma's ring, sitting proud in the oyster, with its diamond eye that has seen so much. The pregnant teenager crowds in. She is standing on Susan's dress. 'We thought you could use the shell as a necklace. See if you put a wee hole in it?'

'But . . . how?' Susan looks to her dad for inspiration. His mouth hangs open like the poached salmon awaiting them in the Masonic.

'Ours not to reason why.' The ned doffs his baseball cap. There are teeth missing when he smiles. 'Oh fucksake, Collie – no!' He shoves the dog, who has started squatting on the sand. Stops him just in time.

'I hope you'll be very happy,' the crop-haired woman says, pressing her gift into Susan's hand. And then they turn to leave. As they walk off, scrunching the banked-up shells, tramping on the dog's molehills, the pregnant teenager begins to chant, fist pumping in triumph.

'Here we go, here we go, here we go.'

Then the man and the woman join in. They seem animated with joy. Walking away, shouting and rambling, out of Susan's life. With her new life about to begin.

*

You walk, shouting and rambling, through the night. Your breath is ragged in your breast, lungs swimming in the sluggish ichor that used to be your blood. How could it have stayed rosy and wholesome? Diluted beyond measure, there is not much left in there of the original you.

Hunger is a constant, hunger and exhaustion so present that you are permanently dizzy and your brain cells buzz without recourse to the drink. Of course, the drink is also a constant, so how would you ever tell, Kelly?

You have not eaten, washed or slept properly in weeks. You weave through your city like a pinball, lurching from the night shelter to the soup kitchen to the park. Parting your lips to receive bread and prayers, then outside, later, for the sharing of the wine. A communal cup of Buckfast – made by actual monks.

You want folk to know you tried. Those people who pass with pity or disdain – you wish you had a photo of your wee house sellotaped to your forehead, or the means by which to play them the highlights of your life, a kind of spooling aura of faces and experiences that have touched you, to give witness to what you were before.

You did try. That tarty cow Ellen never pressed charges. Garry never came home. The glove factory gave you a lukewarm reference; it was sufficient to get zero-hours cleaning work from an agency who would take a cut of the money you didn't receive.

You can't do anything on zero hours except wait. When

you go to their office, because they wouldn't answer your calls (and you are running out of credit), they send you away. Too aggressive to be on their books, when all you do is ask. You go to the job centre. You are desperate. They don't give you a job, though. They send you away, in order that you can contact them by phone. But you don't have enough credit? Well, then, you can contact them online. You don't have a computer.

God bless libraries, and kind librarians who are patient and used to providing quiet comfort – even if you've no intention of getting one of their books out. You don't have to pretend, like hovering near the counter of a coffee shop before using their toilet. You just go in, and they help you. Libraries are beacons in the dark, you think. You find, in the months and years to come, that you will use them often.

After your online claim is processed, the job centre still does not give you a job. They give you an appointment and an adviser. The adviser does not give you a job; they give you a Jobseeker's Agreement, which the adviser completes and you are told to sign.

You sign. You do not get a job and you do not get money. You get seven 'waiting days'. A week of sweet fuck all. Then . . .

Sanctioned.

—Why?

—You left your job voluntarily

You hang on. You sell some of your clothes. You buy six bottles of White Lightning at the Co-op while you have money in your pocket. You buy oven chips. You are not going on the street again, no way. You go to the doctor. He offers you sympathy and a note for the food bank. You decline. You do your job search stuff. You send off CVs and go down the library and log in to Universal

302

Jobmatch like it tells you on the form. You get no matches and no replies. You don't know how to elide over the gaps in your CV. You ask if you could go on a CV writing course. There is a waiting list. You will be sanctioned if you don't write your CV. Your housing benefit claim has been held up, you don't know why. You are tired now, and scared to ask. You think they think Garry still lives here: his name is on their records. It is all in your file.

Lots of files. How many files does your life occupy, Kelly?

You go back to the job centre, homework done like a good girl. You fix on your smartest smile.

Sanctioned.

—Why?

—You haven't adhered to your Claimant Commitment agreement.

—I have.

—No, you haven't. Failure to log in to your Universal Jobmatch account.

But you did, you did.

—You'll have to apply for a revision of an outcome decision. I'll send it to the judgement team. *The adviser shows you, shell-shocked, out.*

—Write it down, *says an old man in the waiting room. He wears a shirt and threadbare tie. You can see where he's cut himself shaving.*

—What?

—Get the woman to write it down. Say exactly why she's sanctioning you.

—She says I didn't state the dates I applied for work. But I did – right here at the top of the page.

—Aye, that's the week dates. They'll want the actual days.

But nobody said.

—Change the bloody goalposts every time, hen. Ask them to give you a hardship payment. Eighty pounds. That'll tide you over.

—Ho, old-timer, *shouts the security guard*. This is nothing to do with you. Button it. Don't be getting involved.

—I'm just helping the lassie.

—I'm warning you, pal, I'll put you out. And you'll no get to sign on either.

—Can I get a hardship payment then? *You plead with your adviser, who is calling someone else through. She is distracted. You are a buzzing fly.*

—You can apply. But we can't arrange an interview to begin the process until next week.

—But how do I pay for food? Or electric?

—Not my problem. You should have adhered to the agreement. Next.

Every day, you log in to Universal Jobmatch. It's in your contract. Except they don't update the jobs every day. It's in their contract. You take up the doctor's offer of the food bank chitty. You are feeling a bit down, you could do with some pills too? The doctor is reluctant. He knows your history. You go to the food bank. It is full of lovely people, who make you tea and lead you to shelves of tins and pasta.

—Cooker? *a lady asks. You are confused.* Have you a cooker in your house, pet, or do you need stuff you can rehydrate? It's amazing what you can cook with kettles.

She fills a bag for you. You go home. Take a drink.

You go to the library. Universal Jobmatch, check, check, check. You post CVs through the doors of local employers. (You wait till it is dark, so you don't have to talk to folk. You are getting really knackered with talking to folk. With making yourself supine.)

You go home. You are in arrears. It tells you so, in bold red print. You bin the letter. Take a drink.

You are assigned a work placement, to 'enhance your employability skills'. It is unpaid. It is sweeping the floor of a glove factory. The one remaining glove factory in Glasgow. You laugh, at first. Then refuse. You try to explain.

Sanctioned.

You go home. Take a drink.

You drink until you vomit. You wake from the blackout, your hair crusted to your mouth. Your lips are glued numb. Your body bucks and jitters; it is fighting with itself. Kelly, your head has swollen until it fills the room. It is too weighty to be carried. Off with her head. *Yet you carry it still, you carry all this weight, and it clanks in chains around you, all the need and the thirst. It will drink you dry, then it will suck your eyeballs, suck up your soul.*

You need to be unburdened. You need to make yourself light.

You make a pile of all the letters, the angry red ones, the reproachful black. Mandatory *and* compliance. *Those are their favourite words. You think you'd like a world where the words are* kindness. Care. *Maybe* listening. Or simply help. *You pile the letters in the sink. Strike a match. Take a drink.*

Burn, baby, burn

You think of your doll, Libby-loo, dying. Malki burning her, you dousing the flame with water from the tap. There is no drink left. You put on two jumpers, your jacket and your walking boots. Post your key back through the letter box.

Outside, you walk. You walk and walk and walk. Away from Grovepark Street towards the canal. It leads you

through the top of the city. You pick a street, any street.
Glasgow has a gridded heart: up, down, across. This is a
down street, you follow it down. There is the Clyde,
lapping brown. You could slide under there.

Drift.

Or you could take a drink and walk.

Down on the walkway, by the bandstand, you find your
tribe. Overcoats, red eyes. They are huddled by a burning
bush. When you squint away your double vision, the bush
is a metal dustbin.

Burn, baby, burn. *You sing it, loud.*

—Fuck off, *shouts a voice. It lobs an empty can.*

Ha. Not entirely empty.

You take a drink of someone else's saliva, or maybe
piss.

You walk, shouting and rambling, through the night.
And this is your life.

Your life.

Chapter Twenty-Two

'Are you sure you want to do this, doll?'

They are parked in Mr Lu's van, Kelly and Dexy and Aleisha, with Collie pawing Aleisha's lap. The dog is transfixed by her belly, keeps trying to sniff it. It is a new wonder to him, this person within a person. To him, Aleisha is wonder-full. He can see and smell vibrations far beyond Kelly's range. Does he smell her differently too? Because Kelly feels she is vibrating slightly; every scale on her skin is risen and fizzing to catch the air. It is a combination of the high of being on the beach, at the wedding, and the low of what is to come.

'Can we no just go up the road now? We've given that dame her ring.' Aleisha pushes Collie down. 'Gonny sit, you? Didny say much but, did she? Stuck-up cow. All that effort and we didny even get a thank you.'

Kelly lives a life of take, not give. She had forgotten the simple pleasure of making someone smile. Making them wonder-full. Because Kelly was there, the bride was glad.

'I think she was very happy.' She is looking through the windscreen at the grey and brown houses that bend out of sight down the road ahead. Council houses on one side, neat bungalows on the other. Of course, most folk bought their houses back in the eighties, so council house isn't strictly accurate, but how else to describe the serviceable four-square rows? Built with underfloor heating, which never worked, so your mum had to get storage heaters, which hissed at night as you and Mandz tried to sleep. But the rooms were broad and airy, the gardens generous. That's what you see when you look down Castledykes Road. Lots of greenery: trimmed hedges and hydrangeas. Lawns with birdbaths in the middle. In spring, it is a riot of flowering cherries. Even the bins out on the pavement, waiting to be emptied, are neatly placed and clean. Kelly thinks if you give folk nice places to live, then they'll keep them nice. What is wrong with giving decent homes to people who canny afford them? How does that damage them or make things unfair?

No, what is not fair is when you take those chances away. When your community doesn't belong to you any more. When they sell off your nice broad-roomed homes and your solid sandstone schools. Your parkland, your libraries. There is a fund at the council called the Common Good. Kelly knows this because her dad was chairman of the allotment society one year, and they applied for help to build raised beds so the old folk could still plant stuff. That phrase has forever stuck.

The Common Good. She thinks about it whenever she's sitting in a doorway, eyes down and hands outstretched. When folk drop litter as they scuttle past, or when they swear at the foreign beggars, or shut doors in people's faces. When young mums and old men are left standing on the bus. She thinks, *But what if it was you?* And she wants to shout it, over and over again.

The Common Good. That's a far better way to say it. Douce and polite. It feels proper Presbyterian. Old-school Scotland.

'How about we go for fish and chips?' Dexy starts the

engine. The van jumps, and a baseball bat rolls from the gap between the seats.

'Why is there a baseball bat in a fruit and veg van, Dex?'

'Fuck knows. Guess it's a tough life selling vegetables in Glesca.'

'Collie! Quit it! Stop sniffing, or I'll teach that wean to bite you when it comes out.' Aleisha is very snappy. Hormones probably. 'Och, guys. I'm tired. No offence, Dex, but you snore like a fucking warthog. I don't want to spend another night in that B&B. How about we just go home?'

'But this *is* my home, Aleisha. Least, it was.' Kelly unclicks her seat belt. She is still wearing the white, sand-stained smock. She loves how it drapes and shimmers as she moves; it is a princess dress. 'We've sat here twenty minutes, and not a single person has come down that road. Or a car. Dex, if there was a posse of reporters or folk waiting to ambush me, I think we would've seen them by now. Don't you?'

He shrugs.

'I just want to chap the door, Dex. Please? Just in case. I've come all this way.'

Dexy stares at the ceiling. 'I know you have. I just don't want you getting upset again.'

'Hand on heart, I don't think my dad will be there. I think . . .' she picks at one of the glittery sequins sewn into the embroidery, 'I think my dad's dead. In fact, I'm pretty sure he is, but I just want to check. You know? He stopped writing to me, you see. I think . . . if he was . . . I think he would have still kept trying to contact me.'

'He was writing to you?' Dexy sounds amazed. 'How? When? It's no as if you've got a letter box.'

'It doesn't matter. But . . . what if he was still here and I went away without ever seeing him?'

'And what if your sister's there?'

'She won't be.'

'How d'you know?'

Oh, Dex. You want him to stop being so achingly gentle. You are not a china doll.

'Because of my truly horrible therapist called Shirley, right? She opened one of my dad's letters once, she bloody opened it in one of our very first sessions, fucking sitting there on her fat arse, and I could see her eyes move over the page, and I was screaming at her to stop, but she kept on going. Said I had significant issues around denial. She said I should be pleased, that my sister had moved on, and so should I. *Why don't you let me read it out to you? Mm, Kelly? Shall I? Why do you not want to hear what your father wants to tell you?* Bloody well guilt-tripping me. Like she always does. Wanting me to face up to . . . what was it? Oh aye. Fucking "accept the past in order to process the present, then build on those foundations to construct your future". Or some shite.'

'That's some right good bollocky-talk, doll. Pure poetry. And did you find those helpful words cured you?'

'Oh aye. Model citizen now, me.'

'Did you let her read the letter out loud?' asks Aleisha.

'Did I fuck. Told her she was totally unprofessional and that I'd be reporting her. Then I ripped it up in front of her face.'

'But that wasny the end of your Shitty Shirley sessions, was it, doll? Cause you're aye moaning about her.'

'Naw. The woman clings like a bloody limpet.'

'Shirley not?

They smile at one another, her and Dex. Then Dexy leans over her body to open the door. 'Out you pop then.'

'But I don't want you guys watching me. Go for a wee drive round the block. In fact, away and get chips. There's a cracking chippie down by the harbour.'

'No way,' says Dexy. 'I'm no—'

'Dexy, please? Ten minutes. This is my life. I want to do this alone.'

Aleisha sighs. 'Will you at least take this bloody dog? He's driving me mental.'

Kelly and Collie get out of the van. Kelly licks her lips. Collie licks at a damp patch on the pavement. 'Dirty boy. No!'

He raises one ear at her; it's more of a flick. In human-speak, she suspects it would be a middle finger. 'M'on, Collie Dog. Let's do this thing.'

She fills herself with false energy, strips the tingling from her skin and pumps it all inside, so that when she walks, she bounces. Shoulders set, a certain slackness in her arms, for the benefit of the watchers, she moves with liquidity down the street. She knows Dexy will wait until she reaches the bend in the road and disappears from sight. There's nothing she can do about that; the man is thrawn.

I've got your back, doll.

Kelly will not dwell on the thing she is about to do, will not unpack and map out the various scenarios and outcomes, because if she did, her steps would falter, and she would turn and flee. *What if Dad what if Mandz what if Dad whatifif.*

What if you were not here.

And this will just keep on coming. She will be forever here, with her dad's house round the corner. If she doesn't go in.

For more than half her life, Kelly has not wanted to know. The unbearable is only unbearable if you stop and weigh your burden. If you literally don't go there, you can set yourself free. Aye. So you can, Kelly. You have no idea how this choice will worm and rot inside you, gnawing a cavity that grows and blackens. Until the need to know becomes greater.

There it is. Her ain wee hoose, at the end of a block of four. The grey harling has been painted a pleasant pale green. There are still two trees in the front garden – a crab apple for Kelly, a Kilmarnock willow for Mandz. A family tradition: to plant a tree for each new life. Maybe Kelly will plant a tree for Aleisha's wean, when it comes. In fact, bugger it. That's still her tree. She opens the gate (also green). Takes the path to her own front door, and casually reaches up into the crab apple's boughs. Pinches her finger and thumb into the stalk of a small, hard fruit. Twists. It comes away easily. She puts it in her pocket. There will be plenty of seeds in that.

She looks round for her mum's gnomes, but the garden is gnomeless. The only ornamentation is a pair of green ceramic pots flanking the door, wide-bellied and tumbling with blue asters. Kelly stands on the step, her dog snuffling round her feet. She feels Collie's breath hot through her white dress. Imagines he is gently blowing her forwards.

She breathes. Knocks on the door, a new PVC one, with mock Mackintosh roses in the glass. There is a pause of nothing, then a darkening behind the glass. A click as the handle turns. And a man in a T-shirt is standing in her hall. He's about the same age as Kelly. Middle-aged.

'Yes?'

She hasn't thought this through. Hasn't reckoned on the plummeting spill of all that energy, how it simply drains from bright to grey.

'I'm sorry.' She turns away.

'Can I help you?'

Kelly's finger curls to rub against the ring; she finds it comforting. Of course. The ring is no longer there. 'I was just looking for someone,' she says. 'He used to live here. Alex McCallum?'

'McCallum? Huh, you're the second person to ask that. Popular guy, eh?'

'Yeah. He was, actually. He was really nice.' She notices their hall has been opened up; they've taken the wall into the living room down, so it is all open plan. It's bright. Bright and light.

'Well, like I said to the other woman, I've only been here three years. Bought it off a couple called Adams. But I said to her—'

'Sorry? Who?'

'The other lady. Jennifer? She was round here earlier. I said to go and ask Mrs Grey next door. She's been here for ages.'

She has and all. Auld Witchy Grey, who would burst your balls and shout *wheesht* over the fence. Who always said the McCallums were *a bad lot*. You wouldny touch her with a bargepole. No. It is enough. You tried, Kelly. Dad is gone. End of story. It is what Shirley would call 'closure'.

You came. You saw. You closured.

Go on, Kelly. Laugh. Did you think your brittle heart would mend? The man continues to talk at her; she can tell he is trying to be kind. She nods at cotton-wool words, ears full with the sound of the sea. She thinks she would like to be there, on her beach at the end of the world. That is the place she misses the most. You can't really hear the sea from their house, though the harbour is just down the road. Her cowboys boots clip on such familiar slabs. Clip-clop is the sound of wooden clogs, and toy high heels made of glittery plastic, and the shoes you wore for the school dance, and smart winter boots to walk you to your mother's funeral. She and Mandz helped her dad lay these slabs, ferrying sand on their plastic spades. She won't walk on them again.

Out on the street. She told them ten minutes, has no idea of time. She will walk, slowly, to the top of the road, then she will decide. The sound of a car crawls past; it is a low, throaty judder. Kelly clicks her fingers. Collie answers. The tip of his nose against her hand. Her brittle heart softens; she'd forgotten he could do that to her. 'We'll be all right, boy.'

She is not leaving him behind. That's one decision made. She guesses others will flow from that. That's how choices give you choices. The noise of the engine changes. It was fading, but now it's louder, strident and whining as if it is going backwards. At the edge of her vision is a blur of green. A brief flash of red, white and blue. Green Land Rover reversing, sleekit as a predator, the camouflage green of neat trees and mown grass. Before she can think straight, it has mounted the pavement, and the shape of him is out and looming, Major fucking Tom all red in eye and face, and he is shouting at her, fucking frothing at the mouth and pointing, no, the pointing is lots of fingers, he is sweeping in and grabbing; he has Collie by the scruff. Collie writhes and snaps, but the man has a hangman's noose, and he lassoes it round her Collieflower's neck, Kelly rootless and rooted; she sees it all and is powerless.

Is slow. Slow and low, she goes to kick at the man, screaming, she is screaming for Collie. Folk are opening their doors, she sees terraces and gaps and blocks of open black holes, then Dexy is there, she hears him yelling from Mr Lu's van. Aleisha too, they have stopped the van alongside the Land Rover, blocking up the road, they think they have, but YOU CAN GET OUT THE OTHER WAY, she yells. Aleisha slithers from the van, arms aloft. Baseball bat in hand, she swings as Dexy shouts: 'What you doing? What are you fucking doing?'

'This is my dog,' shouts the major. 'I have paperwork, you hear me? Paperwork to prove it.'

'Christ, man. Can we no talk about this?'

'You were hurting him!' Kelly is on her knees, trying to

314

touch Collie, but all she sees is the white of his belly as the man drags and bundles him away.

'He's my dog!'

Up and down the street, people are watching them.

'You tied him up. You were beating him! Please, please don't hurt him.'

'You can get another dog, pal.' Dexy is squaring up to him.

'Why? Why should I when this dog is mine?'

'Look, I'll gie you money for it. How much?'

The man has Collie wriggling in his arms. Struggling and whining, Kelly pushing to get through. There's bins in her road, and bloody Dex, all elbows and jutting chin.

'Do you no fucking get it, pal? You can get another dug. But what about her? What if she canny get another chance?'

The man hesitates.

'Give him back, ya auld cunt!' Aleisha is a banshee, is Boudicca swinging her club. She reels with the force of her efforts, and the baseball bat flies from her hands, looping like a caber over the Land Rover and onto the windscreen of Mr Lu's van. Glass shatters; it is a crumping, tinkling distraction in the background, but not to Kelly. All she can hear is Collie, and the slam of a door, then the roar of an engine. Dex and Aleisha gawp, helpless, at the damage as the Land Rover scuds towards the bottom of the road.

Burn, baby, burn.

Kelly pokes at the fire she's built on the sand, from driftwood of varying shapes. They'll be coming for her soon. Any minute now.

Dex and Aleisha have driven off in search of a garage. Dex punched the windscreen out to see, but there's no way you could drive home like that. Imagine battering up the motorway, getting the face tore off you by the wind. She asked them to drop her here. Took Dexy's lighter.

315

'You're no gonny torch yourself, are you?'

'Nope.'

This beach, the Dhoon, is different from the one in Gatehouse. The Gatehouse beach is curved and scenic. The Dhoon is more rugged. Rough around the edges. She wonders what the wedding party will be doing now. Toasts and speeches, probably. Cool champagne in a frosted glass.

She was going to be her sister's bridesmaid.

The tide is coming in. Fast. Soon all this wide mudflat will be sea again. A sharp line of sea, travelling on the diagonal; it will swagger in to slap the mud. It will wipe all these sandy ridges from the face of the earth, make new ones. Move on. She stares towards the sun, puts her hand up to make a brim above her eyes. She can see Darren and Katie Carruthers' old cottage, stretched along the rocky outcrop. Remembers dancing with Darren one long-gone summer, as the bonfire blazed and they burned their school blazers. The family who live there now have added a conservatory. How wonderful that would be. You could enjoy the beach all year round with one of those. Often they'd come here in winter too, to make a fire, muck about. Her and Mandz. But it always seemed to be a better idea than it was. They'd stick it out, but it would be freezing: too sore to sit on the bone-chilled rocks; sand turned to petrified yellow froth that you would slip and skite your arse on. Or on a stormy day, when school had been really bad and you wanted to shout at the sea, you'd come here then too. Battle the wind to face the water. After that initial primal scream, you aye felt deflated. And a wee bit daft.

But to sit inside four walls of glass and watch the weather seethe while you were toasty warm. That would be the life.

Kelly leaves her fire behind, walks the length of the Dhoon beach. Stones click underfoot. Mud clags. Then sea strikes over sand. She sees her dress rise with the first inrush of the waves. Her cowboy boots are ruined.

So?

She goes in a little deeper, the current snaking round her knees. It feels like Collie is still there, shepherding her in a figure of eight. Her princess dress becomes a mermaid's tail, then a jellyfish with stings. Further in she goes, and further, far enough in until it starts to scare her: not the depth, it's never deep here, but the strength of the water. Its relentless might.

Might.

She might just have a wee lie-down. That would be nice, to have the Solway bob beneath her. Kelly stands with her back to the oncoming sea and drops.

And drops.

And drops.

And drops.

And drops.

Tumbling into water, your face is spurting gargoyles, sea is up and sky is down, you are stone on parapets, you are the angel on top of the library, you are seaweed in your mouth and on your back.

You are back. You float spread-eagled. Safe, because the sea will carry you on. Here, in this moment and this place, it can only carry you in, not out. And you know this, and so you float on salt, your fingertips dancing as you rock and drift. You rise in ripples, you dip in breaths. The vast-acred sky is the colour of oyster shells. When you kick, the diamonds sparkle.

You feel your backside scrape along the sand. You feel a sharp stab. Quite deliberate it is. A stab in your left tit. Open your eyes and she's there. Your other half, set against the sun.

'You took your time.'

The sky somersaults, smashed light cartwheeling above you. Above her.

317

'Yeah?'

She is ankle-deep, walking with a stick. 'I heard you were coming. Bloody reporters at my door.' She gestures behind her. 'I've been watching you from the window. Always were a drama queen, Kell.'

'I knew you'd be here. In the Carruthers' house.'

'My house now. Me and Darren.'

'Of course.' Kelly paddles her hands, but all she does is churn up sand. She has definitely run aground. 'I like your conservatory.'

'You know Dad's dead, right?'

'I stopped getting his letters. I guessed.'

'I never knew where he sent them. If you even got them.'

'Was it . . .?'

'It was quick. A stroke. Six years ago.'

A heavy tear runs down the side of Kelly's nose.

'You getting up then?'

Kelly floats on mountains ground down by glaciers, on the wash of granite moors and golden fields. She floats at the upright feet of her sister. It is a miracle, nothing more.

'No. I don't think so.'

'My dress is getting wet.'

'I'm glad you're here.'

'Did you think I wouldn't be?'

'I heard you went away.'

'I did. For treatment. Et voilà.' She lifts her stick, crashes it down on the water. Silt and Solway splatter into Kelly's mouth and hair. Kelly drinks it in. If she could burrow down inside the mud, she would. If she stands up, it will make her sister small. Stooped.

And it will make her face her.

'Hey, Ophelia. You'd better get up. There's a bloody great shark coming to get you.'

'No, there isny.'

318

Too delicate. The lapping water is ice and cloud. Kissing this unbearable surface. She is waiting for the storm to break.

'Get up, you fanny. Why are you making yourself cold?'

Kelly sits up, dripping. Amanda takes her arm and, leaning heavily on her stick, helps pull her from the sea. Her princess dress cloys in alabaster folds. Translucent.

'Here.' Amanda takes off the cardigan she's wearing, drapes it to hide Kelly's pinpoint nipples. Underneath the cardigan, Amanda wears a blue sleeveless smock dress, embroidered with sequins. They are the same.

'Did you get that in the hippy shop in Gatehouse?'

'Yes.'

Peas in a pod.

Which one's which?

She knows you, and you know her. The line of her jaw. Lips that are bramble dark. The long nose that you consoled each other was exotic. She is folding the cardigan over you, tenderly patting and tucking you in.

'I'm so sorry,' you whisper. 'Oh, Mandz. Forgive me.'

Amanda makes a sound. Not quite a word. A fraction. A fragment. A hairline fracture that splits stars.

'Just come home,' she says, soft in your ear.

Kelly and Mandz. Your two heartbeats, echoing with life. The water keeps coming. You stand in the Solway, entwined, your wet body dampening her dry one. Where you end and she begins melts away. The oyster-shell sky races the sea. Kelly brims with things she cannot say. She feels like she is dissolving, that it's only her sister's skin that keeps her tethered to her own bones. How to live when you are split? How to be so happy and so sad? How do people do this?

'Stop!'

A man's voice is shouting from the car park on the shore. Kelly and Mandz lift their heads to see. Wrong, this is a wrong thing to see, it's not allowed. The man is driving his white van (illegally) onto the beach, is screeching at them through a glassless window. Mr Lu's van. Unfixed.

'Don't fucking do it, Kelly! We got him!' Dexy steers to a skidding halt.

'Kelly!' shouts Aleisha. She is out the van and running like a duck. 'If you fucking kill yourself, I'll kill you. And that'll kill me. And *then* you'll have murdered my wean. You want that on your conscience, ya bitch?'

'Is that the A-Team?' says Mandz, releasing Kelly. But the water is past their knees, and Kelly sees how her sister wobbles. She holds her steady. Together they paddle towards her motley crew.

First Dex, and then Aleisha – *I canny even swim!* she shrieks – come splashing in to save her. They are swiftly overtaken by a streak of running fur. Silky black and blazing white, her Collie Dog is coming. He has never tackled a sea before, but he does it with panache, biting the waves that try to impede him, blinking as the salt stings his eyes, and never once slowing his pace.

'Oh my God. Collie! But how?' she shouts. 'Collieflower! Baby! Here, boy, I'm coming.'

'Fucking Dexy.' Aleisha raises her fist. 'He was brilliant, Kell!'

'Ach. I just had a wee word.' Dexy's face is flushed. Uncertain. He holds his arms out like a tightrope walker, moves gingerly. Steadily. She doesn't think he can swim either, but that's not stopping him.

Her kelpie dog, bounding home. Collie leaps onto her chest, sending Kelly back under the water. She doesny mind. They tumble in the surf, she and Collie. *From Here to Eternity*. Hands reach down to pick her up. Dexy, brushing the water from her eyes. Cheeky bastard kisses her.

She doesny mind.

'Fuck me.' His arm is round her waist, solid as a rock, but he's looking at Amanda. 'Are yous two twins?

'I'm the eldest,' says Kelly.

'Aye, but I'm the best.'

'No.' Dex nods his head. 'I can see that. All right then, doll.' He lets Kelly go, actually tilting her so she falls back into the water. 'You're chucked.'

She hears Amanda laughing, or perhaps it's Kelly laughing, then a wave tumbles over her head. Unsteady gasps, the grey-brown sandy water breaking, Collie barking. When she rights herself, she notices how carefully her friends tend to her sister. Aleisha has caught Amanda's stick, which was drifting, and Dexy is slowly walking her back to shore.

'Ho! What about me?' Kelly rises, floundering and flashing almost everything she's got. Which isny much, let's be honest.

But maybe it's enough.

She follows her family, feet squelching inside knackered boots. Collie keeps circling up and down, until he's got them all in one herd. Kelly budges her way into the middle. 'Room for a little one?'

And they move forward in a fluid arch. Each bearing the others' weight.

Epilogue

You are lying in your bed, with the covers pulled tight. Tight, because there are shadows on the wall, shadows of people. You peek out and you are on a stage and they are all cheering, waving, tons of cheers and the crackle of applause, and you're waving back, and then they wheel on a man in a hospital bed. You feel your arm shake—

'Kelly!'

Your arm is being shaken.

'Kelly! Ho, Rip Van Winkle!'

You wake up.

Your sister leans over you. 'Were you asleep?'

'No.' You shuffle yourself into a sitting position, making Collie grumble. He moves, marginally, resettles himself. 'Maybe. I was only dozing.'

'You were making funny noises. Kind of like cheering?'

'Was I?' You shake your head. 'Weird.'

'Anyway, I made you tea.' Mandz sets a cup down on the small rattan table next to your chair. Fragrant steam rises. On the saucer (Mandz has saucers) is a Tunnock's caramel wafer. 'My favourite,' you say. You don't know when you last had one of those.

'I know,' she says.

And she does.

'Did she phone again?' you ask.

'No.'

You nod.

'You could be passing up a great opportunity, you know.'

'You think?'

'Aye. Who knows – this week a chat, next week you're on the telly: one woman and her dug. Maybe a heart-warming movie to follow?'

'Oh aye, deffo. *A Pilgrimage on Six Legs.*'

'Hmm – nah. That sounds too much like *The Human Centipede.*'

'Fair enough.' You think a minute. 'What about *There and Back Again: A Wee Hobbit Wumman's Journey*? Starring Chou-fleur et Raquel.'

'Who?'

You shake your head again. 'Nothing.'

Your sister returns to her kitchen, which is Shaker style, with wooden worktops. Swanky. Mandz is very particular about her worktops, freaks if you leave a ring mark anywhere. Hence the saucers. There is a drawer in her kitchen packed with painkillers – amitriptyline, gabapentin, Sevredol, Co-dydramol – and a cupboard full of wine and other booze. She has offered to lock it. You'd shrugged, then said, 'Up to you.'

'I'll lock it,' she said.

'Boot.'

'Alky bitch.'

You'd both burst out laughing, leaving poor Darren all confused.

The wind is picking up outside; you can see trees bend against the sheeting rain. You stretch out your feet, causing Collie to sigh and open one eye. 'What?' you say. 'Sorr-ee.'

He shakes his head at you. Well, he doesny really, but you know he does, inside. You poke him with your toe. You have

324

slippers, Kelly. Big fluffy beasts that trip you when you walk. Ridiculous things. You don't like them, but they were a gift from Aleisha. And you like her. So.

You wonder how she's doing. Any day now. You'll definitely go up then, when baby Harley Alba or Hiccup or whatever Aleisha finally decides to call her makes an appearance.

Water splats across the windows. It's just the rain, but Mandz says some days if the tide is high and the weather wild, the house gets doused in sea-spray. Apparently the salt's a bugger on the paintwork, but you think it would be amazing. To watch the elements come and batter you and never feel a thing.

You lift your teacup. The saucer rattles. You are so thirsty. The tea smells of perfume, so you put it down again. Take the caramel wafer instead. Collie whimpers. You check, but he is drooling on your slippers. Surreptitiously you stuff the biscuit into your mouth before he notices. He is becoming a right wee pig.

She hasn't phoned. That's good.

They've been trying to get you to do a 'reunion'. That bloody journalist and her paper. That Jennifer Impatience. She keeps calling the house, trying to set it up. A meeting: you and the man with the tan office shoes. Martin, his name is. Martin Grey. Senior partner at Mellick, Grey & Strutt (Accountants). Been hinting they'll give you the reward if you do.

You don't want it. They can give it to the Outreach; you've told Mandz to tell her that. You've never actually spoken to Jennifer Patience. All calls have been fielded by your sister. She knows the right things to say. They have fobbed Mrs Impatience off with a photograph, of you and Amanda having a hug. They staged it so you can hardly see your face at all. You don't want the fuss. Mandz said Jennifer Patience wasn't happy, but they put it in the paper all the same. Called it

325

an 'exclusive'. Full of phrases like 'amazing discovery!' and 'long-lost twins!'

Too many exclamation marks. Too bouncy. But nothing . . . bad. You are grateful she has written nothing bad.

You hope they will leave you alone now. You are nothing special.

You luxuriate in your comfortable chair (also rattan, but with nice big padded cushions). You think this is your favourite place in the entire house. You are inside and you are out. The rain beats down on the conservatory roof. From here, you can see the beach. You love watching it, the sea. Tides passing. Sand exposed. Sand swept clean. Sand exposed. Sand swept clean. It is a neat trick.

You close your eyes again. Other than the drumming rain, it is entirely silent. You and Mandz have talked a lot. You'll keep talking now, you know that. You never really stopped. But there is time for silence too.

You don't know if you'll stay here. This is not your space; it is Amanda's space, Amanda's and Darren's. You know Darren does not like you, and you don't blame him. Oh, he never says, but it is there, in his stiff politeness, in his skirting round you instead of screaming. You wish he would scream at you.

Collie licks your hand. You open your eyes to find him staring. Deepest brown eyes, which can see your soul. And the chocolate crumbs on your fingers. Bonios and Tunnock's. You could have a biscuit shelf, you and Collie.

Dexy has told you about a scheme called Housing First. He's sent you a link (you have a phone now, Kelly – a wee marvel in your hand). Dex is aye pinging you links and videos, near daily, daft messages, now he has your number.

I've got your number, Kelly doll! He thinks he's funny.

Man's a nightmare. This link he's sent promises priority access and flexible support. It seems to suggest you get to keep your house, no matter what. Even if you 'disengage'. Imagine that. Not having to subject yourself to Shirehorse Shirley, and they still give you a hoose!

It sounds too good to be true.

Or you could always just stay wi me.

Like you say, Dex is a nightmare.

Dex thinks you should maybe meet the man with the tan office shoes. Privately. Says it might help. But you cannot . . . you haven't gone there. Up to Glasgow. Not yet. And why should you meet him anyway? Mr Martin Grey (Accountant) wouldn't give you his panini. Guy's a fanny.

'What? What is it, boy?' Collie has jumped up, is quivering at the patio doors. Tail stiff and wagging.

'Is it the birdies?' You can see a skein of geese arrowing over the bay. You stand, to look out with him. But it's not the geese that transfix him. It's movement down below. Two mad weans are rampaging across the beach, under the pouring skies. Hoods up, wellies on, they are chucking ribbons of seaweed at each other. One of them holds a long streamer of kelp above her head. Her hood falls to her shoulders as she runs, the seaweed triumphant green and glistening in the rain.

You open the door to let the weather in. And to hear the children playing.

Acknowledgements

This book is a sum of many parts. Big thanks to:

Karine Polwart for permission to steal some skeins of geese and wise, weatherly inspiration.

A fan-girl hat tip to Kathleen Jamie's magnificent poem *The Queen of Sheba*, which I pinch echoes of in a beach scene . . .

Scottish PEN's Many Voices project, and all the good folk I met at Move On, especially Linda Stewart and Denise Talent, Kerrie O'Brien, Jenna, Stephen, Terry, Stacey, Fynn, Kyle, Brian and Ryan.

Righting Welfare Wrongs by the Scottish Unemployed Workers' Network – a harrowing but very helpful book.

Kirsty McCrindle for advice on housing issues.

Jan Smedh for correcting my Swedish.

The Whithorn Trust Visitor Centre.

My lovely agent Jo Unwin, Milly, Donna and all at JULA. Jo Dingley, Francis Bickmore, Anna Frame, Alice Shortland, Jo Walker, Rafaela Romaya, Leila, Vicki, Jenny, Megan, Alan, Melissa and all at Canongate for making me feel so welcome and for their love and care for Kelly. Jane Selley for meticulous copy-editing and Alison Rae for proofreading.

My family as ever – the more we've been distant, the closer we've become. My girls Eidann and Ciorstan and my husband Dougie for unstinting support and love. And my boys, Wren, Xander and Phil. The clan continues to grow. Finally – to Sam. This one's for you.